THE SHOCK OF THE LIGHT

The SHOCK of the LIGHT

Lori Inglis Hall

PAMELA DORMAN BOOKS • VIKING

VIKING
An imprint of Penguin Random House LLC
1745 Broadway, New York, NY 10019
penguinrandomhouse.com

A Pamela Dorman Book/Viking

The PGD colophon is a registered trademark of Penguin Random House LLC.

VIKING and VIKING ship colophon are registered trademarks of Penguin Random House LLC.

Designed by Meighan Cavanaugh

LIBRARY OF CONGRESS CATALOGING-IN-PUBLICATION DATA

Names: Inglis Hall, Lori author
Title: The shock of the light / Lori Inglis Hall.
Description: New York : Pamela Dorman Books, 2026.
Identifiers: LCCN 2025036139 (print) | LCCN 2025036140 (ebook) |
ISBN 9780593834251 hardcover | ISBN 9780593834268 ebook
Subjects: LCGFT: Novels
Classification: LCC PR6109.N454 S56 2026 (print) |
LCC PR6109.N454 (ebook) | DDC 823/.92—dc23/eng/20250919
LC record available at https://lccn.loc.gov/2025036139
LC ebook record available at https://lccn.loc.gov/2025036140

First published in hardcover in Great Britain by The Borough Press,
a division of HarperCollins*Publishers* Ltd., London, in 2026.

First United States edition published by Pamela Dorman Books, 2026.

Printed in the United States of America
1st Printing

The authorized representative in the EU for product safety and compliance is
Penguin Random House Ireland, Morrison Chambers, 32 Nassau Street,
Dublin D02 YH68, Ireland, https://eu-contact.penguin.ie.

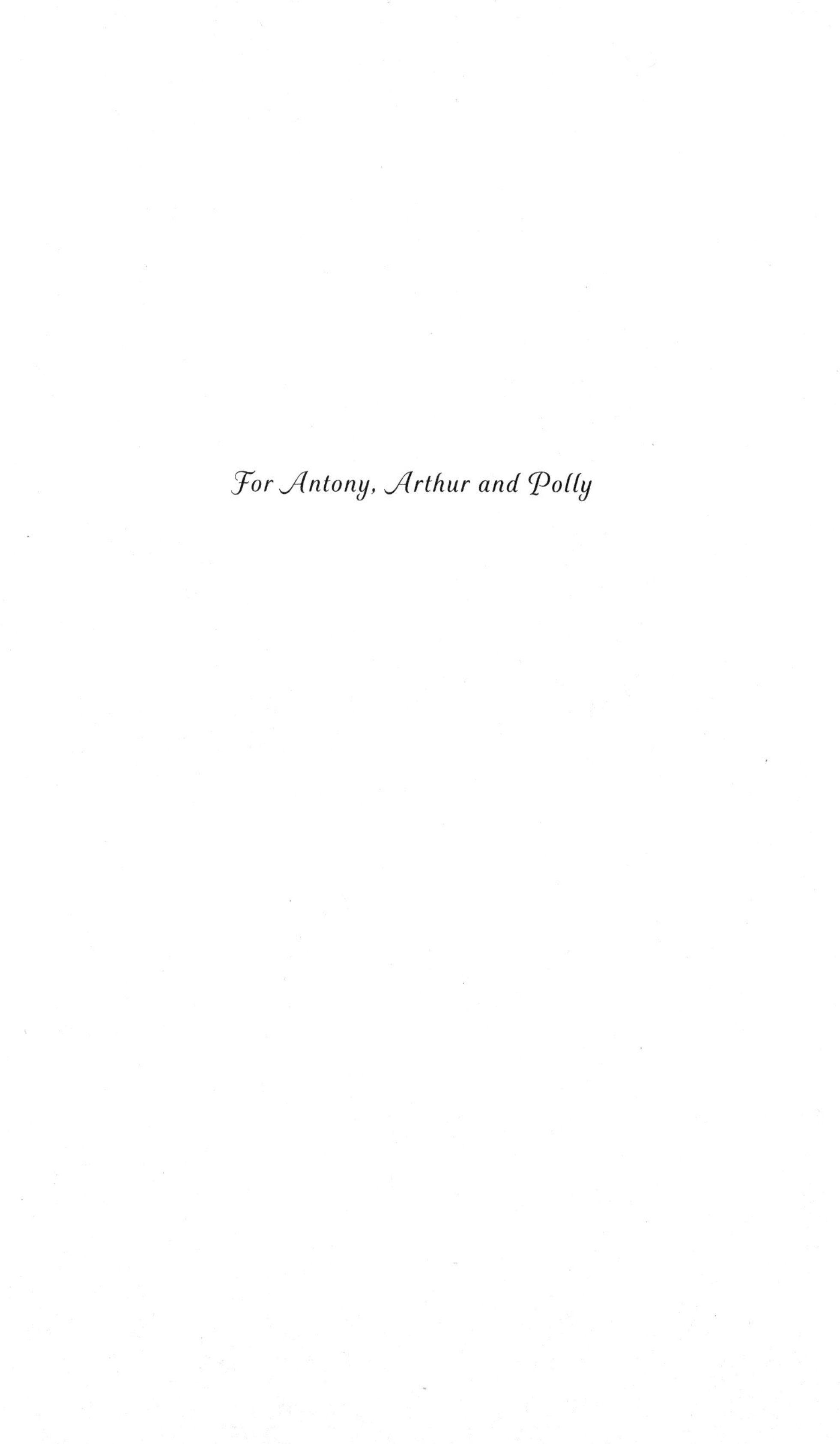

For Antony, Arthur and Polly

For every atom belonging to me as good belongs to you

Song of Myself, Walt Whitman

Prologue

The first time the twins are separated is birth.

The boy is born first, howling, red-faced, lashing out at the doctor. His hands are searching for the other—his mother Adela sees this; how lost he is without his twin. The girl is born soon after, more pink than red, and calm. The midwife places her next to her brother, who clasps her hand and stops crying. Everyone laughs at the sudden silence except Adela, still prostrate in bed. She is trying to comprehend what has happened, the change, the stinging between her legs.

"Would you look at that," says Dominic, from the doorway. He goes to the crib, despite the midwife trying to usher him away, birth being no place for the father, after all. He places his hand on the girl's chest, smiling. He has always longed for a daughter.

"Mother and babies all well," says the doctor, packing his bag, not looking up. Adela has found his cold, brisk manner at odds with the experience. How can something so transformative be dealt with so curtly? She will never understand the English and their ways. In France, she's sure they would have let her scream.

There is a flash. Dominic taking the first photograph.

The picture is framed and placed on a mantelpiece in the same room as the crib where the babies are clutching hands, legs entwined, not a sliver of light between them. Their father names the girl Tessa, for Hardy's Tess. The boy he leaves for his wife, who names him Theo after her father. She pronounces it the French way, as her father did, the way that feels natural on her tongue—*Théo*, with a hard T—but no one else will.

In time, more photographs join the first. Here are the twins at school in the smart blazers of the local grammar, where Theo uses his brain and Tessa learns how to make a home, furious at the injustice of it. Here they are climbing trees, swimming in the river; the land is theirs, they've claimed it. Theo in his academic gown, Tessa in Paris, her arms full of books, smile blazing.

In the fields beyond the house in which they grow, crops rise and fall with the turning of the earth.

They were linked by a single thread but now the thread divides, two twins, two lives. As the space between the twins widens, they don't notice it at first. The light that stands between them.

Part One

TESSA

Paris, 1938

One

Tessa is crouched at the top of the narrow stairwell leading up to her bedroom, which she's always called a *garret* in letters to her brother, if only for the romance of it. She runs her fingers over the new line of her stomach and cranes her neck.

It is a colossal pig's ear of a mess. *Disaster* feels fitting. *Catastrophe* better still.

Downstairs, her landlady is on the telephone. Through the spindles of the banister, Tessa can make out Madame Vernier's expression as she strains to hear the voice crackling across the Channel from a house 500 miles away.

No, I don't know when she'll be back. Yes, I passed on your message. No, I have no message for you. Désolée.

She is struggling to get a word in edgeways. Tessa knows the voice on the line will be barking questions, as it has throughout her childhood. Her mother will be crouched on the stairs too, in Cambridge, the wall next to her lined with family photographs. The stairwell in which Tessa is hiding is covered in yellow paper, which in places is torn, peeling back on itself in little wave-crests. Through a window no bigger than her head she can see the rise and fall of grey-tiled rooftops, and beyond, the spire of the great cathedral on its island.

She had always wanted to live in Paris, the city in which her mother grew tall.

She told her mother the truth a week ago, when she could no longer ignore the nausea and the tightness of her waistband. The most god-awful telephone conversation, which she'd realized within minutes should have been a letter. Her mother was certain she knew what to do—certain, but quietly so, meaning Tessa's father must have been nearby. This morning the letter in her hands arrived, written in English to ward off prying eyes, repeating all the things her mother had said on the telephone. *We will go away for a time*, her mother wrote, *arrangements are underway*—but all without further elucidation, leaving Tessa to wonder briefly if a page was missing. *Your father is not to know*, her mother went on, and then—*nor Theo.*

But Tessa tells her brother everything, it is the twins' way. Then she thinks, no—it *was* their way, because she hasn't told him. This is another break with the past, the first being her move to Paris three years ago . . . The acceptance letter from the Sorbonne on the table, Theo pacing up and down in the parlor. The blazing row.

"How could you?" he'd hissed. She couldn't look at him, couldn't bear the desperation in his voice. The twins had never spent more than a few days apart.

"I thought we'd agreed," he said. "Cambridge. We both said we'd stay. Law for me, Literature for you. We said we'd do this together."

Tessa snatched up the letter, reading it again, unable to believe it was real. "I didn't say that," she said. "You did."

Time, that great healer, will repair the rift between them.

But if Tessa keeps something from her brother again, she knows it will change everything. Impossible to think otherwise—if she shuts him out, he might not come back. At school, a girl in their final year had fallen pregnant. Of course no one was told, but all the signs were there. The weight gain, the sudden disappearance from class, the girl's mother pushing a pram a few months later. Everyone knew the child wasn't hers. Tessa had listened as her peers passed judgment, along with her brother. She remembers his words in particular: "*Girls like that, they can never escape the shame. It lingers like a bad smell.*" He probably hadn't meant it to be cruel—but it was, it was. It still has its sting now.

Her mother is right. Theo cannot find out. He'd never look at Tessa in the same way again.

Besides, the point of coming to Paris, of the life she'd sought, was that it was just hers, something she'd no obligation to share. The city in its entirety has been an education. Has it been the same for Theo, she wonders, still in Cambridge? He'd put a few miles between himself and their parents. She'd put an ocean. Now look at the state of everything. Twenty-two years old, and with nothing to show for it but this god-awful mess.

Her mother is certain it cannot be undone. She won't hear about the doctor Tessa found, carbolic soap and a hook. It is too late for that, her mother says.

In the hallway below, Madame Vernier has her hand to her mouth, her staccato French changing, softening.

I know, we never stop worrying for them, do we? They never seem grown to us.

Yes, thinks Tessa, I am a bad daughter, I know.

Her mother had wanted to know about the father, and Tessa almost answered, almost reached for the obvious. Luc doesn't even know. He wouldn't understand.

Luc is a sensation on her skin like the sun, he is heat.

Tessa had wanted to say, I love him, I loved him—I did, I swear. *Until.*

Her hand is on her belly, and how queer they are, these instincts, this need to protect something she doesn't want and never ever asked for.

Already her silhouette is changing, her belly rounding beneath her breasts. *Finish your studies*, her mother wrote, *it's only a few months. For God's sake, hide it.* Tessa lets go of her belly, twisting her skirt into a knot, because how simple her mother makes it sound, this shifting of the earth.

Downstairs, Madame Vernier hangs up the phone and Tessa treads silently back upstairs.

A great shame, her mother called it. Oh yes, Tessa thinks, that's exactly what this is.

Cambridge, 1942

Two

Tessa is always the fastest and bravest—it is a matter of pride (though her brother might call it recklessness). She is the first to reach the top of the oak tree, where from the tallest branches the land's divide is clear: rooftops one way, a great stretch of green the other. Her victory is simply one of technique, because while Theo climbs steadily—one foot, one arm, other foot, other arm—Tessa swings her way to the top.

On the terrace below, her parents' friends are gathered around her father. *Fifty*, she hears one say, *but you've only just been born!* A group of girls she'd known at school are hovering by the edge of the lawn, where she can hear them laughing and chatting. Lily is there. Years ago they'd been as thick as thieves, only now Tessa can't remember the last time they had a conversation. Lily is married now, has children, Tessa knows that, at least—how different their lives have become. Go over, join in, her mother had said, but since Paris she's forgotten how. Her schoolfriends raise their hands and wave, and she pulls her lips into a smile, quickly looking away in case it's mistaken for an invitation, knowing that the old Tessa would have rushed over, full of tales and escapades. In the midst of it all her mother is fussing over the lunch spread. Tessa is reading her lips, watching her direct and explain; perhaps she thinks the concept of a buffet is beyond her friends. For a quick second their gazes meet and her mother falls silent, her hands caught in a gesture in mid-air.

Tessa is astonished her mother can look her in the eye.

Theo is laughing when he finally appears beside her. "Typical Tessa," he says.

"I took it as slowly as I could." She's unable to hide her teasing smile. "Wanted to give you a fighting chance."

Every time he comes home could be the last. Tessa tots them up, unwelcome lists in her head. Last swim, last climb, last breakfast. His going away had sent her crashing to the ground in its unexpected reversal of roles. Theo leaving this time, and Tessa clinging on.

She catches the twitch of his lips; knows he won't give in so easily, his smile and the glint in his eyes mirrored in her own. "The uniform is a handicap," he says.

Tessa laughs. "You're on leave. No one's forcing you to wear it."

RAF blue, he almost disappears into the sky—Theo, the birds and the rooftops. She can see the river below, a darker slate blue from this height.

She reaches out and touches his hand. "I've missed you."

She hadn't needed to say it; so much between the twins exists unspoken. Or did, because there was a time when she wouldn't have let him reach the tree. She'd have thrown herself at him the moment she spotted him crossing the lawn, curling him into a tight hug. Tessa wants to reach back through the years, reach her arms out to him, but she can't. Theo might realize she's turned to stone.

"Maman is going to say we're being rude." He's looking down through the branches to the party, squinting at the guests, trying to reclaim people's names from his memory. She knows, because she did the same earlier, while lying on her back on the lawn. Her body language—learned these last four years—had been quite enough to keep the guests at arm's length.

"She's going to give us a thorough ticking-off," she says now, tartly.

Theo guffaws. "A clip round the ear."

"So impossibly childish." She mimics their mother's accent, pursing her lips, sucking in her cheeks.

Theo looks thoughtful, and she thinks—no, he doesn't have it in him to be truly mean.

"Still, she's put on a good show, hasn't she?" he says, proving her point, and she smiles but as much for being right as for him. "I mean, despite everything."

Tessa, who has no guilt to assuage when it comes to their mother, uncurls her smile into a frown. "People will think it's decadent. Inappropriate. They'll enjoy the party, thank her with one breath and condemn her with the next."

Theo nods, severely. "The WI will be up in arms."

"The parish council have already called a meeting."

Somewhere in the garden, a man lets out a hearty laugh, and they both look down.

"Anyway, who cares if she thinks we're rude?" she says, because this is what matters. Tessa hasn't seen her brother in months. He takes a cigarette packet from his pocket and passes it to her, followed by a silver lighter.

"It suits you, you know," she says. "The costume."

"The fabric's as stiff as a board. I feel as if I'm made of wood. Still, thought I'd make an effort for Papa's birthday. It's not my fault he's sulking."

"I know, I know."

"And it's not as if I've ever claimed to be a pacifist. Papa's principles are his own, they're not mine."

Tessa doesn't say anything and this makes it worse. Theo looks away and she knows he's gone back to the row; the moment Theo announced he'd joined up. Their father's eyes wide with fury. "Violence is never the answer," he'd said, almost spitting out the words. "Hate never wins."

It hadn't made a blind bit of difference. Theo was determined.

Their mother calls from the house and they can see Michael waving from the garden. Tessa rolls her eyes and Theo is laughing again, his hand over his mouth so Michael won't see. "Maman invited him, or he invited himself—how should I know? You know what he's like."

"I do know what he's like, yes. He's so . . ." She pauses to search for the right word. "So *smug*," she finishes.

"He's important, Tess. Doing good work, by all accounts."

"Or at least that's what he wants us to think."

She begins to climb down, amazed at how easily her twenty-six-year-old body reclaims the movements of her childhood. She starts to mimic her brother. One foot, one hand, so slow and methodical, typical Theo. Michael's at the bottom, probably trying to see up her skirt. From her vantage point she can see how much his hair has thinned, the desperate brush-strokes taming the remains across the void. She adds this weakness—not the thinning hair but the attempt to hide it—to a list of faults two decades in the making. Michael would say he is there for his old friend Theo, but he fools no one.

Then, a memory. Every year, their father made them stand silently in the back garden, waiting for the nightingale's song to break through the pitch black. He had a recording from the BBC, a woman named Beatrice Harrison playing the cello in her garden, a nightingale in the trees above singing along. He'd play the recording all winter "to get them through."

Imagine being in the woods, listening to that song, they'd said. And so a plan had formed. Tessa can see them walking into the woods, lamps aloft. The twins must have been thirteen, fourteen years old.

In the memory, Theo was dawdling, whispering behind his hand so only Michael could hear. Michael, who'd appeared from nowhere at school and rarely left her brother's side, who always seemed to be in their house yet never invited them to his own. ("Don't force him. It's not somewhere we'd necessarily encourage you to visit," their mother said, to which their father replied, aghast, "Adela, you bloody *snob.*")

Tessa's best friend was there. They saw each other almost every day, although Lily wasn't interested in the natural world. Already she looked bored.

"Can't we just go to the flickers?" she'd asked, when Tessa first put the idea to her. In the woods, Lily wore two cardigans and a coat, even though the weather felt mild. She kept looking at her watch and huffing.

"You can go home, you know," said Tessa. "No one's forcing you to be here."

But Lily wouldn't leave, and Tessa knew why. She'd seen the way Lily looked at Theo, the blushes whenever he addressed her, although this was in itself a rarity. Theo had not yet developed the passion for the opposite sex which had begun to consume their friends, and how Tessa loved him for it. Everything changing around them, but Theo steadfastly unmoving. There was a lot to be said for Theo's dependability. Tessa considered it an undervalued quality. No, dear, reliable Theo only had time for his own friends. And Tessa, of course. Tessa above all else. In the twins' hierarchy everyone else tailed behind.

Movement, then. A shadow in between the trees. Lily let out a scream. All around them birds scattered from branches.

"Well, that's gone and done it," said the shadow. "Nice one, Lily."

"Stephen," said Theo, pushing past Lily. In the lamplight, Tessa could see the red in her brother's cheeks, the smile she wasn't sure she'd ever seen on his face before.

At thirteen, she had no word for it.

Stephen was another of Theo's waifs and strays (Tessa had no idea what compelled her brother. He was, after all, a popular child). A farm boy who smelled like one, to Tessa at least.

"*Sorry,*" said Lily. "Look, where's this ruddy bird? I'm freezing."

They threw down a blanket the twins had found in the boot of their father's motor, and lay down shoulder to shoulder. Stephen, then Theo, then Tessa, then Lily, who didn't hide the fact she'd rather be next to Theo, bottom lip pushed out, another huff. Michael had slunk off for a wee, and in the silence they could hear his stream hitting the forest floor. When he appeared out of the trees Tessa thought he'd lie on the end of the blanket, next to Lily. Instead he planted his knee between Tessa and Theo, forcing them apart.

The twins exchanged a pained look, separating to allow Michael between them.

Damn, Tessa thought. She didn't care about the others, not really. This was something she wanted to experience with Theo. If she closed her eyes, she could pretend it was just the two of them. So she did, the others vanishing in the black behind her eyelids.

"And now we wait," said Stephen, in his gruff voice, snuffing out the lanterns. They could barely see their fingers in front of their faces.

"Oh, bloody hell," whispered Lily, and they all sniggered.

Tessa raised her head. Even in the black she knew Theo would be looking back at her. Her eyes adjusted and she could just make out her brother's, shining in the dark. Here we are, she wanted to say, another year, another spring. She hoped he'd understand, knew he would—knew he had when he gave a little nod in acknowledgment. Dropping her head, she realized Michael was gazing at her intently. He parted his lips, mouthed her name, *Tessa*. For a moment she felt too stunned to comprehend his meaning. Oh no, she thought. Absolutely not.

Why did everyone seem so obsessed with this sort of thing all of a sudden? *Romance*. Where had it come from? Lily used to be *interesting*. Now all she did was gossip about boys, and who had the hots for whom, and who'd been spotted sneaking off together at the end of school.

Tessa had no inclination to sneak off anywhere with Michael.

Michael took her hand, lightly squeezing his fingers between her own.

Tessa snatched it away, pretending she had an itch just behind her ear. How long could she keep scratching, she wondered; where else could she put her hand so he couldn't claim it?

Then they heard it, loud and clear through the trees. The nightingale. No one said a word. Everything else faded away. The song cascaded octaves in whistles and trills, delighting in its twists and turns.

Theo, Theo, Theo, she thought. Can you hear me, Theo? Isn't this magic?

All change, everything changing. But the stillness of that moment. The quiet. Tessa doesn't think she's ever felt a sense of peace like it.

In the garden, Michael reaches out a hand to help Tessa down, so she jumps—it's the only way to avoid touching his flesh—landing solidly on two feet. In haste, Michael stuffs his hand into his pocket, as if she'll forget he ever offered it if she can't see it. Theo has yet to appear, which is telling in itself. Tessa knows he'll be listening.

"How's the foreign office, Tee?"

"Tee" is a name reserved for those she likes.

"Marvelous, thank you, Michael."

"You're doing well, I hear. Making quite a name for yourself by all accounts."

"Am I? Yes, I suppose I am. Turns out three years at the Sorbonne is excellent prep for the secretarial pool. I've really no idea why they don't include it in their prospectus. Forget academia, forget knowledge, three years within our hallowed walls and one might just reach the heady heights of *pool typist*."

"Ha. Still bored, then."

Tessa hesitates, glancing up to where she can see Theo's legs, swinging back and forth from a branch. "I wish I hadn't told you that."

"It's written all over your face." He puts his hand on her elbow and draws her toward him. "Have dinner with me, Tessa."

She shrugs him off. One graceful movement. "Honestly, I'm starting to think you have a fetish for rejection."

Michael's eyebrows rise to the heavens because she's excited him, that word. "As it happens, I need to talk to you about something. A solution to your current predicament, perhaps. Have dinner with me."

No one knows what Michael does, only that his "war work" keeps him exceedingly busy and provides him with no uniform or insignia to give one a clue. Questions are met with a smirk and such obvious delight in the mystery that Tessa can't bring herself to ask any more.

Two thuds behind them make them turn around. Theo does not land solidly. "Maman's ready with the cake," he says, stalking off ahead.

"Theo!" Michael exclaims, his smile widening. For the first time it looks genuine. "How marvelous you could be here."

Theo doesn't answer. Tessa turns to follow but Michael takes her arm, again. He looks at her, more a study than a glance, before taking a square of paper out of his pocket and pressing it into her hand. "Don't read it here; don't read it in front of Theo. Wait until everyone has gone to bed, and take it to your bedroom."

Tessa looks down at the paper lying flat on her palm. "What is—"

"Now, now, let's not spoil it by asking questions."

On the terrace, Tessa kisses her father on the cheek and he squeezes her hand, a warm smile just for her.

"Here they are," someone says. "The twins, together again."

Their mother is watching them. She makes a point of greeting Theo, kissing his cheek, tracing a finger over his blue uniform.

"Of course he goes straight to his sister. Nothing for his *maman*," she says, and her friends laugh. "Although I suppose I should be grateful if they notice me at all," she goes on, warming to the subject. "We could barely prize them apart when they were little."

Their father joins in. He looks strained in his garden chair, won't look at Theo, not in his blue. Pacifism has widened the wedge between them.

"Adela had them at the doctor when they were four because they didn't talk. At least, not to us. They had their own language. Grunts and hisses, the strangest thing you've ever heard."

"Of course the doctor wasn't interested. I remember the two of you, sitting on his rug, playing with blocks. *Théo* stacking them up, Tessa taking great delight in knocking them down. The man barely looked at you. A complete waste of time. That's twins for you, he said. Always in their own little world."

She looks at Tessa, but Tessa won't hold her gaze, refusing to give her mother the satisfaction. "Twins feel they only need each other, that's what he said. How nice it must be, to have a little world that is just yours. We do feel so grateful, when they allow us inside."

Tessa swallows. Theo is scratching his head, looking bemused, Michael grinning manically next to him, pretending he's in on the joke. She takes her place at the piano, tucked just inside the open French doors, striking the first notes of "Happy Birthday," much louder than she intended. Michael's note is burning a hole in her pocket. She focuses instead on the cake—pink icing and not enough candles because Maman didn't want to be cruel.

Although it's not yet eight, their mother retires to bed with a novel, as she does every evening now that she can't telephone her sister behind the lines in France. Their father disappears to his study to work, casting tall shadows on the walls in the evening light. This splintering is done behind closed doors, the togetherness on the terrace just for show.

The twins are in the library, its shelves heavy with philosophy, history and poetry—the "meat of thought," as her father might say in one of his curious but original analogies. Michael's note is still in her pocket. Theo is sprawled on the floor beside the record player. His tastes have changed since he joined up—more populist, less jazz, and worse, he's lost his delight in introducing her to something new. They smoke cigarettes from the chrome-plated case in his pocket, Air-Force issue, not his brand. He'd always wanted to be a pilot but their father's fury, at one time effectual at least, propelled him to Cambridge and the law. Tessa suspected the war was a gift in that sense, giving him the opportunity to strike out away from their father. Theo had always been the more obedient of the two.

"What did Michael give you?" he says, keeping his voice light, but Tessa can read him like a book. "The note, I mean."

She looks down, stretching her hand against her legs, curling a fist, unfurling her fingers. "His telephone number," she says, avoiding his eyes so that she might hold on to the lie. "You know what he's like."

He takes a drag of her cigarette before passing it back. "He's consistent, at least. He's been sweet on you for years."

They sit in silence for a while, Tessa's head resting on her brother's shoulder, leaning against him, arm to arm. She can feel her eyes closing, her breath softening.

"Tell me about London," he says, idly. "About your life."

Her breath catches in her throat. Four years ago, as sunlight danced across yellow sheets, her mother had made her promise she wouldn't breathe a word to Theo. But sometimes, in the quiet of an evening, she wants to tear down the wall between them and tell him about her shattered heart, and how it is still quite shattered, and how, if she lets it—which she rarely does—it aches for what she lost.

"Same as it ever was, save for the bombs and the rubble. Do you miss it?" she says, hoping he'll say *yes, Tess, but not as much as I miss you!*

"The rubble? I'd say that's more of an acquired taste."

She nudges him, unable to stop herself from laughing. "London, idiot."

Theo doesn't say anything for a while. "I find it helps not to think about the things I miss."

Tessa wants to tell him not to go back but finds she can't make her lips form the words. When the offer of a life in Paris presented itself, *she* hadn't stayed. Besides, it's not as if Theo has a choice. They speak instead of the birthday party, they've no desire to consider the rest, not really. But Tessa finds she cannot calm her anxiety; their father might outlive Theo, Theo has seen war, has seen death. Her brain is forever calculating odds and chance.

"How is Maman?" says Theo, stretching his arms above his head. She knows he's desperate to go to bed, but they have so little time together. It has to count, every moment.

"Depressed. She says the world is too dark, that she's losing hope."

"And Papa?"

"He'll forgive you eventually."

"There's nothing to forgive."

"Yes, yes, I know."

Tessa knows what it is to feel a parent's disappointment. How it weighs on the shoulders with strange, discomfiting pressure.

When they finally say good night, Tessa follows Michael's instructions to the letter. How she has grown to loathe this man. Has he always been so bad? No, manhood did that, she thinks; it's the way he's grown. Tessa sits down on her bed and unfolds the square of paper, the sense of possibility like an electric shock. Because the truth is, Tessa would have followed Theo into the air if she could, if it wasn't for the space between her legs, where the powers that be seem to think men keep their strength and bravery. Tessa looks down at the note.

Five words, typed. "The War Office, Thursday, 9 a.m."

Three

Did you get a cup of tea, Miss Armstrong?"

"Sorry?"

"Tea, Miss Armstrong, from Miss Norman outside—or would you perhaps prefer a glass of water?"

The room is painted white and kept bare. If she looks up she can see the pavement outside, just visible through a slit of skylight. She's been to the War Office precisely six times to deliver messages. Like all government buildings, its impact quickly fizzles into a disappointment of sterile corridors and harsh lighting. This is her first time in the basement.

"You'll be pleased to hear you come *fortement recommandée*," says the man, Mr. Joyce.

Tessa smiles, because he's right—that does please her, but she's thrown by this sudden lurch into her second language. "Recommended for what?"

Mr. Joyce takes off his glasses, a grave expression on his face, although as she's known him for all of five minutes she can't be sure he doesn't always look like that. Tessa can't help but glance at her watch, even though she telephoned her office to say she'd be late. She wonders if she's to return to the Foreign Office or if this is a line in the sand. Smiling to herself, she thinks: a beginning.

"I'm told your French is excellent," says Mr. Joyce, sticking entirely to French this time. "I'd love to hear it, if you'd be so amenable."

Tessa obliges, although she can't think why he's testing her, because that's undoubtedly what is happening. "My mother was born in Paris and always spoke French at home, and we spend most summers at my grandmother's house in the Loire. At least we did."

He nods, jotting down notes. "And you studied at the Sorbonne?"

"Yes. Literature."

"You weren't tempted by Cambridge? Your father is a don, I see."

Tessa shakes her head. "Not really, no. You see, I wanted a degree. Three years of study only to be refused a qualification on the basis of my sex seemed somewhat pointless." She smiles apologetically.

"And you returned to England from Paris toward the end of 1938?"

Tessa hesitates, flustered. She doesn't think about Paris; she can't. "Yes," she says, after a moment. "I came home."

"You didn't want to stay?"

Tessa shakes her head.

"Because of the situation in Europe?"

"Yes," she says, hoping he can't read the lie.

"Terrible business, France. No one expected it to fall to the Germans so quickly. How do you feel about it?"

When she doesn't answer straight away, Mr. Joyce clears his throat.

"It makes me sick to my stomach. My brother told me there are swastikas hanging from the buildings along the grand boulevards."

"Your brother . . . ah yes, Theo—a twin, I see. Charming. He's in the Royal Air Force."

"Just gone to North Africa." The thinking behind saying this being that Mr. Joyce might inadvertently give away Theo's exact location, as if that will change anything, as if it will make any difference at all to how worried she is.

"Yes, good man. Doing rather well for himself by all accounts."

Tessa's shoulders sag. She doesn't mind if he notices. "So I hear." But there is something else, amid the worry. A pang of jealousy, that Theo can have this experience and she cannot.

"You must be terribly proud."

It's too painful, speaking in her mother's tongue. In quick, deliberate English, she says, "Forgive me, Mr. Joyce, but am I being redeployed?"

He responds with another lurch, his French undeterred. "How would you describe your politics, Miss Armstrong? You're quite an active member of your local Labour Party, I see."

Tessa starts, surprised. "I-I am . . . yes."

"Your father's influence, I suppose?"

"Well, I wouldn't say . . . I mean I'm quite capable of forming my own . . ." Tessa nods her head. "Yes."

"Would you describe yourself as left wing?"

"I'd describe myself as a socialist."

"You called yourself a Marxist at school."

The air leaves her body. "I'm sorry?"

"You wrote a rather remarkable essay, did you not, in which you described education as a mechanism used by the ruling elitist class—your words, I hasten to add—to create a compliant future workforce—"

"I can't believe I put it quite so simplistically but—"

". . . thereby reinforcing and legitimizing class inequality."

"How do you know about that?" It dawns on her that she might be losing her job, rather than gaining a new one.

"Caused rather a stink, by the sounds of it." Mr. Joyce puts down his pen. "Would you say your politics have evolved since then?"

Tessa smiles, ruefully. "Solidified is perhaps a more apt word. But rest assured, Mr. Joyce, I love my country. That's why I want it to become a fairer, more just place."

She's looking longingly at the sliver of pavement beyond the skylight.

This is Mr. Harris the head teacher all over again. His office, which one only visited if suspected of the most heinous crimes, like stealing or plagiarism. Or Marxism.

"But how exactly do you define a fairer country? What is the metric?"

"A place where everyone can enjoy the privileges currently reserved for a minority because of the accident of their birth. A country that works to the benefit of the weak and poor, not just those lucky enough to sit at the top of the heap."

"Like you?"

"Like you, Mr. Joyce. As a woman I wouldn't be allowed anywhere near the top of the heap."

His cheeks redden, and she feels a momentary rush of satisfaction.

"But you attended a good school, Miss Armstrong. You have a degree. Privileges afforded to you because your father works hard and makes use of his great brain."

"Which he is able to do because as a scholarship boy he had a fine education bestowed upon him. But it shouldn't be charity, it should be a right."

Mr. Joyce doesn't say anything to this. Tessa can hear a clock ticking, a telephone ringing. She hears the sound of feet on the street above, the repetitive march of the commute.

"Would you be prepared to join the fight?" he says.

"I was rather under the impression that I had." She thinks of the long hours spent in front of her typewriter. The clack-clacking of keys fifty times over in the office.

"I'm trying to understand if you share your father's pacifism."

"I'd say I'm sympathetic to it. Peaceful options should always be fully explored—that's just common sense, isn't it? But we've done that, haven't we, and look where it's got us."

"Your brother risks his life every time he climbs into a plane."

"Yes."

"Many would say he's a hero."

"I . . . yes. He's very brave."

"And would you, if you could, risk life and limb for your country in its time of need?"

Tessa looks up, surprised. "I would, of course I would. But perhaps you might tell me what this is about, Mr. Joyce?" she says, because she can't think of any redeployment that would involve putting her life on the line. Air-raid warden, perhaps. The searchlight operators, who stay put no matter what comes raining down from the sky. Except she wouldn't be sent to the War Office for a role like that.

"You'll need to make your way over to Lillywhites," he says, in crisp English. The interview must be over, she thinks.

"I'm late for work as it is, Mr. Joyce."

"But you work for us now, Miss Armstrong, and you need to get measured up for your uniform. They'll be expecting you."

"Uniform?"

"Yes, for the First Aid Nursing Yeomanry."

"The FANYs?" She feels a thud of disappointment in her stomach. Is that what this is all about? The FANYs are drivers and mechanics. They're usually debutantes, too, which Tessa most decidedly is not.

"We find it helps to have an official place in the hierarchy," he says, but he won't say more.

Since leaving France, Tessa has resided in the spare room of her aunt's house in Bloomsbury.

"There's a telegram here for you," says Violet, when she spots Tessa in the doorway. "Are you up early or home late?"

"I'm exactly on time." Tessa helps herself to a buttery soldier from Violet's plate. The telegram is propped up against the salt in the middle of the table, but as soon as her eyes happen upon it she forces herself to look away. Nothing good ever arrives in the form of a telegram. "May I have an egg?"

"Yes, if you make it yourself. Good evening, was it?"

"I stayed with a friend. Didn't want to wake you."

"Gosh, you are considerate. I was out myself, as it happens."

"Oh yes, which chap was it this time?" Her aunt smiles beatifically and doesn't answer. "I've no idea how you keep track. Your date book must be an organizational masterpiece."

Violet changes the subject. "Your mother rang, wanting the news. I told her I hardly see you."

This sends Tessa's stomach into a flip, because the whole point of staying at Aunt Violet's is to keep out of trouble. Except last night trouble found her in the guise of an airman named Colton, which is an absurd thing for anyone to be called, or so it seems the morning after. Tessa can still feel him on her skin, his smell lingering in her nose. The sensation, even if it's nothing but a memory, makes her flinch, although her aunt doesn't seem to notice. As soon as Violet pops out, she's going to run a bath. She's going to scrub her flesh until it is red and raw, and she's rid of the feeling of him, of *it*.

Every time, she hopes sex will feel like it used to with Luc. Often it feels like a punishment.

"She assumed I meant you're overworking," says Violet. "Don't worry, I didn't say anything to the contrary."

"I do work hard, as it happens. Any news of Theo?" Her eyes are on the telegram again. Telegrams can mean death.

"You tell me—you're the one he writes to. Aren't you going to be late?"

Tessa shakes her head. "Day off."

"Another one? I didn't think people had days off during a war." Violet nods at the telegram, which Tessa still hasn't acknowledged. "The girl said it was urgent."

The envelope is marked "CONFIDENTIAL." She scoops it up, closing her eyes briefly. Two threads run taut from Tessa's body, one tied to Theo, the other to her parents. She's tried to break both in the last few years. But no, it's not Theo; it is not world-ending, not this time. In black print is an address, Orchard Court, today's date and a time, 2 p.m.

Orchard Court is a tall and rather nondescript building of yellow bricks and white stucco. Inside, mirrors hang on marble walls. For a moment Tessa is everywhere, five, ten of her, all with the same look of unease. She is directed to an apartment on the second floor, which from her position in the doorway seems just as luxurious as the rest. Plush carpets and walls of black marble, a floral perfume in the air. In the sitting room, a man hastens out from behind a desk and grasps her hand.

"Ronald Stenwick, how do you do?" he says, in what her father would call "public school monotone." Though she hasn't said a word, he adds, "We shan't do questions yet and we do try, Miss Armstrong, not to ask too many."

Now she's here, she can't help but feel this is a bit overblown for the FANYs, which is, to Tessa's mind, little more than debutantes chauffeuring around well-heeled major generals. So, this must be something else—she was right to be suspicious. The fake FANYs. Something in need of a cover story. She feels her shoulders tense and thinks, a secret. Nerves rise in her stomach.

Stenwick nods at a chair.

"Thank you," she says, sitting down.

"How did you find your meeting with Mr. Joyce?" he says, opening a khaki cardboard folder. "I hear you strongly defended your political views."

A pang of alarm. "At least you know I mean it."

Perhaps this is his apartment, she thinks, always curious. Except no, it doesn't look lived in. There's none of life's detritus scattered around.

"And do you feel able to work alongside people who don't share your strong opinions, who—and this is just an example, mind—might share your goal but not your motivation?" His nose twitches. "What I mean to say is, you might need to work with communists."

Tessa nods. "I imagine a desire to rid the world of the fascist right is something we all share."

"Sometimes people have more personal reasons."

"Yes."

Stenwick looks up from his folder. "Miss Armstrong, what we are asking of you goes beyond any conventional notion of warfare. It is, as you may have surmised, a position from which I cannot guarantee you will return."

Tessa places her hands very carefully, palms down, on her knees. Well, she thinks, at last. "Am I allowed to ask questions now?" she says.

Stenwick frowns. "All right."

"From where might I not return?"

"From France, Miss Armstrong."

Tessa takes a deep breath. Her insides are riddled with the bruises of the past.

"You have a fine grasp of the language," he continues. "Apparently you sound like quite the native. You know the country well and I believe you should have no trouble assimilating. But let me be clear: should the enemy happen upon you, it is entirely possible you'd pay with your life."

The conversation is too much; it is, quite frankly, ridiculous, like little boys playing at war. "What exactly would I be doing?" she says, feeling numb.

"Special Ops. Sabotage, to put it plainly. A disruptive force, right under the enemy's nose. But look, these are details for Miss Jones . . ."

The numbness dissipates. Tessa feels a bolt of excitement run down her spine, but perhaps it's not that, perhaps it's fear. Fear would be sensible, she thinks. Fear would be expected, in response to such extraordinary words.

"Miss Jones?" she asks.

"Yes. I rather expect she's wondering where we are."

He stands up and fastens his jacket. Tessa follows him through a door into another room, which is a little more frayed at the edges. A woman a little younger than her mother sits behind a desk. She sticks out her hand, saying, "Hello, Emmeline Jones," in a crisp accent that brings to Tessa's mind thoughts of empire and Queen Mary.

"I'll leave you to it, shall I?" says Stenwick, slipping away before anyone has a chance to object.

"This must be difficult to take in," Miss Jones says. She has a pot of tea standing ready on a small white tray. "Milk, sugar?" she asks.

Tessa asks for milk only as she sits down, eyes still on the just-closed door. "Mr. Stenwick asked if I'd be willing to go to France."

Miss Jones nods and passes her a cup.

"But how? France has been occupied for more than a year. Paris is crawling with Nazis."

Miss Jones looks Tessa straight in the eye. "War is many things, Miss Armstrong. For the past year our organization, the Special Operations Executive, has been engaged in a secret battle across Europe. Specially trained agents collaborating with local Resistance groups in occupied areas to disrupt German operations—with much success, I might say."

It takes a moment for this to sink in. "And that's what you'd like me to do?" she says, in disbelief.

"We'd like you to take on a role as a courier, moving between different parts of a network of our agents and French Resistance groups, carrying messages and such, as directed by staff at our headquarters on Baker Street. It's a dangerous role—you'll be tremendously exposed, and you'll need to think on your feet, but it's one we believe you to be eminently capable of. Your reports from the Foreign Office are excellent, Miss Armstrong. You're a clever girl and that's what this organization needs." Miss Jones lets her sit with this for a moment, before she says, "Besides, France is important to you."

Tessa nods. Perhaps they want people hardened by loss, she thinks.

"People I love are there," she says, simply, even though there is nothing simple about her situation. Her heart is in France. Her heart, shattered like glass.

"It's a lot to ask of you."

Tessa straightens her body. Makes herself feel tall. "I'm not afraid, if that's what you mean."

"There's nothing wrong with fear, Miss Armstrong. Are you worried about deceiving your family? You'd have to, I'm afraid."

"No, that's not . . ." Tessa stops. "Theo, I suppose. My brother."

But she's been lying to him since she left Paris. The shame of her deception washes over her.

"You're very close to him?" says Miss Jones, misreading Tessa's expression. It is a salve, the misdirection.

"Yes, very. We're twins."

"I wonder, would you need to elaborate on your ostensible move into the FANYs? Perhaps don't think of it as deceiving him, but rather as not giving him the entire truth of the matter until later on."

Tessa places her teacup down on the desk. At once, and without breaking her gaze, Miss Jones moves it onto a saucer, wiping away the small wet ring with a handkerchief whipped out of her blazer pocket.

"If I say yes, what happens next?"

Miss Jones smiles. It is neither pleasant nor cold, more an impression of someone smiling, as if she'd once observed someone do it and remembered what it should look like.

"We'll send you for training. It won't be easy, I'm afraid. It's designed to challenge, to make absolutely sure you're the right . . ."

Tessa's attention wanders. Perhaps she is simply incapable of absorbing anything more in that moment. Outside a window framed by thick brocade curtains, she can see the top of a bus driving past. Life going on completely as normal just a few feet away, as hers is inextricably altered. But no, she thinks, that is done; the alteration is in the past, this is simply another layer of change.

The only thing she can do, she decides, is move forward. She'd wanted to be just like Theo, contributing to the war effort in a way that mattered. Well, she thinks, now is your chance. Look how it's fallen into your lap.

Besides, she is not who she used to be. She will never be that person again.

Four

Tessa slides her finger along cold black metal. She's held a gun before, years ago when Theo found a new crowd at university. Shooting weekends at friends' grand piles, and balls with women called Lettice and Eugenie. Sometimes, if she was home, she'd tag along. Curiosity, she called it, and it was. Like peering into a goldfish bowl. At a supper one evening she'd offered up a passage from *The Communist Manifesto* in lieu of grace, and Theo declared himself "perfectly dead" from shame, taking their tone of voice, their disdain, as his own.

Those guns weren't like these, but the sensation is the same. Power, for there's no mistaking that's what it is, arrives in the form of a small pistol and a machine gun, which hurts her arm whenever she fires it.

"Take aim," says the instructor. "Aim for the chest, the largest area, although a head-shot is kinder, if you can. Remember we're not the monsters, they are."

She fires, hitting her target on her first attempt. "Good job," the instructor says, unable to hide his surprise.

It rains that afternoon. Tessa is in the woods, water leaching through her khaki overalls, the sodden fabric sticking to her skin. She feels as if she'll never be warm again.

Across a path strewn deliberately with piles of wood and rocks, her fellow trainee Inès is trying to catch her eye. She pulls an anguished face, mouthing, "I want to go home," and Tessa stretches her lips into a comedic, exaggerated grimace. It's a far cry from that morning, when they'd joked about "PE this afternoon!," because this is nothing like schoolyard games. Once they've cleared the forest, Tessa and Inès have to cross a narrow rope bridge above a river and scale a wall on the other side, all without an instructor declaring them "caught." She cannot help but look back, looking for "them," whoever they might be, tracking her through the forest.

"Where the bloody hell are they sending us—the Pyrenees?" hisses Inès.

Tessa's stomach is churning. "Try not to look down," she whispers.

"One foot in front of the other," says Inès.

"That's it. Just keep going."

In the dormitory that evening, the women huddle by the fire with contraband gin.

"The instructors are nicer here," says Brigitte. "At Wanborough they seemed positively insulted by the mere notion of training women."

"Remember that one fellow who wouldn't look any of us in the eye?" says Tessa.

"At least these chaps don't think we're only here to snag a husband," says Inès.

Fleur, who is at least ten years older than the rest, has a ripe belly laugh. "It doesn't occur to them that some of us might be quite happy to have left behind the husbands we do have."

Inès flashes a wicked smile. "But if we *are* on the lookout, I hear the Balkan section is the *crème de la crème* in terms of both beauty and brains."

Names are forbidden at Beaulieu. Inès is not Inès; Brigitte is someone else. Tessa, in this world, is Marianne, a new person with no ties, no obligations. No roots. Her aunt and her parents think she's on a training course for the FANYs, that she's going to be a driver or a translator or perhaps both—Tessa has tried to be vague, despite her mother's insistence on questioning her every move. She hasn't mentioned a word about it in her letters to Theo.

Brigitte pulls a packet of Rich Tea biscuits from the pocket of her dressing gown and passes them round the group.

"It certainly beats the secretarial pool," says Tessa, eagerly taking a biscuit from the pack.

"I was a typist too," says Inès.

"I worked in a shop," says Brigitte.

"I was a drunk's wife," says Fleur.

They are wide-eyed. This is as forbidden as the gin. The women are an odd assortment, all of them either French, half-French or with an unusually good grasp of the language. Mongrels the lot of us, Tessa thinks. Inès had grown up with a father in the diplomatic service. Brigitte, like Tessa, has a French parent. Fleur escaped life under the occupation, smuggled out by boat. Little details keep slipping out—they know, for example, that Tessa is a twin. But they could say anything, Tessa thinks, and I'd never know if it were true.

"I heard after jump-training it gets really interesting," says Inès, eyes flashing. "They send us on a dummy mission in a city we don't know. And it'll feel like we're on our own but really, they'll be spying on us the entire time to see how we cope."

Tessa raises her eyebrows. "Heard from whom?"

"Someone who should know better," says Fleur.

"Or someone who can spin a tall tale," says Brigitte.

"Apparently, they ply you with booze and see what secrets you spill," Inès says, and Brigitte pretends to spit out her gin.

"*And* they listen in at night to see if we talk in our sleep. I mean there's no point in us gadding about the Left Bank if we're singing the National Anthem in the King's English come midnight."

The Left Bank. Tessa takes a slug of gin and, when it burns, another.

When the bottle is empty they climb into their beds, into the space between what was and what will be. It takes Tessa a long time to fall asleep, moving between nerves and excitement. That she can be outwardly one thing but in truth something different is nothing new, but it has never occurred to her before that this ability might be worth something.

She drifts between sleep and not, turning her body toward the window, which frames a bright moon. There's too much in her head to grasp a single thought; in the turbulence, she can't get a hold of how she feels about anything. About Theo, about her training, and Paris, and ten toes and ten fingers, that blazing memory.

You seem amused.

Another memory in her mind's eye: a bookshop on the rue de l'Odéon, a crowd straining to hear the words of a man sitting in a small leather chair. She holds on to this memory. This Tessa, the Tessa of before, considered the author Ephra Laurent a genius. She'd expounded on his work in class at the Sorbonne, much to the horror of her professors, for whom writers like Laurent remained a step too far. Too new to be decent, too different to be accepted. She'd sent his work to Theo, who'd had precisely nothing to say on the matter, but then Theo feared change, always had, and she wouldn't want her brother any other way. But in confrontation with the author, because that's what this reading felt like, Laurent's importance was quickly transmuting into self-importance, its no-good cousin. The thought must have made her smile, because the man next to her leaned in and whispered, "You seem amused."

When Tessa turned her head, she was surprised to discover the voice belonged to the painter Luc Langlois. She'd seen his work at a gallery on Cork Street, canvases of bold dream sequences, lighthouses in deserts and castles afloat in vast oceans. She'd read profiles in magazines, seen his portrait taken by Lee Miller. Tessa forced herself to look away. "I stayed up all night reading his book. I couldn't put it down. I felt that I wouldn't be the same person when I finished it, and it's a rare piece of literature that has that power. But I'm not sure I feel that way any more."

"Why?"

"He's so . . . grand."

"He's a very great writer."

"Yes, and he's ruining that impression with his personality."

Luc snorted a laugh. People turned around and told them to be quiet. "He'll be remembered for his words, that's what matters. It's all he cares about."

Tessa frowned. "He doesn't get to decide how he's remembered."

When Luc invited her to a celebration at his apartment, she said yes. When it transpired the party was a celebration for Ephra Laurent and the pair were good friends, Tessa felt so mortified she thought she'd have to leave the party, and possibly Paris too.

"Ephra, this is Tessa," said Luc, before she could slink away. "She thinks you're too full of yourself to be any good as a writer."

Tessa ground her shoe into the paint-splattered floorboards. But she didn't deny it. Ephra Laurent pretended to consider her words, stroking the patchy black stubble on his chin. Even his beard is pretend, Tessa thought; a hint rather than something whole.

"She needs me to be humble," he said, confidently, to Luc.

"*She* has a voice of her own," said Tessa.

Ephra put his hands around her waist. Even when he felt her tense, he didn't let go. He dug his nails into her waist, making sure she could feel him make his claim. Then he slid onto his knees and pressed his head, nose first, into her crotch.

"I believe in my own greatness," he said, tipping his head back to meet her eyes.

Tessa clenched her jaw. "So I see."

People started laughing. Luc was looking at her, shaking his head and mouthing, "Ignore him."

"But in this I have become monstrous—forgive me!" Ephra cried, but it wasn't serious, it was theater. Eventually, when he had bared his soul and confessed his ego, and his audience had begun to tire, he let her go. He was just a clown, he said, baring his teeth in a tight, wide smile. He was not to be taken seriously, he added, but she'd noticed the glint in his eyes.

Tessa would always remember the sensation of his nails against her skin.

She is awoken by something solid and cold against her skin. "*Laisse-moi tranquille*," she mutters.

The cold comes again. Metal against her forehead. Then a voice, "*Oben! Oben!*"

The moon is centered in the window, round and white. She draws her robe from the bedpost and says, "*Je me lève*."

"*Komm mit mir.*"

The owner of the voice, as poor an imitation of a German accent as she's heard, hooks a hand beneath her elbow and drags her from the room. She hears Inès roll over, catches the muttered, "*Pas encore*." The man shoves Tessa into a cold metal chair, which hurts her shoulder and she cries out, looking accusingly at the instructor before she takes in her surroundings. They've dressed the room by undressing it. Plain white walls, a single table and two chairs, the beam of a bright Anglepoise lamp now angled into Tessa's face.

"We know who you are," he says, in English now.

"*Je suis Marianne Bonaly*," she says.

"We know you are an English agent. Your accent is terrible."

"*C'est drôle*, I was just thinking the same about yours."

The man slams his fist down on the table, a few centimeters from her hand. This being a beautiful English country estate and very much not a Gestapo prison, Tessa is finding it difficult to take him seriously.

"We know everything. There is little point in resisting, it will only bring harm upon you and your friends. You will give us the names of your coconspirators. I suggest you do not wish to discover the consequences of noncompliance."

"Why do you need their names if you already know everything?" she says, because she knows how it goes now, has the routine down pat. As hard as they might try, there is no way to make these mock interrogations feel real.

Besides, he's a good egg really, this chap, when not in his Gestapo get-up.

Breakfast is spent in the "French house," in which the trainees have to adopt French customs, and behave as naturally as possible in a foreign environment. It is a conspicuously modern building in the grounds, with slim chimneys and Crittall windows. Tessa is devouring a breakfast of pastries and coffee with Inès and Fleur. Blink and it's a holiday, she thinks. Blink between the real and this.

"Bad luck last night with the midnight Hun. He must have eyes for you—you've been interrogated more than the rest of us put together," says Inès.

The trainees speak French exclusively now. It's strange how it helps with the pretense; another layer of camouflage to go with the fake name and the French food, and the French labels sewn into her clothes. Fleur considers it her duty to iron out the faults in their accents, "which you English cannot or refuse to hear."

Tessa shunts her chair along a few inches to make space for the new arrivals. Jean, with his shock of white hair and round face, is known to all as

"The Moon." Victor is a somewhat dour man with a look of permanent anxiety. Victor, she thinks, is English and Jean is definitely French because Fleur worked with him before her escape.

"You look as if you had a restful night's sleep," says Jean, nodding at them one by one.

"Awful, actually," says Inès. "You wouldn't believe what we have to put up with. Night drills, dirty tricks, interrogations . . ."

"It'll be different, over there," says Victor. "They can't be rough with you here."

"I shan't say anything, no matter what they do," says Tessa.

"No one knows how they will react in that situation," says Fleur.

"If it helps, just remember that if you're captured, you're probably dead anyway. Might as well keep your mouth shut," says Victor, ripping up a croissant and dipping a piece into the strawberry jam. Definitely English, thinks Tessa.

"That doesn't help," says Inès.

After their first lecture of the day, Tessa and Fleur are given the task of packing away crates of materials for making plastic explosives. Tessa attends classes with extraordinary names such as "Murder," "Arson" and her personal favorite, "Codes, Ciphers and Secret Inks" (one day she intends to flummox Theo with her new skills).

"Here's a tale for you," says Fleur. "Did you know that Jean and I were supposed to leave France together?" Tessa shakes her head. "But we didn't. He didn't turn up. Apparently he needed more time to sort out loose ends with his family. He appeared for training two weeks later as if nothing was amiss."

Tessa seals a box and gets started on the next. She has no wish to be drawn into a conspiracy.

"A fortnight is a long time when you've declared yourself a subversive, no matter how much of a secret it's supposed to be. People talk. They are watching all the time." Fleur is speaking very slowly and deliberately, her fingers tapping against the metal box she's stopped packing.

"They wouldn't let him get this far if they weren't sure of him."

Tap tap, go Fleur's fingers against the metal. "Did you know Ronald Stenwick used to work in France? For a publisher in the south."

"I didn't know that, no."

"Our moon, Jean, was his right-hand man. They've been friends for years. The point is, we only know what they want us to know. Whatever they might promise in these classrooms, don't ever forget you're on your own."

Two weeks later, and Tessa is striding across the grass at RAF Ringway, nausea churning in her stomach. She has leaped from a rope strung from a gym roof and from a metal tower, her fall broken by a heap of old mattresses. She has practiced jumping through a rectangular hole cut into the fuselage of a stationary Whitley airplane, taking care not to catch her nose on the sharp-cut edge, a mishap so common it is known as "ringing the bell." She has learned how to curl her legs, how not to brace for impact, and how to roll on landing.

Today she is to parachute from a plane.

Inès is handing out cigarettes. "That's a whole pack already this morning. They've turned me into a chimney. Can't they bloody well hurry up?"

"Probably checking for cracks," says Victor, dryly. "These planes are about as old as I am."

"Are you all right, Marianne?" says Inès. "You're rather green."

It's a curious thing. Tessa's never had a problem with heights before. Toward the end of her training, she will have to throw herself from a plane, again and again, until she's totted up four training jumps. In dreams her parachute doesn't open. In dreams, she is subjected to a perpetual agonizing fall, the ground moving further and further away, except perhaps it's not her after all. Perhaps it's Theo.

Jean, who is struggling to contain his wild white hair beneath a leather flying cap, nudges her gently with his elbow. Fleur's words of warning are ringing in her ears.

"The plane won't be flying too high," he says. "They have to stay low to avoid detection. You'll hit the ground in ten, maybe fifteen seconds, and then it's all over."

"Hit the ground . . ." she echoes, wanly, when he turns back to the others.

Their instructor directs them toward a large boxy aircraft, painted in thick green stripes. Behind a stretch of glass, she can see the pilot checking his controls. It's not Theo, of course it's not Theo, but she feels a surge of hope whenever she sees a flash of blue uniform, even though she knows her brother is thousands of miles away. What would I say to him if we ran into each other in a hangar, she thinks, glad to steer her thoughts away from visions of plummets and bone-mangling landings. How on earth would I explain my presence here? She is an interloper in Theo's world.

The instructor quietens them down and runs through the procedure, demonstrating sliding open the hatch in the fuselage, making sure they've checked their parachutes. As they take their seats, the propellors either side of the cockpit whirr into life, and the plane lurches forward.

"Oh God," Tessa whispers. Someone squeezes her hand and she looks up, surprised, at Jean, who keeps his eyes focused on the land outside the window.

The point is we only know what they want us to know, Fleur had said.

"It's a practice jump, that's all," says Jean.

Tessa smiles but takes her hand away, folding it into her lap. She looks out on the disappearing land, the people at the aerodrome shrinking from sight. The flight is rough, the unsettled air bouncing them against their thinly cushioned seats.

I don't want to do this, she thinks.

"Time to go!" the instructor shouts, signaling to the pilot, after what feels like no time at all.

He opens the hatch on the floor of the plane. The group unclip their seatbelts and line up.

"You," the instructor says, pointing at Victor. "Go!"

Victor shoots them a grin and jumps. Tessa can see through the hatch for a few short seconds before Victor releases his parachute, a cloud of white silk erupting above his head. She feels the bile rise in her throat, feels her legs weaken as if they've hollowed out. I've lost my bones, she wants to say. So sorry, how inconvenient.

Inès, muttering the Lord's Prayer, jumps next, then Jean.

"You!" shouts the instructor, pointing at Tessa. "Go, now!"

But she can't. Her jelly legs won't respond and as fierce as the instructor is, with his roars of "Go, *go*!," the voice in her head warning of certain death is louder and more persuasive.

"But I can't," she says.

With a roll of his eyes, the man slams the hatch shut and points at the row of empty seats. "Sit!" he shouts. "Seatbelt on. *Now*."

Tessa bites her lip, determined not to cry. All this work, *all this work*, she thinks.

"Can I try again?" she says to the instructor, but he doesn't respond.

Back at their billet, a beautiful red-brick hall with peacocks strutting across a wide green lawn, Tessa is relieved to have arrived before the others. She shuts herself in a lavatory, taking off her flying cap and shaking her hair free. *Idiot*, she whispers. And then, in a voice so quiet she barely makes a sound, *fuck*. She presses her hands against the wall, letting her head drop, trying to gather her thoughts. She'll just refuse to go home, she thinks. It is dawning on her just how much she is longing to return to France. People she loves are there, she'd told Miss Jones.

Snap out of it, she thinks. She thinks of Luc, working in his studio. She's just back from a lecture and he turns toward her as she opens the door, smiling. It was such an unguarded expression, that smile, because she'd surprised him in coming home early and he wasn't quick enough to hide how delighted he was. Then she thinks about Theo, because Theo can tease her out of anything. Theo would tell her to calm down. Theo would know what to do.

She faces the others at supper, a chicken pie and green vegetables, in what must have been a grand dining room in the recent past, but in the present is lined with rows of metal trellis tables and uncomfortable chairs. Victor appears first, placing his tray down on the table, sitting back in his chair with his arms behind his head, reading her expression.

"Are they sending you home?" he says.

Tessa shrugs. "I don't know."

"It's a shame. You've the makings of a decent courier."

Jean and Inès appear, Inès's face creased with discomfort. She takes Tessa's hand and gives it a squeeze. "In a way, I think you're rather clever. I mean, it's a most unnatural way to arrive anywhere. If we humans were meant to fly, God would've given us wings, wouldn't he?"

Victor nods. "There's really no point in fearing the jump when it's what might be waiting for you on the ground that'll kill you. I mean, a jump gone wrong and you've still got a chance of survival given the height, but a machine gun?" He shakes his head, drawing a line across his throat.

Inès pales and pushes her tray away, muttering, "For God's sake."

"I've never had a problem with heights. I don't understand where this has come from." Tessa shrugs. "Not that I'd ever been in a plane before this, even with my brother."

"*Ton frère?*" says Jean. He picks up the pepper and shakes it over his pie. He keeps going, until a layer of black disguises the meal.

Tessa looks about to make sure no one else is listening. "He's a pilot."

"I didn't hear that," says Victor, through a mouthful of food.

Jean is smiling. "Your brother is a pilot?" he says.

Tessa nods. "Yes, but . . . I mean, he's not here, if that's what you're thinking. He's not going to be able to give me a pep talk. He's . . . somewhere else."

"But your brother has been through this training, *oui*?"

A vision fills Tessa's mind. Theo plummeting toward the earth.

Jean is still smiling. "So, he's better than you. He can do it, but you can't—is that what you're telling me?"

"I'm not telling you anything of the sort."

She sees Jean and Victor exchange a look. "It's because he's a man," says Victor. "I think we're just more suited to this sort of thing."

"It's our physique," says Jean, nodding. "*Notre caractère*. Our strength of mind."

"One might call it the supremacy of both the male physique and mindset," says Victor.

"I know what you're doing," says Tessa. Fleur was wrong about Jean, she thinks. Fleur must have got it wrong.

"So, you agree that men are better at parachuting than women, *oui*?" Jean says. "After all, more of us are trained to do it. I mean, the powers that be put so little stock in women parachuters they don't even award you your Wings. They don't think you deserve a qualification at all."

"Plenty of women have gone through this training."

Jean nods, sagely. "I see. So you are a disappointment to your sex, yes?"

Tessa feels her face twist involuntarily, and clearly looks so aghast that they laugh.

Victor says, "I think there's only one thing for it. You're going to have to prove us wrong."

The next day, Tessa leaps from the Whitley on her first attempt.

Five

There is an aberration sitting on Aunt Violet's doorstep. It has a face like her own only slimmer, the jaw squarer; but the same eyes, the same color hair tucked neatly beneath a blue peaked cap.

"Theo!" she cries, her suitcase slapping down onto the pavement as she throws her arms around him. "What are you doing here? God, I've missed you."

Theo, it seems, cannot speak. His eyes move over her own aberrations, the khaki uniform of the FANYs, because of course she hasn't said a word. She can imagine the tussle of questions in his head—should he ask about the uniform or the suitcase, has he missed a letter? Instead, perhaps because he cannot come to a decision, he says, "I'm waiting for someone to let me in. I've got a day's leave before I take up a new posting in Sussex."

"Africa too hot, was it?" She pulls her lips into a smile and hopes it looks casual. She isn't prepared for this. The lies don't yet feel natural on her tongue.

He laughs. "Something like that. What are you wearing?"

Tessa looks down, as if surprised.

"What happened to the Foreign Office?"

This is a tone of voice she knows well. He's not going to let it go and he's not going to buy it—even she knows how implausible it sounds. She pushes past him and slots her key into the door. The lies only land if she's not looking at him. "Fancied a change, that's all. Where's Aunt Vi?"

"I don't know. How the devil should I know? But Tess, the FANYs?"

Tessa marches ahead into the kitchen and puts the kettle on the stove, thinking about how her aunt's house has never changed. It is still almost entirely as it was when they were small, and for a moment she envies her aunt's ability to grasp a point in time and never let it go.

"Silk stockings and debutantes," he says.

"What's that?"

"The FANYs. Hardly your scene—you hate debutantes. Or is it some sort of class war thing? Bringing down the *ancien régime* from the inside."

Tessa's eyes are bright with the deception. "Now there's an idea. Tea?"

Theo is here and in her head, eight again, devouring Aunt Violet's chocolate cake at the kitchen table. Thirteen, and sulking about being left there by their parents, even though they both loved it really. Wasn't it simpler then, she wants to say to him, and don't you wish we could go back? They've sat at this table at every age, and she thinks this is probably not the first time Theo's done so while simultaneously trying to decode his sister. Tessa can close herself off, but he doesn't have the gift. The kettle whistles then, making her jump, snapping her from her thoughts. Twisting open the lid of a tin of loose-leaf tea sends a musky, woody waft into the air. Tessa spoons some leaves into the pot, adds water and gives it a stir. Aunt Violet would say, let it be, give it time, but Tessa's never been one for waiting.

She pours them each a cup, adds milk and sits down. "Go on then, tell me everything."

"Everything?"

"Absolutely everything. How many people have you killed since I last saw you?"

He shifts in his seat. If Tessa sees a scab, she has to pick at it, even if it's threaded into someone else's skin. "I'm not flying bombers. I'm not unleashing mass carnage onto populations. It's more about picking them off, one by one," he says in a quiet, low voice.

She smiles, pleased at this glimpse into a side of his character he rarely shows. "How coolly clinical," she says.

Theo takes an apple from a bowl in the middle of the table, and with his penknife begins to peel the skin, a single neat coil. Their father bought Theo the knife at a market. How jealous she'd been. "What do you want with a knife anyway?" Theo had said, looking pleased to be singled out by their father, who normally only had eyes for Tessa. Because of course, why would a girl be in need of a knife, save for in her kitchen drawer?

"It's more a case of 'them or me,' actually," he says.

"Don't spoil it. I adore coolly clinical you. Not a mass murderer, but a sniper. How close do you get? Can you see their fat black hearts pounding beneath their iron crosses and swastikas?"

Theo runs a hand through his hair. "Jesus, Tess." He's right, it's too far. "What's this all about?" He gestures at her peaked cap, sitting on the table between them.

Tessa feels her shoulders tense. "I told you, a change."

"You're not a driver, surely?"

"There's nothing wrong with my driving."

Theo laughs. "My nerves and that dead sheep say otherwise."

Tessa shoots him a look. "Translating, that sort of thing. I want to do my bit, like you. Typing and fussing around with paperclips didn't feel enough."

"It's not really *like me*."

"Thanks for that."

"But the FANYs . . . ?"

"I don't know why you keep saying it like that."

"Yes, you do." Theo grins, spying the wavering of her resolve. "If you wanted to see some action you'd join the WAAF. The FANYs is just a way to keep society girls amused while they wait for all the eligible chaps to return. Everyone knows that."

"An outrageous and classist generalization."

"Is it? I thought I was quoting you."

He passes her a piece of apple and keeps the rest for himself. "This isn't anything to do with Michael, is it?"

Tessa makes a show of rolling her eyes. "I'll have you know I've been recruited for my superior language skills . . ."

". . . which they couldn't utilize in the Foreign Office?"

"Which they had little desire to utilize in the Foreign Office."

She's up out of her chair then, pouring them both more tea and setting a kettle of fresh water on the Aga. She can feel Theo's suspicious gaze burning into the back of her head.

Later that evening, Aunt Violet dishes up lamb—sourced, she says with a wink, from *a contact*.

"That's the greengrocer, the baker and now Mr. Tims the butcher all head over heels in love with her," says Tessa.

Theo is devouring the meal at a rate they'd normally consider quite rude, but all is forgiven in the current circumstances. For the last few years every sentence, every action is forgiven due to the current circumstances. Aunt Violet and Tessa sit mesmerized.

"What do they feed you at your base?" says Tessa.

"*Do* they feed you?" says Aunt Violet.

Theo shrugs it off. It's the journey, he says, it's being relaxed, it's just what a decent meal does to a fellow. He says, "It's really very kind of you to take such good care of my sister, because you do look good, Tee. You seem . . ." And here he sits back in his chair, his eyes on her face. He looks surprised. "You seem happy."

Tessa looks away, feeling suddenly emotional. She doesn't want to pinprick the mood and spoil even a second of her time with her brother.

"She's the easiest house guest I've ever had," says Aunt Violet. "She's never here. When are you off again, dear?"

"I'm waiting to hear about my posting," she says, chewing on her bottom lip.

"Does that mean you might not be in London?" It's like an itch Theo can't reach, she thinks.

Tessa focuses on her forkful of lamb. "We have to go wherever we're needed. That's the rub, I suppose. The only certainty is uncertainty."

"God, you sound like a training manual." She knows he's thinking, come on Tess, what is this, spill the beans.

"Well, it's obviously gone in then, hasn't it?"

She takes him to a pub. Not the sort of place he'd expect, either, and she enjoys watching as his brain collects the pieces of this jigsaw puzzle, trying to slot them together. At The Crown it is loud, the sort of volume that sees conversations split into the basics of language, convenient for those who wish to keep secrets. The pub is a mass of bodies. Fellow airmen nod and hold Theo's gaze just a second too long, because they're bonded now in all the terrible ways, in ways the twins can never be. But perhaps this is no longer true, she thinks—because she has no idea what her future holds, not any more. Tessa knows that her brother has seen death, and feared that any moment could bring about his own, while Tessa has not. But then, Theo will never comprehend the feeling of watching your body change in the knowledge that you are growing, sustaining a life. It is the dividing of a thread she'd once thought would run straight throughout their lives, and for a moment she is stunned by this loss, of what they had and she'd thought would always be. Theo looks back at her then, and she wonders if he senses it too, the loss, and its permanence.

"Let me introduce you to my friends," she says, quickly, leading him to a back room where it is quieter. Several tables have been requisitioned and crammed together. Colton, the American airman, is there, his face changing as she approaches: she sees pleasure, which makes her feel a little ill, and then confusion when he spots Theo on her arm.

"Stand down, Colton, he's my brother," she says, primly.

There are sweaty handshakes and kisses. Girls from the Foreign Office, Americans picked up from who knows where.

"Him?" Theo hisses in her ear.

"It's a benevolence of sorts. Every day might be my last, and it's even more likely to be his." She slaps her hand to her mouth. "God, Theo, I'm sorry." It is a shock, how easily she stumbles upon the worst possible thing to say.

Theo frowns. "I don't think about it. Besides, that's part of it, isn't it? The risk."

"So you do think about it." She thinks, I know you, Theo. I know how your mind works.

Colton worms his arm about Tessa's waist, the possessiveness of the gesture making her skin crawl.

"Not when my brother is in town," she whispers, and he skulks off toward the crowd, shooting miserable looks over his shoulder. The thrill of disappointing someone who wants her erupts in goosepimples on her arms. It makes her feel powerful, when once she did not.

"You know, if you want to see your chap, I don't mind," Theo says.

"Don't you? I'd be livid if you spent our one evening together with someone else. I've missed you something rotten, Theo. Besides, he's not my chap."

"Does he want to be?"

"It doesn't matter what he wants," she says, more sharply than she intended. She changes the subject, abruptly, because she knows he caught her tone, and she can see the quizzical look in his eyes. "Are there any women at your base?"

Theo leans back against the wall, uninterested. She knows when she's being indulged. "A few, but they're barely out of school. Why, are you worried I'll get lonely?"

Of course he misses her point. The dividing lines of gender mean so little to those on the winning team. "I meant *working* at your base."

"Oh, did you? Some, I suppose. We don't really mingle, or at least, I don't."

Later, as they walk in the cool evening air from Belgravia to Bloomsbury, Tessa tells him how she'd often stay in bed when the air-raid siren rang. It's not that she wanted to die, she just felt calmly accepting of the situation. Those are two different things, she says.

He's looking at her in a strange way, his lips pursing and relaxing, pursing and relaxing, as if he can't quite find the words.

"Some of the men in the squadron," he says, after a while, "they're a mess. It does things to your head, war. It's not all heroics. It's not like the newsreels." He hesitates. "It's hellish, you know. Except that isn't enough, that word, 'hellish.' There aren't words, I think, for this experience, and I'm worried . . ."

Tessa lets the pause hang. "Worried about what?" she says, eventually.

"That I'm going be a different person when this is all over. What it's doing to me."

They are in a garden square, neat lines of plants and oak trees, triangles of green, except the new world is there disrupting this sense of order. Sandbags. A salvage station. A searchlight, unmanned and dark. Theo sits down on a bench, patting the space next to him. It's cool now, a clear evening of coal-black sky.

Tessa drops her head onto his shoulder. "Human beings are very resilient."

He takes a breath. "Look at you and Paris."

"Meaning what, exactly?"

Even though she can't see his face, she knows he is looking down at her.

"You went away one person and came back another."

She doesn't say anything for a while. Theo squeezes her hand.

"Is that why you joined up?" she asks, quietly. "Because I forgot to answer a few letters all those years ago? You didn't do it to get back at me, did you? Because I won't be able to live with that, Theo."

He shrugs her head off his shoulder and looks at her. "You can't possibly think that, not really."

"I don't think you've ever truly forgiven me for leaving."

"Tess . . ." Theo shakes his head. "That isn't remotely true. Of course I forgave you—we moved past it. I adored visiting you in Paris, just as I loved you visiting me in Cambridge. Those are some of my favorite memories."

She smiles, despite herself. "Mine too. And the letters."

"We must have used an entire forest's worth of paper writing to one another. Look, I joined up because it was the right thing to do. Just as the Sorbonne was right for you . . . even if it hurt me at the time, which it did. You know it did, and we dealt with it. We moved on. And then, in your last year in Paris, everything seemed to change again, and I still don't understand why. I don't understand the way things have been since. The way it is with us. Was it the distance, after all—the being apart?"

She is staring determinedly at a patch of grass, a few crumbs of seed still visible, an earlier gift for the birds. A feast for the rats. "I have no idea what you're talking about."

"That's because you think you hide it, that you're this wonderful actress, and I'm sure you do fool plenty of people. Problem is, I know you better than anyone else. And look, you wanted an escape from being part of a pair, fine—I understand that, even if I don't feel the same way. I've never felt that way. But you're different. You *are*. You're shut off, and sometimes you can be cold in a way you never were before, and brittle—yes, you're brittle. I don't know if it was something I did and that's why you wouldn't see me that last summer, or . . ."

"Theo, it was four years ago." She can't look at him.

". . . Or if something happened to you, something that made you unhappy, because you were, Tess, even if no one talked about it, even if you didn't . . ."

"I don't know what else to tell you. Maman wanted one last holiday, that's all, so we spent the summer abroad. We all knew this war was coming. It was our last chance and we took it. We grabbed it. I'm sorry I was so hopeless at writing. I'm sorry Maman didn't invite you, but you were busy with your studies and your pupillage and no one wanted to get in the way of that."

Theo snorts. "The mother and daughter summer tour is the least believable part of it. You'd never put up with each other for that long without a screaming row."

"Look, I know joining the FANYs is hardly comparable to your astonishing feats of bravery, but . . ."

"I'm not talking about that. Don't turn this into something else."

Tessa starts to cry. She searches her pockets for a handkerchief, but Theo beats her to it, pressing his own into her hand.

"People change. It does happen."

"Not without a good reason, they don't," he says, firmly.

"Besides, it's not as if you don't have any secrets."

He bristles. She knows he's afraid of what she might say next, of the questions she might ask. He knows she means his friend Stephen. Theo's other life, that he can never bring himself to speak of.

Tessa looks him straight in the eye, the light shifting between them. "Theo . . ." she says, but stops. He could never understand. She couldn't bear his judgment. *Girls like that* . . . She remembers his words, has never forgotten them. Her mother was right—it's better this way, even if it hurts, even if it's always there between them.

Like her mother said all those years ago in Paris, it cannot be undone.

Six

The car is leaving London and Tessa has her nose to the glass, wanting to absorb it all in case it is her last chance. Outwardly she is calm, a picture of serenity in fact, although the dart of Miss Jones' eyes suggests this is in itself a cause for alarm. The calm, of course, is a lie, another to add to the pile. Her belly is full of butterflies, because in a few hours she will be in France. In a few hours she might be dead. In the sky, the moon stands white against the blue. Once they have left the suburbs, dog roses roam wild upon hedgerows. Tessa breathes it in, this Englishness; the glory of it feels like a goodbye of sorts.

"I saw my brother when I was in London. He was on leave. Funny when the stars align like that, isn't it?" She thinks about saying goodbye to Theo. Of how tightly she'd clung to him.

"How was he?" Miss Jones sounds amiable, but her eyes are locked on Tessa's.

"Well, thank you. He has a new posting, although you probably knew that. I didn't tell him about this, if that's what you're worried about."

In the rearview mirror, Tessa sees the driver look up and then away, his eyes back on the road.

"No, but it would be understandable if you had. Some of the girls do, the chaps as well. He's the person you're closest too."

Tessa looks out of the window again. Outside, the sun colors everything golden white.

"Are you all right, Tessa?"

"I am, thank you."

"It's all right to not be, you know."

Tessa smiles at this. "Would you prefer me a nervous wreck?"

"I'd expect a glimpse of nerves, yes, at the very least."

"Maybe I'm an even better actress than you'd hoped."

I just want to get away from myself, Tessa wants to say. But she can't; imagine the questions it would invite. Miss Jones is almost as bad as Theo, with her keen nose, digging into everyone's business. She thinks, I just want to get away from the past. I want to erase the last four years. Do my bit. Except it's not just the weight of the past, it's the here and now. It's the butterflies in her stomach, and the thought that tomorrow will be so very different to today.

"Theo did say something interesting. He said that risk is part of what he does, an attractive part. He said he doesn't think about death."

"Do you think about it?"

"Theo's death? All the time. I can't imagine anything worse."

"I meant your own."

Tessa hesitates. "We're none of us invincible, Miss Jones."

The barn at the airfield in RAF Tempsford is neat and rectangular, like a child's drawing, all clapboards and red roof tiles. The others have beaten them to it, two cars parked at awkward angles on the gravel path. Tessa picks up her suitcase, full of clothes belonging to the person she is now—Marianne, not Tessa, not any more—and follows Miss Jones inside. Another woman shakes her hand. Adrienne—not her real name either, Tessa knows. A man, middle-aged and balding, sits quietly in the corner of the barn, a cup of tea clasped in his hands. It's obvious to Tessa's ears that the man is French and the woman is not. She molds her thoughts into her second language, wondering how different it sounds from the voice in her head when spoken aloud.

A table is set with cold meats and cheese. They serve themselves, although Tessa can't think that anyone feels like eating. There's a knock at the door, three firm raps, so uniform and neat that Tessa knows in her gut the hand belongs to a military man. Sure enough, the head that appears around the door is attached to a body clothed in RAF blue.

"Let me introduce you all to Squadron Leader Bridgham," says Miss Jones, as Bridgham sits down and helps himself to a plate of food.

"Fine weather today," he says, and they nod their heads.

How odd it feels to hear someone speaking English in this environment after sticking so rigidly to French for months. Tessa wants to laugh at the absurdity of it, but it wouldn't be received how she wants it to be, which is lightly. Danger is no longer an abstract set of instructions written on a blackboard in a Buckinghamshire country house; it is an hour away and here they are, behaving as if it's a dinner party. After supper, Squadron Leader Bridgham sits them down on metal seats, the signifiers of war around them. The black telephone, just like her father's but with a Green Hornet scrambler attached. A map of France marked with red flags, Bridgham pointing here and there, as he begins his briefing.

"We've just heard from the Met Office and you'll be pleased to hear conditions are ideal for the drop," he says.

Tessa's stomach lurches. She wants to reach out and squeeze Adrienne's trembling hand. The woman is trying hard to hide it, clasping one hand within the other, pressing her flesh as if willing it to behave.

Bridgham produces a photograph of the landing site, a strip of green in the middle of a forest.

"It's so small," says Tessa.

"It is, and you'll only have a narrow window in which to make the drop zone," says Bridgham. "The site is approximately two miles southeast of the city of Poitiers and its transport links. It might seem dark now, but you'll be astonished by how quickly your eyes adjust. And I dare say the lack of light won't stop you finding the bottle of whisky we've stowed in the fuselage for you to share."

A ripple of laughter runs through the group, but the smiles don't reach their eyes. Within no time at all Miss Jones is rising to her feet, thanking Bridgham for his contribution. She turns to the group.

"Before we say goodbye, I want to say to you how brave, how extraordinary I think you are for accepting this mission, and to thank you for the courage and tenacity you have shown thus far. You all have your own reasons for being here but I know that you all, without exception, want your country, be it Britain or France, to be free."

They are dismissed from the room, before Miss Jones calls them back one by one. Tessa goes first. This time, Miss Jones speaks in French, checking each item in Tessa's open suitcase, the labels, the buttons, the novel tucked in between blouses and stockings.

"Tell me about yourself," she says. "What is your name?"

"Marianne Bonaly," says Tessa.

"Where are you from?"

"I was born in Paris and educated there—at the Sorbonne."

"And now?"

"And now I'm looking for work. I'm prepared to go wherever that work might be."

"Oh? Are you not married?"

"I was . . . I am. He's a prisoner of war in a work camp in Germany."

"You must be dreadfully worried."

"Of course. He used to write . . . but it's been a long time since I've heard anything."

"Go on."

"Before the war I was a secretary to a lawyer in the city, but now . . ." Tessa takes a deep breath. "Now I do what I have to, to survive."

Miss Jones snaps the suitcase shut. "Good. But try not to answer questions you haven't been asked. Folks keep their heads down in France. Don't volunteer information."

Tessa nods.

"A party of local Resistance members will be waiting to welcome you in France. They'll give you a meal and a bed for the night. Then you're on your own, and you'll need to get in touch with our network on the ground as soon as you can. Your contact is a chap named Basile. Have you memorized how to contact him?"

Tessa swallows, and nods again.

"Basile will have instructions as to your next move. Tessa, this is our last moment together. I've been following your progress and want you to know how proud I am of you. You've done very well in training, and you should know that a lot of very senior people are impressed by you."

Tessa, unable to suppress a surge of pride at this praise, takes a wad of envelopes from her coat pocket. "These are the letters for my parents and Theo."

Miss Jones takes them. "We'll send them at plausible intervals. I imagine you'll be able to get letters sent back from the field on occasion too, which we'll forward on to your family."

"What's the point? I won't be able to say where I am or what I'm up to."

"Indeed, but you may be away for some time. Some agents find it helps to feel they have a connection to home. And of course, you'll be able to comment on the news, the latest with the war. It'll give your correspondence a more realistic edge."

There is little to do but shake hands. Tessa climbs into her flying suit, smoothing down her clothes beneath so that she might appear presentable when the moment comes, a pistol strapped to her waistband in case things go wrong from the off and she needs to defend herself. But could I pull the trigger, she has wondered. Could I take a life? She straightens her hair beneath her leather flying cap and adds a fresh layer of red to her lips. She vomits her nerves into the porcelain toilet bowl, hoping nobody can hear through the walls, all horsehair and rot. They are driven in an old Ford station wagon to the runway, where a Halifax bomber, its undercarriage painted black, sits gleaming in the moonlight. They all comment on the moon as they huddle by the plane's cold metal ladder. It is their good luck charm, they say, a beacon.

Bridgham talks them through take-off, showing them where to store their luggage. He mentions the whisky again and they laugh tight laughs. They will all take a sip before the plane leaves the ground. Bridgham shakes their hands in turn, as does Miss Jones, and they climb aboard. Suddenly no one can meet anyone's eyes. Now it is real. Tessa forces herself to breathe slowly, her parachute weighing heavy on her back. The engines roar into life and then there is movement, the aircraft lurching forward and picking up speed. They wave at Miss Jones from the windows, as the plane rises into the air with bone-juddering vibrations, Tessa feeling as if she might at any moment split in two. She thinks, how can anything so loud, so cumbersome, fly over a country undetected?

Bridgham was right about their eyes adjusting. Suddenly there is detail. Bridgham and his copilot visible through the gloom; and the controls, little red lights and gauges. The navigator poring over maps. No one speaks, there is little point in trying above the sound of the engines, so they pass the whisky back and forth in silence. It doesn't help, the drink, it only encourages the panic rising through her body. It's as if she has a cinema behind her eyelids, constantly replaying an imagined scene, a spiraling plummet to the earth, the land rearing up toward her. Little beads of sweat begin to sprout on her forehead, above the goggles fastened too tightly. Her hands are shaking and she hopes the others don't notice. Minutes pass, hours. Through the moonlight she can see the fields of France below, the loops of the Loire. She squints through the darkness at the others but no one seems moved, no one seems shattered when she is quite shattered. Heart, mind, resolve. She looks once more from the plane window and thinks of Paris. She thinks of the dappled sun on her grandmother's linen sheets, and of being with Luc in his studio, when every moment had felt like a dream. Then Bridgham is speaking to them in his low, calm voice and the others are moving in their uncomfortable seats, unbuckling their lap-belts and shifting their packs against their backs. Tessa feels the bile rise. Two rows of torchlight illuminate the ground below. The plane dips slightly, and she feels it slow down. Then the hatch is open and below is the earth and those lights, two rows of people guiding them. The crates go first, supplies, armaments, and letters from home for those who came before her. The crates fall, pops of white parachutes disappearing into the black. The green bulb illuminates, meaning it is time.

"Go, go," says Bridgham, through the radio. Adrienne jumps, then the balding man.

"Go," says Bridgham to Tessa. She knows what to do but her feet won't move. Her minds fills with visions of the land below, rising up to devour her as she plummets. Not again, she thinks. Please not again.

"Go, now!" Bridgham shouts.

I've done this, she thinks. I know I can do it. Four jumps, four landings. Why is this happening again? Perhaps the floor is glue. Perhaps the floor will save her.

"Too late, don't go," says Bridgham. The green bulb goes dark, the red lights up. It happens that this is all she needs to overcome the images behind her eyelids, the flickering imaginings of death. Tessa launches herself through the hatch. Bridgham shouts, the radio crackling, "No, no. You'll miss the site!"

Then her body is in flight. Cold air rushes into her mouth, her nose, her ears, and even if she wanted to scream, she couldn't. The dots of light are behind her, the ballooning silk of the other parachutes, like barn owls, silent and white.

Tessa presses the release on her own parachute and it unfurls, wrenching her upward. Then, with the most incredible crack of noise, the land below explodes into flames.

Seven

She is caught by the outstretched branches of a beech, her weight straining against the thick straps of her parachute, the fabric cutting into her arms. Branches tear through the silk with an almighty rip, which in the sudden silence of the forest sounds like thunder. Then her brain begins to catch up. The explosions of light, the thundering rat-tat-tat of machine guns.

Tessa manages to brace first one foot then another against the tree, so that her parachute straps no longer bear her full weight. Tugging against the ropes, she tries to dislodge the parachute from the branches but it is stuck fast. Something warm is sliding down her face. When it reaches her lips she recognizes the metallic taste as blood, but she can't feel any pain. She tries to steady her breath. Calm down, she thinks. Don't panic. She *is* panicking. With effort, she slides her arms from the parachute and leaves it suspended in the tree, the wind catching it, inflating the silk like an enormous white beacon. Where is her confidence, she thinks, why is she now her brother with this one-hand, one-foot motion, so slow, so painstaking when she knows there is no time. There are voices at the edge of the trees. Torchlight.

First things first, they'd said in training, weeks ago, which feels like a lifetime ago. Take off your flying suit. Bury your weapon. Try to look as normal as possible, as quickly as possible. Try to look like one of them, because you are one of them.

Tessa reaches the ground with a thud. She can see the moon, it's still so bright. She thinks of Bridgham in the Halifax, London-bound. Does he know, she thinks, did he see the explosions, hear the guns? *You'll miss the site*, he'd screamed. Tessa might have no idea where she is, but she is alive at least. She can hear the rustle of an animal, she can hear footsteps. Tessa starts to run. Why do her feet slap against the earth with such force, why is her heart like a beating drum? Don't panic, she tells herself again. Stop panicking.

Tessa keeps running, her fingers tight around the cold metal of her pistol. She's doing everything wrong. Hasn't made herself look normal, didn't hide the parachute. They'll find it, they'll know she's there, they must have seen her falling through the sky. Keep going, she thinks. She wants to say it aloud, needs to hear the sound of her voice to know she is really there, is really doing this, in France. France! Her feet hit a gravel track and skid to a halt. The driveway of a house which bears no light. A dog begins to bark. It's perfect but too obvious. It'll be the first place they look.

The woods go on and on. The soft crunch of debris, twigs and leaves, beneath her. She thinks back to the maps they studied in training, and tries to place the woods, to remember where the road is, and where the enemy is likely to be congregated. The enemy, she thinks. Nothing is making sense, her senses are scrambled by the silence, the descent, the darkness. The fear. It occurs to her that she is running in a straight line, that this is wrong, so she veers off the path carved by deer and other creatures, into the narrow spaces between the trees. It seems unfathomable they have not caught her yet; they must have vehicles and dogs—power, when she has none. Pain begins to wind its way from her feet, traveling north through her veins until it spreads across the entirety of her body. It is in her lungs, in her ragged breath. Tessa stops, letting her body sag against an oak, ivy knotted around its trunk. Who holds who, she thinks, the ivy or the oak?

It's too quiet. Is it possible that with the lights and the guns, they didn't notice her? This seems too good to be true. She tries again to catch her breath and resumes running. She thinks, stop panicking. She thinks, oh God, oh God, oh God. The trees are thicker in this part of the wood, her eyes struggle to adjust to the blackness. Tessa can hear water. She slows down, walking with her arms outstretched to keep the branches from her face. She can hear an owl, the wind in the trees, the gentle crunch of movement, the language of the woods.

The water is a stream, the moon has two faces, in the sky and mirrored in the water. Why haven't they come? The roots of another oak have burst free of the earth, coiling over the river like a spider's legs, matted with mud and plants. Tessa shuffles down the bank and crawls into the space beneath the roots. If she sits with her legs folded against her chest, the water laps at her shoes but doesn't touch her clothes. She is so cold. For the first time she feels grateful for the flying suit, even though she knows she should take it off. If they found her now she could be a runaway. Or a local woman who went out for a walk and got lost, and thank heavens they have come. Her mind conjures a scene, the landing site strewn with supplies and other things, the others from the plane, the reception committee with their lanterns, which she blinks away because it is too much to comprehend. They are dead, surely. There is no way they could have survived such an onslaught. The Germans will have her suitcase. She combs her mind through its contents: clothes with the right labels, stockings, undergarments, money and books. Nothing with a name, nothing to give her away save for the fact there is one suitcase too many. Her papers are in her pocket. She has a little money. She has the pistol.

A voice calls out through the black, then another and another. German accents. German words. Tessa gasps, unable to stop herself. She winds in her limbs, making herself as small as possible, and clamps her hands over her mouth to stop herself from crying out. Her pistol has only six bullets. Will they kill her straight away, she wonders. Is that what has happened to the others, to Adrienne and the unnamed man, to the people waiting on the ground?

When Tessa opens her eyes, it is to the soft light of a new day. The water is still lapping at her boots but it has a color now, silvery grey, like home. Tessa and Theo used to swim in the Cam every morning. The water on their skin like ice, a rush of sensations. She can picture her brother pushing through the water, ripples spreading wide from his body. I wish we were there now, she thinks, and that none of this had happened. Silently, she folds her lips around his name, *Theo*.

It takes a moment for her to comprehend that they did not discover her, despite the engines, the guns and dogs. And yet she feels no relief, no sense of calm, because she knows with the skidding, thudding beat of her heart, the tightness of her breath in the shallow well of her chest, that relief would be foolish. They might be watching her right now, their cruel smiles becoming gleeful, as they wait for her to emerge. It takes another moment for her to comprehend that when the footsteps and the voices and the torches disappeared, her eyes had somehow closed and remained so. I am a fool, she thinks, a lucky fool, because at no point in training had her instructors recommended falling asleep as a strategy. Summoning whatever strength or bravery she has remaining—to Tessa they are one and the same—she crawls out of her hiding place, shocked at the difference between the woods in daylight and the woods at night. A few hours ago it had felt like a never-ending forest, thick and medieval, a place of wolves and roaming deer. In daylight she can see the trees away from the stream are not so old, nor are they tended to, the oaks and beech standing thin and weak. Bright streams of light speak of openness. Tessa scoops up water with her hands and washes her face, removing blood and dirt. Her fingers map a long cut on her cheek. Not easy to explain and she has no makeup with which to cover it. She pulls the leather cap from her head and combs her fingers through her hair, clipping it back into shape. She slides the flying suit from her shoulders and pushes it with the cap beneath the spider-leg roots, hiding the pistol inside the fabric as instructed. Young French women going about their business are liable to be searched, and they do not carry weapons. Tessa needs to appear as normal as possible. Her clothes, a jacket, cardigan and cotton dress, are crumpled but passable if she can smooth the worst wrinkles away with her hands. She has no hat, which feels strange and might attract looks, but perhaps her youth will excuse it. She'll say she forgot it. She'll say she thought the day too warm.

Tessa makes her way through the trees until she finds her way back to the narrow deer path. She looks first one way and then the other. Logic suggests they will be waiting, but she can think of no other way of escaping. The leaves are green and new, the woods riven with the promise of hope, but all Tessa can feel is waves of nerves. This isn't happening as it is supposed to. Nothing is going to plan.

Eventually she reaches a road, the woods behind her, fields in front, the road dividing them. The countryside feels too quiet; they should be everywhere now it's light. Tessa makes a decision. She turns right, no rhyme or reason to it—to her eyes, there is little difference either way. The air holds a chill, despite the light, and she pulls her jacket tight around her. She's been walking for ten minutes when a car appears, slowing down beside her as she walks along. Tessa feels her nerves, or maybe just bile, rising in her stomach.

A man with a beard, streaked with grey, unwinds his window. "Are you lost?" he says.

"I'm trying to get to the city," she answers, feeling conscious of her accent. "A man stole my things. He knocked me over and I hurt my face." She is providing answers to questions he hasn't asked.

"You shouldn't be out here." The man is stroking his beard, looking her up and down. "The Germans are everywhere."

Tessa looks down the road, and back toward the woods.

"I can drive you to the nearest station," he says.

This is a choice she will face daily, she realizes. To place or not her trust in strangers, people who might very well be *them*. She looks into the man's eyes, and into the back of his car where a Labrador lies asleep, unbothered by her presence at the window. There is a green blanket draped across the seats, an empty crate, nothing to aid her appraisal. Instinct, after a night of little sleep, feels a risk in itself.

She rocks back and forth on her feet, before climbing into the car. "Where are you going?" she says.

"To the market," says the man. "Not that there's much to buy."

The view from the window begins to change from flat arable land to the occasional house, squat and square, until she can see the red rooftops of a village. A crowd seems to be forming, and she is about to ask the man what it is when she spies the blockade. The French police, not the German army.

"For God's sake," says the man. The skin around his eyes is pinched. "Do you still have your papers?"

"Of course," says Tessa, but too brightly, because no one should seem relaxed in this situation. She takes the proof of Marianne's existence from her pocket, willing her hands not to shake. At the checkpoint the police are questioning and searching people, their bags and vehicles.

The French police have a reputation for helping the occupiers. They spoke about it in training, the police willingly serving up busloads of Jews for deportation.

The man is still squinting at her, reading her mind. "They used to be bad but now, who knows? I think the police are as sick of the Germans as the rest of us."

An officer approaches the car and raps his knuckles against the window. "Papers, please," he says.

The driver passes his papers and then Tessa's through the wound-down window.

The officer scrutinizes their faces. "You are together?" he says.

Tessa wants to say yes but before she can summon the courage, her companion says, "No, I picked her up about a mile back. She's been robbed."

The officer is staring at Tessa. "Wait here, please," he says, gesturing for a colleague to join them.

"I'm sorry," says the man.

"It's all right, I'll be all right," says Tessa. She turns away until she feels she has driven the panic from her eyes because no one must know how scared she is, even the man in the car.

A different officer approaches the car and opens the passenger door. "Come with us, please," he says. He takes Tessa's arm and pulls her from the car, as his colleague does the same to the bearded man.

"No, wait, stop. What has he done? What have I done?" she says. Her head is turned away and she is marched toward the open door of a police car. She does not see what happens to the man, or his dog, no longer sleeping but yowling on the back seat.

Eight

Tessa is driven several miles to what appears to be a small town. Her eyes map the journey from the car window, the way the roads divide and merge, the woods, the lay of the land. A house there, a barn. The car stops in front of a modern building, all grey stone and hard edges, at odds with the historic blur of the surrounding buildings.

"Excuse me, but what have I done?" she says, amazed at how steady her voice sounds when inside she feels sick with fear.

They have taken her papers. Tessa looks up at the sky from which she fell not twenty-four hours ago. Perhaps the supper in the airfield barn will turn out to be her last meal. The men in the front seats do not answer her question. The door is opened and Tessa is pulled from the car. She manages a quick glimpse of her surroundings before her head is pushed down against her chest, a bar catching her eye. *Chez Emile* is painted in thick red letters above the door. She knows the name, has filed it away as a safe place, all those hours of training finally paying off.

She wonders how this scene appears to the people in the street, and how often they have witnessed it. Do they even notice any more? Tessa is marched into the narrow entrance hall of the building, a row of hooks on one side heavy with coats and jackets. The chairs along the other wall are occupied but no one looks up.

The young officer at the front desk examines her papers and writes down her fake name in a ledger.

"What is this about?" she says, trying to sound annoyed rather than terrified, but neither the officer behind the desk nor the one holding her arm react. She is led to an office, painted green, with a desk in the center and cabinets along one wall. A French *tricolore* hangs from a stand in the corner of the room, but it is not alone. It is joined by the Führer's standard with its furious red, its black swastika. The truth is a slap in the face. This is no longer her France, the country she once loved; it has been stolen. She cannot drag her eyes away.

Tessa sits down on a metal chair in the center of the room, clasping her hands together in her lap and willing them to stop shaking. Her eyes scan the desk, alight on a photograph of a woman and two children, blond and perfectly formed. How well they'll fit into this new world, she thinks. A notebook, closed. A golden pen. She can't help but imagine what they will do to her. A memory seeps out: a farmer back home, dragging a dog into his yard and shooting it dead because it had mauled his sheep.

Then the door opens. It is a different gendarme, young and eager, she can see it in his eyes. Too young, surely, to be married to the woman in the photograph, to be the father of those children. Perhaps it is his mother, his siblings.

He sits down at the desk and looks at Tessa. "The Germans are looking for you," he says.

Tessa forces her lips into a frown. "Have you found my things?"

"Excuse me?"

"I was knocked to the ground and robbed. Look . . ." Tessa draws her finger along the cut on her face. "I'll happily testify against the man who did it. I doubt I was the first."

How easily it rolls off her tongue. The man just stares at her. "How insulting," he says.

"No, I wouldn't say I was insulted, just cross. No one likes to be robbed."

"Of course, of course. No one likes to be deceived either, wouldn't you say?"

"I'm sorry?"

The gendarme is smiling back at her. "Go on then, tell me your story."

"My story?"

"Yes." He looks down at a sheet of paper. Her papers, it turns out. "Marianne Bonaly, *qui est-elle*?"

This is nothing like the mock interrogations by the midnight Hun.

When she has introduced Marianne, trying not to trip over the details she has committed to memory, trying to make it sound natural, the man laughs, a hollow, cruel sound. "Yes, we love to hear these little tales. Do you think we don't know who you are?"

Tessa swallows. "You know who I am. My papers are in your hand."

The man clenches both hands into fists, his knuckles turning white then red. "You people . . . it just makes me so angry. It makes me furious, in fact. Who are you to tell a nation what is right? The arrogance of it, the entitlement. Who do you think you are?"

"I've told you who I am. My name is Marianne—"

The gendarme slams his fist against the desk, making her jump. "No. One man, two women but only one woman found at the site. One crate of ammunition. The Germans thank you, by the way. I'm sure they will put it to good use. What else? Ah yes: crystals for a wireless transmitter. Perhaps you might know for whom they were intended?"

Tessa blinks. "I don't know what you are—"

It is a shock when he hits her. Standing up, his feet square, he swings his arm into the strike, knocking her to the floor. It takes a moment for the pain to arrive. She puts her hands to her face, blood dribbling from her nose and over her fingers. She has cried out, but it feels as if the noise came from someone else. She thinks of the people coming and going in the foyer, wondering if they even broke their stride.

"You're a monster," she spits, through the blood, as he comes around the desk.

When he kicks her in the stomach, she can tell from the look in his eyes he is enjoying it. Stenwick had warned her she might pay with her life but she hadn't prepared herself for the possibility of failing quite so quickly.

She thinks of her brother, all the while trying to keep her breath steady. Theo will never forgive her for keeping this from him.

"Now you talk," says the gendarme, pulling Tessa up by her arm and throwing her back into the chair.

"OK," she says, "OK, my name is Marianne Bonaly. I was born in—"

He hits her again, but this time she is determined to stay upright. The door opens. It is an older officer, the husband of the woman in the photograph, Tessa is certain of it.

The older gendarme looks from his colleague to Tessa and back again. His eyes track the blood smeared across the floor. "For heaven's sake," he says. "This is my office."

The younger gendarme is irritable, but Tessa cannot tell if it's because his authority is in question, or because his fun has been curtailed.

"If you want to do that, take her somewhere else," says the elder gendarme. To Tessa he says, with a noncommittal shrug, "Go and clean yourself up."

Tessa crosses the hallway, past the desk, to the bathroom he points at. There are people milling about but she reads it differently this time, sees how determinedly they are not noticing her. Tessa examines her face in the mirror. Blood is streaming from her nose. Tears carve a line through the mess of red. I have a mask now, she thinks, the smear of blood rendering her unrecognizable. She squeezes her eyes closed, trying to recall her training. First things first, check for danger, look for a way out. Tessa opens her eyes, exhaling slowly, watching the rise and fall of her chest in the mirror. She blinks away the remainder of her tears and checks the small rectangular window, but it won't budge. She scoops water from the tap and sweeps it across her face, pressing her fingers against her cheek and wincing. When she is finished, she steps back into the hallway, into the small crowd spilling out from the metal chairs. Are they locals, here to report crimes, she wonders. Or are they under suspicion too? No one is guarding them, no one is taking any notice of them at all. The door to the office is now closed. The gendarme on the desk is a different man to the one who welcomed her—if that is the word, which she's sure it is not. He has never seen Tessa before, at least as far as she knows, and that small grain of doubt is enough for her to form a plan.

Tessa takes a coat from a hook on the wall and slides her arms into it. She's waiting for a shout, a hand on her shoulder, but it never comes. She swipes a burgundy beret and pulls it down over her hair, and then—as if it is nothing at all—pushes open the front door of the gendarmerie and leaves. Then she is on the steps, looking out onto a strange town. Sometimes eyes are weapons, the hurried look about the street as they hauled her from the motor. Now, thanks to that snatched look, she can step out of the gendarmerie and appear as if she knows exactly where she's going.

She can hear her breathing, shallow and ragged. Her lips are wet. The nosebleed marks her out; the cut on her cheek, too. It's what people will remember if they're questioned. Have they seen a strange woman? Well yes, there was the woman with the blood all over her face. Except, people do get nosebleeds. It's hardly a rare affliction. I just have a nosebleed, she thinks, nothing more. Wiping her hand across her face makes her flinch. If it's a nosebleed and not an injury, then, thinking logically, there should be no pain. There is no pain, she decides, every word punctuated by ever deepening resolve. The bruises won't be far behind.

There is the bar she'd spotted from the car, despite the hand pushing her head down into her chest. It is, she thinks, astonishing how much the eye can detect from such a poor start.

People are watching but pretending they're not, well versed in feigning disinterest by now. Not drawing attention to oneself is the first rule of life under occupation. Tessa is trying to keep the fear from her face and tension from her body, because she knows at any moment a hand might grab her arm, forcing her back to an almost certain fate. *An almost certain fate.* She feels a swell of tears which she swallows down—grateful for this skill she's acquired these past four years. Had she truly comprehended the risk before now? No, she thinks, appalled by her own naivety. She thinks again of the farmer and his dog, because that's how they'd do it, isn't it? A quick shot to the back of the head, clean and quick. She wonders, unable to stop the thought: is there any awareness as the bullet penetrates or is death instantaneous? But then, what is an instant if not a moment, a passage of time, however brief. She thinks, oh God oh God oh God. Despite the warnings from Miss Jones and her instructors, despite the constant reminders of what they were taking on, Tessa realizes now that she'd assumed she'd be all right. Because no matter what has happened in the past, she has gone on, she has simply gone on, dragging the wreckage behind her.

Tessa keeps walking.

As she crosses the street, she adds details to her rudimentary map, trying to regain her focus. Keep going, she thinks. The gendarmerie is behind her, its steps of thick stone. An ash tree, its branches run barren, creeping up against a window with bars. There's an alleyway to the left that leads to God knows where, and one to the right leading nowhere at all. Bins, boxes and a high wire fence.

In training they'd said to expect the unexpected. Gently pressing her face with the tips of her fingers, Tessa hopes the swelling hasn't started to show, turning up the collar of her stolen coat to hide the worst of it. They thrill in it, men like him, especially when it's a woman. In hindsight she doubts she was the first. A young mother to her left is hurrying children along the pavement. A *tabac*, a *boucherie*, a *pâtisserie*; a French town is a French town is a French town. An old man with a stoop, and how painful it looks but the thought only lasts for a sharp second, because there are so many thoughts behind her calm eyes. They may appear too calm with a nosebleed like that, so she adds a twinge of distress, there for them to read in her eyes and posture.

The door to *Chez Emile* is heavy. Putting her weight into it just to gain an inch sends a cascade of pain through her body, but it's all right, with the breeze it could be a shiver. Two men sit as far apart as the bar allows, heads bowed to their newspapers. The barman—Emile?—gives no response but locks his eyes on hers. That's the giveaway. Friend or foe—one day of tiptoeing behind the lines, and already it can all be said with a look.

"I'm sorry, but I have a dreadful nosebleed. Might you have a bathroom I could use?" she says.

The barman flips open the hatch on his thin wooden bar. Glasses are piled high to the ceiling on dusty shelves. Metal signs hang in between boxes of cigarettes, coffee and aperitifs. A glass shattered against the bar could be a weapon. A knife to slice lemons. Hot coffee in a pot. She walks through the open bar as if she's supposed to be there and look how effortless it is, the movement of her body within this space. Doesn't it seem as if she's always been there, with the furniture and the dust on the shelves, as she walks into a back room as if she knows the way. A desk to the left is piled high with paper. A box of soiled towels and cloths on a dirty floor. Cobwebs above and all around, sticking to her coat sleeves as she moves through. Then another open door, then daylight, then fields. A bicycle to her right, not in great condition but it will do. It has a basket, what joy, but she has nothing now.

There's a tap on her shoulder. The barman presses a handkerchief and a few francs into her hand. A square of paper, an address, brief directions.

"Go quickly," he says, his face so riven with worry that she wants to say it'll be all right, don't fret, but she can't because he's right to fear the worst.

Then she is on the bike, heading south through the woods. She'll follow the river, can't risk the road. Behind her they are discovering what she has done, the fact that she is gone. She knows it is inevitable that more are coming.

Across the sea, from the sky, through fields, and lanes, and villages. Her life before is a dream that feels more unreal by the day. Theo, Maman and Father, who know nothing but the lie. She wonders, perhaps for the first time, if she will make it home.

Nine

Her parents are the metric against which all adults are measured. That is to say, her first thoughts about Agnès Roue are to compare her to her mother. Agnès is younger and lacking her mother's style, being more practical in her trousers and waistcoat, which are in any case more suited to her circumstances. Tessa is thinking such thoughts to distract herself from the giggles of a child coming from behind the bedroom door, and the sharp sting of an iodine-soaked rag on her cheek.

"A few more moments should do it," says Agnès, from the stove where she is warming a stew. It smells delicious, but Tessa is so hungry it could be a thin gruel and she'd devour it.

Agnès ladles the stew into a bowl and passes it to Tessa. "Incredible what one can create with nothing," she says.

"I feel terrible taking your food."

Tessa has only the money from Emile in her pocket. Unless Agnès is an actress of extraordinary skill, she was warned to expect Tessa's arrival at her door, pulling her into a warm embrace and drawing her quickly inside.

Agnès lights a cigarette, running her eyes over Tessa as she shovels food into her mouth. "You're good, you know. Better than some we've seen."

Tessa shakes her head. "I don't know what you mean," she says, which makes the other woman chuckle.

Agnès pours a small glass of yellow liquid from an unlabeled bottle and passes it across the table. "Drink this, it'll help with the pain."

It smells pungent and sour.

Agnès pulls hard on her cigarette. "Has a man ever hit you like that before?"

"No," says Tessa.

"Then you're lucky. You'll be all right in a few days."

Tessa looks around in case anyone might be listening, not that there is anyone else in the small apartment, save for the giggling creature in the bedroom. The facts: she has no papers, no money, and probably the Gestapo on her tail. Her only options are to trust Agnès or go it alone, with nothing. The benevolent bartender at *Chez Emile* evidently trusts Agnès, and it's funny how that seems to mean something, given the man is a stranger.

"I just walked out," says Tessa. "The Germans looked for me all night, and the police just let me slip away."

"Sounds like you had a friend."

Tessa thinks. The older policeman? The gendarme on the front desk? "I have to get in touch with my contact. He'll tell me what to do next."

"You have the bicycle, but I'd wait for the bruises to go down. You should probably get some sleep too."

Tessa's shoulders sag, the movement almost automatic, as if she's lost control of her bodily parts. "They've got my papers," she says. She wishes Agnès would pour another glass of the yellow liquid. It's given the scene a pleasant blur.

"Then we shall have to get you more. It'll take a few days. Let's say you're my cousin, come to help with the baby. You'll need a new name, though." She reaches out and tugs Tessa's hair. "And you can't look like you any more—the Gestapo will have your picture everywhere." At Tessa's horrified expression, Agnès laughs. "It grows back, so I'm told."

"*Au revoir*, Marianne," says Tessa.

There is a wail from the other room. Agnès slips away, returning with a dark-haired infant on her hip.

"This is Eliana, although we call her Elaine now," says Agnès.

"How old is she?" Tessa can't quite look at the child.

"A little over a year. Do you want to hold her?"

"No . . . no, thank you. Not right now. Where is . . . I hope you don't mind me asking . . . where is her father?"

Agnès snorts. "She's not mine. Her parents lived in Paris."

"Where are they now?"

"God knows. There one day, gone the next. Mercifully, Elaine was with a cousin at the time. They took everyone, big and small."

The child has pink circles for cheeks. Green eyes beneath long lashes.

Tessa's throat is dry. "Were her parents in the Resistance?"

Agnès shakes her head. "Jews. Their neighbors couldn't wait to see the back of them. Are you sure you don't want to hold her?"

Tessa shakes her head. The child's legs are like doughnuts, one on top of another. Her hair falls in fat ringlets.

"I'm sure that's not true," she says. "About the neighbors, I mean."

"Talk like that is a giveaway you're not from here. No, the French have turned denouncing their neighbors into an art form. Sometimes I wonder what I want for Elaine, justice or revenge?"

Tessa scrapes back her chair and stands. The noise startles both Agnès and the child, who is sucking hungrily at a bottle, the rubber teat clasped between her few milk teeth.

"I think I'll go to bed now," she says, abruptly. "Thank you so much for the food. It was delicious."

She carries her stolen coat through to a back room and draws a curtain over the door space. She dresses in the nylon slip Agnès has laid out for her and climbs beneath the sheets of the narrow bed. It's no good. Sleep, when it comes, is ambushed. There will be no rest, her unconscious mind decides. Dreams form around the memory of the birth, the pain, and the splitting of skin.

The next morning, Marianne is reduced to heaps of brown hair on the floor.

"It's not that bad," says Agnès, which does little to raise Tessa's spirits. "You look a little bit like Louise Brooks."

Tessa laughs, although she doesn't feel like laughing. "I shan't worry about standing out, then."

Agnès is looking at her, eyes narrowed. "If only we had some dye, but . . ." She throws her hands in the air with a sigh. "This life."

It feels like a loss, a ridiculous one, but a loss all the same. As if her sense of self is bound up in the piles of hair. It is an unraveling, see how it unspools, womanhood and identity. Now I really am someone else, she thinks, but it sits uneasily in her gut. When her hair is dry and makeup has been caked over her cut and bruises, Agnès takes her picture with an ancient-looking camera and disappears again. The child is nowhere to be seen; she seems to move through a rotation of houses in the village during the day, an assortment of women, always women, picking her up and dropping her off. Tessa thinks she should offer to watch the child, but this is impossible—she knows her limits. So, she cleans the apartment and prepares food for this woman she does not know, who might not be who she says she is, who might at any moment arrive with the Gestapo, a fat bounty in her pocket to see her through the rest of the war.

Tessa wants to move on, but she cannot without instruction and she can do nothing without papers. On the third evening, as Agnès settles the child in her crib, Tessa serves up a meager meal of cheese, ham and bread. A pile of food coupons is stacked high on the table.

"I encountered the most annoying woman in the queue for the butcher today," says Agnès, speaking in the low voice she uses whenever the child has just fallen asleep. "She's seen me with Elaine, and even though we don't know each other from Eve, she felt it quite appropriate to tell me how little we look alike. Does she have her father's nose, she said. His *nose*. You know what she meant, yes? I should have got Elaine out when I could. There are networks—it's doable but difficult. The Germans are everywhere here. It was stupid of me to think I could pass her off as my own."

"What are you doing with all these coupons?"

Agnès smiles, grimly. "There's tobacco too, look." She pulls out a crate from beneath the sink. "Can't spare any, I'm afraid."

Tessa feels her cheeks grow hot. "No, no . . . I just . . ."

"Ha! I saw the way your eyes lit up." Agnès is pouring herself a glass of wine and grinning. She slides the bottle across the table toward Tessa. "It is for those left behind. There are a lot of women with a lot of mouths to feed and barely the means to do it. All the men are gone. Vanished. We women have to look after our own, see? It's not like anyone else will—not the Vichy government and certainly not the Germans."

This is not the sort of thing they taught in training. Resistance means sabotage, not support.

"Where do you get the coupons from?" asks Tessa.

Agnès waves her hand airily. "There's ways and means for almost everything if you're determined enough."

"And shopkeepers just give you a little extra?"

"Absolutely not. That would interfere with their black-market trade. You see, some of us are starving and some are doing very well. No, you just have to ask in a way that leaves them no room to say no."

"How do you do that?" Tessa asks, quietly, because she's not sure she wants to know.

"By not asking at all."

Later, Tessa helps Agnès to divide the coupons into equal shares for a network of women whose husbands have, for a variety of reasons "vanished."

"Are you married, Agnès?" she asks, knowing full well the answer. There are photographs in drawers and cupboards, she's looked.

"Yes," says Agnès, not looking up.

"Is he in prison?"

"He was in a camp not too far away but they moved him."

"To where?"

"I'm not sure. Somewhere in the east, I think. I haven't heard from him in a long time."

Tessa wishes Agnès would keep a few coupons back for herself and Elaine, but knows she won't. She wants to leave this place knowing they will both be all right, but the likelihood is they won't be.

"What did you do before the war?" she says.

Agnès shrugs. "Same as I do now. Social work."

"You look after everyone."

The woman laughs. In the harsh electric light, she looks incredibly tired. "But I used to get paid to do it," she says, quietly.

On the fifth day, Tessa's bruises have faded enough for her to leave the apartment. Agnès applies makeup, a thick beige paste, to disguise what remains. It sits on Tessa's skin like a layer of wax. It makes her feel brand new and perhaps she is. Her papers call her Isabelle. She wonders, when all is done, just how large her collection of aliases will be.

Tessa rides cross-country on Emile's bicycle, following a route dictated by Agnès. No roadblocks, no crowds, no one to wonder what on earth

Louise Brooks is doing riding through the Loire Valley. She keeps catching sight of herself in shop windows, her hair falling just above her chin. Who is this person, mirroring her every move? She wonders what Theo would think if he could see her now, if he'd be proud or appalled. She hopes he'd be impressed. Her mother would probably say that Tessa is doing what she does best, causing trouble, getting involved when she should stay quiet. Tessa is the problem child, whereas no one need worry about Theo, and how easy it has always seemed to be for her mother to divide her children in this manner. Tessa tightens her grip on the bike's handlebars. She hopes her father, the pacifist, will understand.

It's easy to find the dead letterbox, a small hotel in a nearby town where she can leave a message for her contact. A group of children are hovering outside, arguing over a skipping rope: it's my turn, no it's mine. A little girl snatches the rope toward her with such righteous indignation that Tessa stops and smiles, even though she knows she should get away as quickly as she can. The girl must be about five, just about the right age, dark hair, although obviously it's much longer than in the image in Tessa's mind. Someone, the child's mother she supposes, has brushed the girl's hair through and tied it with a green ribbon. Tessa shakes her head and shoulders to be rid of the thought. Would I recognize you, she thinks. If I saw you, would I know?

Tessa deposits her note with the woman on the front desk, who takes it and places it in a pigeonhole without so much as glancing at it or Tessa. When she steps back outside into the light, into the fresh air pulling in and out of her lungs, there they are. Germans, a whole convoy of them. It is an odd sensation, like a cooling of her blood, a wave of hatred and anger rushing through her. Where are they going, she thinks, in their tanks and armored cars, when the closest battle is in the sky? A crowd is gathering on the pavements, it's still enough of a novelty for that, it would seem. Tessa wants to absorb every tangible detail—the shape of the helmets, the cut of the uniforms, the sound of the panzer's tracks and leather boots against the dirt road.

The next day, after another night with Agnès, she returns, waiting at the allotted hour in the allotted place—a ruined church near the edge of town. She'd scouted it the morning before, deciding it was a place for lovers, which in Tessa's mind is one and the same with what she'd been searching for. A place for a clandestine assignation. She'd said two o'clock, but when her contact—an agent she knows only as Basile—does not arrive, the doubts set in. Had she, after all, written three? Dog roses smother many of the ancient graves, ivy claims the rest. It reminds her of those Sussex hedgerows, the last journey with Miss Jones. The smaller hand on her watch inches to three, and a feeling of dread descends into the pit of her stomach. She is twisting her fingers together, looking about, trying to keep her expression neutral. She's doing what she's supposed to, but it's still going wrong.

At half past three she decides to leave, concluding that Basile's absence might suggest something sinister. Dislodging her bike from its perch against an old poplar tree, she pushes it through the undergrowth toward an iron gate set into a high brick wall. She will later wonder, the memory sheared down its center by shock, if she heard the crunch of a footstep before the leather-gloved hand clamped across her mouth, or if the hand came first. The bike goes one way and she the other. She is forced against the wall, face first, the mortar full of stones and bits of glass.

"When I got your letter, I thought I wouldn't come," whispers a voice, in English, into her ear. "Then I thought, no, I want to stand face to face with the person who betrayed us. I want to look you in the eye and see if there's even a trace of guilt."

Tessa tries to make a sound, but it only makes him press his weight against her, the rough brick scraping against her forehead.

"I thought I'd see if you brought the Germans with you—just so I'd know for certain. Are they here, Marianne? Do you have them hiding in the bushes, waiting to pounce? Let them take me, I say. It's worth it for the chance to tell you what you've done."

He loosens his grip, flipping her round so they are face to face. He must be in his forties, hair peppered with grey, cheeks riven with blood vessels, giveaway enough without his hot whisky breath. Tessa tries to breathe through her mouth. This time she is determined to get it right, even if he is not. "*Quel temps fait-il?*" she says, hoping he'll detect the steely edge to her voice, hoping it isn't muffled by panic.

The man takes a step back, laughing, though he doesn't smile. "Yeah, all right. If you'd rather. It's humid. There'll be a storm tonight." The words fall from his mouth in a low, flat tone. He pats his coat pocket. "I wouldn't run if I were you."

"There's no one here," says Tessa, quicker than she'd have liked, still stubbornly in French. "I haven't brought anyone with me if that's what you're worried—"

"They're all dead. All of them." He is equally stubborn in sticking to English.

The breath catches in her throat, although she'd known it must be the case. "The landing committee, the others . . . ?" she says. She tries to stop the images but she's too slow, the darker corners of her brain claiming victory. Adrienne's nervous hands back at the airfield before the flight to France, the noise of the machine guns.

It should have been me, she thinks. She closes her eyes but Adrienne is there too, in the darkness.

"All of them. Good people they were, too. And we had one of ours on the ground, in the landing committee. He's dead and all." Basile wobbles off balance, taking a moment to regain his composure. Tessa wonders how much he had to drink to decide this suicide mission—if indeed he really did believe she'd sold him out to the Germans—was a good idea. "White-haired fella named Jean," he says.

Tessa takes a step back. "The Moon," she whispers. She drops her head, putting her hands on her knees to stop herself from keeling over. She feels sick.

"Knew him, did you?"

Tessa can't escape the vision of Jean, tearing at a pastry with his teeth, strawberry jam caught in the corners of his mouth. The shock of white hair and his big, round face. His hand squeezing hers on the parachute flight. His kindness. Then she thinks of Fleur's suspicions as they'd packed away the crates during training, Jean fleeing France weeks after he was supposed to—well, she needn't worry now. Basile begins to pace up and down, one hand against the gun in his pocket—if it is a gun; he's offered her no proof. The gate is a foot away. If she forgets the bike she might just make it.

"They're all dead. All gone. Except you. I've been wondering . . . I came all this way to ask you. When did you turn? And why? Or have you been on the enemy's side all along?"

Tessa takes a step toward the gate. An inch, an inch, she thinks, but too late, it's too much. Basile's hand is back on his pocket. "I haven't turned, and I haven't told anyone anything," she says, insistently. "I missed the drop zone, that's all. It's the only reason I'm alive."

"Bullshit. You were in the gendarmerie. We hear things, you know. There are eyes everywhere. Why didn't they kill you like the rest? Thought you had more to offer, did they?" He stumbles again, this time toward her. Tessa allows his body to make contact with her own, before twisting and shoving him back against the brick wall with all her might. Before he can protest, she slides her hand into his coat pocket, wrapping her fingers around the pistol. Remembering her training, she raises the gun until it is level with her midriff, keeping it close to her, anchoring herself with her feet spread hip-width apart.

Basile throws his head back and lets out a peal of laughter. "Here we go," he says. Then he slumps down against the wall and begins to cry. "Look at you—all this and you're so calm. Like stone."

"This isn't calm," she says. It is always a surprise to discover how others perceive her. Her heart is thudding in her chest.

Tessa crouches down on the grass, upsetting a pale blue butterfly. It flutters around Basile's face, but he doesn't seem to notice. "Pull yourself together," she whispers, holding up her hand when he opens his mouth to speak. "And for God's sake stop blathering on in English or you'll get us both arrested. *En français, oui?* Yes, I was picked up the morning after the drop, and then I escaped."

"Yes, how did you do that then?" he says, in French, surprising her with his obedience.

"I've no idea—luck, mostly. I must have had help, but I don't know who from. One of the gendarmes, perhaps."

Basile laughs. "Not bloody likely . . ."

"A man in a bar gave me an address and I've been there ever since. I haven't told anyone anything. Even if I'd wanted to, I didn't have a chance. It all happened so quickly."

Basile whips his head away and vomits on the grass. She thinks, is this really Ronald Stenwick's army? Bringing down the axis of evil from within, one drink at a time. Taking hold of the man's chin, she angles his face toward her own. His skin is warm and sticky. His breath turns her stomach.

"There's no one waiting, no Gestapo hiding in the bushes," she says. "It's just you and me, so snap out of it, will you?"

Basile takes a hip flask from his coat pocket and takes a swig. "Seems you haven't heard," he says. "Funny, I thought your Nazi pals would have been bragging about it like mad."

"Heard what?"

"It's all gone to shit, that's what. Mass arrests. Networks collapsing. Paris is a goner, by the sounds of it. Long and short of it is London wants you home. There's a flight next—"

"No. I just got here, I'm not . . ."

She hasn't achieved anything yet, she thinks. What is the point of not dying like the others, to then just give up? Theo hasn't given up, she thinks, curling her fingers into a fist. Theo wouldn't go back.

"Those are your orders. I'm to make sure you get on the plane."

Tessa sets her mouth in a firm line. All those months of training. The break with everything that went before. "I won't go. I refuse."

Basile shrugs. "Fair enough. I couldn't care less."

"What about you? Are you being sent home too?"

"Oh no, lucky old me, I'm to stay and rebuild. London doesn't quite seem to appreciate just how often the Germans happen to be waiting for us."

"Meaning what, exactly?"

"Meaning London has a bloody mole. Meaning we're blown. Good luck getting them to believe it, though."

"If you're staying, then why can't I? You'll need a courier—"

"No."

"You can't do it all by yourself. Besides—and look, I'm sorry for being blunt, but my French is a damn sight more convincing than yours—"

"No."

"Why?"

"Because I don't trust you. You're right, though, your French is good. How's your German?"

Tessa looks Basile straight in the eye. "I'm not a traitor."

"Good for you, of course you're not. It doesn't matter." He hands her a square of paper. "Those are the flight details. Memorize them and destroy it. Personally I'd leave you here to rot, but what can I say? They don't listen to the likes of me."

He staggers to his feet and brushes grass off his coat. "I'll take that," he says, reaching for his gun. Still reeling from his accusation, and against her better judgment, Tessa hands it back.

"I won't go," she says, jutting out her chin like the little girl stealing back her skipping rope outside the hotel.

"Fine by me."

Tessa feels a thud of alarm. "But what do I do, where do I go?"

Basile shrugs. "Not my problem. As far as I'm concerned, dear, you're on your own."

He walks away, leaving Tessa alone in the graveyard. Theo—she'll think of Theo to stem the panic. She wants his voice, but there is nothing. Birdsong and insects, the unsettling quiet of solitude. All that effort spent blocking him out, and she wants nothing more in that moment than to undo it all.

Ten

She is on a train, going south.

Agnès has set it up. Tessa was frantic. It's not the danger, nor the being cast out, it is the thought this opportunity might be taken away because she has nothing else. She cannot go back to nothing. She will not go back to the secretarial pool. Agnès has solved many problems, including the infant Eliana, and Tessa will not be the last. "There is a man," she says. "He is one of yours. You'll go to him."

Tessa admires her determined way of speaking. There are no shades of grey. This is what will happen, and this is how we will do it. "I can't, they won't trust me," she says.

"But he trusts me. I'll tell him you're no traitor."

Tessa can't help picking at the scab. "But you don't actually know that."

Perhaps that is the worst of it, the danger she brings to Agnès. Every day she remains in the apartment increases the risk.

Agnès taps her head. "Instinct. It never lets me down. Go to him, he'll be able to use you. I should think he'll be glad of the help. I'll let him get in touch first, and then you'll know, won't you? That he wants you." She takes out a pencil and writes down an address on a scrap of paper. "You'll need to remember this, don't carry it with you. There will be a room for you, although you'll have to work for it."

"How do you know they'll take me in?"

"Because it's what they do. They provide shelter when people need it." She is busy sorting through her coupons, tidying away the breakfast things, shooing Tessa away when she tries to help. "I haven't told them who you are. I mean, who you *are*—they know you are Resistance, one of us. But they won't get in your way—in fact I doubt they'll even ask. And that is Resistance too, do you see? We all play our parts, and those parts can be quite different. But we are all opposed to this murderous occupation."

And now Tessa is on the train. The carousel turning again. Marianne before, Isabelle today, Tessa hovering like electrical interference between the two. She shows her papers to a young SS guard, who looks pale against his grey jacket, trying to strip any sign of hesitation from her movement, wondering if she comes across as too forceful, too eager. She knows to smile just so, to maintain eye contact a fraction of a second longer than the norm. It pricks his interest, distracting him from thoughts of duty and suspicion, just as she'd intended. Before she knows it, he is carrying the suitcase filled with clothes borrowed from Agnès, and checking the ticket bought with Agnès' money, and making sure she is settled in her seat.

Tessa squashes her nose into the glass. She wants to breathe it in, this view. It disperses the panic.

The train is pulling into a station, but not hers, not yet. She watches people disembark, weaving their way between the soldiers and swastikas on the platform, their eyes lowered. France is so quiet, that's the main difference between before and after—no one speaks any more. Conversations beyond the necessary—how much is this bread, do you have any butter?—are kept safely behind closed doors. Her eyes are alert to children clinging to their mothers' hands; she is searching their faces, because she is here, somewhere, in France. What would I say, if I saw her, she thinks. And would she believe me?

If she ran into Luc, how would she stop herself from calling out his name? She tells herself to stop it, to pull herself together, because one-two-three villages ("Count them!" Agnès had warned), and she is there.

"There" is an abstract concept. There is nothing there. The platform is a strip of concrete set into a bank. No buildings, and none on the horizon. No soldiers either, or people shuffling along, eyes down, hoping this won't be their day. One man stands on the platform, wearing a low cap and a black jacket. He does not look down: in fact, he meets Tessa's gaze in a way she has come to understand is quite dangerous. The man has dark curls which spill from beneath his cap, olive skin and tufts of black hair visible beneath his open shirt collar. Tessa feels herself blushing as she approaches him. His beauty is a shock.

Up close, she can see his eyes are hazel with a flash of green.

For God's sake, she thinks.

The man nods and sets off toward a white Citroën parked at an awkward angle on the side of the road, which is more of a track. He pops open the boot and climbs into the driver's seat. Tessa drops her suitcase into the boot, slamming it shut with more force than she intends. It is amazing, she thinks, how often she has to rely on blind trust. She stifles a laugh, a smile—because it is ridiculous and the ridiculousness is easier to comprehend than fear or danger—as she climbs into the motor with this handsome stranger, who could be anyone. She can't remember the last time she laughed, realizing that she is exhausted, worn through from being someone else. She has been in France for just over a week.

"My name is Isabelle," she says. The man glances at her out of the corner of his eye, the skin around his mouth tightening and relaxing as he purses his lips, as if he is tussling with something in his head.

"Welcome," he says, after a moment, a hint of a smile vanishing so quickly Tessa can't be sure she didn't imagine it.

They follow a winding track down into a valley, the path like a spring unfurling. The land is green, luscious and alive. Fields are planted in wide strips, vegetables and sunflowers, it's all the summer's promise. The farm, when they arrive, is small. A house of rough golden stone and an oak-framed barn, with stables and pigsties arranged around a yard. It reminds her of a farm near her parents' house, but how it must have been fifty years ago, before machines replaced men and thick-bodied horses. There is a lopsided cart loaded with hay. Chickens scatter between her legs, somehow both frightened and curious. In the low-beamed farmhouse kitchen, an old woman is serving bread and cheese to a man with wild grey hair and a girl who looks no older than fifteen but must be—surely—given the girth of her pregnant belly.

No one looks up. Her driver takes a slice of bread from a plate and begins to slather it with a rich, brown pickle.

"I'm Isabelle," she says, after a moment.

The woman stops and looks her up and down. From her expression it is obvious the verdict is not good. "You will call me Madame Delon. This is Monsieur Delon"—the old man does not look up—"this is Claudine, my only daughter still at home"—Claudine offers a wan smile—"and of course you know Gabriel, our farmhand."

"No, I don't actually," says Tessa, feeling somewhat awkward. "Hello, Gabriel, thanks for the lift."

The man nods and raises his hand. His eyes remain on hers for a moment, and she feels heat creeping into her cheeks again.

"Help yourself to some food and then we'll get to work," says Madame Delon. "Plenty for you to be getting on with around here."

Tessa is starving. She paces herself so as not to cause alarm among her new hosts but in truth, she wants to eat her share and steal the food off their plates too. Above the table, herbs hang drying from brown string, but they're not the ones she's used to seeing above the Aga at Aunt Violet's.

"What is this?" she says, pressing a yellow bud between her fingers.

"*La tanaisie*," says Madame Delon, briskly. She is eating but cleaning the kitchen at the same time.

"It keeps the flies away," adds Claudine.

After lunch, Tessa is handed an apron and told to get on with the laundry. This seems a simple task, but it soon becomes clear why her mother and Aunt Violet delegate it to a laundry service outside of the home. Madame Delon, visibly frustrated at having to explain the process, unwraps a bar of homemade lye soap (the making of which Tessa quickly comes to understand is also her responsibility) and explains.

"Claudine's done the mending, so that's one less job. You'll do the soaking today, then you'll need to be up before the sun tomorrow for the actual washing."

"Tomorrow? You mean, it takes two days?"

Madame Delon smiles. "If you're quick it does."

Tessa gets to work, submerging each item, bed linens, clothes, underthings, in a vat of warm soapy water, feeling a sense of rising irritation. How is this helping the war effort? If she wanted to work in a laundry, she might as well have stayed at home. She wonders if they know that others can be paid to do such things, then realizes that of course they do, that's why she is there. Wistful thoughts of armament training and subterfuge float through her mind, passing messages undetected between Resistance networks, planting bombs, the escape she thought she'd have.

Late in the afternoon she's called into the kitchen, her forehead throbbing with a persistent ache. The air is thick with the rich smell of roasting meat. To Madame Delon's weary instructions, Tessa sets to work chopping onions, carrots and celery to accompany the beef. Claudine is pounding dough into a ball, her belly wobbling with every thud against the wooden board. Tessa keeps noticing it, although she's trying to look anywhere but.

She catches sight of herself in the mirror by the door. Her skin is red and blotchy, her hair flattened against her scalp. She asks Madame Delon if she might borrow a headscarf and is grudgingly obliged; when Tessa ties the cotton fabric around her head she feels herself take one more step away from her past self. Despite the sweating, despite the cracked and sore skin on her hands and her earlier irritation, she cannot deny it is a welcome feeling.

Gabriel appears in the doorway. The sight of Tessa inspecting a pan of roasting meat makes him smile. "It's like you've always been here," he says, sitting down at the kitchen table. "No one would think you'd just arrived."

"Already part of the furniture, you mean?"

It's the first time she's seen him laugh, and she is surprised at the way it transforms his face. He lights up when he laughs. For God's sake, she thinks, again. He is just back from the fields, skin glistening with perspiration.

"She'll be able to take over Hélène for you," he says to Claudine.

Claudine's expression erupts into a wide, genuine smile. "Yes, would you? It makes me ache all over."

Tessa hesitates. "Who is Hélène?" she asks, warily.

"The cow, of course," says Gabriel, with an infuriating smirk. "But you've got farm experience, haven't you? That's what the Delons said. A new kitchenhand, raised on a farm, good with her hands. So you'll be fine, won't you?"

Tessa smiles, tightly, because funnily enough animal husbandry hadn't been covered in training. Perhaps this is Agnès playing a joke on her. Or perhaps she just said whatever was necessary to guarantee Tessa a place to stay, a cover story.

"Of course. Marvelous. Anything I can do to help," she says to Claudine.

"Spoken with grace," says Gabriel.

Tessa puts her hands on her hips. "They say sarcasm is the lowest form of wit."

Gabriel's eyes flash. "A kitchenhand who quotes Wilde. Whatever next—

Baudelaire in the laundry? Literature *and* chores. Goodness me, we are blessed."

"The pleasure is mine, honestly," she says, smiling sweetly. A *farmhand* who knows Wilde and Baudelaire, she thinks. How curious. Tessa and Gabriel regard each other for a moment, but neither presses the point.

Claudine squints at them both. "What on earth are you talking about?"

When Gabriel disappears to clean himself up, Tessa says, "How long have you two been together?" wondering why it suddenly seems so important to understand the relationships between the farmhouse's inhabitants.

"What, me and Gabriel? I don't think so. I mean, it's not as if I haven't thought about it—look at him, *magnifique, non?*—but no, we're not." Claudine points at her belly. "He's not the father."

Tessa shakes her head, feeling, to her surprise, a kind of relief. "I'm sorry, I didn't mean to pry."

"Now you're wondering where the father is."

"No, I'm not, honestly. It's none of my business."

"Of course you are. The answer is I don't know where he is. Germany, possibly, or maybe he just wants me to think that."

"Same as my husband," she says, but this time the pretense feels like an insult. "I'm sorry."

"Yes, well. Same to you." Claudine continues to pound the dough onto the board. "We weren't married. I think my parents are hoping he won't come back. It's an easier explanation, isn't it?"

Tessa smiles, although she doesn't feel like smiling. Finally, she allows her eyes to settle on Claudine's pregnant belly. "Not long now," she says, almost to herself.

After supper, Madame Delon asks Gabriel to show Tessa to her room. Her suitcase is still sitting by the door, the coat stolen from the gendarmerie in a heap on top of it.

"Remember, up before the sun," says Madame Delon.

Tessa tries to smile but finds it is beyond her. She wonders if she is still a courier, still employed, because she won't know until someone—Agnès' mystery person—makes contact. And perhaps they won't, perhaps they've been told to cut ties with her, and she'll spend the rest of the war as Isabelle the laundry maid.

To her surprise, Gabriel leads her out of the house and toward the barn. It's mild outside, a wide gloaming moon high in the sky. Perfect for a drop, she thinks, which sends a torrent of images into her brain. The bright lights, the roar of gunfire.

"Are you all right?" says Gabriel, the softness in his voice another surprise. All she can do is nod.

She follows him up a narrow stone staircase to the top of the barn. One corner of the room has been turned into a small bathroom: a lavatory, basin and washtub behind thin wooden walls. The other end is stacked high with hay, but in between stand two narrow beds.

Gabriel points at one then the other. "This is mine, that's yours." He tugs a ratty curtain along a rail between the two. "And this is to stay drawn. Don't get any ideas."

Tessa rolls her eyes. "I shall do my best to resist."

Gabriel could be anyone, she thinks. For all she knows, he could be a collaborator. Don't trust *anyone*, that's what they said in training.

She watches his outline through the curtain as he undresses, his shirt becoming the ripples of arms, trousers becoming legs lean but muscular. She wonders, as she slips into Agnès' nightdress, if he is doing the same.

The beams in the barn are dark and scorched with age. Symbols, circles and triangles, are carved into the wood—witches' marks, there to protect from evil. In the heat Tessa cannot sleep. Gabriel's breathing comes slow and even, breaching the thin curtain, the additional warmth of another person floating up and around her. Sleeping in the same room as someone else makes her think of training, of the women in the dormitory. With the turning of the wheel, her thoughts land on Luc. Lying in Luc's bed, somewhere she'd never wanted to leave, a new feeling back then. The crackle of the gramophone, the slip of the needle, Charles Trenet filling the studio. Luc rolling over, his head on his arm, asking to paint her.

"Which part of me do you intend to capture in your painting?" she said. "My lips, my neck, my breasts?" Because he belonged to a group of artists renowned for reducing women to body parts. And now Tessa wants nothing more than to crawl into bed beside Gabriel, just to experience the feel of his chest beneath her hands, even though it'll make her feel disgusting, as it always does now. Not him, not Gabriel, but it—what her mother had called "*the act*" in those awkward, dreadful conversations when it had all come to light. Gabriel seems fine, better than fine actually—although yes, she's noticed the glint of anger in his eyes. But then she'd be angry too if she'd lived through what the French have. Then she remembers: she *is* angry, she has been for years. Paris and the war that came after, the intolerable limitations of womanhood, it goes on and on. It courses through her, a livid red torrent.

Eleven

It's been over a month and there's been no word from anyone. Tessa thinks of writing to Agnès, but it is too dangerous. She could try to seek out the network herself, but cannot risk the exposure. What is going on? It's like being trapped in a vacuum. And so she becomes Isabelle, a helper around the house and on the farm, cooking, baking, cleaning, astonished at how such menial tasks can swallow days. Endless as it feels, she considers the work a blessing for the simple fact it stops her from looking inside herself. For the first time in her life, she doesn't have a minute to spare.

In town she's managed to find a few cheap, thin dresses more suited to the weather in the south, rinsing one out in the sink each evening and leaving it to dry outside the barn. She wraps her bobbed hair beneath a scarf or borrows a wide-brimmed straw hat to keep the worst of the sun from her face. Most days, Madame Delon sends her out to work in the kitchen garden, to weed between the orderly rows of cabbages, cauliflowers and beetroot. A fledgling swallow often sits atop a ladder, calling for food, swooping away in great crescents over the barn. Her favorite patch is enclosed within a low fence of woven hazel. Gabriel calls it "the witches' garden." It is where Madame Delon grows the herbs and flowers she dries over the stove and kitchen table, concocting salves and poultices to heal seemingly any ailment. Comfrey is mixed with water and used to feed the soil. Calendula for all manner of skin complaints. There is feverfew for fevers and headaches, and soothing chamomile, which is steeped in hot water and sipped from mugs. Tessa can see this is not a family to contact a doctor willingly, and why would they, when the land offers up its own cures?

At breakfast one morning, Monsieur Delon is fussing over an old box camera, parts strewn over the kitchen table as Tessa is trying to prepare breakfast—bread and cheese from the farm's dairy.

"The mess, the mess!" Madame Delon is saying from her place at the end of the table, waving her arms in the air, waiting for the coffee, which in this time of deprivation is more acorn than bean.

Tessa is slicing bread and cheese as thinly as possible because everything has to last longer, stretch further. Gabriel is behind her, trying to reach his favorite mug from the shelf above. They find themselves in a strange dance, Gabriel going one way, Tessa the other, until they end up moving the same way, at the same time. Tessa is briefly trapped between his body and the wooden work surface. This is not a position she enjoys; automatically her eyes start planning her escape route, needing to know there is a way out because once there wasn't, and that experience bleeds into everything that's followed since. Except she isn't panicking, her breath hasn't quickened, she doesn't feel the wet warmth of stress on her forehead. She looks up at Gabriel and finds he is looking at her. He smiles, quickly. "Sorry," he says.

Tessa can feel heat in her cheeks. "No, no, it's my fault."

He's gone then, a cough, a frown, his fingers in his hair, and she's picking up the bread knife and placing it back down on the board, trying to find her sense of purpose.

Gabriel sits down, looking uncertainly at the dismembered camera before him. Monsieur Delon catches his expression.

"I know where everything goes," he says, indignantly.

Gabriel puts up his hands in mock surrender. "I didn't say a word."

"*Le désordre!*" says Madame Delon again, from her place at the end of the table.

Tessa has finally finished and lays the table with her meager offerings.

"Is it even possible to find film for these old things?" she says, of the camera.

"This old thing," Monsieur Delon begins, affronted, "is an exemplary piece of engineering and will last my lifetime."

"I'm not sure that says much for your time left on earth," says Gabriel, between bites.

Monsieur Delon ignores him. "The film I have. I just need to work out what's wrong."

"I don't know why we'd want to capture this time," says Madame Delon. "I don't think I will want to remember."

It's a big day on the farm, one Tessa has studiously avoided since her arrival. She's been getting the hang of the laundry, which is arduous, tending to the garden, running errands for Claudine, knowing how unpleasant pregnancy can feel in the heat. There hasn't been time for anything more. Madame Delon has accepted these excuses with grace, but no longer, she says, her hands on her hips. *Enough is enough*. And now Tessa is standing in the doorway of an old stable. Hélène, the cow, walks back and forth across the rough stone floor, an area so small she is practically walking in circles.

"You're making her nervous just standing there." Gabriel comes striding across the yard toward her.

Tessa shields her eyes with her hand, sifting through the scant information she has gathered about Gabriel these past five weeks. He grew up nearby, he says, although his accent doesn't fit. Sometimes he speaks of a sister who moved away. Late at night, he slips out of the barn when he assumes Tessa is asleep, and doesn't return for hours.

She daydreams about Gabriel, and it makes time slip, teasing the day along. Sometimes, she catches him staring at her. Sometimes, he doesn't look away.

But he could be anyone, she thinks. I can't trust anyone.

"You've no idea how to milk a cow, have you?" He makes no attempt to disguise his pleasure at what is to come.

"Fine, I admit it. I've never milked a cow before." To show how lost she is, she throws her hands into the air, startling Hélène into letting out a low wail, proving her point at once.

Gabriel pats the cow on its haunch. "There we are, there we are," he says, in a soft, patient tone of voice. He turns to Tessa. "That's all you needed to say. It's hardly a prerequisite to having grown up in the countryside, is it?"

His condescension winds her arms against her chest. "Are you going to help me or not?" she says.

"Yes. When you ask so charmingly, I can't think of anything I'd rather do."

Gabriel takes Hélène's harness in one hand and scratches behind her ear with the other. Immediately she calms down. "First thing you need to do is secure her to the low beam there. Trust me, it will make life a lot easier. You need to be quiet and calm, and then she will be too. See?"

Tessa nods.

"My goodness, you do look serious when you're concentrating." He laughs. "Don't stand behind her—our Hélène here has a good kick. Normally I'd say that doesn't need explaining, but with you I'm not so sure."

Tessa bites her lip, fighting the rise. "Thank you."

"Look, there we are, she's much happier now. Pat her on her side, so she knows you're there."

"Hello, Hélène," she says, rubbing the beast's side.

"Good, you've brought a bucket of soapy water," he says. "Sit on the stool here—don't look so scared, I won't leave. Keep talking to her as you clean her *pis*."

Tessa's head shoots up. "Clean her . . ." *Pis.* Tessa doesn't know that word. Don't let it show on your face, she intones silently. She examines the cow, her shiny coat, bright eyes, pink muzzle, even pinker . . .

Tessa points at the bright, full udder.

"Her udder, yes. Why else would Madame Delon give you the water?"

Pis. Udder. Don't forget, she tells herself. "I thought it was in case I spilled any milk."

Gabriel closes his eyes, just briefly. "We don't want any hay or dirt to get into the milk. We do drink it, after all. Besides, a gentle wash can encourage the milk to let down."

Tessa washes the udder and starts drying it with a clean rag. If Theo could see me now, she thinks, which makes her smile.

"What is it?"

She shakes her head, because she cannot put words to it. Missing Theo is an ache that nothing in Madame Delon's garden can aid.

"Careful not to hurt her. She'll let you know if you do."

Tessa finishes drying the udder, which is smooth and rubbery, rather like a very lean steak. This, she supposes, makes sense.

Gabriel kneels beside her, places his hand around one of Hélène's teats, and begins pulling down rhythmically on each in turn. "What I'm doing here is making sure any dirt passes through. We don't want that mixed in our milk either. There, there, Hélène. Keep stroking her, won't you?"

Tessa rubs her hands against the cow's surprisingly soft coat. "Sometimes it's all we need." She looks up, and Gabriel is staring at her.

"The human touch?" he says.

"Comfort."

He thinks about this, and nods. "Have you got your milk bucket?"

Tessa places it beneath the cow.

"Sit on the stool and put the bucket between your legs."

"Pardon me?"

"It's to stop her kicking it over."

Gabriel takes her hand and clasps her fingers around a teat. His touch is a shock. She wonders if he can hear the change in her breathing.

"Gently squeeze the teat and pull down, using your thumb and forefinger. You don't need to be rough, but you need a steady grip to stop the milk flowing back into the udder."

To Tessa's delight, white-gold liquid begins to spray into the bucket.

"*Voilà*," says Gabriel.

"Now what do I do?"

"Keep going until each part of the udder begins to look deflated. You should be able to tell from sight."

"Gabriel, I'm milking a cow!"

He pats her lightly on the shoulder, but she can see out of the corner of her eye that he is shaking his head and biting his lip against a laugh.

Her exuberance doesn't last long. It takes so long to milk Hélène that she is late for the rest of her errands. She rushes into town on her bicycle before the morning market ends, clutching a list drawn up by Madame Delon.

Tessa's eyes track two enemies now, the grey uniform of the SS and the dark blue of the Vichy Police, although the real danger is those who hide behind plain clothes. As she dismounts, her head is turned by a fracas in the square. A man is being marched from his market stall, twisting his body against the hands that bundle him into a black car. He looks like anyone and no one, fifties, grey hair, a slight stoop, not someone who'd normally draw the eye. A woman shouts, "Leave him be, leave us be!" and the men go back and grab her too, dragging her screaming by her wrists, her knees scraping across the paving stones. Everyone stops for the few slow seconds it takes for this incident to transpire, and then everyone carries on with their shopping as if nothing happened. No one wants to be seen as interested or concerned—or worse, angry—because look where it gets you. No one makes eye contact either, because this risks acknowledging the truth of the matter. They have witnessed something and done nothing.

Tessa, too, turns away, but her eye is caught by a young figure across the square. A girl, no more than five, her hair in tight, neat pigtails. Tessa can see she was wrong, there is one person refusing to pretend that nothing's happened. The girl is watching the departing car and looking up at a woman who Tessa supposes is her mother. Tessa thinks, yes, you're right, we are cowards, but perhaps self-preservation is the only sensible choice. She thinks, blonde hair. The baby was born as dark as her father, her probable father, but perhaps that doesn't mean anything, perhaps nothing is static or set in stone.

Tessa swaps eggs and vegetables from the farm for meat and other luxuries, this being the new economy of bartering and need. She visits the chemist to buy lye for soap-making. Monsieur Bernard, the pharmacist, takes a brown bottle from a shelf, but before placing it down he pulls out from beneath the counter a small package wrapped in brown paper. He sits the bottle on top of the package and names his price, as if nothing is amiss. And because nothing *is* amiss, at least not to anyone looking on, Tessa simply pays and puts both bottle and package in her basket. In her chest her heart is a beating drum.

There's a roadblock on her way home. Of course there is, they rise like weeds from the earth. Tessa stands silently, heart still thudding, in a line of people waiting for permission to leave the town, well versed in the etiquette by now. You do not speak in case it is your turn to be interrogated. You do not speak in case you implicate others in line, even if all you've done is say hello. Tessa arranges her features because this is the Milice, the French military police, and not the Germans. The Milice have a reputation for ruthlessness, for cruelty beyond even that of the occupier. Flirting will not help her here, as it had with the young German soldier on the train to the south. The small package from Monsieur Bernard sits at the bottom of her basket. She considers sliding it into the waistband of her skirt—it's certainly small enough—but what is the point, when a young officer is diligently patting down everyone who crosses this imaginary demarcation line. All she can do is hope for the best. She wonders how her expression reads to those around her, if they can see her fear, if they can tell she has something to hide.

Finally she is called forward. The officer flicks his eyes back and forth between her face and her papers.

"What is in here?" he says, casting his eyes over her bicycle basket.

"Ingredients for soap-making, a little food." She feels she could at any moment be sick.

The officer runs his fingers over each parcel in the basket, lingering on the small package. There is a pause, a beat. This is it, she thinks, this is the end.

"OK, you can go," he says, with a shrug, handing back her papers.

Tessa smiles, but not too brightly, not enough for him to see the relief in her expression. She mounts her bicycle and cycles as fast as she can. She doesn't look back.

Back at the barn, she stashes the package beneath her thin mattress. Gabriel walks in as she is tucking the coarse linen sheet back into the bed frame.

"What are you doing?" he says.

"Making my bed."

He looks at her quizzically. "But you've been up for hours."

Tessa turns toward him and smiles. "It's true, I'll never make a man a decent wife."

When Tessa goes back to the kitchen, for she might not be a wife but all the duties of one remain, there is a small white envelope addressed to *Isabelle* on the table. Claudine is there, chopping a large cabbage into chunks.

Tessa has become adept at hiding the tension she feels in her body whenever the pregnant teen is in the room. The memories stirred by the sight of her. If the family notice, they might mistake it for deference, she hopes. A servant, and her betters.

"It arrived about an hour ago," says Claudine, nodding at the envelope. "There's no postmark. Someone must have dropped it in the box themselves."

Claudine has caught a scent.

"Who's it from?" Gabriel is an observer, she's noticed, but his face never gives a hint of his inner world, where the information he gathers goes and what he does with it. He takes an apple from the fruit bowl, the crunch of his teeth sinking into its flesh landing between the thuds of Claudine's knife. He sits down and starts fiddling with Monsieur Delon's camera, which remains in pieces on the table.

"From my brother, I should think," says Tessa.

But this will not do, not for Gabriel. "Hand-delivered?" he says.

"She has a man, Gabriel." Claudine speaks as if it is the most obvious thing in the world.

"Do you?" says Gabriel.

Tessa does not look up. "Do *you*?"

"Have a man? I don't, as it happens."

It's time, she realizes, to let Gabriel, the ever-present observer, know how much she sees. She raises her head. "I mean, if I did—and I'm not saying I do—when should I see such a person? While I'm scrubbing the bed linen? Perhaps a quick rendezvous in Hélène's milking stall?"

The atmosphere thickens around them. Claudine considers this and shrugs. Tessa turns to Gabriel and settles her eyes on his. "No, I'd have to sneak out at night, wouldn't I, Gabriel?"

He doesn't say anything, but she can see a muscle in his cheek pulling taut. Tessa pockets the letter, pushing it deep into her skirt pocket, as far as it will go. She'll read it later, when there's no audience.

The letter is a map only someone who knows the farm could decode. It leads her to a barn, set away from the main buildings, four fields and an orchard in between. The barn appears to have once been used as a workshop, rotten benches lining one wall, vises left open and waiting. There is a disused saw pit outside, the carcass of a long two-handled saw still resting against the timber, its metal now a dull, rusted brown. Nowadays the barn holds shelves of crated apples, the remains of last year's haul, and barrels of preserves. Tessa is sometimes dispatched to unwrap the apples from their brown-paper cradles, which gives her a convenient excuse when it comes to slipping away from the farmhouse.

There is a small drawing of a sundial in the corner of the note, a shadow cast to tell her when to arrive. Tessa is prompt, glad of the afternoon sun illuminating dark corners. She wishes she had a weapon, her eyes appraising the potential of the long saw propped against the wall.

She sees him first, which she prefers, but only from behind. She's come in the other door, around the back of the barn, beneath its cloak of rambling rose and brambles. This person, with greyish hair and square shoulders, probably doesn't know it exists, which is an oversight on their part, a lack of preparation which does little to settle the nerves in her stomach. But there is something about those square shoulders, the hair, which pricks a memory, sending images she'd long left behind into her consciousness.

"Victor?" she says. She hasn't seen him since training. His sudden presence makes her think of Inès and the other women she shared a dorm with, Brigitte and Fleur. Might they be with him? Are they in France? She thinks: are they alive?

Victor whirls around, a hand on his waistband. I might not be armed, she thinks, but he is. He straightens himself, settling his bones. He's embarrassed at being caught off guard, she can tell. "*Quel temps fait-il?*" he says.

Tessa smiles. She doesn't want to, but she can't help it because this is the very first time that anything has played out the way it's supposed to.

"*Il fait humide.* There'll be a storm tonight." This is what Basile was supposed to have asked her, so she'd know who he was—in the event she'd been the one to pose the question. This is how she was supposed to answer. Victor can only have got this from Miss Jones in London.

She thinks of Victor in training, his dry asides, his seriousness. He'd warned her that the enemy would be rough with her if caught, that training couldn't prepare them in that way. She wants to tell him how right he'd been.

He leans back against a rotten workbench and looks her up and down. She submits to his silent consideration.

"*Ça va?* You look well," he says.

"Yes. I liked the sundial. It was a nice touch."

"You've had London in apoplexies."

Tessa stiffens. "Have I? What's the verdict?"

"You know London, everyone deserves a second chance. Nothing is ever as bad as it seems. The Paris networks have fallen—did you know that? Because you wouldn't know it from London. But then, perhaps all those drops gone wrong—and my my, you know all about that, don't you? Perhaps it was just bad luck, after all."

He knows, then. Basile's accusations have spread. Does Victor truly believe she'd do such a thing, she wonders. Except—of course—he doesn't know her at all. He doesn't even know her name. A few weeks of training, pretending to be other people, practicing how to lie. Why on earth *should* he trust her?

Victor lights a cigarette, a glow of red in the dim light. "I suppose the question is, do you deserve a second chance?"

"I haven't used up my first. I didn't . . ." She pauses, twisting her fingers together. "Are they really all dead? The landing committee. The others. Jean." She releases her fingers and clasps her hands behind her back, pinching the skin on her wrist as hard as she can, thinking of Jean, "The Moon."

Victor shrugs. "I only know what I hear."

His nonchalance makes her fierce. "I didn't betray anyone."

"Yes, but see, you would say that, wouldn't you? Still, I'm not dead yet. Perhaps you might give me a little warning. A wink, or a nudge."

"Victor . . ." It is exasperating. She has no way of proving her innocence. She only has her words.

"Truth is, I don't have a choice," he says. "There's hardly anyone left, and God knows I need a courier. The previous one didn't last long, though she did try, poor love."

How easily it slips off his tongue, the loss of a colleague. She wonders if he's always been this way, or if it is a learned behavior, rooted in the times in which they live.

"I'm sorry," she says. She wants to say, not Inès? Not Brigitte or Fleur? But she doesn't, because it won't help to know.

"Yes, me too. She was good, as it happens. Do you have something for me?"

Tessa nods, handing over the small package from Monsieur Bernard.

"You've done one thing right, then."

"What is it?"

"Crystals, for Alain's wireless transmitter. He's one of us, came over on the plane with me. You'll meet him next time."

"I'm not supposed to. I'm supposed to keep my distance from the others in the circuit."

"Yes, well, nothing works as it's supposed to—haven't you noticed? You'll need to set up a dead letterbox so I can contact you. I can't keep posting notes through your fucking door."

"I was starting to wonder why I was even here. I'm more a laundress than a—"

"You know what we're here to do—light flames, etcetera. Can I trust you, Isabelle? That's what we're calling you now, isn't it?"

Tessa shakes her head. "You can't trust me, just as I can't trust you."

He looks worn out. There are wrinkles where three months ago there were none. "You've learned something, then," he mutters.

"Yes." She hesitates. "Is it true then, about the Paris networks?"

If a person is a sum of their experiences, and she might well be, then winding through it all now is horror, a sensation she doesn't think she'll ever be able to keep from her eyes or the tightness of her shoulders.

Victor opens the barn door, looking first one way and then the other. He says, sneering, "I heard they sat around in cafés speaking *en anglais*. Don't do that, will you?" His expression is severe. "I'll be in touch. Try not to get anyone killed in the meantime."

Twelve

Victor is an empire-builder. They're sitting in the barn, now known as "HQ." Alain, Victor's wireless operator, is in the corner, the only dry spot, tapping out a message to London with a morse code key. Tessa pictures the message arriving in the Baker Street signals room. Does it provoke a flurry of activity or are they jaded now, repetition washing intrigue from the dots and dashes?

They must be quiet. Alain insists he cannot concentrate otherwise, and they need to be careful. The barn is isolated but it is a busy time of year. Men in the fields nearby tearing crops from the earth, toiling from sunrise until after dark, the fields spotted with yellow lamplights. Anyone could betray the group at any time—they cannot count on the farm workers turning a blind eye. They must be ready to run. They must never drop their guard. *Trust no one*, Victor intones. In the distance, they hear the rumble of a tractor, an urgent voice shouting instructions, which makes them press their bodies back against the walls, out of sight—an audible release of breath when the tractor passes by. Harvest is a stressful time. That morning a row erupted at breakfast because Gabriel announced he had to slip away for an hour in the afternoon. Tessa can see this is not done, that harvest is a compulsory sacrifice of time and energy, no ifs or buts. She keeps her time away from the farm as brief as possible, finding a moment here, a half-hour there—evenings are better, if they can. Her orders—which she follows to the letter, so stern is Madame Delon—are to cook hearty meals, potages thick with garden greens and pulses. Food for keeping on.

Where does Gabriel go, she wonders. Who does he meet?

Victor cannot keep still, despite the need for quiet. Empire-building, she can see, is an exertion. His task is to draw together groups of local resisters. A clandestine army, disrupting both the domestic activities of the occupier, and their defensive preparations against the Allied invasion they all suppose will come. Tessa imagines Theo above her in his plane, wonders if he knows yet what she has done. Sometimes she sees him in a dark room, his body red with fire, but it's just a nightmare, a fear, not a vision. A feeling of hopelessness rushes through her during these moments, and despair. She wants her brother here, alongside her. She wants to know that he is safe, picturing him opening her letters full of pretense. Is it kinder, she wonders, letting him think that all is well? She hates the idea of Theo not knowing if she is alive or dead.

She's keeping watch. Although Alain will broadcast for less than a minute, they are vulnerable. It is foolish for them to be together, but today is a day unlike any other. Tonight there will be a drop of supplies, except "drop" is the wrong word. The plane is carrying such fragile cargo that it must land, unload, and take off again. Victor runs the sums over and over, calculating manpower, risk and mistake. The risk is death, mistakes can mean death. He wants it over and done in six minutes.

Alain packs up his Marconi transmitter, the final coordinates sent. The set is hidden in a leather suitcase for which he has fashioned a hiding space in the boot of his car. It's heavy to carry, and extremely dangerous to have in his possession. The life expectancy of a wireless operator is six weeks, he tells Tessa, the first time they meet. The occupiers can detect the transmissions, which is why he can only transmit for moments at a time, and why he has to keep moving. Alain is exceptionally proud of his three months.

"How does Baker Street know it's you sending the transmission?" she asks. "What's to stop the Germans capturing your set and impersonating you? They'd get all sorts then, wouldn't they? Information, agents, ammunition, delivered straight into their hands."

"Good grief, you're right." Alain rolls his eyes, but he's only joking. They are comfortable enough with one another now for rudeness to pass as a tease. "Funnily enough, they thought of that. I include a coded security check, a sentence known only to me and Baker Street, at the beginning of the transmission so they know it's me. If I'm captured, God forbid, I have a second check, a bluff I can pass to the Germans. As soon as Baker Street receives the bluff security check, they'll know I'm a goner and the network is blown."

"God forbid," she echoes.

Both she and Alain have objected to this foolish meet-up, especially so close to the drop, but Victor insists on fine-tuning the plans for the evening. Tessa has pieced together the bits of Victor's character he has let slip. He is excellent with details, but also obsessive. He mines any problem until he has explored all possible resolutions. He is stubborn and convinced he's always right, and often he is. He's what her father would call a serious man.

Alain speaks up, says they must leave, and she can see what a wrench it is for Victor to keep from running over the plan one more time.

"Before you disappear, I need you to run an errand. It won't take long, but it's important," Victor says to Tessa.

He directs her to a derelict house, not far from there, and tells her what to say on arrival. Alarm bells sound in her mind. She reels off her reservations. "It's too close to the road, and I'll have to go straight there to make it. What if I'm being watched?"

Alain is already gone, no pause for farewells. He'd parked his car in a spinney a little way from the barn.

"Then lose them. I know you know how. Look, I wouldn't send you if it wasn't important. It's something that's to go back to England tonight on the plane. It's not heavy."

He won't tell her what the plan is beyond that evening, but his sallow cheeks, the grey beneath his eyes, have not escaped her notice.

"Victor, is everything all right?" she says, even though dawdling is a risk.

"Yes. You should go now." He puts his head in his hands and does not look up until she leaves.

She takes an odd route even though time is against her, weaving her bike in and out of lanes, cutting through the woods, picking a sprig of wildflowers in case she needs a reason to be there. She's going to be in such trouble when she gets back. Even with the excuses Tessa invents to explain her absences—she is gathering lavender with which to scent soap, collecting vegetables, delivering post—Madame Delon can be severe. Scrubbing the floors takes a morning? She'll want it done in half that. Tessa dreads to think what she'll have in store for her today.

The flowers take her back to her mother's garden, the sloping land before the silver water of the Cam. The twins are young children, wading through the river, Tessa's hand clasped in Theo's, pollen and insects thick in the air. The sensation of missing her brother is a force. It weakens her knees, it sends her heart racing, and it is all she can do to dismount from her bike and wait for it to pass.

She decides to leave the bike hidden behind a thick hawthorn dotted with ripening fruit, making her way through the brambles on foot, cuckoo-pint and ivy beneath her. In truth, it's not a bad place for a meeting, despite the proximity of the road. Nature has walled the abandoned house with green. Tessa walks in a deep circle so she can approach from the rear, away from the road. Traffic is rare around here, but the land is busy with men at work.

There's a man by the building. His shape is the giveaway, the outline, broad-shouldered but long and lean. He's looking about, clearly nervous, no trace of the false calm Tessa has worked so hard to master.

"Gabriel?" she whispers.

He stands up straight, shoulders square. "Hello," he says, his voice laced with panic and surprise. She stays silent while he scrambles for specious excuses. "I'm just looking at this house. Thinking about moving out of the farm, you see. Not that I mind living in a barn, and you're a very quiet sleeper—I don't know if anyone's told you that before. Thing is—"

It is the bare bones of a house. An outline, like Gabriel in the shadows. It has walls but no roof. Paper hangs from the lath and plaster which has burst open, spitting horsehair innards across what remains of the floor.

There is no time to wait for him to cotton on. "Are we to expect rain today?" she says.

In any other situation she'd find his expression comical: widening eyes, his mouth hanging open. It takes what feels like a full minute for him to pull himself together and say, "Not till nightfall, I believe."

Then he says, "Christ. You?"

She replies, "You," in a voice so soft it takes her by surprise, that she is capable of such tenderness. Gabriel is not the enemy. Gabriel is one of them. Possibilities spring forth in her mind. The shape of his body through the ratty curtain. The feel of his hand against hers in the milking shed. She shakes them off because there is no time. "Do you have something for me?"

Gabriel claps his hand against his mouth. "I fucking knew it. How could she be so stupid?"

Hope shrivels into nothing. Tessa looks about, because she's always looking about. "Who, Madame Delon?"

He doesn't say anything.

"Agnès," she says. Agnès said she'd sent someone to the Delons before, someone in need of shelter. Tessa had presumed she meant Victor but now she sees, it was Gabriel all along. Gabriel is in the Resistance. Gabriel must be how Agnès knew that Victor was building a Resistance network.

"Did she send you here?" he demands.

"She did."

A beat, as he comprehends this. "She shouldn't take such risks, not with other people's lives. Sheltering one person is bad enough, but two? The Germans will kill the Delons if they discover us."

"Perhaps they think it worth the risk. After all, we're fighting for the same thing."

His lips tremble. "The Delons have already done so much."

She'd never considered before that much of the Resistance, far from bombs and machine guns, would be so quiet. And yet it is just as important as the rest.

"Too much," adds Gabriel.

"I don't know where I'd be without them."

He is searching for the words but looks calmer now. "All this time. All this time we've been under the same roof and working together."

"Yes, working together." Her breath catches as she says this.

"*Pour la France*," he says, emphatically. He puts his hand on her shoulder, smiling in a way she hasn't seen before, an open, unembarrassed, and—yes—relieved way. There is heat in her cheeks, and she hates that he must be able to see, might be able to read her thoughts when she is thinking about his smile, about how much she longs for him to smile that way again.

She pulls herself together. Instinct, Agnès had said, never lets her down. She was right before; this isn't a good spot. It might feel hidden, but it's not. Voices, shadows, carry further than you think. "Give whatever it is to me and let's go," she says. "Put your arm around me and we'll walk back together. If anyone sees us, they'll think we're courting." From his jacket pocket he takes a sheaf of paper, tied with string she recognizes from the farm's kitchen. Tessa slides it into the waistband of her skirt, adjusting her blouse over the bulge. She can feel Gabriel watching, even though the white of her stomach must only be visible for a quick second. Their eyes meet, and neither looks away. There it is, a sensation across her skin, an old feeling, not unwelcome. They walk back, his arm around her shoulders, hers around his waist. She's surprised by how natural it feels. Gabriel's story comes in dribs and drabs. He's hesitant, wary of whoever else might be listening. In an occupation, even the trees might well have ears.

"I was a journalist, in Paris," he says. "Left-wing politics, so you can imagine how popular I was with our uninvited guests. When France fell, I established a small press with a few friends. Poetry, editorials, the sort of thing that very quickly became forbidden."

"You're a writer," she says.

"Yes, why? Wait, don't tell me, you don't like writers." He squeezes her shoulder. There it is again, an electric shock. "I've seen you gazing at the novels on the bookcase upstairs. Your nose in the Flaubert, breathing it in."

He mimics this, his palms flat to his nose, inhaling with his whole body.

Tessa, abashed, laughs. Madame Delon had caught her gazing at the books too. "You've no time for that," she'd said, and Tessa had felt like crying when she'd realized it was true.

"Do you think I haven't noticed you watching me?" she says, raising her eyebrows to keep it light.

"Of course I've had my eyes on you. I didn't believe your story. You appeared one day out of thin air, our mystery kitchenhand quoting Wilde but with little knowledge of even the basics of laundry. Obviously there was more to it."

Yes, OK, that's why you were staring, she thinks. "Not necessarily," she says.

"But I arrived in much the same way. It's the way these things work."

They are quiet for a moment.

"Tell me about your newspaper," she says, but what she means is, tell me about *you*.

Gabriel shakes his head, embarrassed, which she finds unbearably endearing. She wants to wash her mouth out, chide herself, because anyone could be listening. There is no time for this.

"I know I should be proud, but our work was angry, too angry. We showed our bones," he says.

"You were honest."

"We only made three issues, but each was a call to arms. We called it '*Résistance*'—I know, a triumph of the imagination. A friend managed to smuggle a copy to England, although it's about as difficult to publish there as it is here, with the paper rationing."

Tessa feels a stab of recognition. She'd bought *Résistance* in a London bookshop.

"But then they—they, them, the Germans—came upon us and the whole thing fell apart. Someone talked, I think. A few of us got away, some were not so lucky. These days I write at night, poetry mainly, about the importance of resistance. I have my typewriter in the stables. That's where I go when I sneak out. There's no woman, there's nothing like that."

"And Agnès helped you to escape down here?"

His face softens, momentarily. "Agnès helped, yes."

They must be lovers, she thinks. The sun is so bright on her face. "Is your name really Gabriel?" she says.

"Yes. Are you British?"

Tessa hesitates and shakes her head, surprising herself with the lie. *Never break cover*, they'd said in training. Besides, why would Gabriel think she might be British—is her accent a giveaway? What if other people have picked up on it—the people in the market, say, or the men who come to help in the fields, who might not be who they say they are either?

It is difficult to trust anyone when they're all pretending to be something they're not.

It's dark by the time Gabriel returns from the fields. He treads lightly on the floorboards, shutting himself in the bathroom to scrub the toil from his skin. Tessa squeezes her eyes shut until he is the other side of the curtain. Time is tight, but she can do nothing but wait for his breathing to fall into a slow rhythm. Beneath her bed sheets, she is dressed entirely in black. Money from Victor has allowed her to add to her meager wardrobe: Isabelle favors light dresses for housework, and black for sabotage.

The moment she creeps out of bed, the curtain rattles back on its rail.

"I'm coming with you," Gabriel says.

"No." Tessa firmly shakes her head. "You said it yourself, it's too dangerous. Besides, you do enough." She lifts her sweater and pats his pamphlet, tucked into the waistband of her trousers.

"Jesus, who cares about fucking poetry?"

"Oh, stop. A poem is a profound form of protest; it lasts forever."

She's noticed that when Gabriel is amused, the corners of his mouth pinch, resisting a smile.

"My father said that. He's a pacifist. Gabriel, I'm sorry, but I have to go."

He reaches out and takes her arm, pulling her back. It is thrilling, that touch.

"I can't keep on playing at being a farmer," he says. "We both know the Germans are going to find their way down this track sooner or later. The villages around here, the communities, they're decimated. They walked into my country, practically unchallenged. Please, let me do this. I need to be useful."

Fine, but she makes him carry the lantern, which is heavy and always butts against her legs, a line of purple bruises lingering long after a night is over. At least the drops are few and far between, the bruises fading before the lantern is needed again. As it is, they've no need for the lamp just yet because the moon, plump and white, is enough. Tessa leads and Gabriel follows. Whenever she gets too far ahead, he reaches out to draw her back.

"What's true?" he whispers. "The name, the background, the husband in prison?"

"We shouldn't talk," she says, but then cannot, after all, stop herself from saying, "I'm not married."

"You'll forgive my curiosity, what with you being involved in getting my pamphlet to England—an extraordinary feat at this moment in time, with the borders closed, the country occupied. That's one thing I know about you. The RAF are going to drop thousands of copies over France, I know that too."

They reach the clearing then, shapes moving from behind the trees and from the undergrowth. Tessa puts her finger to her lips, glad to put an end to Gabriel's interrogation. There is a soft tread of feet, black shadows against the moonlight. Quiet, but for the sounds of the forest; owls above, movement all around, and in the air the sweet, sticky scent of pine. To protect them, Tessa doesn't know the names of the others in Victor's group. It means that if she is caught and tortured, she won't be able to give them up. She shudders, unable to prevent the movement of her body.

Victor appears at her shoulder.

"Who is this?" he says, of Gabriel, before hissing, "There is a plan, Isabelle, a *plan*."

"As it happens, this is your author." Tessa takes the pamphlet from her waistband and thrusts it at Victor's chest. "He wants to help. I believe his exact words were, 'Jesus, who cares about fucking poetry?'"

Just imagining the indignation on Gabriel's face is enough.

Victor takes a step toward Gabriel, making no bones about sizing him up. "Fine. *Christ*. Follow Isabelle and for God's sake, don't fuck it up."

It begins then, a noise in the sky, a hum which becomes a roar. Victor is directing them into position with exaggerated gestures. They light their lamps. Tessa can feel the tension in the air, the electricity of fear. Anyone could be in the woods, watching. They could be surrounded by the enemy, waiting to pounce. Then the plane is in sight, so close the force of it almost knocks her off her feet. It is quite a thing, she thinks, to land a plane, its lights extinguished, in a forest clearing between two rows of humans bearing nothing more than oil lamps. How easy they make it look, the men in the cockpit. She cannot stop herself from peering in, in case one of them is Theo. But Theo doesn't fly Lysanders. For all she knows, Theo is dead.

The thought is all it takes. Images fill her mind, the worst she can conjure. Theo in the wreckage of his plane, bloodied and broken. Eyes like glass, staring into nothing.

Life without her brother is no life at all.

"Isabelle, come on," whispers Gabriel, snapping her out of it.

They set to work, their group ranging from teenagers to the middle-aged, all drawn from the surrounding villages. She doesn't know how Victor's done it, gaining their trust. Perhaps it is better to call them an army—after all, they are in almost as much danger of dying as any soldier. Victor hisses instructions and they load small crates from the plane into wheelbarrows, wheeling them across the uneven forest floor to a van. Everyone is quiet, going about their work, looking back toward the woods because any moment could be the last. Tessa remembers the night she arrived, the deafening sound of violence, the machine guns, the bursts of light.

"Be gentle, go easy," Victor keeps saying. He's looking at his watch, tracking the six minutes in which all must be done.

There are people on board the plane, hastily climbing out of flying suits which fall discarded onto their seats. Tessa is helping Gabriel to load a box into a wheelbarrow when her arm is taken in a firm grip. She swings around and there by the light of the moon is another, a silver moon, a shock of white hair.

"Jean," she says, her chest tightening with alarm.

"I didn't expect to see you again." Jean has a wide smile. She remembers it now, the way he bares his teeth. "But you made it! You jumped!"

"I heard you were dead." She is thinking of Fleur's warning all those months ago, and his kindness during parachute training. There are so many thoughts competing for light at this moment.

"But I'm not, and neither are you. *Nous sommes pareils.*" He takes her shoulders in his hands briefly. And then he is gone, into the darkness. The engine of the hidden van roars into life and they cower against the earth, dropping as one, because they all think in that moment, that roar, they are done for. Victor's six minutes is up. He passes Gabriel's pamphlet into the cockpit. Gabriel takes Tessa's hand and she squeezes his, because they do matter, his words, his protest. Then the Lysander is turning around, the pilots nodding at the group as they re-form into two rows, lamps aloft.

When the plane takes off, she tells herself something has gone right, something has happened, but there is another sensation, heavy in her belly. She looks back toward the woods, where Jean has disappeared into the darkness. Jean who should be dead. Jean who survived the ambush the night she dropped into France, despite being caught slap-bang in the middle of it.

"Who was that man?" says Gabriel, as they make their way back to the farm. "The one who knew you."

"A ghost," she says.

Thirteen

In between their farm duties, Tessa teaches Gabriel how to hold and fire a STEN MK2 submachine gun. An extraordinary thing, to possess this knowledge, unthinkable just a year ago. Not for the first time she wonders about the women she trained with, where they might be now. Are they safe, are they alive?

This is Victor's big plan. His army is ready and waiting, armed thanks to the recent drop and trained—somewhat—by him and Tessa. She's being bossy, moving Gabriel's arms into a better position and straightening his back, enjoying the feel of his skin beneath her fingers. "If you're not confident, then aim two shots in quick succession at the chest. It's the largest area, see? Otherwise, if you think you can, I'd go for the head. Nice, clean and quick. They're the monsters, not us."

Gabriel lowers the weapon. "Am I supposed to attribute this knowledge to your rural upbringing, too?"

The plan is two-fold, its target a large armaments plant outside a nearby town, which sends its wares of destruction north in preparation against

Allied invasion. Tessa and her group will destroy the telephone wires so the guards in the factory are unable to call for help.

One day, in the falling-down barn, she asks Victor, "How on earth are you going to smuggle the explosives into the factory in the first place?"

Victor is head down over a blueprint. This is not enough to draw his eyes away. "Via an employee," he mutters.

Tessa can see too many red flags to blithely accept this. "How do we know we can trust them?"

"Because it's me," he says.

"You?"

"I've been working there for a few months." He still won't look at her and now she knows why.

"Doing what, exactly?"

"Working the production line."

Victor has assembled the bombs used by the enemy. He has built the weapons aimed at Theo. She thinks then of the threads that run from Victor—her and Alain, Gabriel, the Delons, the other resisters. The entire network is at risk.

Victor, clearly reading her mind, smiles. It's supposed to be reassuring but she can see the effort it takes. "It's worth the risk."

Tessa keeps her arms folded against her chest. "You should have discussed it," she says.

"I did. Just not with you."

The explosives are on a timer, set to trigger at night to protect the French workforce.

Tessa keeps her voice light in an attempt to mask her worry. "Did you discuss it with Jean?" she says. In her peripheral vision she can see that Alain and Gabriel have paused in their own work to listen.

"Jean again. Ever since he got here, he's all you've spoken about."

"That's not true, Victor."

"When, as far as I can see, Jean has been nothing but kind to you. One might even say you're here because of him." He fixes her with a hard stare. "But look, I'm happy to put your mind at rest. Jean isn't involved in this."

She can't hide her relief. "I don't think you should tell him."

"Why?" ask Victor and Gabriel at the same time.

Tessa looks around the barn. Victor to Gabriel to Alain. Again, she feels the dead weight of certainty in her stomach. "Enough people know already, that's all," she says.

"What is it about that man? Jean. You've been acting strangely ever since he got here." Gabriel and Tessa are walking back across the fields. He stoops to pick a cornflower and for a moment she thinks he'll hand it to her, but is disappointed when he slips it into the buttonhole of his jacket.

She looks at him out of the corner of her eye. "Strangely?"

"Fine, even *more* strangely."

"I don't trust him."

"I can see that," he says. "I'm asking why."

"He's supposed to be dead. Killed in a drop gone wrong, they said. I don't understand how he wasn't, and the only ways he plausibly survived are very bad for the rest of us."

"I don't suppose you'll tell me what happened?"

"I don't suppose I will, no."

How can she gather proof of her suspicions against Jean? If he has forged a deal with the Germans in order to escape—or perhaps he was rotten all along, Fleur certainly suspected so—then there must be evidence somewhere. Communications, perhaps. There must be others involved. But Jean is clever, and she doesn't know anyone in the circuit except Victor and Alain, who both think she's being ridiculous. Basile, perhaps, except she has no way of contacting him and no idea if he's even alive. She could write a letter to Miss Jones in London—there are ways and means—if it weren't for the fact that Jean, who seems to have placed himself in charge of this, will presumably have been told to check their letters.

When they get back, she is immediately thrust back into her routine of bread-making and supper preparations. Gabriel sits at the kitchen table, sharpening knives and farm tools. The door flies open with a bang to reveal Monsieur Delon with his cobbled-together box camera, raising it triumphantly into the air. "It works!" he says, before spying Gabriel at the kitchen table. "Where have you been?" he says, his eyes narrowing.

"I've been here, doing as you asked," says Gabriel, gesturing at the pile of gleaming metal before him.

Tessa is pounding the dough into a piece of board, which sends up a cloud of flour into her face. She cries out in surprise, then sneezes, wiping her hand across her nose, making herself sneeze again because her fingers are covered in flour. Gabriel cannot stop laughing, while Monsieur Delon just looks weary.

"I think this moment needs to be captured," says Gabriel, trying to catch his breath. "I think it would do us all good to remember this extraordinary lesson in how not to bake bread."

Monsieur Delon nods, handing him the camera, even though Tessa is protesting. Gabriel holds the camera at his waist, looking down into the lens.

"I really wish you wouldn't," she says, but Gabriel is still laughing and it's infectious, and suddenly she is having trouble focusing on the dough, the click-click of the camera bringing heat to her cheeks. She wonders if Gabriel can see it, beneath the flour.

Gabriel stops laughing, in fact he's grown quite serious, his eyes still locked on the camera lens, an image of Tessa laughing reflected and refracted across the distance between them.

"What is it?" she says, self-consciously sweeping an errant strand of hair from her face.

He looks up. "You're so ridiculous," he says, but he's smiling, the words softened with such affection that Tessa drops the dough in surprise, sending up another cloud.

Later, as they are changing into their darkest clothes, Gabriel calls her around to his side of the curtain. He's kneeling on the floor, looking into a black chest drawn from beneath his bed. Tessa is again disappointed, is again surprised at her disappointment, but she's not yet ready to follow that thread. The truth is, she often finds her thoughts straying when she's undertaking her myriad of chores, wondering what Gabriel might be thinking about as he works the fields. But it is a forbidden thing, kept at arm's length. This is not why she is here.

"I thought I'd share my secret stash," he says, holding up a handful of books.

Tessa falls to her knees, picking up a copy of *A Farewell to Arms*. "I bet you know Hemingway."

Gabriel looks pleased at her reaction. "I met him in Spain, as it happens. We were both reporting on the war. *Des collègues*, in a way."

"But why do you hide your books beneath your bed?"

"I don't know. Have to keep up the pretense, I suppose."

"Because farm laborers don't read? Gabriel, I never had you down as a snob."

He nudges her with his elbow, sending a current of excitement across her skin. "It's not about my perceptions so much as other people's. I'm very aware it's only farm work that's keeping me from being sent to slave labor in Germany, like most men my age. How will the occupiers get fat from our land if there's nobody to harvest food for their tables?"

This is when Tessa sees the book. She lifts it from the pile, tracing a finger over the familiar racing-green cover with its black Dadaist font.

"Ah, a fan of Ephra Laurent," says Gabriel.

"Absolutely not," she says, but she doesn't put the book down straight away. She thinks of Luc, defending his friend the first time they met. *He's a very great writer.* Inside, she feels like ice. "He was friends with someone I knew in Paris."

She thinks of Ephra's fingernails, digging into her skin.

She wonders how many times she said no. Fifty, perhaps; a hundred.

Tessa drops the book back into the chest and closes the trunk.

"I have to get back to work, and so do you." She says it quickly, before he has a chance to ask.

They drive to the woods in Monsieur Delon's car, and set off on foot, keeping the wick of their oil lamp low until their eyes adjust to the black. There are no roadblocks; indeed the roads are empty. Luck or fallacy, she thinks, because it might well be a trap. That afternoon Victor left a signal, a rose in the letterbox, so they'd know he'd set the explosives in the armaments plant. Alain told her Victor had planned to smuggle them in his lunch canteen, a baguette with a putty explosive filling, but Victor won't be drawn as to whether or not this is true.

In the dark, Tessa shows Gabriel how to adapt his walk: wider steps, relaxed knees, toes down first then heel, allowing him to feel his way across the ground in the absence of sight. Six months ago, walking through the woods at Wanborough Manor in the treacle black, she had learned how to navigate by the moon, to leave as little trace as possible. Tonight is not a clear night, a bank of grey distorting the stars—perfect for sabotage but dangerous when on foot. And yet it is incredible how quickly their eyes adjust, making out the treeline, discerning a path carved by foxes or deer between the trees. The blackness is a connection to Theo. It reminds her of those six short weeks every year as teenagers, when they'd take to the coppiced wood near to home and listen for nightingales, sitting quietly on the wet earth as the trees erupted with golden song. For a moment she allows herself to bask in the comfort of the memory.

Eventually they clear the trees, guns slung over their shoulders. This time, if caught, they will fight and undoubtedly lose, but the plan is to try and take out as many of the enemy as possible while doing so. Nobody mentions the coda to this, *and then die*. Perhaps it is too strange or too abstract to face, or just too horrible. Victor and the others in their group are already there, hunched low to the ground. In the valley below, the armaments factory could almost be a town, its roots running long across the land. Three large buildings in the center, spreading out into smaller units and huts. The explosion, if it works, will target only a small area—small but crucial, says Victor. They cannot stop the factory's work, but they can disrupt it.

They move into position and wait, Victor's eyes shining in the dull light. Tessa can see he's in his element, and perhaps she is, too. Is this how it is for Theo in his plane? It's not just the doing, it is the taking back of control, even in a small way. It is power. The group is giddy with it, excitement pulsing through them. It makes them forget themselves, speaking too much, when they really shouldn't speak at all. Gabriel hushes them with a whispered, "For France."

Victor indicates for her to join him behind a gorse bush, and they set about adding fuses and detonators to the explosive putty. Gabriel's eyes are wide. It is only a matter of time, she knows. The truth, or at least something in that orbit, hangs in the air between them.

"Go, go," mutters Victor, and the group move into position. The telephone wires are to be cut in several places before the poles are blown. Gabriel shimmies up the closest one as Victor leads two other groups further down into the valley. Tessa hoists her gun onto her back, and crouches down to shape the explosive around the pole's base.

Then, in the distance, an explosion. The sky floods with orange, a cloud of white mushrooming over the middle of the armaments plant. The noise comes at a delay, tearing across the valley toward them.

"My God," whispers Gabriel, as he slides back down to earth.

Tessa lights the fuse and they run, the crunch of their footsteps the only sound except there, a tawny owl, a low hooting call from somewhere in the clouds. Then it comes, more explosions, the telephone poles crashing to earth behind them. They cannot stop and marvel at their achievement even for a moment, even though they are alive with the thrill, smiling for the first time in a long time. But no, back to the car, back to the house, the roads are still deserted but the countdown is on. They know the enemy will be coming.

Gabriel parks a little way from the farmhouse so as not to wake the others. His arm is against hers, and when he moves away she feels the loss. There is silence in the car but a roar between them, there in the gap, the space for breath. If she moves just an inch to the left, he'll be there. If she raises her hand, he'll take it. She knows that, knows the rest too.

They sneak into the barn, Gabriel lighting the oil lamp only when the door is safely closed behind them.

"That was something," he says. His cheeks are flushed.

He's gone then, behind the curtain, his silhouette illuminated by the lamplight. Tessa taps her fingers against her iron bed frame, unable to stop moving, her hands, legs, shaking. The night's not over, she's certain. It all unfurls before her. Taking back control is addictive, it lights something inside her which runs a blue current right down to her toes. It is a sensation she recognizes, and wants, and greets like an old friend, because it's been a while since she has felt this way.

Tessa draws back the curtain on its rail, the hooks rattling one after another across a kink in the metal. Gabriel stands half undressed. Tessa goes to him, can see in his eyes that he wants her to. How neatly they fit together, her forehead beneath his chin, his breath and then his lips against her skin. She slides the shirt from his shoulders, placing her fingers on his chest, his arms, every part as it is revealed. He pulls her sweater over her head, until there is nothing—trousers, undergarments, everything to the floor. It shocks her how much she's missed this feeling. She slides his hand between her legs, just so he can tell how much she wants him. It is important to her that he knows.

For the first time in a long time, Tessa knows exactly what she wants.

Fourteen

They hear of the reprisals at lunch the next day. It is a scene of two halves. Beneath the table, where the only roaming eyes belong to the dog, two sets of fingers are entwined. Above, they dare not meet each other's eyes. One dropped piece of cutlery and the game is up.

It is Monsieur Delon who tells them about poor Bertrand, a worker from the next farm over, who Tessa feels sure must be a member of Victor's army.

"Dragged from his house before the sun rose," he says. He is trying to fill his pipe, dropping tobacco on the kitchen table, scooping it into his hand and aiming it at the pipe's bowl with pinched fingers, a move he repeats several times. "They took his wife, his children, left his front door hanging off its hinges for all the world to see. Bastards."

Victor is already at the barn, pacing about. Alain is in the corner, clutching his wireless set to his chest. If they're caught, all the evidence is there with them, waiting.

"Bertrand, Camille, Amory, Pascal," says Victor. He takes his cap from his head and throws it to the ground.

"Nathalie too," says Alain, looking stricken. "I recruited her."

"I know them," says Gabriel. "Bertrand and Nathalie weren't even there last night."

"Were they at the last drop?" says Tessa, and when Gabriel nods, she knows what has happened. They were at the drop, *as was Jean.*

I should have done something, she thinks. I shouldn't have doubted myself. Why hadn't she written to Miss Jones in London—why hadn't she found a way?

Victor knows too, but he will not have it. He scoops up his hat and points it at Tessa, then Alain, then Gabriel. "We were at the drop too and we're still free. Besides, it's not just us. They're arresting people all over the district. Ten at least, in the last two weeks."

"There's a rat," says Alain. "Someone has turned."

Victor bites his lip. "We don't know that."

"But we do. People have started to talk about your friend Jean. Isabelle was right to be worried about him," says Alain. Tessa puts her head in her hands. She feels sick. "He didn't know about last night, did he? You said so yourself. But he was at the drop with Bertrand and Nathalie."

Tessa and Gabriel exchange a look. Their closeness is irritating Victor, she can tell from the way he's watching them, the way he grinds his heel into the earth.

"What else are they saying?" says Gabriel.

"That Jean can't be trusted. That people are rounded up after meeting him. That he miraculously evades capture every time."

Victor points at Tessa. "She got away too—perhaps she is the traitor."

"Victor!" she says, affronted.

He can't look at her while he lays out the accusation. "It's plausible, isn't it? The point is, London trusts him. They've looked into it."

This is new. "They've looked into it?" Tessa says.

"They called him back. There was an inquiry. There were . . . accusations against him. We're probably not supposed to know about it." He shakes his head. "We should be talking about the drop."

"Victor, for God's sake," says Alain.

"The drop can't go ahead, surely?" says Gabriel. "It's far too dangerous."

"And Jean organized it," says Tessa.

"We need supplies, we need money." Victor is picking up his jacket, he has no time for it, for them. He carries on as if they haven't spoken. "The moon looks good for tomorrow. Alain will message London to confirm."

"And who do you expect will be there to meet the drop?" says Alain, gently. He knows Victor, knows how to proceed. "Everyone is terrified."

Victor rests his head against the doorframe. He's lost weight, she can see it in the sharp lines of his cheekbones. "I'll do it by myself if I have to," he says. "Just send the message."

Looking first one way and then the other, he takes off down the path.

"The man has a death wish," says Gabriel.

But Tessa knows the pressure Victor must be feeling. "He has orders."

"We should lie low for a while," says Gabriel. "Let the Germans think we've given up."

"We need to cancel the drop," says Tessa. "It's a trap. Whatever Victor says, we need to warn London about Jean. How could he?" Anger rushes through her, a blistering red rage.

"Who, Victor?" says Gabriel.

"No, *Jean*. How could he turn on us? How could he . . ." She wants to scream. "People are dead because of him."

Alain nods, grimly.

Gabriel reaches out and touches her shoulder. "Except we don't know that for sure."

"But it makes sense, doesn't it? We have to warn London. We have to get a message to them."

"But if the Germans are listening," says Alain, "they'll know he's blown. We'll be rounded up within the hour."

Tessa looks from one to the other. "Better get on with it then."

Gabriel makes sure the coast is clear as Alain starts to unpack his set.

"It needs to be something only London will understand," she says. "Something the Germans won't be able to unscramble straight away, even if they've cracked your code." She claps her hands together. "Tell them the Moon is bad," she says, and in response to Gabriel's confused face adds, "It was Jean's nickname during training."

"The Moon?" says Gabriel.

"Yes, because of his white hair and big, round—"

"Yes, I see," says Gabriel. "How original. Well done."

"Is it too obvious?" says Alain.

"I don't know, perhaps. Send it in Latin, make the Germans work for it," says Tessa.

"Perhaps it's not obvious enough," says Gabriel. "London might just think you're talking about the weather."

"Then perhaps they'll call off the drop," says Alain. "Either way we win."

Tessa can see the plan unfurling in her mind's eye. "That's the beauty of it. We only need one person to understand the true meaning of the message, and she will."

Alain smiles, tightly. "Miss Jones." He puts on his headphones. "You should go, in case they're nearby. I'll try and transmit a few times throughout the day. That alone should tell them something is amiss."

"Should we leave?" says Tessa, as they walk back to the farmyard. "We're putting the Delons at such risk by staying here."

"We should leave," says Gabriel.

But they don't, not at once. The farm is quiet. Monsieur Delon is out in the lower fields and their mistress is gone from the house.

"Let's slip away together," he says. "Over the Pyrenees to Spain."

"It's safer if we separate," she says.

"It is, but I don't want that."

There is a noise, a low moan, from the stable. At first they think it's an animal, but then it comes again, more intense this time. Gabriel looks into one stall and then another.

"Quick, quick," he says to Tessa.

Claudine is leaning against the wall, her face flushed and beads of sweat sliding down her cheeks. Her breathing sounds odd. It comes in short, ragged bursts.

"Oh God," says Gabriel.

"The baby is coming and no one was here," says Claudine. "I looked everywhere for you." She lets out a sob. "I want Maman. I want her now."

"We're here, don't worry." Gabriel turns to Tessa. "Do you think we can get her to the house?"

But Tessa doesn't answer. Her eyes are fixed on Claudine's.

"Isabelle," says Gabriel.

Claudine lets out another moan, louder now. Tessa wonders if they'll hear her in the fields when the labor really gets going.

"Isabelle, for God's sake!" shouts Gabriel.

Tessa shakes her head. She pinches the skin of her arm, because she can't lose herself in the past, not now. "You have to get her onto the floor," she whispers. "On her hands and knees." Tessa had been forced to lie on her back and it had felt wrong, unnatural. It had made the pain worse.

With effort, Gabriel maneuvers Claudine into position on the floor. "Towels, cloths," she says, quickly. "And hot water." Gabriel sprints from the stable and she can hear him clattering about in the laundry, banging cupboard doors open.

"Isabelle, I'm frightened," says Claudine, on all fours, in the blessed gap between surges.

Tessa lifts up Claudine's skirts, rubbing her back, wishing someone had thought to do that for her, four years ago. "Do you need to push?"

Claudine is looking back at her, wide-eyed. She nods.

"Good, don't fight it. The baby is ready to be born. I need you to summon all the strength you have and then push as hard as you can with the next wave. Don't hold your breath, OK?"

Claudine nods again and lets loose an almighty roar, her whole body tensing. Tessa wraps her hands around the baby's head, pink, slimy and warm. She can see a button nose, two ears, the eyes screwed tightly shut. There is a noise behind her and she turns her head to see Gabriel in the doorway with a bucket of water, towels slung over his shoulder.

"Gabriel, put a towel underneath her, will you?" When he doesn't move, she says again, insistent now, "*Gabriel.*"

Snapping to attention, he lays down a towel, keeping the other in his hands.

"One more push and I think we've got it," she says.

Claudine is panting, red-faced and dripping with sweat. She roars once more, and the baby slips into Tessa's hands as Claudine collapses onto the floor. Trying to keep her grip firm, Tessa passes the child to Gabriel, who has another towel ready.

"It's not making a noise," gasps Claudine, starting to cry.

"It is a he," says Gabriel, softly.

"I think we have to slap him," says Tessa. She reaches out and taps her hand against the baby's bottom, once, twice and then a third time. Almost at once, he starts to wail.

Tessa stops running at the river. It is narrower than the Cam, but more blue, more inviting. Theo would race her in. Theo would tell her to stop being ridiculous.

Stop being ridiculous, she tells herself, in Theo's absence.

It has been so long since she's allowed herself to succumb to it. But the pain is too great, the pull of the past too strong, and she is exhausted, worn down by these last few months in France.

Dropping to her knees, Tessa digs her nails into the dry earth, crying out for all that was taken from her. Her child, the daughter she'd named Béatrice but only in her mind, because her mother had said it was inappropriate when the child belonged to someone else, the paperwork signed before her waters even broke.

Gabriel finds her down by the river. Peeling her fingers from the earth, he wraps his arms around her. He doesn't ask the question. He doesn't say a word.

They sit around the wireless with the others that evening in an impression of calm, their shoulders tensing at every sound in the yard outside. They haven't left, haven't fled as they'd agreed. One last chore, one last hour of work turns into another and another. They both know it is more of a risk to stay.

Madame Delon insists on opening a bottle of wine in celebration of her new grandchild. She keeps squeezing Tessa's hand, and hugging Gabriel, kissing them both on the cheeks in thanks.

As he does each night, Monsieur Delon tunes in to the Free French radio station Radio Londres, and they all say together, "This is London, the French speaking to the French!" But on this evening, Tessa and Gabriel cannot find the words.

Claudine sits by the radio, the baby asleep on her chest. No one says anything when Tessa declines to hold him, but she notices the pause, this breach in what is expected.

The broadcaster clears his throat. "And now for some personal messages," he says.

This is how they begin each broadcast, a string of nonsensical phrases, coded messages for the resisters, sent from London. Tessa had been taught how to decode the messages in training, with each network given a specific code with which to identify messages intended for them. Sometimes the Germans jam the station (one evening with a Tchaikovsky concerto which Tessa found rather pleasant). There are several coded messages this evening.

"Louis has long arms," "The cat is in the parlor," and then "Alphonse telephoned his mother and all is well."

This is wrong. This is a message intended for them, but the words are wrong. This is an instruction to proceed, not abort.

Tessa takes a deep breath. Gabriel sits up.

"I'm tired," she says.

"Me too," says Gabriel.

"You realize that you lovebirds aren't fooling anyone," says Claudine, to their departing backs.

In the barn, Tessa strides up and down on the thick, worn planks. "Miss Jones must not have understood. It was foolish to send something so abstract."

"Or they didn't believe you."

"Or Alain couldn't send the other messages. What if he's been picked up? They might be on their way here right now."

"Or they didn't believe you."

The magnitude of the situation is overwhelming. Tessa feels frantic, gripping her fingers, twisting them, flexing them. "Victor and the others will go to the woods to meet the drop."

"Yes."

"We have to warn them."

"Isabelle, we have to get away from here."

"We can't just abandon them! They're walking headlong into a trap. If we don't do something, they'll be killed."

Gabriel gets to his feet, matching her strides across the floor. "Except Victor's right, we don't know that. Instinct and suspicion, that's all this is."

Tessa sits down. Inches open the door to the truth.

"Gabriel, when I was dropped into France . . ." She sees the explosions, hears the noise, for a moment it is all she can do to find the words. "Everything went wrong. The Germans were waiting. There was so much noise, I couldn't even tell what was happening at first. Everyone was killed, it was a massacre, but somehow Jean escaped."

Gabriel folds his arms. She can tell that he is concentrating on his breathing, keeping it steady. "And you?" he says.

"I missed the drop site. I hesitated . . . I panicked. It saved my life."

"You can't be good at everything, I suppose. And then?"

She tells him about the gendarmerie. "It's why no one can quite bring themselves to trust me. They think I betrayed them to secure my release."

"Did you?"

"No, of course not! I'd rather die than help fascists."

Gabriel looks at the darkening sky beyond the window, a line of pink separating the blazing red and the grey. "Did Agnès know?" he says.

"Yes, all of it."

Gabriel nods. "Are you French or English?" he says.

"Does it matter?"

"No, I suppose it doesn't."

"Jean betrayed us, I'm sure of it. How many times do we have to hear it? Every time he's involved, people are rounded up, they die. Gabriel, the Germans will be waiting. They'll kill them."

"I know." He wipes his hand across his mouth. "Jesus Christ."

They leave earlier than normal, their clothes too dark for the changing sky. It is hazy, a mist rising from the earth, their silhouettes casting in and out of the grey. Claudine is singing to the baby in her room, a low gentle sound that follows them into the woods. Tessa settles her gaze on what is ahead. She thinks of weapons training, of the bullet through the dummy's head. How simple it had seemed.

Some way into the woods they hear it. A boot against the forest floor.

They crouch behind a beech, glad of its girth. Tessa stops breathing, because it suddenly feels so loud, her lungs inhaling and expelling, the movement of breath across her lips. A gale tearing across the flat land. Gabriel is looking at her with wide, panicked eyes, mouthing something—a warning—but fear distorts the words, she can't take any meaning from the movement of his lips. She sees the grey of the uniform before she sees the soldier's face. He's young. Is this it, she wonders, is this how it ends? She watches the soldier's fingers tighten then flex around his rifle. *What does it feel like to kill someone*, she'd asked her brother all that time ago, a different year, another life. Gabriel is further around the tree, he can't see the soldier.

She doesn't want to do it. It is a surprise, given everything is on the line, how certain her moral position feels. Can she even do it?

It's them or me, her brother had said.

It is a quick movement, the drawing of her pistol, the pressure and release. The impact to the man's—no, she won't be generous to herself, the *boy's*—skull. Time freezes, blood oozes from a wound. The sound of bullet penetrating bone reverberates around her.

The boy soldier falls face first onto the earth.

"Oh God," she whispers.

I don't think about it, Theo had said. "I won't think about it," she whispers. But she knows she will. It all bleeds out in the end.

She has just killed someone. She has killed a boy. Her hand is shaking. The tremor spreads along her arms and down her torso. She will never forget that sound, she knows even now. She hears it over and over again. Perhaps Theo lied; perhaps it's impossible to ignore such horror, the sound of a bullet breaching a human skull. Perhaps Theo is as much a failure as she is.

Gabriel crouches by the fallen soldier.

"We have to warn the others," she murmurs. She puts her hands to her ears, as if this might stop the scene playing and replaying in her mind.

"Gabriel," she says, and he stands up, putting a hand on her arm. "What have I done?"

His muttered words cut across hers. "The woods are crawling with Germans. We have to get out of here."

"But the others . . ."

"They're already as good as dead. Captured, gone."

She shakes her head. "What have I done?" she says again, to herself this time.

Gabriel grips both her arms and shakes her. "He isn't alone, do you understand? He's watching the perimeter of the woods. There will be others with the same task. There will be more of them *in* the woods, in which you've just fired a very loud shot. Now having gone to the trouble of dispensing with this man—"

"Boy," she says.

"This *enemy soldier*, and undoubtedly saving us from capture, possibly death, let's not wait for his friends to arrive. Yes?"

Tessa nods. She looks back into the woods, where Victor and the others will be lying in wait for the drop. A ring of Germans watching, waiting for the signal to proceed.

"Run," she says.

Fifteen

In the long years since her last visit, her grandmother's house has gained as much as it has lost. Neglect is everywhere, in the closed shutters and the weeds up to their kneecaps. She directs Gabriel to leave the car at the back of the house, where it can't be seen; even though the house sits alone at the bottom of a lane, Tessa has been in France long enough to know that any change is a red flag, attracting eyes and ears.

In her mind, the bullet cracks the boy's skull. Blood leaches into the earth.

They fled the farm just before midnight, the roads empty. Where are the Germans, she kept saying, where are the roadblocks? She'd been worried they wouldn't have enough fuel, but, Gabriel explained, Monsieur Delon had hoarded a few tanks in case of such a scenario.

"For fleeing into the night?" she'd said, and Gabriel nodded.

It took six hours to reach her grandmother's house, six hours of holding her breath.

I killed someone, she thought, over and over. He was there and now he is not.

They became quiet in their fear, both of them shrinking down in their seats whenever they passed another vehicle. Perhaps that made it more obvious, perhaps driving without lights marked them out, but they couldn't bear to risk it. They were both astonished when they made it to the house unimpeded.

The past roots Tessa into this earth; she can feel the binds tightening around her feet, because she hasn't been here since it happened. It is the only place they were together.

"So, this is your grandmother's house?" says Gabriel, as Tessa searches for the key beneath cobwebbed flowerpots in an overgrown bed.

"It was. My mother and aunt own it now."

Gabriel is looking around, shielding his eyes, taking it in. "Where are they?"

"My mother is at home. My aunt lives in Paris." Her fingers clasp the cool, thick metal key. Triumphant, she raises it to the sky.

"And the rest of your family?"

A beat, because it will always take her a moment when it comes to Theo. Where is he, she thinks, almost automatically. It is like a tic. Is he alive? "My father is at home. I don't know where my brother is. He's in the RAF."

Gabriel nods, grinning. "I knew it, I knew you were British."

"No, you didn't. Besides, I'm both, a mongrel."

He helps her up, squeezing her hand because it is still unspoken, just how scared they are. It is one thing to know one's fate and quite another to face it. For a moment she rests her head against his chest, he wraps his arms around her and everything is still. There are insects humming in the grass, the garden waking up with the day.

Even with the key, the door will not give. Tessa pushes her body against it, tries to mimic her grandmother, remembering the way she'd angle her body as she encouraged the door open. As it moves, it scrapes against the tiled floor, a wretched noise that makes them both flinch. Everything sounds louder here. Inside, the house smells of damp, of emptiness. Gabriel takes a match from his pocket and lights it. There are mouse droppings on the floor, bat droppings on the cabinets. She wants to go upstairs and sit where it happened, but there are more practical matters to attend to. They dare not risk opening the shutters, so she explores the larder by candlelight. There are jars of dried beans and lentils, cans of salted vegetables. Outside is a country riven with deprivation and yet no one has discovered her grandmother's bounty. She is astonished it has not been stolen. She would not have judged such a desperate theft.

It is the last gasps of summer, but she makes a thick soup in her grandmother's cast-iron pan. The soup bowls the twins made from coils of clay one summer, their names emblazoned in blue glaze. She almost ladles soup into Theo's dish, but finds she cannot, rinsing it clean, putting it to the back of the cupboard, saving it for Theo who is alive, he must be. She would know, she's sure, if the worst had come to pass. While she cooks, Gabriel explores, taking books from the shelves, dusting them off and reading aloud in both French and English. Each revelation opens the window an extra inch. How Tessa longs to bathe Gabriel in light.

He takes up a photograph in a gilt silver frame: Tessa and Theo, Maman and Papa. It is all she can do not to cry out. She is braced against her own memory but not this, the leaping of her heart. Taking the photograph from his hands, Tessa moves her fingers across Theo's face. It has been such a long time, she thinks.

"You look so different," he says.

She thinks of the girl in the photograph, the person she used to be. The difference between that and who she is now. Someone violated by another. Someone's mother. She can hear the gunshot as the boy's skull splits in two.

"You have the same eyes as your brother," Gabriel goes on.

"We're twins. His name is Theo," she says. Another inch of light.

They eat the soup at the kitchen table.

"We can't stay here," he says, in a low voice, his tone tight and urgent. "We should head to Spain."

"Why, are the fascists nicer there?"

He throws a balled-up napkin at her head. "I know Spain. I can get us to Portugal and from there, who knows? We could try and get to England. We could go to America."

She doesn't look up. "Together?" Can she see a space for Gabriel in her future? It is a surprise to realize she can, and that this is something she wants.

"I hope so," he says.

"I have to get in touch with London. I have to tell them what's happened."

"And how do you intend to do that?"

"If Alain escaped, he'll get a message back. He'll . . ."

Gabriel frowns. "If he escaped."

They head to bed with full bellies. Tessa opens the linen cupboard and there it is, the yellow sheet, in the dark away from the dappled light. Taking out a different sheet and a blanket, she shuts the door and turns back to Gabriel.

"Not in there," she says, spying his hand curling around a door handle. She leads him instead to her grandmother's room, where her pot of pens, notepaper and inkwell still stand ready on her desk. Her clothes are in the wardrobe because no one could ever bring themselves to enact change in a house always standing still. Tessa takes a nightgown from a drawer and slips it over her head. Silk against skin, like wading into the sea in a fierce heat. She trails her fingertips over the fabric, remembers doing the same as a child—her grandmother had always seemed the pinnacle of elegance. She'd have been distraught, Tessa thinks, to see what had befallen her country.

Tessa thinks they'll sleep but they don't, at least not at first, and perhaps it's a place for them to hold their fear, in the heat of their bodies, her fingers in his hair, his lips on hers.

Then they sleep for ten hours. It is an astonishing, unfathomable feat, given the ticking clock and the inevitable any-moment-now state of their affairs. The late-afternoon sun brings with it a moment for the taking. It might be the last opportunity she has, and Tessa counts lasts, those unwelcome lists in her head. Gabriel is sleeping, his hair hanging over his eyes. She wants to reach out and sweep it back, in case, in case, in case. Just in case it is the last time she can. She wishes they had more time. I just woke up, she thinks.

They eat more of the high-summer soup, sitting together on the floor beneath a shuttered window because they fear their shadows might be somehow visible from the road. They keep checking the clock, as if the Gestapo have an appointment.

"We weren't followed," says Gabriel, and she wonders if it is as much for himself as it is for her. "No one knows we're here."

"No one."

"I wish I knew you," he goes on, topping up her wine. She's never seen him so delighted as when he opened the door to her grandmother's still-stocked cellar. "I mean the person in the photograph, with your family."

She rests her head against his shoulder, breathing him in, hoping he doesn't notice. "Honestly, I don't know where one ends and the other begins."

"Are you close to your brother?"

"Because we're twins? It's not a given, but yes, we were close."

"Don't use the past tense, we're not gone yet."

"We're not, but Theo might be." Tessa looks away. How awful it is, to give voice to the thought.

Gabriel is determined they will make it to Spain. Tessa has a sense of indulging him, thinking how pleasant it is to close one's eyes to the truth.

"We keep parts of ourselves hidden from the other, my brother and I," she says.

"Isn't that just a part of growing older? OK, next question."

"Oh God, you really are a journalist." Tessa might roll her eyes, but she's laughing, despite herself. She can see he's in need of distraction as much as she is.

"Next question . . . Don't pull that face, this is a good one. Have you ever been in love?"

Tessa thinks of her heart as a leaden stone strung around her neck. "Have you?" she says.

He can't quite meet her eyes. "There was a woman I knew in Paris."

"Agnès Roue?" Tessa thinks of the woman in the small apartment, balancing a toddler on her hip and solving all of Tessa's problems.

Gabriel starts. "What? No! No, you thought . . ." He laughs, running a hand through his hair. "Agnès is my sister."

"Agnès is your sister," she repeats. He hadn't told her, had only revealed what was necessary. She wonders when he decided to trust her, when he crossed the line from suspicion to this.

"I'm talking about someone named Caroline."

How glorious it is to feel jealous of a stranger. She's missed it all, the good and the bad. "What happened?" she says.

He explains that they were happy, then less so, and then they grew apart. "What often happens, I think. I've no idea where she is now, although I hope she's all right. And you?"

Tessa swallows a mouthful of wine. "Yes, there was someone in Paris. I lived there for a while."

"And it was a big love?"

Tessa nods.

"What happened?"

"Next question."

Gabriel laughs. "I see. Oh dear. All right—why are you here, why are you doing this?"

"Why are you?"

"Do you know, answering a question with a question is incredibly grating for an interviewer. I'm here because I want my country back and because I object, most strenuously, to authoritarianism. You?"

"Well, like you, I'm extremely noble," she says, sarcastically, and he snorts. "I had a job in London but it wasn't enough. It didn't feel enough. I had to do more." She takes a deep breath. It all unravels, in the end. "But the truth is always more complicated, isn't it? There's always the big reason and then lots of smaller, selfish excuses floating beneath. It didn't seem fair that my brother could contribute in a way I couldn't—there, that's one. And then . . ." She shakes her head. "I don't know how to describe the last few years to you. A slow suffocation of the senses. Like I was losing my voice and I couldn't get it back."

Gabriel sits up. He reaches for her hand but she shrugs him off.

"I came here because I have to atone for what I did. I have to make it right so I can be me again. I'm so fed up with being numb, of being this sharp, unfeeling creature with no capacity for tenderness. No softness. You really don't know how good it's felt to be afraid. I know that sounds strange." She looks up at Gabriel. "To feel other things too. I genuinely thought I never would again."

Then she bites her lip and says it aloud for the first time in her life.

"Gabriel, I had a baby, and then I gave her away."

She wakes early the next morning. Gabriel sleeps so soundly she wonders how he ever stirred himself to rise with the birds for his farm work. They plan to make their way to the border, although Tessa isn't sure they shouldn't wait a few days until the dust has settled.

Tessa carries her shoes down to the kitchen, not wanting to wake him, wanting him to have all the sleep he can in this, the calm before the storm. She doesn't put her shoes on in the garden either, wanting to feel the wet grass beneath her feet. It's not yet six, and the sun isn't high enough to burn off the dew. She can see the outline of her grandmother's planting in the borders, but the edges are blurred, everything bigger and wilder with interlopers brought in on the wind. The pond is an ominous black, where once they could plunge their hands beneath the surface and grab frogs and crested newts. Theo is everywhere here. There are two views across the garden, one real and one in her head. She wonders again where he is and instinctively looks up at the sky. Tessa lets her hand slip beneath the surface of the water. There, there he is, a tangible link. Theo, if you could see me now, she thinks. Theo would know how to get to Spain, but he'd find a way to do it properly, *officially*. He likes rules and order and that's why he's so baffled by who he is, deep down. That's why she couldn't tell him about the child. It's his disappointment, his judgment, she can't bear.

"Tessa?"

She snatches her hand from the water, sending ripples across the black. Tessa stands and smooths down the front of her dress. Here is another ghost, walking across the garden.

"Madame Daunay, what a pleasant surprise," she says to her grandmother's old friend, her nearest neighbor, trying to keep her voice steady. She is thrown by this sudden arrival. They will have to move on now, she's sure. Nowhere is safe, not even her grandmother's sanctuary.

The old woman takes a step forward, wringing her hands together. "Your mother asked me to look in on the house every now and then," she says.

Tessa smiles but she knows it is too bright, too wide. "I didn't know that. I'm just visiting from Paris with my husband. My mother probably didn't mention that I live there. We wanted to check on the house too, although I can see you've done a wonderful job of taking care of it."

"Your husband?" says Madame Daunay, warily.

Tessa threads a needle through the holes in her story. Keep it brief, she thinks, keep it plausible. "My husband has a rather important job in Paris, so it's fine. It's all above board us being here."

It sounds desperate, she realizes.

The woman comes closer, and now Tessa can see the mixture of apology and defiance in her eyes. What has she done? Oh God, how could she? Surely Madame Daunay knows by now what it means to make that telephone call. "I've known you my entire life," says Tessa, quietly.

"I didn't realize it was you," says the old woman, pleading.

Tessa takes a step back toward the house, and another and another, until she is running across the lawn. She can hear movement in the lane, tires against the gravel. Her heart is thudding against her ribcage. She flings open the door but before she can call his name, sees that Gabriel is already standing by the window. He has his gun in his hand, a look of wretched despair on his face. "It's over," he mouths. Tessa slips on her shoes and stands next to him, sees what he is seeing. Three—no, four, here's another—cars in the courtyard; black, gleaming machines designed to impress. I am going to die, she thinks. They will kill us. It is what they do to people like her, the Resistance, the spies. There are ten men standing in the courtyard, some in thick grey uniforms and some wearing a uniform she hasn't seen before. Long black leather coats.

Gabriel looks at the men, looks down at his gun and then back again. Tessa takes his hand and squeezes it. At least we had each other, she thinks, at least there was something else, something good, these past few months. What an odd, flat feeling it is, the certainty of death. There is nowhere to go, no way out. Gabriel places his gun on a high shelf, because what is the point, when this is so clearly at an end.

They keep holding hands until they are wrenched apart.

They fight for each other, reaching out their arms, grasping for a final touch.

Madame Daunay is in the courtyard, still wringing her hands. Her eyes are wide and contrite. "Tessa," she says, and Tessa sees Gabriel look back toward her, because in all of this, the spilling of secrets and blood, she'd neglected to tell him her name.

"I'm sorry," she whispers.

Gabriel is bundled into one car, Tessa into another.

I'm going to die, she thinks again, straining her neck for one last look at Gabriel—who could have been a big love, could have been a person she'd know forever. He is, she thinks, this being the last of time, and love and all its possibilities.

"We all have to follow the rules," Madame Daunay calls out, as the car doors slam shut.

Sixteen

The drive takes three hours, with the convoy making one stop. Tessa presumes this is because the Gestapo don't want either of them pissing in their elegant motors. As she squats, one of the men holds on tightly to her arm, his nose wrinkling in disgust.

She is offered no food or water on the journey. Nor do the men speak to her, though she asks, several times, why she has been taken and where they are going.

"It's outrageous, manhandling a woman like this," she spits, feeling fierce and terrified, and everything in between.

Of course, she knows where they're going—Paris, after all these years. She hasn't been back since her mother sneaked her away to hide behind the thick stone walls of her grandmother's house.

Through the car window Tessa can see that everything from the banlieues to the grand boulevards is overlaid with German and draped in the Führer's Standard, just as Theo had said.

Will her death be clean, like the boy soldier's? A quick death is a blessing. She tries to read the men's expressions, but they give nothing away.

Driving along avenue Foch pricks a memory. Tessa and Theo had walked this street together, laughing about something, probably some tale about Theo getting into a scrape with his university friends, who—to Tessa's mind at least—often seemed dumbfounded by the world around them.

Her body is jolted to the left as the car turns at speed into a courtyard. When the door opens, she digs her fingers into the leather seats until they drag her from the car.

"No!" she shrieks, as birds scatter from the window ledges. "*Lâchez-moi!*"

"Please, there is no need for such behavior," says a man in the doorway, his English delivered in a rapid Teutonic volley.

Then she is face to face with Gabriel, who is twisting his body, trying to free himself from two men's grasp. He is mouthing something to her, but all she can see is the purple bruise pooling beneath his eye and the fact that unlike hers, his hands are chained behind his back. Even so, she thinks, he is alive, he is still alive. They're taken up a grand staircase to the fifth floor, which seems to take an age, the two of them struggling, digging their heels into the stairs. The floor she can see is divided into multiple small rooms. On the wall of the corridor is a written chart displaying what appears to be a family tree, branches linking names and titles. Except it's not a family tree, but a comprehensive overview of the SOE Baker Street Command. In a snatched glance she can see Ronald Stenwick, Emmeline Jones, the training schools Tessa attended.

They push Tessa into a room, slam the door behind her and lock it. There is a bed and a small window with bars which overlooks the small courtyard. On the walls, previous occupants of the room—the cell—have scratched names and dates into the plaster. Here is someone called Lucien, a Brian, a Diana. It's impossible not to wonder where they are now. Because she cannot think of what to do, Tessa sits on the hard bed, places her hands on her lap and tries to catch her breath. Her brain is a runaway train, this-is-it, this-is-it, this-is-it.

After about an hour spent running over the worst possible outcomes this predicament might yield, Tessa is taken to a large office on the floor below, where gilt chandeliers hang from pristine molded reliefs. One of the men from the courtyard is waiting for her in the doorway. He's short and stocky, and reminds her of the photographer Man Ray—although she can't think of a bigger insult, to be compared to a Nazi. "Welcome, welcome!" he says in thick, accented English, holding out his hand, but Tessa will not take it.

"I am Colonel Hans König," he says, although he's not wearing a uniform. The man takes a step back and beckons her inside. "It's a reunion, no?"

The view is nicer here from the expansive, barless windows: white clouds and the Paris skyline. Victor and Alain are sitting bolt upright at a round table filled with French delicacies, cream cakes and macarons. A coffee pot sits steaming in the center. It is a party, perhaps. Prisoners, probably soon to be condemned to death, having tea with the Nazi high command. It is the strangest party she has ever attended.

Victor is glaring at her, a purple vein throbbing on his temple.

"Although I believe you called each other by different names. Remind me again, Paul?"

The man she knows as Victor hisses, "Victor and Alain." Tessa can't recall having heard him speak in English, which he does with a crisp Home Counties accent. Speak French, she thinks, trying to communicate this with her eyes. Don't give up.

König slaps his hand on the table. "Ah yes! Victor and Alain."

Tessa's knees are weak, her mouth dry, although as she has no intention of talking, perhaps it doesn't matter.

"And they knew you as Isabelle. How nice it is, that we are finally able to take off the masks and get to know one another." König nods at Tessa, his expression changing in an instant. Now he is severe. "You will sit down, please."

Tessa does as he says, and he pours her a coffee and offers her the plate of cakes. When she doesn't respond he places them down in front of her. "Just in case you change your mind," he says, sweet again. "Now of course, Tessa, I know you by reputation. I know about your little escapade at the gendarmerie. I think you know Agnès Roue, yes? I'm excited to speak to you about her."

Tessa stares straight ahead. If she doesn't meet anyone's gaze, perhaps they won't see how terrified she is, especially at the mention of Agnès' name.

König is still speaking, despite her silence. "But it is through your own words that I feel I have really gained a glimpse into your character." He takes a letter from his pocket and begins to read. It's a letter to Theo, smuggled back home via one of Jean's contacts, or at least so she'd thought. How painful it is to hear her words aloud, the strain of the lie evident, the invention of nights out in London, chatter with friends, none of it sounding quite plausible now she hears it. She tries to keep this from her face because she is still determined to be Isabelle, not Tessa.

Then Alain snaps his fingers and bursts the delusion. "They have copies of our letters home. Nearly every single one I sent," he says, in accented English. So you are French, at least, Tessa thinks.

This isn't just bad luck. Something has gone catastrophically wrong. Clearly they know exactly who she is and why she is there.

Tessa knows she has to make a decision. Does she carry on with the lie, knowing it will likely infuriate König, or does she drop the pretense? She isn't going to tell them anything, she is determined not to crack, and yet—what is left for them to find out when they seemingly know every detail of the operation? "Where is the man I arrived with?" she says, in English. How odd it feels in her mouth after all this time.

"At last, she speaks," says König, but before he can answer her question, although Tessa feels certain he wouldn't have, there is a knock at the door.

"This is Doctor Katz," he says. No one looks at the man, who is wearing thick spectacles, and he does not acknowledge them, even König. "We've been playing a little game, haven't we, gentlemen?" König is beaming at them around the table. "Remi, why don't you tell Tessa all about it?"

The man she knows as Alain is eating a chocolate éclair. He puts it down, shoots Tessa a pointed look, and says, "It's quite simple really. Colonel König asked me to send a message to London on my wireless set, so I did."

Why is he so calm, Tessa wonders. What on earth has happened here? Victor, in contrast, is trembling with fury.

König claps his hands together. "Doctor Katz has tried transmitting on your wireless sets before—with . . ." he shrugs, nonchalantly, ". . . some success, I should say, wouldn't you agree, Katz?"

The other man is shaking his head. "You people are so careless with your security codes."

"You see, Tessa," says König, "this is the first time we've been able to send a message to London via the actual wireless operator himself."

"London will think the message is from us," the man she knows as Victor interjects, bitterly. He won't look at Tessa. "And when they reply, thinking they're replying to us, they'll be passing information directly to them." He nods at König and Katz. "They'll know about our drops, our people. They'll know what equipment we have. The enemy will know everything, and they'll be getting it directly from the source."

"It is a good plan, no?" says König.

It is at this moment that Tessa remembers the conversation she had with Alain in the barn. The true security check and the bluff check—if London receives the true check in a transmission they'll know it is their agent, but if they receive the bluff check they'll know the agent is compromised. Now she understands the look in Alain's eyes. It won't save them, it's too late for that—but it should alert London to the situation.

"You will be delighted to learn that London has responded," says König.

The three of them stay silent. Victor looks at his hands. Alain continues devouring his cake.

"Doctor Katz, will you please read the message from London?"

Doctor Katz nods, taking a slip of paper from his pocket and clearing his throat. "You seem to have forgotten your security check, dear chap," he says. "Please be more careful in the future."

Alain goes very still, the remains of the éclair an inch from his lips. Victor closes his eyes. So implausible is it—all those hours of lectures, the constant reminders about security—that it takes Tessa a few moments to comprehend what has happened. Baker Street, having failed to follow their own rules, have informed the Germans of Alain's use of the bluff check.

"*Ça y est*," says Alain, dropping the éclair onto his plate and smacking his hands together. He looks at Tessa and draws a finger across his throat.

Victor slams his fist into the table, making them all jump. "It was over the moment we took up with her." He is so enraged his voice is breaking. "How could you? Did they pay you? What price did you place on our heads?"

König dismisses Katz from the room and looks at them one by one. He's not smiling any more.

"You and Gabriel were the only ones who didn't turn up for the drop," Victor says, damning them both in one fell swoop. "Alain was there to warn us, but where were you?"

"That isn't what happened," she says, astonished at the steadiness of her voice. There is no need to say anything more.

But König is even more interested now, rocking back and forth in his chair like an excited child. He claps his hands together and the door is opened by one of two guards, who must have been waiting just outside. "The gentlemen will be leaving us now," he says, and Victor and Alain are hauled to their feet. Alain flashes her a smile, but it's weak, and she can see from the way he looks up and down the corridor that he is wondering if this is the moment, the end. She wonders what they'll do to him to force him to reveal his true security check, and if it will work.

Victor pulls away from his guard and points his finger at Tessa. "You've killed us," he hisses. "You might not be pulling the trigger, but you killed us. Traitor."

And then he is gone.

"Just so we're clear, there is little point in maintaining aliases and cover stories," says König. "That should be more than apparent to you now. Have some cake, won't you?"

"I've no interest in playing whatever game this is."

"No?" He shrugs. "It seems a shame to let it all go to waste. I bought it especially for you, for your reunion with your friends."

"You could have told them I wasn't a traitor."

"But why would I? I think it will be useful, perhaps, for them to feel they have been betrayed from all sides."

"How do you have my letter to Theo?" says Tessa.

"I think you love your brother, yes? How difficult it must be, to lie to someone you love. But as to how it got into my hands, well, I think you know. I think you tried to warn London, and despite what Victor says I think you tried to warn your friends that night in the forest."

Tessa closes her eyes. There's no satisfaction in being right, not now. "Jean," she says.

König is nodding again. "A most helpful man."

"Where is my friend?"

König sits back in his chair. She can see he is taking in every detail, trawling through them for usefulness. "He is important to you," he says, and when she doesn't reply, he adds, "Tessa, I want to help you, but to do that I need you to help me."

"You don't want to help me."

He looks disappointed. "But I do, and you will soon see how well the agents here are treated if they cooperate. They understand this must be a relationship that works both ways. Many of them have been most helpful."

She wants to be sick. "Then they have betrayed their country."

"Have they? Or has their country betrayed them? There is no shame in fighting for your life, especially when you've been so badly let down." At this, he indicates the paper read out by Doctor Katz. "I want to help you and your friend, I do. We are all soldiers, it's just that your uniform is a little different. I respect that. If you help me, I swear to you I will ensure you and your friends are treated as prisoners of war, with all the protection that status affords." When she doesn't answer, he cocks his head to the side, and says, "No one *wants* to hurt you, Tessa. For one thing, I have daughters your age. I couldn't."

Tessa sits with this for a moment, then says, "I'm not sure that speaks highly of your sex or your creed, Colonel." König scoffs and raises his hands. "No, no I'm glad you told me," she continues. "I'm glad you told me that, because if you didn't have daughters, I'd just be a woman to you, and then I'd be in real trouble, wouldn't I? God knows you Nazis love your hierarchies."

"Tessa, you are in real trouble," he says, his expression darkening.

The switch flicks, the mood changes. She wonders if that is all it takes to push him too far.

She is returned to her cell, but not before König promises to speak to her the next day, and the next, "until you trust me."

She wonders who is behind the other closed doors on this floor. The women she trained with? They'd never talk. But remembering that detailed "family tree," does it even matter any more? Clearly many people *have* talked.

But is it really a betrayal, the agents revealing what they know? Perhaps

König is right: perhaps it is the agents who have been betrayed. The British, their superiors, have condemned their own men and women through what appears to be complete and utter incompetence.

What would I do, she thinks, to save my own life? How far would I go? It is an astonishing thing, the instinct to survive.

From her cell, Tessa has a view of the courtyard. A man—not Gabriel, not anyone she knows—is standing facing the wall down there. She's so taken with the hunch of his shoulders, the white of his ears, that she doesn't at first register the presence of a second man. Then things begin to topple onto each other, like a collapsing house of cards, until she is so busy noticing the details of this scene that she forgets to breathe. The way the first man's hands are shaking is one. The other man's uniform, storm-grey, is another, as is the gun in his hand. Tessa wants to take a step back from the window but finds that after all, she can't look away. Something morbid has awoken inside her. How simply it plays out, one action, then another, then another. The man in the uniform forces the shaking man to his knees, presses the gun to the base of his skull and fires. An explosion of red and grey hits the white-rendered wall. The man on the ground slumps forward, his head sliding down the wall until his body lies in a heap. There is a sound in the air, not just the shot but a cry, and how astonishing that it is her own voice. The spray of blood on the wall forms the shape of an oyster shell. I'll remember that, she thinks, and the sound, and the brightness of that red.

There is more movement below. König, the sun radiating off his black hair, steps from the shadows and looks up at her. He is smiling.

Part Two

Nine Months Later

THEO

Normandy, 5-6 June 1944

Seventeen

Armstrong," says a voice, a whisper. "Theo . . ."

Theo opens his eyes, closes them, opens them once more. It's dark, still crow-black outside the billet's thin windows, Barnes' eyes like beacons in the next bed. There's such warmth in his gaze, Theo wants to reach out a hand to see if Barnes will take it. In his mind he does. In his mind the two men linger there, fingers entwined, not speaking because there's no need for words—it's all there in the way they look at one another. Barnes has sandy blond hair which curls over his eyes when not swept back beneath his cap. His creamy skin is butter-soft—Theo's sure of it. He's thought about it a great deal.

And then it hits him. It is *that* day. It is *now*, finally happening. The squadron had gone to bed after supper to try and catch a few hours of precious sleep. Theo glances at his watch. It's nearly ten. He's managed two hours of sleep.

"I know," says Barnes. "Took me a moment too. They'll be in here any minute, bellowing at us to get ready."

Theo swallows. Barnes is still looking at him, but his smile has a pinched, forced look to it now. "Armstrong," he says, again.

"Barnes?"

"I wonder . . . I don't know if this is stupid. I'm not sure if I should . . ."

Theo raises himself up on his elbow, checking over his shoulder to see if anyone is listening. But the rest of the men seem to be asleep, their snoring a low hum beneath the sounds outside. The slow, sliding grate of aircraft hangars opening, the slamming of doors. The distant chat of the ground crews getting ready.

"Please say it," says Theo, as quietly as he can. It's been there for months, a current pulsing between them. It is what gets him through the day. "I want you to say it."

"I don't want to get your hopes up."

Theo shakes his head. "I know how it is." It's not like I haven't been here before, he thinks.

"It's just . . . do you . . ."

"Yes?"

"I just wonder . . . do you think we'll get a special breakfast before we go? Or is it lousy rations whatever the day's significance?"

Theo flops down on his back, so Barnes can't see his expression. He laughs, though he can hear how forced it sounds.

"I don't think I can eat," he says. "Whatever they might dish up."

It is the biggest day of the war.

That's what they say, the men, as they climb into their cockpits an hour later. These are the words spoken: *This is it, here we are, we made it, lads.* The biggest day of the war and they are to be part of it. The atmosphere at the airfield is electric, it thrums beneath everything else. If anyone is feeling trepidation, and surely they are, they do not voice it. No one wants to pin-prick the mood by showing their fear, although Theo supposes they all feel it, the thud of nerves beneath the bright eyes and the backslapping. Barnes puts his hand on Theo's arm. Should I say something, Theo thinks.

It is all there, isn't it, in Barnes' touch? The two men speak eagerly and often, about everything. They seek each other out. They bunk next to one another, and Barnes is the last person Theo sees each day. Five floorboards separate their beds; he knows, he's counted. There are looks that breach that divide, eye contact lingering. Once, Barnes allowed his fingers to graze the back of Theo's hand and didn't immediately snatch his hand away.

I should say something, he thinks.

Except maybe he's imagining it, and this is hope not reality, want not truth. Because there is a want, aching, burning inside of him. No, after all, it's too much of a risk—the rejection, the exposure, the shame. It is a distraction from the matter at hand, the magnitude of which is almost impossible to comprehend. The squadron hasn't been able to leave the base for months in case they let something slip about the ops, the plan. No leave, no telephone calls, no letters. Theo exists in a bubble of stiff, blue uniforms in which there is no before, no outside, only this. The potential of a future, the anticipation, the waiting, waiting, waiting.

So if Barnes rejects him, there'll be nowhere to go, no way of escaping, unless Barnes reports him—and then the only place Theo will be going is prison. So Theo has said nothing and has been fucking a ground engineer instead. The ground engineer approached him, that's the difference. The risk felt almost tolerable.

But here, now, on this dark, not-quite-new day, this is the moment, because chances are there will be no other. Months of raids, multiple targets across the northern coast of France, and here it is. The biggest day of the war. Aerial cover again but this time the gliders he's accompanying are loaded with men, not bombs. This is liberation from above, the mission to secure the roads beyond the Normandy beaches before the invasion proper.

Within an hour of their late-night breakfast, the squadron has been briefed and they are on the runway, preparing to depart.

"Barnes," says Theo. "Richard."

Barnes nods. He smiles. Is there something in that smile, Theo wonders. An acknowledgment? Is it there or is he seeing what he wants to see?

"See you on the other side," says Barnes in his shifting accent, which Theo has never quite been able to place.

Theo smiles tightly, knowing the moment is gone, that he doesn't have the nerve.

Stop it, he tells himself. It's all in your head.

But what if it isn't?

"Make sure you do," he says, because it feels like bad luck to say goodbye. In their minds the squadron are already up in the clouds, but here on the airfield there are people milling about, the ground crews, the airborne crews. The tension and excitement are palpable. Theo can feel them surging through him. This is what it has all been leading toward.

He climbs into his Spitfire, shooting a last look at the base he's called home for the past few months. He looks around, looks at the other men climbing into their planes and gliders, the pilots, the last tranche of paratroopers. Some of them are in their teens—boys, not men. Theo, at twenty-eight, is considered the elder statesman of his squadron.

Most of the pilots he trained with are dead now. They barely lasted a month. Shot down, blown to pieces, butchered. Theo has witnessed ending after ending after ending.

Human beings are very resilient, Tessa once told him. Theo isn't sure this is true. He knows well the fragility of the human body, has seen men maimed, their lives forever altered. He is not the person he was before. He is changed, he is changing so quickly it leaves him breathless. These experiences, the endings he has witnessed—no, Theo shakes himself: deaths. He's seen death. He is not some stuffy Victorian needing euphemisms for the most profound of human experience. Theo has seen death, and it is hollowing him out, the person he was before replaced with anger, and hatred, and an inexplicable and overwhelming urge to let men do whatever they want to him, whenever they want. Risk is part of it. Risk makes his heart beat faster. It's how he knows he's still there, that he isn't stone cold inside.

One life, two lives, all the way up to nine. Theo is somehow still going. See you on the other side, he says, to no one in particular.

Before him, beyond the glass arch of the cockpit, a bank of cloud smothers everything, the land, the sky, in grey. If he strains his neck, wrapped in a burgundy knitted scarf—a present from his mother, who by no stretch of the imagination can be said to have a gift for the craft—he can just make out the white peaks of waves below. Sometimes he imagines dolphins, leaping in great arcs, or he makes his brain work harder and a whale, a great black beast, skin glinting in the low light, erupts from the depths of the Channel. The air in the cockpit is bitterly cold against his skin. He is glad of his misshapen scarf, and gladder still of his thick socks. Barnes had teased him something rotten about them back at base.

"Look at you in your granny's hand-me-downs," he'd said, prodding Theo's foot with his toe. A glancing touch can hold the full spectrum of human emotion.

His mind is twisting between whales and socks and white peaks. It keeps other thoughts at bay. It's coming up on midnight, but the sky remains dark. The enemy, his squadron hopes, will be caught unawares. There, now he's done it. The enemy. There goes his stomach, somersaulting with fear.

The Battle of Britain. North Africa, and now this.

The liberation of France.

Theo is gulping in oxygen. He pushes gently on the throttle. Moves lower, as per his orders, beneath the reach of enemy radar. The wind unsettles the plane—the lightness of the Spitfire continues to astonish him four years in—but the rudder quickly brings everything to rights. He can't see the others, can't hear anything above the engine. Disorientation is always a danger; it can come quickly and powerfully if you're not careful. He'd once spent five minutes wondering why his head was pounding and his ears throbbing, before he'd realized he was flying upside down. Theo keeps his eyes flicking back and forth between the instruments and the thick bank of grey. The landing crafts will be leaving soon to cross the Channel, crammed their full length with men, young and old. He imagines the push and pull of the tide, the ripple back and forth of green tin hats. For some, this is their first time leaving England. Imagine that. The poor buggers.

"Theo?"

"Tessa?" His shoulders tense. His hands freeze mid-maneuver. In response, his radio crackles, firing a blush into his cheeks. Did they hear? They'll tease him unmercifully about it later, if so. He can hear it now: *Oi oi, who's Tessa?* But no, nothing, silence and cold air. Tessa isn't there. Of course she isn't there. It's a memory, that's all, a longed-for reality. He used to hear her voice in his head all the time. It stopped, though, when she went to France, as if she'd severed the thread between them. How did she do that, he thinks, and how come she has that power and he doesn't? Ahead is a blinking light, a flash, another. Yes, France. And what is that sound beneath his ribs? Is it really his heart pounding, longing for a place he's always considered a home away from home? The last few months have brought him back regularly, attacking warehouses, railways, but this feels different. Below his plane, tens of thousands of men will soon break free into the waves. *This is it.* Land, the inky wobble of the coastline. Can he make out the shapes on the beaches? Has his imagination taken over again? He opens the throttle fully and pulls up, keeping his speed steady at a textbook 185mph.

The first tentative shots from an anti-aircraft gun on the beach rip through the air. Theo banks left to avoid them. "Shit!" he shouts. And then, "Fuck you!" His language is astonishing in the sky, a torrent of filth pouring from his lips. Tessa would be delighted, he thinks. Tessa would laugh and join in. He can't feel the cold now. His breath is ragged, shallow beneath his thick flying suit. Thank Christ for the clouds. The enemy might be able to hear him, but they can't see him.

Theo circles over the line between land and sea. There's Barnes—his plane, like Theo's, newly painted in black and white stripes. Barnes is a veteran too, there from the beginning. Not many have the stamina or the luck, but Theo is addicted to the adrenaline of flying. He can't give it up and doesn't care to try. Any day might be his last; it is a strange but potent high.

Shapes move in and out of the grey. British aircraft, the coming Germans. An enemy plane appears on Barnes' wing. It takes Theo a moment to grasp what is happening.

"Barnes!" he screams into the radio, just quickly enough. Barnes loops back, taking the enemy craft by surprise. He is behind it now, his plane disappearing into a cloud of black smoke as he hits the other plane with a hail of fire. The fighter spirals toward the water and disappears into the grey Channel below.

"Yes!" Theo shouts, punching the air. "Bloody good show!"

Gliders, odd, noiseless beasts, move alongside him. Paratroopers en route to their drop zones. Imagine dropping into the unknown. Christ. Theo shudders, he can't help it, but perhaps it is the cold after all. He circles again, but nothing. Where is the enemy? Have they really caught them unawares? He's had countless dreams of this dogfight—he has barely slept in months—and is this it, is this all they've got?

"We've surprised them," he roars into his radio. Like many, he'd been perplexed by the order to proceed, the weather just as rotten as the preceding few days. But no, what genius—the Germans, it seems, are just as dumbfounded.

The percussion of battle reaches his ears. Moving softly on the rudder, he circles again to the left. His heart is thudding harder now. Theo feels almost gleeful. Sea, beach, green, he flies toward the green, squeezing his fingers around the trigger, sending a volley into a mounted gun. Flames rise into the air, black, then orange, then a fierce red.

"Do you think about the people you've killed?" Tessa once asked him.

Movement catches his eye. An enemy aircraft, an SKG 10. Theo circles back but it's too late to intervene. He doesn't see the Dakota or the glider until the flames tear through them. Theo squints, trying to spot the British roundel, the circular identification mark on the aircraft. There it is. British, no doubt.

"Shit," he says, under his breath. "Shit, shit, shit."

The glider turns orange, then red. It comes apart, splintering into the air, the disassembled parts crashing into the sea below.

Just boys, he thinks. The paratroopers. The pilot. The navigator.

A sharp volley from his machine gun sends the German fighter into the sea. Theo doubles back. It's hot now, the coldness gone, beads of sweat multiplying on his brow. The enemy is outnumbered in the air; even with the morning's poor visuals it's obvious. Theo goes low, aiming his gun beyond the beach; he has to take out what he can while the paratroopers make their drop zones. Barnes is on his right again. He knows it's Barnes, can just make out the markings on his plane.

If we get out of this alive, I'll tell you how I feel, he thinks.

Does he jinx it? Does his promise to himself damn Barnes? Because seconds later Barnes' plane is in flames. Theo doesn't witness the impact, but he feels it. His plane juddering, tilting from the blast, it takes a moment for Theo to regain control.

"Jesus Christ!" he shouts. "Barnes, Jesus Christ." He watches the plane—at least, what is left of it—spiral toward the beach below. "Bail out, Barnes, for Christ's sake, bail out!" he yells, knowing that it is pointless, that Barnes cannot hear him now.

The air is alive with bullets, and with planes ducking and diving through the cloud. Theo can't see a parachute. He wants so desperately to see a parachute emerge from the falling plane. Except how will that save Barnes? Parachuting straight down onto the enemy below.

There is no parachute. Just flames, and the remains of the plane exploding when they hit the beach. Maybe he did get out, thinks Theo. Maybe I missed it. It is perfectly plausible that I missed it.

And then from the corner of his eye he catches a flash before the impact sends his plane into a spin. Again, he hadn't spotted the enemy fighter. Too busy thinking about the Dakota, the boys. Barnes. Nine lives, ten lives, eleven, twelve. Here he goes, spiraling toward the earth. Today's the day, he thinks. Adrenaline sends blood pulsing around his body. Theo looks back and sees the tail of his Spitfire blown clean off, shards of metal burning black in jagged peaks.

"I'm going down!" he shouts, as if anyone can do anything. With the battle raging around him, they probably aren't even listening. Below. He'll be part of it now, like it or not. Managing to regain some semblance of control, Theo steers the plane as far inland as he can. Images repeat. Men disappearing into the flames, black, then orange, then red, the spindly details of life on Earth growing more distinct. He can see roads winding from the beach, toward the first signs of French normality beyond the bunkers and the barbed wire. Houses painted in cream and red. Garden fences. A farm, perhaps, with a large vegetable patch, neat lines of artichoke plants.

He thinks of Barnes, of loss. He thinks of his sister, of the strangeness of her peaked cap sitting between them on Aunt Vi's kitchen table. I'll never know, he realizes. I'll never know what she was up to. I'll never know what happened all those years ago.

How will she go on, once he is gone?

Eighteen

A voice whispers, "He's coming round."

The biggest day of the war. Theo reaches out to take the controls of his plane but his fingers are grasping at air. He remembers a blinking light, a flash, another. Thirty thousand feet below him, tens of thousands of men in landing crafts, bracing against the surge of the waves. The memories come orange, then red, then black. It is so hot.

There's a noise in the air which sounds alien and forbidding.

"Can't you shut him up?" says a second voice.

Some of the noise, Theo is astonished to realize, is him. He must have been dreaming of his plane, of the invasion too, because everything else is missing. The juddering of the plane, the crackle of the radio, the ferocious roar of the engine. There is movement though, wherever he is now, thin vibrations through the earth. The noises seem to be outside, at a distance. Outside, he thinks. And then, I am inside. He can't seem to open his eyes. Around him feels solid and damp when he stretches out his arms. The smell is familiar but not like the Spitfire; there's no fuel in his nose, the smell often lingering on his hair and flying suit, which his hands tell him he is still wearing—although why is there a wetness there, and what is this metallic taste on his tongue? He can hear his heart beating, there it is, tearing, skidding, the sound of something out of control. The air is damp but no matter, there is heat deep inside him keeping him warm.

"Shh, shh, Denis, please," says the voice that brought him out of his dream.

The other voice says, sounding panicked, "He's going to get us killed."

Theo tries to shuffle back, away from the voices, the vibrations and the sounds outside, but his back seems to be against something solid and his legs won't move. "Who's there?" he hisses into the blackness. He fumbles at his waistline, but his pistol is gone.

"Be quiet," comes the first voice again, firmer now. A woman, he thinks. It occurs to him that this might not be a dream, despite the haze, the almost unreal voices. Where is he? The voices remind him of home, of his mother. They are speaking her language, he realizes. They are speaking French. His mother keeps a furious grip on her native tongue, conversation at the dining-room table dancing between English and French, Theo and Tessa switching between the two. He'd give anything to be back there now. Debating a book with Tessa, their father offering his opinion as if it were fact, their mother chipping in with a droll "*vraiment?*"

The pain strikes then, like fire, making him beat at his legs. "Oh God," he gasps. "Oh my God." His voice doesn't sound like his own.

"Hold on, don't move," says the other voice, which sounds different, male. Then there's a warmth on his face, stinging—iodine, he knows the smell. Theo tries to turn his head away but it is held firm.

"Tessa?" he says, although he knows, he knows. Hope doesn't always run with logic.

The blackness retreats and turns to grey, and then a woman's face comes into view. She's close to his mother's age, and holding an oil lamp. Her hair is wrapped tightly in a headscarf.

"It's just dried blood," she whispers, holding up the red-sodden rag for him to see.

"*Qu'est-ce qui se passe?*" he says. He looks about, still blinking, trying to breathe through the pain. The room is built of brick, streaked with dark stains. It is some sort of barn, an outbuilding at any rate. He can see wooden beams, the tiles of a gabled roof. He's lying on an old, ratty mattress, which seems to have absorbed the wetness in the air.

The woman raises the lamp, squinting at him. "You can't remember?"

He thinks of the orange, then red, then black. The juddering of the plane, and the stench in his nose. Barnes' plane slamming into the beach below. He thinks, the heat of those deaths.

The woman shakes her head. "Maybe it's for the best."

The man takes the lamp from her, swinging it back and forth, a spray of shadows across the walls. He's older than the woman, greyer. Two fingers are missing from the hand gripping the lamp. "You came down in our field, parachuted from your plane. It's a wreck," he says. In case he hasn't been understood, he places the lamp on the floor and mimes the descent, slapping his large hands together at the point of impact.

The woman shoots the man a look. "We did what we could with your leg, but it's a bad break. You need a surgeon to set the bone." She's watching his eyes, making sure he's keeping up. He doesn't like the way she's looking at him. Pity, he thinks, and fear.

He reaches down and touches his leg, wincing and gritting his teeth against the pain. His flying suit and trousers are torn below the knee, the fabric of his uniform soaked black, a rag tied around its source. By pressing his fingers against the fabric he can tell the wound is wide and gaping, and solid in the center. The woman swiftly clamps her hand over his mouth to stifle his cry.

"Water," he says, when she releases him. Taking a flask from her jacket pocket, she leans over him, wetting his lips. The whisky burns his throat but softens the pain. "More," he says, and the woman nods.

The man tuts. "Don't waste it on him. I doubt he'll last the night." He is shaking his head, the lamp still swinging this way and that. "Your leg is infected," he says, shrugging his apology. "We've cleaned it as best we can but if it gets into your blood . . ."

The man looks like he might be a farmer. Farmers know about these things.

"How long have I been here?" Theo asks.

The woman smiles, patiently. "A few days."

A few days. He tries to think back through the blackness, gripping his hands either side of his head, which hurts, which makes him grip harder because the pain is proof that he's still there, clinging on.

"Here . . ." he says. "But where . . ." and the woman whispers, "*La Normandie*."

There is an explosion outside, and another and another. His rescuers dive to the floor, but Theo's stuck fast on his mattress, cradling his head in his hands. Dust falls in clouds from the rafters. He can taste it on his lips, his tongue. The woman takes a pistol from her pocket, while the man goes to the door, looking about. Theo wants to ask if he's going to die, but looking down at his damaged leg he's afraid of the answer. His father would say something profound in this moment. Tessa would be furious, and unafraid of her fury because she'd be right. It is unfair. He's never going to solve the problems in his head now. He's never going to see his sister again. He thinks then of Yeats, "all changed, changed utterly."

The woman inspects his face through narrowed, concerned eyes. Taking Theo's hand, she guides his fingers across a large gash on his temple. "It's not so bad," she says. Sitting down next to him, she takes a packet of cigarettes from her pocket, lights two and passes one to Theo. It hurts to breathe but he takes the cigarette, coughing into his fist at the first inhale. The woman puts a finger to her lips.

"It'll hurt more if they find you," she whispers, tilting her head toward the door. She takes the flask from her pocket, but this time she doesn't offer him any. "I can't tell you how long it will be until they get here," she says. "I can't tell you if it will be friend or foe."

"It sounds close."

"Yes."

"They might be looking for me," he says, and he can't stop himself from laughing, because it is obvious from the sounds outside that they won't be, not at this stage of the operation. Besides, they probably think he's dead.

The woman presses lightly on his arm. He begins to cry, trying to hide behind his free hand. He hasn't done this in years. He can feel the heat creeping up his neck toward his face. There is nothing he can do but hope—*pray*, he thinks—but Tessa would tell him to stop being silly. She'd call him a hypocrite, only summoning God in the worst moments.

"I have to get back," he says, weakly.

He thinks, the invasion of France, all that prep. Despite the wounds and the fogginess, he wants to claim his place as a liberator. He has to find out if Barnes is alive. Again, he sees the flames rising from Barnes' plane. But it was chaos, he thinks. Maybe he got out, and I didn't see. After all, he himself has survived. I am alive, he tells himself. Perhaps Barnes is too.

"I'd like to see you try and get out of here," says the man. "Normally we have our ways and means—I mean, Christ, you're not the first person to appear out of the sky. But as it is, right now, in this moment, there is nothing to be done. Just listen to that racket out there. We're surrounded by Germans. Trust me, you're safer here."

The woman says, "The British are having difficulties with the enemy's tanks. It will be the Americans here, I think. You strayed quite far in your plane."

Despite the pain, this irritates him. "It's quite difficult to stay on course . . ." He takes a deep breath, his French momentarily failing him. ". . . when the rudder has been blown off." He wipes the back of his hand across his forehead. "It's so hot in here."

"Not really. Not at all. It's the middle of the night." She places her hand on his forehead. "It's just you, Denis. You have a fever."

Denis.

"Do you have my identity papers?" he says, and the woman takes them out of her pocket and places them next to Theo.

"I wanted to know your name," she says.

Another explosion, another crash. The woman presses her hands against the wall, steadying herself.

"Liberation," mutters the man at the door, grimly.

Another crash sends a shelf of glass bottles to the floor, shards scattered.

"You should go," he says. "Both of you. It's too dangerous." But in his head he's desperate to say, please don't go, please don't leave me, because he's afraid of the visions behind his eyes which keep growing in color and intensity, and scared too of the end, of facing it on his own.

"It makes no difference if I am here or there," she says. "If the Germans find you, we are dead. Perhaps we are dead anyway. If you lose."

He looks at her for a moment, although he's having a hard time keeping his gaze steady. It's becoming difficult to breathe, as if a weight is pressing down on his chest, but it's just his uniform. He thinks, no, it is fear. Eventually he says, "My name is Theo," pronouncing it the French way, *Théo*, like his mother does, and feeling another stab of homesickness. "They give us fake papers in case we have to land behind enemy lines. It's to give us cover as we try to get back home. I expect there are British pilots in France right now, living under cover, trying to make their way through enemy territory."

"Enemy territory," she says.

Theo tries to sit up. The pain is unbearable. "Not you."

"You don't know anything about us."

"I know you're helping me."

The woman smiles, but grimly. "Perhaps, but when people are caught, they talk. It's not a judgment. We all say we won't, that of course we'll keep our mouths shut no matter what they do, but when the time comes, we talk. It is human nature, self-preservation."

Theo winces. "It might not come to that."

"Maybe not. But we have been occupied for a long time. You know France, yes? You speak the language well. But France has changed. Perhaps none of us can go back."

"I can hear the guns."

She places another cigarette between her lips. "Yes."

Another sound beyond the window. They both turn toward the glass.

The man is keeping watch at the door, a rifle in one hand and in the other, a beer. Theo thinks he should sleep, but it feels so abstract, as if he's forgotten how. His mind won't stop. The orange, then red, then black.

It's getting hotter, he's sure.

"Tessa," he says. It strikes him it will feel good to say her name, that it might help. As children they'd show off at school by reading each other's thoughts. "We're the same person," Tessa would say. They aren't, the past few years have been proof enough of that, but the line between them sometimes blurs. Last time he saw her, they had lain on their backs on Aunt Violet's sitting-room floor, listening to records, Puccini's "*O soave fanciulla*," stretching out the time because they'd both known that would be it for a while. She'd reached out and taken his hand, just like she used to.

Beneath the heat, the wet, the thoughts tumbling over one another, panic begins to rise. "Tessa," he says again.

"Keep your voice down," the man hisses.

"She is your love?" the woman says.

"She is my sister."

"She is at home, waiting for you." The woman shuffles toward him, patting his hand and stroking his brow, tenderness replacing formality, because—it comes upon him in that moment—hers might well be the last face he sees. He focuses his mind on a single image, the garden at his grandmother's house in the Loire. They'd both loved it so. He thinks, he will undress and bathe in the pond. They will eat oysters for lunch. He can taste salt on his lips.

"She is in such a dark room," he says, but the woman shushes the words from the air.

"That is you, *Théo*. Your sister is at home."

Distance quietens, he thinks; time severs.

He can hear the sound of engines, of vehicles carving up the earth outside, and boots thudding as one. Men are shouting and calling but he cannot tell what language they are speaking. Somewhere a baby is crying and he looks at the woman, at the turn of her expression, wondering if the child is hers, why she is here and not there. The woman begins to weep, but there is no one to comfort her, Theo has forgotten how. Sometimes the earth shakes and more dust pours from the ceiling. It is hours, it is minutes, later he will discover it was days. The building is aflame, but no, that's just Theo, flailing against his sodden makeshift bed.

At last, with the careering beat of his heart, the door is pulled open wide. Light floods the room. They all turn toward it, blinking, holding their hands to their eyes.

Cambridge, September 1944

Nineteen

Theo insists on taking the train, more for him than for them, though it's true his parents would probably rather meet him at home. How can things be different if they keep it normal? He adjusts his position, has to keep the leg straight as much as possible—no, not has to, has no choice. Lucky not to lose it, or so said the doctors in a makeshift Normandy hospital, a godforsaken heaven-sent place. Lucky old Theo, he thinks, who didn't lose his leg, didn't die with the rest, and was found by the right side. He maneuvers to a new angle so he can see the view from the window, thinking about autumn and the turning seasons so he doesn't have to consider the rest. Why did he get away with it, why was he spared, why not them but him? They fell into the flames, he did not. His parachute opened, Barnes' did not. So much left up to fate—the parachute, the wind, the landing that only buggered up one leg. Lucky—he shapes his mouth around the word. He is home, and they are not.

Theo takes a taxi from the station—he'd insisted—through streets of yellow brick and hardly any cars but people everywhere, milling about. He thinks, hell and back but little change here. He's expecting it, home, but somehow it still takes him by surprise. Peaks of box hedging carved by his father, and grudgingly maintained ever since by a man in the village for a few pennies every month. Green gate, green windows, the apple trees where fieldfares devour a fallen bounty come October. His mother is waiting in the doorway, shielding the worst of her emotions with a handkerchief.

"*Dieu merci*," she says, drawing him into a hug.

"Hello, Maman," he says, biting his lip because Tessa wouldn't cry. He is looking over his mother's shoulder, waiting for her wry "You're not dead, then?," but all he sees is his father coming down the stairs.

"You're a sight for sore eyes," his father says, placing his hands on Theo's shoulders. Perhaps there is change, beneath the quiet.

Familiarity is a comfort, after all. The tiled floor where as children they'd see how far they could slide in their socks, and again as adults who should have known better. Paintings by artists his mother had known in her youth. Where are they now, Theo wonders. Denounced as degenerates and on the run, or worse. We can do nothing but hope for the best, Tessa had once said.

Tea is served in the parlor. His mother's favorite cups, bright glazes of red and yellow, and the best cakes she can manage given the constraints.

"I thought she'd be here," he says, once his mother is assured the "butcher army doctors," as she terms them, have not ruined Theo's leg for good.

There is a beat. His mother closes her eyes. "The war is not over for everyone," she says. Her eyes when they open are wide and ashamed. "*Théo*, *chéri*—I'm sorry, I didn't mean that the way it sounded."

Theo shrugs. He's used to maneuvering his body around the blows. There's no reason why this morning should be any different, buggered-up leg or not.

"Do we know where she is?" he says. "I can't remember the last time I heard from her."

Tessa likes to shock, so much so that she has rather lost her ability to do it. But credit where credit's due, joining the FANYs was a twist he had not anticipated.

"Won't you take more tea?" says his mother.

Theo is suddenly alert. "I've barely taken a sip."

His mother is very interested in her napkin, threading it through her fingers and scrunching it up into a ball in her fist. "She is here and there," she says.

A feeling settles in the pit of Theo's stomach. "Is she all right?" he asks.

His father scowls and stands up, knocking over his chair in his haste to detach himself from the scene.

"What's the matter?" says Theo.

His mother reaches out and squeezes his hand. "Nothing. Your father is feeling a lot of emotions, that's all. We all are. We're so pleased that you're home, at last. It's been such a worry."

"I know it has. I really do. But will you please tell me what's going on? Where is Tessa?"

The feeling in his belly is joined by a familiar sensation in his chest, because he'd known something was wrong, has done for months. It's been gnawing at him, like a beetle attacking a wooden beam, only he's done everything he can to ignore it. It's the distance, he'd thought, it's the silence; it's natural to worry.

"Jesus Christ," says his father.

"Dominic, please," says his mother.

"Adela, we have to."

Theo follows the conversation back and forth, knowing full well they're speaking aloud only the bare minimum, doing all they can to keep him at arm's length.

"How can we?" His mother begins to cry.

"Tell me," says Theo, quietly.

His mother expects him to comfort her; he can see it in her eyes, the surprise that he hasn't, the disappointment that he won't. But she doesn't know yet that he's all switched off inside. Then she nods her head and his father walks over to the bureau, the keeper of everything deemed important. Passports, tickets, bills, letters. The boring bits, as Tessa would say. When his father retrieves a letter from the pages of a notebook, he closes his eyes. Theo clocks that, and the way his hand shakes as he grips the paper. His father puts the letter down on the table and goes over to the window.

Theo picks it up and reads the two sentences of type. "I don't understand," he says.

His father doesn't turn around. "Don't lose your temper," says his mother.

But he will and he does, because he is Theo, not the other half of the coin. Tessa is impulsive and brave; Theo is quiet but sometimes hotheaded. Today, he is dramatic. He stands up, brandishing the letter. "What does this mean?" he shouts. He's not going to listen to his mother. He's not going to do what she wants.

She knows this. She looks him straight in the eye. "We don't know, Théo."

"We regret to inform you that your daughter Tessa Armstrong is believed missing behind enemy lines in France. Inquiries are ongoing and we will inform you as soon as we receive news of her whereabouts." He holds the letter out to his mother. "What was she doing in France?"

His mother becomes flustered then, making big gestures with her hands, her eyes wide. "There are field hospitals there . . . evacuation stations . . ."

"Not behind enemy lines, there aren't." He turns to his father. "Papa?"

His father's skin is grey. "I don't know."

Theo sits down but no, it isn't right. He stands up again, even though his leg is beginning to throb. "I knew it didn't make sense. All that talk about the FANYs and . . . and *purpose*."

"Purpose?" says his mother.

"Have you asked anyone?" he says. "You must know someone, surely?"

"No one will tell us anything." His mother takes the letter from his hands, folds it, and rises to place it back in the bureau.

"That letter is a month old," he says. "How long has she been missing?"

His mother sits back down, twisting the fabric of her skirt into a knot. His father wipes a hand across his brow and says, "Do you think we haven't tried to find out more?"

"I forgot," says his mother, clearly eager to change the subject. "A letter came for you too."

She hands Theo an envelope. At once, he recognizes the handwriting as that of his commanding officer. Theo knows then what it must be. He doesn't want to open the letter—his parents are watching him intently—but he cannot bear to wait a moment longer.

"It arrived a few weeks ago. We weren't sure whether to forward it to you at the hospital," his mother says.

Weeks ago. Theo's been to hell and back and his parents have had the letter for weeks.

Theo slices open the envelope with his father's paper knife. He reads the few short lines. Tells himself to breathe, not to give anything away to his watchful parents.

There it is in black and white. Barnes, dead. Confirmation. The British had been unable to recover his body from the beach, if there was a body left after that explosion. Theo doubts there would have been. Barnes blown to bits. Barnes melted into nothing. No evidence his parachute deployed, the letter states. Not a single witness able to provide even a small grain of hope to the possibility of Barnes' survival.

Barnes dead. Tessa missing.

But I love them, he thinks.

Blow after blow after blow, they come raining down.

His mother takes his hand, concerned. "Theo?" says his father.

He tells them he needs some air but he just wants to be away from them, from the letters and the photographs on the mantel. Tessa receiving her degree at the Sorbonne. The two of them waving from the high branches of the oak tree in the garden. He wanders down the lane into the village, trying to get used to the walking stick. People keep nodding their heads respectfully. Yes, beyond the grief—is this grief, he wonders—there is the other Theo, uniformed and commended. What if people ask about Tessa? He's neglected to find out the family line. Is she well or not? Abroad or not? He thinks, is she dead? *Dead like Barnes*. But he'd know, wouldn't he? He'd know if she was dead, he'd feel it inside, he's certain.

The telephone box is unoccupied. He can remember the number—funny, that, since he hasn't dialed it in years. "I'm glad it's you who answered," he says into the receiver. If it had been the father, he'd have hung up the phone. He feels like he is speaking into the past, beyond the boundaries of time.

There is a long pause.

"Are you there?" he says.

"I heard you got shot down," says the voice on the other end of the line.

"I did, but . . ."

"I checked the death notices in *The Times* for months. That's where your folks would put it, isn't it—*The Times*?"

Theo hasn't anticipated this. Can't they just skip it, can't they just jump ahead?

"I checked it obsessively," says the voice. "And you didn't even write."

You told me not to, Theo thinks. "Can you pick me up?" he says.

"You come here."

"I can't. I mean, I can but you'll still have to pick me up. My leg . . ."

"Oh. Oh right, I see. Is it bad?"

"Some people say I was lucky." Theo clears his throat. "It's not too good, no."

Stephen finds him standing by the phone box. "Well then," he says, when he opens the car door.

Theo has an image in his mind, Stephen, Tessa, and Michael, on the bus to school; they must be about thirteen, although time slips, memories blur into one. They are laughing at something Theo has said, teasing but affectionate. And in the woods, where they'd all gather after school, Stephen trying to roll a cigarette with tobacco stolen from his dad, but the tobacco keeps bursting free of the paper, spilling onto the mossy earth. Tessa has her head down in a book, Michael is looking about nervously, always convinced they are about to get caught. Stephen lights the cigarette, handing it to Theo first. Their fingers touch when the cigarette passes between them. It sends an electric shock along the length of Theo's spine, which irritates him. He doesn't want these feelings, can't comprehend them, not yet.

He remembers his fascination with the line of Stephen's neck against his shirt collar, wondering what it'd feel like to place his lips on that exact piece of skin.

But now, in the car, Theo can't bring himself to look at Stephen properly until the final bend before the farm. He looks the same, the farm looks the same, like everything else. Disused machinery sits in heaps about the yard. The hay barn has a bowing roof, more moss than tile. They'd fucked in there, years ago, when everything had felt so different. Now the world is transformed and Theo is too, but Stephen remains unchanged. Same clothes for working in, boots covered in farmyard. Same red hair shorn into a sensible crop. The farm might have kept Stephen the same, but as a reserved occupation it's also protected him from the war. And yet keeping people fed in a war must be its own fight, Theo thinks, with its own struggles. Stephen is Theo's age but seems older. Once upon a time the relationship had felt so wrong but now it might be different, what with Theo being changed. He's never spoken about Stephen with Tessa, and perhaps that's part of it too. Something that's just his.

"Where's your family?" Theo asks.

"Hello, Stephen, how have the last two years treated you?"

Theo laughs, but he can't get out of the car until he knows. He doesn't want to deal with pleasantries—*how are you, Theo? And the war, and the leg, and the rest.* He wants to be alone with Stephen.

"Gone to see a man about a dog—they won't be back till late," says Stephen, striding toward the farmhouse door.

Theo maneuvers himself awkwardly out of the old motor, putting his weight on the stick as he hauls himself up. He's glad Stephen isn't looking. The air is thick with horse shit, woodsmoke and hay. Hay always makes him think about sex. He's thinking about it now. Tessa would be proud—she's always had a filthy mind.

Stephen sits down on a tatty sofa in the too-full sitting room. Bits of oily equipment on the table leach black into the rough oak.

"Can I have a drink of water?" says Theo, sitting down next to him.

"Afterward, maybe." Stephen is unbuttoning his shirt.

"No, that's not . . ." Theo can see a sliver of Stephen's skin. "That's not why I'm here."

Stephen laughs, cupping Theo's chin with his hand. "What is it then—do you want to talk?"

"Is that so difficult to believe?"

"You had your friends, your sister, for that. I always knew what you wanted me for." Stephen shrugs, turning his head away. "You're not the only one to see me that way. I know what I'm good for. The fellas round here . . ."

Theo feels a twinge of guilt then because he does want him, only now he's ashamed of it. "I can't believe you're still sore about it," he says.

"Not sore, no. Livid."

"Jesus, are you really?"

"How casually you threw me away."

"The work was in London, Stephen. My job. That's all it was."

Theo folds his hands together on his lap to hide his excitement. If he can't stay here and he can't go home, he doesn't know what he'll do. Stephen takes this as his cue. Straddling Theo, he puts his lips against his neck, not kissing, not quite touching, just enough for Theo to feel his breath on his skin. It feels wrong, like it used to, but perhaps that's what he wants, after all.

Then Theo says, "I do like you, as it happens. It was never just sex," as if that somehow makes it better.

Afterward they take a walk around the farm, sex loosening their limbs and tongues.

"You're out of practice," says Stephen, to wound, but Theo knows it's not true.

In the cattle shed, the Jerseys poke their slim, elegant noses through a grille to feed. A lumpen pig with a wiry coat plods back and forth between troughs either side of the yard. Stephen scratches it behind its pink ear and the creature rolls onto its back, like a dog in ecstasy.

Theo taps a cigarette from a pack.

"Yes please," says Stephen. "Thanks for asking."

"You don't smoke."

"You don't know a bloody thing."

Theo hands over a cigarette.

"When did you get home?" says Stephen.

The question makes Theo flinch. "About three hours ago."

Stephen stoops down, still scratching the supine pig. "Jesus."

"Why do you say that?"

"I don't think my parents would be so understanding, that's all. Casting them off after all this time away in favor of a casual—"

"Don't say that," he says.

Stephen shrugs. "Well."

The ache in his leg has spread to his chest. But no, he thinks, this is something different. "Tessa is missing," he says. "In France."

It takes five seconds to recount all he knows of his sister's predicament.

Stephen considers this for a moment, and then to Theo's surprise, he laughs. "Your sister always did tend toward the dramatic, but that seems a bit over the top, even for her." He pauses again, and takes a drag of his cigarette. "Goodness me, it's the end of days but Tessa finds a way to outdo us all."

Twenty

The next day he's on the first train to London, his mother objecting the entire length of the journey from the house to the station. "But you've just arrived," she says, whining and needling when he doesn't respond. Though it is barely dawn, she has taken the time to put up her hair and powder her face. For the journey, Theo has chosen a book from his parents' library: *Of Human Bondage*, Tessa's of course, a declaration of ownership in her neat script inside the front cover. He traces a finger across the blue ink. Where are you, Tess?

"I have to look for work," he says to his mother, eyes down because he never could lie. "You said it yourself—the war's not over yet."

"Yes—after all, leaping from a burning airplane is of little consequence. It's about time you did your bit."

She's made him a sandwich for the train: crab paste, his request. A man with a briefcase and a copy of the *Telegraph* tucked tightly under his arm joins him in the carriage. Theo's trying to read but finds he cannot focus on the words. The problem being he cannot escape his memories, and no matter where he directs his thoughts, the shadows intrude. No, not shadows, a blinding light. His hands lose the page. A thread has worn its way loose in his trousers, and his fingers work at it, picking, pulling. When he looks up, the man has stopped reading his newspaper to watch. The man keeps eyeing him, and Theo knows what he must be thinking. Theo's youth, the lack of uniform, the stick adding new possibilities to the equation. Theo's either had a good war or a bad war, and if it's bad then at least it's over.

London is a comfort in its differences. There is none of Cambridge's sameness, seemingly unmarked by the past four years. Here the war is everywhere. Sandbags and taped-up windows, sudden breaches between buildings, experience etched onto the faces of passersby. Theo pauses in front of a department store, examining his reflection in large panes of glass. It astonishes him how much he has aged, the lines drawn tight near his eyes, the carved edges of his cheekbones.

This is not where he thought he'd be.

Petersham Place is a road of mews houses, hemmed in between white stuccoed embassies and mansions. His mother had the address in her book. How sweet it is they've kept in touch, he thinks, with sour sarcasm. It's still early enough for the shock of the light. It was black and now it's not. The house is in the center of the row, its door painted blue. He intends to knock, but doesn't, and nor does he press the bell. Tiredness comes upon him like an ache, but perhaps that's just his body telling him to slow down. In desperation, Theo shifts from one foot to the other to keep the blood pumping, leaning his walking stick against the wall. Dots connect in his head; the pain, the injury, a blinding light.

Michael opens the door, his briefcase held like a shield against his body. He's wearing the uniform of the professional, a pinstriped suit, well fitting, not cheap. Michael had developed a nervous twitch at school, continually pulling down the sleeves of his blazer to hide his frayed shirt cuffs. Theo takes it all in, from Michael's thinning hairline to his unlined face.

"Theo?" Michael takes a step back and places a hand upon his chest, all affectation.

"I knew you were involved the moment I read the letter." Anger comes quickly; it had been there all along, waiting to bubble to the surface. Theo forces Michael back against the door, his arm across his throat. His leg, his hip, scream in response. He's missed it, the adrenaline, the thud of his heart against his ribs. People stop to watch, exchanging whispers behind hands. "Where is she?" he says.

The color drains from Michael's face.

Theo pushes harder. "Where is she?"

"Theo, I don't know. Come inside and have a drink, and we can talk."

"It's half past eight in the morning."

"A cup of tea, then."

Theo considers this for a moment and nods. Reclaiming his stick, he follows Michael into a hallway of doors, the walls patterned in florid paper turned yellow with age or smoke.

"You'll have to mind the mess," says Michael, unlocking the door to his flat. "I've no help."

"You mean your mother doesn't visit often."

"Ha! No, sadly not."

Theo thinks how often Michael says "Ha!" instead of actually laughing. Tessa used to mock him for it, though never to his face. What does it say about Michael, he wonders, that he can't drop his guard enough to show true emotion. Or is it that he's just humorless through and through?

"Tea then?" Michael is examining the contents of various cupboards as if he's never been there before. The flat does have an air of abandonment. Clothes not put away, a thin layer of dust on the sparse furniture.

"I realize you're upset, old chap, but poor show out there. This is my home, those are my neighbors. It doesn't help to draw attention . . ."

"I'm not interested in your spy games," Theo says, sharply. He's not going to be told off by his old schoolfriend. Michael's air of superiority is incredibly grating. Doesn't Michael realize how wound up he is, he wonders. Was his behavior outside not enough of a sign? Michael places a mug of weak tea down on the table next to Theo. "Gather you've been through something of an ordeal."

Theo tenses his shoulders but doesn't answer. An ordeal—as if such trite words could ever come close to conveying the things he's seen. *An ordeal*. It's so sanitized, so tidy, but perhaps that's how men like Michael comprehend it.

"You left France a hero," says Michael.

Theo blinks. Clearly Michael has no idea of the reality of Theo's experiences. The pain, the deaths, the absence of hope. "Is that what they're saying? Jesus."

Michael nods. "I don't know anything, I'm sorry to say, but even if I did, I couldn't tell you."

Theo laughs. Perhaps it is a play, and this a theater.

"You might well laugh, but you do realize they could prosecute me if I told you anything?"

"Christ, you're so *important*."

Michael leans his full weight into the kitchen counter. "I'm terribly worried about her, as it happens."

"She told me she'd joined the FANYs," says Theo. "Was that a lie?"

"No, she did join the FANYs."

"Then what was she doing behind enemy lines?"

"I told you I can't . . ." Michael looks straight at Theo. "She was working."

Theo opens his mouth to speak.

"I can't tell you any more," says Michael, quickly.

But Theo will not be put off. He will follow any thread, no matter how weak. "Who was she working for?"

"The same people you and I are working for, I imagine." Michael takes a sip of tea, looking relaxed again. Perhaps, Theo thinks, he believes the worst is over.

"War is a machine with many, quite different moving parts," says Michael.

Theo knows he's being patronized but cannot, after all, stop himself from saying, "Meaning what, exactly?"

"Meaning your sister is incredibly capable and intelligent, with a working knowledge of France and a near-native fluency in the language."

Theo stands up and moves stiffly about the flat, maneuvering with his stick through piles of books and other detritus suggestive of a disorganized life. Dostoevsky for show, pristine, he clocks that. No pictures or paintings, no real giveaways as to the personality of its inhabitant. Michael's a shell, he thinks, a limpet. He always has been.

"Is she dead?" he asks. He can't not.

He doesn't know what he'll do if the answer is yes.

Michael drops his head. "I don't know. It's possible. I can't say any more."

It is as if an alarm is sounding in his mind. It is the worst thought, the worst reality. "Blink once for alive and twice for dead," he says.

This makes Michael wince. "No one's heard from her in a long time. She might be in a camp."

"A camp?" It is hope, and Theo grasps it.

"POW. But it's complicated."

"Why is that?"

"She wasn't wearing a uniform, for a start."

Theo wraps his arms around his head. If he can just shield himself from the light bleeding from a break in Michael's curtains. If he could just not be here at all, in this shambles of a room, with this man he'd once considered a friend. "I don't understand what that means. Are you saying . . . ?"

"I'm not saying anything, Theo."

"No uniform, in an enemy-occupied country. If she's been captured in civilian clothes, she won't be considered a prisoner of war."

"No."

"But she was a FANY."

"In name only. She doesn't have a commission. Very few women in the FANYs do, as it happens. It means they're not formally members of the Forces. Bit of an oversight on our part, I'll admit."

"Oversight?" Theo is aghast.

"The women were recruited to the FANYs to provide them with a cover story, but unfortunately it means Tessa likely isn't protected by the Geneva Convention."

"So if she has in fact been captured, she'll be considered a spy, with no legal protections at all." It is unbearable sometimes, possessing a lawyer's brain. There is no hiding from the implications of Michael's words.

"Theo . . ."

"*Is* she a spy?" She'd never have kept that from me, he thinks.

"Look, war isn't a homogenous—"

The alarm is sounding in his head again. "Do fuck off."

Michael bristles. "You've become rather coarse, dear boy."

"Three years as a cog in your bloody war machine will do that to a man. Are you, are they . . . Jesus, is anyone looking for her?"

"If I were to hazard a guess, I'd say inquiries were ongoing. It's a complicated situation, as I'm sure you can imagine. All we can do is hope."

"All we can do is hope," Theo deadpans. "And where exactly do I place my hope, in finding my sister or merely finding out what happened?"

"If I were you, I'd just hope the Allies take France."

He has too much energy and no way to expend it. His leg is throbbing, his temples too. Barnes' address is written on a slip of paper in his pocket. Theo keeps touching his fingertips to it, making sure it's still there, but he doesn't need it. He has the address memorized. A woman in black answers the door of a house that is grander than he'd expected, tucked down a quiet street in South Kensington.

"Mrs. Barnes?" he says, wishing at once he hadn't come, knowing in his gut it is a mistake.

The woman shakes her head and beckons him inside. He is shown into a sitting room, a plush sofa in deep green velvet, rococo armchairs upholstered in wide stripes. There are photographs on the mantelpiece. Barnes in a morning suit and a top hat, smiling beside a racehorse—the jockey reaching down to pat Barnes on the shoulder. Barnes as a child, a teddy bear and building blocks. Barnes arm in arm with a young woman. Theo reaches out and presses his fingertips to the glass that protects this photograph.

Missing him is such a physical sensation. As with Tessa, it is pain, a blow to the chest endured over and over.

At a noise behind him, Theo snatches his fingers away. An older woman is in the doorway, peering in, grey hair swept up high on her head.

"Yes?" she says.

Theo smiles reflexively, then straightens his lips into a frown, unsure what is expected of him. "Mrs. Barnes?" he says.

The woman bridles. "Cliffton-Barnes. And you are?"

Theo swallows, nervous. "Theo Armstrong. I flew with your son."

He holds out his hand, but she doesn't take it. The woman looks him up and down, her eyes lingering on his stick. "You're injured," she says, softening a little. She moves into the room, sitting down on the velvet sofa.

Theo nods. He is thinking of Barnes' accent, which he could never quite place. He'd never guessed this was his world; it wasn't common in the Air Force, which to Theo had always seemed comfortably middle class. "It's not so bad," he says, gesturing at his leg. He's hoping she'll ask him to sit down, but she doesn't. She is staring at his leg.

"I was so sorry to hear about Barnes . . . about Richard," he says, shifting his weight uncomfortably on his stick. "I've been in hospital. I didn't find out for certain until . . . well, a while after."

The woman frowns. There is a knock at the door and a younger woman in black comes in, eyes wide at the sight of Theo. She takes his hand and holds it in both of hers.

"You're Theo?" she says.

Theo nods, confused. Barnes had never mentioned a sister and they'd spoken about everything, hadn't they? Almost everything, anyway. The time he'd spent with Barnes had been the highlight of every day at the base.

"This is Emily," says Barnes' mother, softly. "Richard's fiancée."

Theo looks down and yes, there is the ring. It is large and antique-looking, all the bearings of a family heirloom. He carefully removes his hand from hers.

Emily takes a deep breath; she steadies herself on a chair. "It's wonderful to meet you finally," she says. Theo can see she is on the verge of tears. He couldn't bear it if she cries.

"Richard told me all about you in his letters. He was thrilled to make such a friend. I think it made being away from us so much easier. Perhaps it felt the same for you. Shall we have some tea?" She looks at Barnes' mother, who nods and rings a little bell on a side table.

Emily gestures to a chair, and when Theo stumbles she takes his arm and helps him to sit.

Theo is thinking of brushed fingers, of the looks that passed between them as they gossiped at night in their adjacent bunks. He remembers the last time he saw Barnes. *See you on the other side.*

Blow after blow after blow.

"He was a wonderful pilot," he says, at a loss for anything else.

Barnes' mother looks away. Emily is nodding, smiling bravely. "Yes," she says. "He was, wasn't he? That's what everyone has said."

Because it's what we say, thinks Theo. They died quickly and painlessly. They died as heroes. They had no idea what was happening as they endured their hideous, bloody deaths.

The woman who answered the door appears with a tray of tea. She places it down in front of Barnes' mother, pours three cups and hands one to Theo.

"And your sister, your twin," says Emily. "She must be delighted to have you back safe and sound."

Theo swallows. He places the tea down and smiles, weakly. "Yes," he says. Barnes told her about Tessa. Barnes told her about him.

"When were you going to get married?" he asks. Emily opens her mouth to answer but cannot seem to find the words.

"Postponed due to this blasted war," says Barnes' mother, from the sofa.

"But it will be over soon," says Emily, quickly. "We're winning now, aren't we, Theo?"

Theo nods. He wants to echo her spirit but he can see it's just pasted on, the desperation leaking through the cracks. He wonders if Emily can see that his heart is shattered, too.

"Richard just adored you," he says, quickly, eager to give her what she wants but hating himself for it. He thinks, I wanted him so intensely. But more, it was so much *more*; he loved him and what is he supposed to do now with that love? What will Emily do? It is different when grief can be known and acknowledged. When it is a public thing.

He's jealous of her, he realizes. Jealous that she can love and grieve in any way she sees fit, whereas Theo's pain must be guarded. To be robbed of a future, one must possess it in the first place.

"I should have written first," he says. "I didn't think."

"Perhaps, yes," says Mrs. Cliffton-Barnes.

"You're welcome anytime," says Emily, who of course has no right to say such a thing, who is perhaps clinging on to this family now her connection to it is gone.

He stands up. It is agony. It takes all his effort not to cry out.

"You're not leaving already?" says Emily. "Please, please, you should stay. We'd love to hear more about Richard at the base. You saw a side to him we never could . . . and . . ." Her eyes fill with tears, which she quickly blinks away.

"Shall we call you a cab?" says Barnes' mother, pityingly.

Theo shakes his head. "Oh, no."

"It's no trouble."

"That's kind, but . . ."

"Really, I shall ask the girl to flag one down. I insist."

"There aren't any bloody cabs. It'll take an age to find one," Emily snaps. For a moment, the room is quiet.

"I shall manage perfectly well," says Theo. "I'll say goodbye."

"Yes, well," says Mrs. Cliffton-Barnes, not standing up.

Emily doesn't rise either. She is staring at her hands in her lap.

"Won't you come again?" she says, quietly, and he nods and says, "Of course, of course, I should love to." But he knows he won't, that he doesn't want to ever see them again. That this—Barnes, all of it—is something he's going to fold away inside himself, out of sight.

Cambridge, One Month Later

Twenty-one

The water is like ice. It stings his skin, and floods his ears with a metallic hum. There is no other sound. Theo hauls himself onto the bank, lying on his back to catch his breath, the grass damp beneath him. The sun is blazing red as it falls toward the horizon. It's so quiet. Just the farewell song of the hedgerows, the low moans of cattle in the high fields, and his own ragged breath.

Stephen sits further up the bank, shivering, his jacket around his shoulders. They should have brought their trunks, they say; they've laughed about it, their unpreparedness. In truth, Theo's are tucked inside his rucksack, but he won't admit it, won't spoil the moment when it feels so nice to finally get along.

"Come here," says Stephen, not looking at him.

They sit together for a while, arm in arm. Theo swims in the river every day. It's good for his leg, he says, but what he means is it's good for his mind. He and Tessa would swim no matter the weather, Tessa plunging in feet first but Theo's advance on the water always more cautious, allowing for the slow acclimatization of his flesh, inch by inch.

"Do you think you'll ever get married?" asks Theo, not looking at Stephen.

There's a pause. They listen to the birds in the trees above them, the cows in the field behind.

Stephen turns onto his side, eyes narrowed. "I'd imagine so."

"Why?"

"Theo . . ."

"No, no, I'm genuinely interested."

"All right, then. Because it's what happens. It's what people do."

"Even when . . ."

"Even when, Theo, yes."

Theo is silent for a moment. "I don't think I can."

"No?"

"It's dishonest."

"Yet here you are, an open book," says Stephen. He laughs to take the edge off, but it's a bitter sound. There is no joy in that laughter.

Theo lets the silence stretch. His inches his body to the left, and the distance between them widens.

"My father once said this landscape was part of his psyche," he says, driving his fingers down into the earth, forcing sand and mud beneath his fingernails until it hurts. Perhaps masochism is a symptom of grief—if that is what he's experiencing. Perhaps it has always been buried inside him.

Stephen rolls over, revealing blades of grass and twigs stuck to his flesh. When he picks them off they leave an imprinted pattern of red lines. "Is that so?" he says.

Stephen's voice has an idle flatness to it, as if he's not quite interested. "What are you doing?" he asks, after a moment's pause which Theo is certain they both spend questioning the timber, clay and river of their bones, despite any seeming indifference to the matter.

Theo shrugs. "What do you mean? I'm not doing anything."

"Exactly. You're not doing anything, except moping. Sulking too, and anger—yes, there's quite a bit of that about."

"Please don't start." Theo closes his eyes, hoping this simple movement will bring an end to the matter.

It doesn't work. Stephen hauls himself up and sits looking at Theo. "Wasn't the war just a pin in everything else? What about your degree, the great career you always said you'd have? All that work and here you are, back at home, not doing anything with it."

"You're hardly one to talk," he says, and the temperature of the air drops. This new masochism must be compelling because Theo plows on, when he knows full well he should stop. "Still working on your father's farm when you always said you wouldn't."

"People have to eat."

Theo runs a blade of grass across his lips.

"Besides, I haven't had the same opportunities as you, Theo."

"We went to the same school."

"And that makes us equals, does it?" Stephen's laugh is incredulous. "At school I was told almost daily that if only I tried harder, I could make something of my life. They didn't realize that my jobs on the farm hadn't magically disappeared because I'd won a place among my betters. I was up before dawn, working. You swanned off the bus bright-eyed and bushy-tailed and there I was halfway through my day. So yes, we might have gone to the same school, but our circumstances could not have been more different."

Theo shifts against the hard earth. He's made his fingers bleed and doesn't want Stephen to notice. "I didn't know that," he says.

"You never asked."

"I'm going to London again tomorrow, as it happens."

"About Tessa?"

"Yes, with my parents. To see this Miss Jones, writer of brief, impenetrable letters."

"I don't suppose there's any news?"

"If there is, Miss Jones isn't passing it on."

What Theo hasn't told Stephen is that he does have a plan. He is going to find his sister, as sure as the moon shines white. He has made up his mind.

Twenty-two

The meeting takes place in a hotel just off Trafalgar Square. Theo likes to look up at the skyline when in London, the parapets of those fine marble-white buildings against the blue.

"Are you sure this is it?" his mother says, who has no doubt been expecting a bland but authoritative government building, one of Whitehall's plain palaces.

His father follows in a daze. He barely spoke on the journey up, but then he's barely spoken since Theo got home. Work provides a convenient excuse for the hours he spends locked in his study, but they can all see the lie. His father can't bear their grief and has no wish to share his own. Tessa was always more his than their mother's, but not as much as she is Theo's.

Tessa, he thinks, would say she belongs to no one.

Miss Jones (Not "Mrs.," the doorman gently corrects Dominic) is waiting for them in a suite. The rooms are quiet, and almost certainly empty. No tell-tale footsteps, no clinks of teacups in other rooms.

"Thank you for agreeing to meet us," his mother says.

Miss Jones speaks in a brisk, matter-of-fact tone of voice. "Of course, of course," she says, opening a manila folder on her desk. They haven't been offered tea, and Theo senses they won't be staying long. "I'm happy to answer any questions you may have, although I must warn you there is much we don't yet know. France, as I'm sure you can imagine, is in a sorry state."

"What was Tessa doing there?" says Theo.

"Tessa was employed by our organization to carry out covert operations."

"Pardon me?" says his father, quickly. "She said she was a translator."

"No, she was a driver," says his mother.

Theo hisses, "She was a spy," and his parents turn to him in shock and disbelief.

"No. No, I'm sorry, but no," his mother says. "That is not possible." And then she bursts into tears.

His father is still looking at him. "Tessa wouldn't . . . she . . ." He takes a deep breath. He hits the desk in front of them with the flat of his hand, making even the stolid Miss Jones jump. "She's a pacifist."

"No, *you're* a pacifist. Tessa has her own mind," says Theo.

He watches as his father absorbs this. "Are you saying you knew about this?"

"No, I'm saying—"

"Please," his mother says, rubbing her temple. "Please stop."

Theo takes a deep breath and steadies himself, turning back toward Miss Jones whose expression is carefully neutral, her eyes cast down. "What sort of operations was my sister involved in?"

Miss Jones purses her lips. "I'm afraid I'm unable to—"

"Fine. Where was she last seen?"

"She was dropped into western France in June 1943, and moved south soon after."

"Dropped?" says his father.

"Parachuted," Theo answers quickly, before Miss Jones can draw a breath. He tries to picture his sister, falling through the air.

"We have a house in the Loire—please, please, have you checked? It is somewhere very dear to Tessa." His mother is wringing her hands together.

"I'm afraid she's not there." Miss Jones does not look up from the file on her desk. She can't stand their hope, he thinks.

"When did you last hear from her?" he says.

"In the autumn of last year."

Out of the corner of his eye, Theo sees his father's head drop to his chest.

"But that is so long ago," his mother says.

"As I say, the country is in a sorry state. As the liberating forces continue their operations, we are likely to see agents reappearing—"

"How many are missing?" says Theo.

"I can't tell you . . . quite a few." Miss Jones looks rather pale now. It is the only discernible change in her composure during the meeting.

"What *can* you tell us?" asks his father, quietly.

"It seems from the communications we've gathered that Tessa has fallen into enemy hands."

"*Alors*, she is dead," says his mother, simply. His father reaches out and takes her hand.

Miss Jones frowns. "I appreciate this is distressing but I urge you not to give up hope. Tessa has shown great fortitude, often in incredibly difficult circumstances. I give you my word I shall do everything in my power to find her."

Miss Jones has the most striking blue eyes. Theo is quite taken aback when she finally focuses them on him. His mother and father stand to leave.

"Thank you for your time," his father says.

"I'll meet you outside," Theo tells them.

Miss Jones somehow manages to convey irritation, despite appearing exactly the same as she has for every moment of their meeting. Inscrutable, he thinks; that's the word for her.

He waits for the door to close. "Is she dead?" he says flatly. He feels utterly numb.

"As I said, we've no reason to believe—"

"Is she dead?" he repeats. Her voice in his mind is not a voice but a memory. Tessa isn't there any more.

"You know, she worried dreadfully about deceiving you."

Theo laughs, a proper belly laugh, and he can tell it shocks her—she isn't quick enough to hide that. "Miss Jones, my sister does what she wants and hang the consequences. What exactly are you doing to find her?"

"A security directorate will shortly be traveling to Paris, to investigate the cases of the missing operatives."

"Then I should like to join them."

"I'm afraid that will be impossible," Miss Jones says crisply. "As I say, I shall keep you informed as best I can."

"I studied law at Cambridge and worked for a chambers of some regard when I graduated. I understand the legal implications and the parameters at play here. And I speak French. Not quite as fluently as my sister, mind, but well enough to be of use."

But a Cambridge degree won't mean anything to Miss Jones, and why should it, he thinks. In these situations you are either in or out, and the families are definitely on the outside.

"That's kind of you, truly, and I shall keep you in mind should a position become available." Miss Jones has a practiced, patient smile. She picks up her pen, opens a different folder and nods her goodbye.

He leaves his parents at Marylebone station. The trip was a mistake, and they all know it. His mother is clutching a sodden handkerchief, his father turned to stone because the not-knowing calcifies those left behind.

"Won't you come back with us?" says his mother.

"Tomorrow, tomorrow," he says, shutting the carriage door.

A woman is leaving Michael's building just as Theo arrives, and she nods him inside. She must live in one of the other flats. What does she think of Michael, he wonders—does Michael even have any friends? In Michael's flat, the same sliver of light splits the sitting room in two. Michael's cheap paperbacks are still piled around the room, dirty crockery in the sink. The room smells of occupation, of sweat and flesh.

"Good grief," says Michael, a washing basket in hand, skidding to a halt in the doorway.

Theo lifts his head. "The door was open."

"And you just let yourself in. I was collecting my laundry from my landlady."

"Bit lax for a spy."

"I'm not a spy."

A new smell to add to the others: Michael's laundry, lavender and starch.

Michael drops the basket on the kitchen table. "Is this a social call? Should I pour us both a drink?"

"If you like."

Theo is hoping for whisky though it's only three o'clock. He counts the drinks he's consumed in the last few days until he runs out of fingers. "I wasn't sure if you'd be here. Do you ever actually go to work?" he says.

Michael's smile is smug. It brings to Theo's mind thoughts of violence. "Not every job happens in an office. How are Adela and Dominic?"

"How do you think they are?"

Michael hands Theo a tumbler of whisky. "And Miss Jones?"

"I feel as if I know less now than I did before."

Michael grins. "Good old Emmeline."

"Why won't they tell us anything?"

"Because they don't know anything. Nothing concrete, at least."

"She said a security directorate is going to Paris to investigate the missing agents."

"Did she?"

"I want to go to Paris."

"Ha! I'm sure you do, but that's not going to be possible for some time."

"No, I mean I want to help find Tessa. I want a job, that's why I'm here."

"Ask Miss Jones," says Michael, shrugging.

"I did."

Michael sits down on the sofa, crossing his legs. "And she turned you down. Try and see it from her point of view, old chap. You're distraught, you're—"

"I'm qualified. I need to be on the inside of this. I want to do my bit."

"And will you? Or will you question every single witness about Tessa, no matter how tenuous the connection? How exactly do you intend to separate your grief from your professional responsibilities—do you think you can? I don't believe I could."

Theo sighs. "What else am I to do?"

"Keep going. Find a way to live your life," says Michael. "I'm sick to my stomach about this."

"But it's not enough. No, I'm sorry, but I've made up my mind. You'll just have to square it somehow."

"Square what, exactly?"

Theo is pacing up and down in Michael's small sitting room. He's aware of how it looks; he can read Michael's expression, the concern and alarm. "I want you to arrange it. I want you to get me in."

Michael looks aghast. "Go against Emmeline Jones, are you mad? She's practically running the shop these days."

Theo has acquired a new component part to his being, but Michael doesn't know this yet, hasn't sensed how the war has changed him. "I don't care one jot how you find me a job, but I'd try, if I were you."

This has Michael sitting up straight. The concern is still evident in his expression but it's different now, because it's focused on himself. "What is that supposed to mean?"

"It means this will blow up into a hell of a storm, should the press get hold of it. Women sent into enemy territory, no uniforms. What were they doing there? I should think there'll be a lot of interest. I should think people will want to know exactly what has happened." Theo smiles without showing his teeth. "And I wouldn't want my name connected to it, if I were you."

The pub in Soho looks normal enough. It is normal, he thinks.

He's been there before, many times, although not in years. He shouts for a pint, the barman reading his lips and tapping the right pump. With his drink, he heads through a door at the back. It's hidden behind a curtain and leads to stairs to the basement below, streaks of damp on the walls, a smell of cat piss and mold. Navigating the stairs is not easy, encumbered as he is by his stick and the full pint, but eventually he knocks on the door at the bottom. A familiar face appears as the door swings open. Frank—Frank with the beard, but it's longer now, straggled and grey. The war has aged him just like it's aged them all. Frank looks Theo up and down. "Haven't seen you in a while, poor love," he says. Theo repositions his walking stick, self-conscious about his new additions—the stick, the limp, the haunted look he's acquired. But when Frank reaches out to tenderly stroke Theo's cheek, Theo wonders if being walking wounded might have its benefits after all. Inside, the music is so loud Theo can feel it in his chest, like he's being impaled by a heavy bass drum. Men, for they are all men, line the walls. On the dancefloor, in silk shirts and too-tight trousers, they are dancing with abandon. Condensation runs in rivers down the brick walls; sweat pools on the floor. Everyone skids and slips; some say you've not experienced the place properly unless you go arse over tit in front of the crowd. Arse over tit? Michael is right, he's become coarse.

His eyes are on a blond. A nod of heads is all it takes and they find a dark corner—a darker corner. No one actually knows what this place looks like because no one hangs around long enough for the lights to come up. Theo doesn't want his drink; this is what he came for. The blond tastes like cigarettes and cheap wine. He slips his hand into Theo's open fly. Please, Theo hears himself say, please please please until the moment arrives, which happens with enough speed to be embarrassing. He takes a handkerchief from his pocket, cleans himself, and goes back into the bar.

Out in the fresh air, he heaves until his lungs are full. He has nowhere to go, hasn't made arrangements with Aunt Violet and can't bear to, he realizes. The notion of spending the night surrounded by Tessa's things is impossible. It is too much.

"Poofter!" calls a man from across the street.

Theo stops so quickly it is almost comical, a Chaplin-esque move, exaggerated for an audience. It radiates in his chest, these new mechanics now entwined with his brain and his breathing. "What did you say?" he asks. It emerges as a growl, from this new animal part of him. Theo doesn't recognize himself.

The rest is a blur, is sounds, is the physical sensation of his flesh encountering another person. Theo striking his walking stick again and again into the face of a stranger, but he has no idea what this person looks like. He's never hit anyone before. There are hands on his body, trying to pull him away. He is aware of a policeman's whistle, because the sound makes him want to run, and yet all he can do is hobble, his leg flushed with an agonizing heat. There he goes again, with luck on his side, getting away with it. He is aware, as he stands in front of the mirror in his childhood bedroom the next day, that what he'd hoped for in life is no longer possible. The things he has seen. Things no one should see. He is changed, undoubtedly and inalterably, his coarse language, his anger, his stick pummeling another man's face. There is no way back from the way he came.

Paris, 1944

Twenty-three

Theo opens one eye and then the other, his room in the boarding house emerging into view. He is conscious of the stench of his breath. Images appear in his mind, possibly from last night but they could equally be snatches of many nights—the pieces are all there but the stitching is gone. Another memory, muscle this time, a sensation on his skin. He reaches behind him to the space between his body and the wall, but there is nothing there but cold, crumpled sheets. Theo thinks of a fingernail dragged over his spine, of hair clasped in his fist, but the memory is as untethered as the rest. Possibly last night, possibly not.

"She left," says a voice.

Theo turns his gaze to the small desk by the door of his room, at which Michael sits in his coat and hat. Theo has learned the hard way to avoid sudden movements after a night on the drink, even when startled by an intruder, lest he unsettle the contents of his stomach.

"What are you doing here?" he says, in a voice that doesn't sound like his, but is hoarse and deep, and somehow older. He tries to arrange his features into an expression of annoyance, but this requires too much effort for the early hour.

"I heard you both come in. I heard one set of footsteps leave about an hour ago. The walls in this old place are paper-thin."

"What else did you hear?" says Theo, and then wishes he hadn't. He wants to remember the boy's face, but it is a vague sketch, an outline with no features. He thinks, "she." Michael's face is marble-still. Theo cannot tell what he knows.

"What are you doing in here?" he says, again. With obvious exertion he raises himself onto first one elbow and then the other. A wave of nausea rises from his belly, and he clamps his lips together and waits for it to pass.

"Best to breathe through your mouth," says Michael. Theo can feel the other man's eyes on his body so he deliberately meets his gaze; Michael blushes, standing suddenly, walking over to the electric heater. "You do realize you're supposed to turn the thing on? Bloody freezing in here. There's no mother to do your bidding now, my boy." He bends down and examines the heater.

"No, don't, please . . ." says Theo, but it's too late. Michael flicks the switch. The grille transforms, orange then red. Theo's stomach churns again. He turns his head and stares determinedly at the window, focusing on the grey of the morning. This makes him realize he'd neglected to close his curtains and the hotel opposite has undoubtedly had a view of the evening past, the rough outline of Theo with another human being. Other images intrude, orange then red then black, the men, the sounds. Barnes, and what he must have looked like in death. Theo closes his eyes and counts to ten.

"Theo, are you quite well?" says Michael.

"Yes," he mumbles. "Could you turn the heater off? I prefer the cold. It helps me get going."

Michael flicks off the heater. "I wanted to make sure you made it to the office," he says, sitting back down. "Given you've managed to inveigle your way onto my security directorate, I'd rather not see you mess it up. It's important work, in case you hadn't noticed."

"Michael—"

"Or don't you want to know why so many of our chaps are missing? Because I do, actually. I want to understand what's happened here."

"Of course that's what I want."

"It's just you're burning the candle at both ends these days, wouldn't you say?"

Theo puts his head in his hands, his temples throbbing against his fingers. He pushes them harder and harder into his eyelids until white spots dance in front of his eyes. Sleep remains a place of fear, something interrupted by images and sounds, some real, some imagined. Sometimes he sees Tessa in dreams that feel like memories. In response, he's developed a self-taught technique. He works until he's exhausted and drinks until he passes out, the blackness swallowing both the passage of time and the surge of his unconscious. Sometimes he awakens with proof of the night's events, sometimes alone, sometimes not.

"Are they unhappy with me?" he says.

"On the contrary, they think your work exceptional. If you can hold it together, you've got the makings of a career. It's put Emmeline Jones' nose well out of joint, as you can probably imagine, given how hard she fought against you being here."

"Then what—"

"I'm worried about you," says Michael. "You almost died a few months ago, not to mention everything that's happened since. I don't think this is the best idea I've ever had."

"Perhaps you might give yourself less credit, then. I'm aware that I'm only here because Miss Jones so vehemently objected to the proposal, and our superiors couldn't resist the opportunity to undermine a woman within touching distance of power. Really, I should be thanking her."

"Christ, you sound like Tessa."

Theo ignores this. "Besides, I want to help."

"It's not helping *you* though, is it?"

Theo raises his head, hoping Michael doesn't notice the effort it takes. "It's not about me," he says.

In Paris, some wounds are more obvious than others—the battle scars, the bullet holes—but it is the lowered eyes that draw Theo's attention. Women in their bright, smart clothes, the sheer defiance of looking good when everything around them has fallen apart. Folks cooking on charcoal stoves on balconies because the electricity supply is unreliable, and nonexistent for many. Theo asks Michael if they can walk to the office. Fresh air fills his lungs; it fills his body with sensations, and sometimes Theo craves sensation. Over the last few months he's felt himself slowly turning to ice, and it is a shock, a good one, to be reminded once in a while of the blood forging around his body, his pounding heart, his hardening cock. Again, he looks at Michael and wonders how much he knows.

They come upon a square where a crowd is gathering.

"Not again," says Michael.

They push their way through furious spectators to a decent view, knowing full well what they'll find. This time it is two women. Barely women, Theo thinks; they can't be out of their teens. One is cradling a wailing baby, her arms wrapped protectively around it as she kneels alongside the other woman. She is crying while the other is trying to look defiant, but the trembling of her lips is obvious to everyone. A man and woman scrape razor blades over the girls' heads, mounds of hair falling to the ground. Each girl has a single suitcase with her. The crowd shouts insults, the more vulgar the better. An older woman steps forward and launches a gob of spit into one of their faces. The girl keeps her hands at her side, still crying as the spittle runs over her cheek.

"They're just kids," Theo whispers.

"Those girls are bloody idiots," says Michael, taking Theo's elbow and leading him out of the circle. They've seen it before, countless times; there's no need to witness it again. The shaved heads, the bleeding scalps, the forced undressing. The painting of insults and swastikas onto the women's bodies before they are sent on their way to God knows where, because who will take them when they wear their crimes so literally?

"Apparently it's worse in the provinces," Michael continues. "Daily show trials, kangaroo courts. The male collaborators are shot."

"And the women are shamed."

"Are you suggesting that's worse?"

"Maybe it is. They have to live with it."

Michael is dismissive. "People get very black and white about these things. It's a good lesson in consequences."

"But suppose those girls didn't think they had a choice in who they slept with? Suppose they felt they couldn't say no. It seems possible, does it not—given the circumstances, that they didn't have much say in it." Theo looks back at the crowd. No, he thinks, the mob. "Hell of a consequence. Shouldn't we do something?"

Michael laughs. "I think the ground is quite shaky enough."

He means, of course, General de Gaulle, the leader of the Free French government-in-exile, who—despite a comfortable wartime banishment in St. James—is determined to perpetuate the idea that the French saved themselves, with no help from anyone. In consequence, Theo's security directorate find their welcome and their access to the evidence in Paris shrinking by the day.

"Besides, France has to deal with traitors in its own way," says Michael.

"Is that what you think they are, those girls?"

Michael looks at him. "I have no idea what they did, and neither do you."

Theo pushes through the revolving door of the hotel, tensing against the screech of the door's mechanics. As he does every morning and several times throughout the day, he sweeps the lobby for signs of Tessa. Agents and operatives are returning in dribs and drabs, broken men and women, directed to the hotel by the authorities or the Red Cross with harrowing tales of prisons, and escapes, and near misses, if they're able to speak at all, which some are not. By the front desk, a gaunt man with yellowed skin is shouting at one of their number, a smart girl named Mabel.

"Where are they? The missing. Our comrades. Where did the Germans take them? Are you even looking?"

"Christ," says Theo, but Michael pushes him toward the lift and doesn't say anything.

The security directorate to which Theo is assigned is based in two small rooms. They are here, they are told, to untangle the mess of post-liberation France, to find the missing personnel smuggled behind the lines by the British authorities. Theo gathers information from interviews and interrogations, preparing briefing notes in anticipation of war crime trials.

This morning's manila folder contains notes of an interview with a man, code name Gilbert, real name Samuel Paul. Paul was arrested three days after he landed in France. Theo puts down his pencil and picks it up again. Three days, he thinks. Paul speaks of a prison called Fresnes, which has come up several times in interviews. He describes the torture he endured—Theo makes a note of the techniques used, of the descriptions of the guards and his interrogators. He adds the information to the index he is slowly collating, a record of misery and abject failure, although as he's only recording the "what-went-wrongs," from the point of view of the Allies at least, he cannot be sure of what came before. Paul describes a miraculous escape from the prison, a window left open and unguarded. Theo cannot help but pencil a question mark next to this section of the interview. So miraculous as to be fanciful. The woman who'd rescued Theo in Normandy had said, *It is human nature, self-preservation.*

He thinks then of the young woman cradling her illegitimate child, spittle running down her cheek.

"I'm interrupting you," says Mabel, the woman from the lobby. She places a mug of tea on his desk. "I thought I best bring you this. You've been looking ever so peaky recently."

Theo nods his thanks.

"Not sleeping?"

"I'm fine," he says, forcing a smile. As she turns to leave, he says, "What happened with that chap downstairs? He seemed to be in a dreadful state."

Mabel takes this as an invitation to sit down. "He was, poor sod. Half dead by the looks of it, hardly a surprise given what he's been through."

"What *has* he been through?" says Theo.

Mabel shoots a look at the open door. "Well, I wasn't in his interview . . ."

"No, but you spoke to him."

Mabel looks at him very deliberately. "I can't, I'm not allowed."

It is a curious sensation, as if he's been holding his breath and someone has given him permission to stop. Has the man in the lobby seen Tessa? Perhaps he worked with her, perhaps he knows where she is. When Mabel leaves, Theo gets up and looks out of the door. No one is around. He pops his head into the room next door, where his colleague Robert is working at a desk identical to Theo's.

Robert looks up, and then he does a curious thing. He puts his arm on his desk and twists his body round, shielding the papers he's reading like a schoolboy in an examination.

"All well, Armstrong?" he says.

Theo shoots him a tight smile. It's hard to keep his eyes on the man rather than the papers. "Just popping out, do you need anything?"

"No thanks, old chap," says Robert, without altering his contorted position.

Theo takes the steps two at a time—there's no time to wait for the lift. Down in the lobby, he rakes his eyes across the crowd milling about but no, nothing. He shoulders his way through the noisy revolving door and looks up and down the street. Back inside, he pushes to the front of the queue at the desk.

"The man who was here earlier. He was upset, he . . ." Theo mimes what he can only hope translates as dishevelment. "Do you know where he went?"

The elderly concierge shakes his head. Theo feels a hand on his shoulder. He turns around and there is Michael, looking stricken.

"You'd better come with me," he says.

Twenty-four

Theo is standing outside number 84 on avenue Foch, the tree-lined street where he and Tessa strolled all those years ago. The trees remain, the sun glowing orange between bare branches, winter a mess of puddles and leaves on the pavement. The building is as smart as the rest, tall and cream, balconies of thin, curled metal, and well-maintained box hedging along the perimeter. Its monied presence speaks of established, ingrained power, which is of course exactly what they'd wanted. "They" being the Sicherheitsdienst, the SD, the SS's counterintelligence agency. Mostly they are lumped together with the Gestapo, the secret police force whose job was monitoring the behavior of the German population—certainly the agents he's debriefed have without exception conflated the two—but they are different beasts, and the SD is undoubtedly worse.

Theo has never been inside this building, but he knows it well. The security directorate have been begging the French to grant them access for months, thus giving De Gaulle another means by which to flex his power. Because it is imperative the British are reminded several times a day that their presence in Paris is conditional, they are forbidden to enter the building. Except today—at the whim of the great General—they can.

Michael cannot stop moving, shifting his weight from one leg to the other. He tells Theo to "be prepared," although he cannot bring himself to say for what. Perhaps Tessa's body is in there, Theo thinks; perhaps this is it, the end.

Michael fills his lungs and smacks his hands together. "Well then," he says, and pushes the door open. In the lobby, an imposing staircase draws the eyes up toward the heavens.

Michael begins to speak in a quick, pinched voice. "They have their own signals room on the second floor. I mean, it could be Baker Street, it's so similar. There's evidence . . ."

Theo waits, but Michael is struggling to continue. "Evidence of what?" Theo says.

"It seems they . . . intercepted . . . wireless operators and played back their machines."

Theo translates this in his head, this new language he's had only a few months to master. "You mean, they sent messages to London on the agents' wireless sets. They impersonated them?"

Michael sniffs. "Exactly."

"Did London know?"

"Only when it was too late. The Germans were kind enough to send a message thanking us for the supplies. All that ammunition, money, *people*, delivered straight into their hands." Michael begins to climb the stairs, Theo following.

"They called it *Funkspiel*—the radio game," he says, but before Theo can speak—and he has a lot to say about these extraordinary revelations—Michael goes on with his tour. "The fourth floor was used by König," he says.

The knot tightens in Theo's belly. König had been the Senior Counterintelligence Officer in Paris. No one knows where he is, and everyone wants to find him. Moving his hand along the banister, Theo makes a note of the sensation, the faint, damp trace of sweat on the wood where Michael's hand has gone before. He wonders if Tessa ever climbed these steps.

"And the top floor?" he says.

"More offices," says Michael. "And cells."

Theo understands this is where they are heading, the final staircase winding up toward the roof. There are two offices stripped bare, the drawers of filing cabinets and desks left open. Theo can see the Paris skyline from the rooftop windows and he feels a sudden urge to flee, because perhaps ignorance is better after all, but Michael is beckoning him on toward a corridor of small rooms. There is an odd smell, a stale, metallic stench. Silvery cobwebs lace across the ceiling above their heads.

"I say cells, but they're more like torture chambers." Michael leans his head against a doorframe, closing his eyes. "In there," he says.

Theo enters the room. There are bars on the dormer window and the shutters are open, just enough to spill light across the bare wooden floor. The walls are covered with rough, carved words. It takes Theo's brain a moment to accept them as names because it is too horrible, this reality, too cruel. A/S/O Millie Brown, reads one. S/O P. Doyle. 4234 WAAF OFF. 17.12.43 6.1.44 another. He traces his fingers across the names, his eyes darting back and forth between the rough walls, the shaft of light, and a dried brown stain on the floor.

She is by the window, of course. Tessa loves the light; even here she'd savor that view. It reads, T. Armstrong 7.9.43 6.12.43. She's curled the tail of the "g," as she always does, he thinks, tracing the final date with his finger. The walls are rough and chalky, a line of dust clinging to his finger when he takes it away. Here she is, he thinks. Here is his sister. There is a clawing at his throat, and it is his own hand, he realizes, his fingernails against his flesh. Because here is his sister, imprisoned by monsters. What has happened to you, he thinks. How has any of this happened?

"We think the dates are when they arrived and when they left. They probably used forks to scratch the dates into the walls," Michael says quietly from the door. "The unlucky few who were still here at the end were taken down into the yard and shot." His voice breaks slightly as he says, "The wall is pockmarked."

"And Tessa?" His voice breaks as he says it. There is another mark next to her name, two Ts curled together. And another letter, a B, below them.

Michael is quiet for a moment. "I'm sorry, we don't know. I wanted to ask you about that little symbol. What does it mean?"

"Two 'T's. We used to sign our names this way when we were children. I don't know what the 'B' stands for."

She cannot be dead. Theo will not countenance it.

He puts his hands either side of Tessa's name and presses his forehead into the wall. She'd known he would come. And then it all comes crashing down, a wave over his head. It is in his ears, his nose, his mouth; this force which he finally recognizes as grief. Theo sinks to his knees, a wail escaping his lips, primal and raw. She is here, he thinks, digging his nails into the wall because she did that, she experienced that sensation, felt this chalk and dirt beneath her fingernails.

"Tessa," he hears himself say. "Tessa, Tess, Tee." He is frantic now, fingers scraping the wall as if it might hold a clue as to his sister's fate.

He hears Michael leave the room, unable to bear it. Theo hears him weep from the hallway.

He's supposed to return to work but he can't. At first he tricks himself into thinking he's walking with no destination in mind, winding off down little side-streets, away from the wide artery of the boulevard Saint-Germain, because what he's really interested in, see, are the cobbled streets and narrow buildings. The architecture off the beaten track. But the current is strong beneath his quicksand denial, and the boulevard draws him back again and again. Before he knows it, he is standing outside Tessa's old apartment building on the rue de l'Odéon, chosen for its proximity to not one but two *extraordinary* bookshops (Tessa had told him so in a letter). The thick wooden doors stand at twice his height. Theo holds his open palms against the wood, but there is nothing, not a flicker. Perhaps he can only sense her in the worst moments. Perhaps she no longer exists at all.

Theo presses on, because there was another address she used to write from. Following an internal map he didn't know he possessed, Theo tracks the streets until he finds himself in front of a large green door. He traces his finger down the doorbells, until he finds the name *Langlois*. The bell rings in the building. A door slams upstairs, footsteps on the staircase, a heavy step. The door opens and Theo finds himself face to face with a man in worn trousers and a frayed corduroy jacket.

"*Oui?*" says the man, looking Theo up and down.

"*Tu es Luc?*" he says, quietly.

The man puts his paint-stained fingers to his lips. "My God," he says. "Are you Theo?"

"Yes," he says. "I'm Theo."

"You have the same eyes."

"Have you seen Tessa?" He speaks quickly. He can't not ask.

"*Comment?*"

Theo shakes his head. He doesn't know where to begin. "Let's get a drink."

They take a table at a nearby bar. Before ordering, the man—Luc—empties his pockets onto the table, patting down his trousers and jacket in case anything has been missed. Theo looks at these possessions spread around the sugar bowl and the ceramic salt and pepper shakers: a tattered notebook, a pencil, a box of matches, cigarette papers, a few centimes.

"It's on me," Theo says, raising his hand and ordering red wine.

"And pastis," says Luc, quickly, like a reflex. "You speak French well." His shoulders have relaxed now. Perhaps because he doesn't have to pay, Theo thinks.

"Not as well as Tessa," he says.

"No, not as well as Tessa," says Luc. He clasps his hands together, framing them around his mouth. "What has happened to her? Something has happened, yes?"

A waiter interrupts, placing four glasses, two with pastis, a carafe of wine and a bottle of water between them. "She's missing," says Theo. He can see no reason to temper his words.

Luc has poured already and is in the process of putting a glass to his lips. He puts it down and takes an obvious, steadying breath. "Missing?"

"She was here, working, but no one knows where she is." He's amazed at how off-hand he sounds. Yes, she's missing, she's probably dead. Isn't this lovely, isn't the weather fine?

Luc swallows. "Tessa was here in Paris?"

"No—well, at the . . ." Theo cannot bring himself to use the word "end." "She seems to have been in custody in Paris. I can't really talk about what she was doing." He can't admit this is because he doesn't know.

Luc closes his eyes and lets out a low moan. He doesn't speak for a long time. It's awkward, people are looking at them, noting Luc's distress. But they don't understand, thinks Theo; it is my loss, my distress.

Eventually Luc looks up, his eyes red-rimmed. "I always find an excuse to walk down her street, even if it takes me out of my way. I met her near there, you know, at La Maison des Amis des Livres, the bookshop . . ."

"I know what it is."

"My friend Ephra was giving a reading. It seems such a long time ago now."

"It *was* a long time ago." Theo's not sure what's come over him, why he feels so angry with this man.

Luc pours Theo a glass of wine, filling the glass almost to the rim so that Theo has to lean forward to drink without unsettling its contents.

"My sister was dreadfully upset when the other bookshop closed," he says, trying to shake off his black mood. He can't stop thinking about Tessa's name, carved into the wall.

Luc nods, the memory bringing a smile to his face. "Shakespeare & Company? Yes, it was terrible. *Terrible*. But you see we haven't been allowed to think or dream for years and that's exactly what those shops are for. Places for dreamers. I know you'll say it's not the worst of it but it is, I think. Five years of prescribed thought, the Nazis telling us what we could think, could say, what we were allowed to believe. *Nos croyances*. We might as well be dead. Tessa would have been appalled by it."

"She was," says Theo.

Luc flinches, and Theo feels a strange rush of satisfaction. The gall of this man, telling him what Tessa would think.

"I wanted to ask you . . . I don't know if you know." Luc downs his glass of wine. The whole glass, thrown back like vodka. "Why did she leave Paris all those years ago? What did I do?"

Theo sips his own wine, trying to gather his thoughts. "What do you mean?" he says.

"I just need to know what happened, what I did."

"What do you think happened?"

Luc shrugs helplessly. "I have no idea, that's why I ask. One moment everything was fine, at least I thought it was. The next, I don't know, she'd left my apartment, she wouldn't speak to me, wouldn't answer my letters. Then, pouf, she was gone. I heard she left with your mother, is that true?"

Theo sits back, thinking of that summer, of the sudden change of plans, of his mother's bright announcement: "We thought we'd travel across the continent while we still can." A grand tour, fascism up close. It was so unlike either of them. And all the time, the few letters Tessa sent that summer all arrived bearing a French postmark. Theo never mentioned it, this anomaly, but he's never forgotten. This proof of a secret, proof they were keeping something from him.

"You must have done something wrong," he says, simply.

Luc raises his hands. "But I didn't, I swear."

"You must have. It doesn't make sense otherwise. People don't just change, not in that way. Think about it, the last time you were together, what happened?" Theo can feel his face growing hot as his voice rises. "Something must have happened." People are turning their heads toward them, murmuring behind their hands. I'd make a rubbish spy, Theo thinks, and the thought makes him laugh out loud. But because he doesn't share this thought with Luc, the laughter sounds hysterical.

"This must be very hard for you," says Luc gently.

Theo wants to sink his nails into the rough, chalky plaster and hold on. He persists. "The last time you saw her, did you fight? Was she upset?"

"No, we spent the evening together, and the next morning I left to visit my mother for the weekend."

Theo slaps the table. To hell with the onlookers, with the barman trying to decide if he should intervene or not. "Right, right. So, something must have happened when you were away."

"Possibly. I thought you might know. I thought she told you everything."

Theo can feel the hot intrusion of tears in his eyes. "You think you know her better than me, don't you?" He knows he should leave, that he's making a scene, but he can't. "She didn't tell me everything. She didn't tell me about you, not really. A few mentions in her letters, perhaps. You're a painter, a surrealist, except you don't like that label, is that right? I know you excited her, you and your crowd. And that's it, my knowledge of her last year in Paris, that is the sum of its parts. I don't know why I didn't push her for more, why I didn't pry."

Luc sits back in his chair. "I'd never presume to know her better than you."

This serious response to Theo's childish possessiveness only serves to increase his embarrassment.

"My friend Ephra said that some women are just like that, that it had never been for Tessa what it was for me. But I don't think that's true. I know we meant something to one another."

Theo looks down at Luc's hands lying flat on the table. They are shaking.

"I thought I'd see her again," Luc says. "I didn't leave when the others did. I thought, why should I? This is my home. Peggy Guggenheim, the art collector, do you know her?"

Theo shakes his head, his breathing steadier now, and forces out a harsh laugh. "Not personally."

"She managed to get a lot of people to America. But I'm stubborn, Tessa would—will—tell you that. It hasn't been easy. I had to hide. Apparently I am a degenerate."

Theo wipes his eyes. And because he is feeling reckless despite barely touching his wine, he says, "I shouldn't worry about that, so am I."

Cambridge, January 1945

Twenty-five

Theo has mastered a series of tricks and techniques to cope with the anguish: "anguish" being the word his mind has settled on to describe this new power in his head, though in truth it isn't big enough for his reality. His grief is colossal, and casts a shadow over everything else.

He's parked his car a little way from the driveway because he doesn't want his parents to know he's arrived. How odd it is to drive again after months of hobbling about with the walking stick. He doesn't need the stick as much now, unless he's tired or needs to walk any sort of distance, but he'll always have a slight limp. A permanent reminder of his war experience, visible to all.

Theo takes a series of deep breaths and a slow count to ten, a routine he has down pat. He wonders what will happen if he doesn't resist, if he just gives in and faces whatever it is that has set his heart racing in that moment. Perhaps fear has the real power. One day he'll let it win, this pain, this panic, just so he'll know. He'll let it wash right over his head and see what happens.

His mother answers the door. "*Mon beau gars*," she says, pressing her face into his collar. Theo puts his arms around her, but it is a perfunctory action. So afraid is he of what might follow, of the emotions it might unleash, he cannot allow himself to hold her properly.

"Hello, Maman," he says, finally. Then she is off, pacing ahead into the kitchen where he catches the silhouette of his father at the sink.

"How long do we have you?" she says, over her shoulder.

"I need to get back to London first thing tomorrow. I've got one more meeting there and then it's straight back to Paris."

"I hope you're finding time to rest, *Théo*. It's important, especially after all you've been through. Now, tea, coffee? Oh!" She claps her hands together. "Peppermint, there is some peppermint in the greenhouse. *Théo*, would you like some, will you share a pot with me? It is so delicious and fresh."

"I'd love some, thank you," he says, his answer sending his mother running from the house.

His father's back is still turned, meaning Theo can lower himself slowly into a chair without it becoming a cause for concern. The drive has made his leg worse, but he'll never admit it.

His father says, "I'd better boil the water for her. It's freezing out there. A hot drink will do you the world of good."

Theo asks, "Has she been drinking?" and his father grips the corner of the sink.

"Please don't start, you've just got here," he says.

"It's not even eleven. She reeks of it."

His father turns around at this. Theo notes the smudged shadows beneath his eyes, the pattern of blotches and broken blood vessels across his nose. "It's been hard, Theo. We all have to find our own ways of coping."

"Of course, but getting half-cut by midmorning might not be an approach to encourage."

Theo thinks of his own evenings. One bottle, two bottles, three. The relief when the edges begin to blur. A noise in the doorway turns both their heads—his mother is standing there, clutching a handful of mint. It's even more obvious now, the hectic flush of her cheeks, her hair in disarray.

"Are you fighting?" she says.

"No," says Theo, quickly.

"I've got the most terrible headache," she says.

His father puts out his hand and gently draws her into the room. "Why don't you have a lie-down? I'll make Theo his tea and wake you up in time for lunch."

Nodding, she says to Theo, "Will you tell me all about Paris?" He's never seen her acquiesce so easily.

When he hears her bedroom door close, he says, "How often does this happen?" but his father puts up his hand.

"She needs a distraction," he says. "A couple of grandchildren might do it. Any luck in Paris meeting someone special?"

Theo is speechless. He laughs in disbelief, because if anything he thought he'd earned a break from this well-worn conversation. "Afraid not, Dad, but I'm sure she's out there somewhere," he says, sourly.

"How's the leg?" His father pours two cups of mint tea and sits down in the chair opposite.

"Almost healed," he lies, blowing on his scalding tea. "It's not looking good. For Tessa, I mean."

He knows the line "Inquiries are progressing well, but there's no news yet" off by heart. Michael made him repeat it three times. "I won't lie," he'd said, but Michael had had little sympathy. "This is what you signed up to," he'd said.

His father closes his eyes, just for a moment. "But people keep appearing. You said so yourself."

"They do, but she hasn't, which suggests she isn't in France any more."

"Unless she's lying low. Tessa's good at thinking on her feet, she'll—"

Theo shakes his head. "She's not lying low, Papa, they arrested her."

"Well, they said they believed she'd been captured but no one really knows . . ."

"*I* know."

"How?"

Theo takes a sip of tea. "I just do." He knows he's being cruel.

"Is that some sort of twin quackery?"

"For God's sake, no, of course not."

His father sighs, pinching the skin on the bridge of his nose between his thumb and finger. "It doesn't mean she's dead. And besides, even if she's a prisoner somewhere, there are rules, aren't there? The Geneva Convention."

"It's not that simple. Tessa wasn't in uniform, and even though she was ostensibly in the FANYs—FANYs don't have commissions—they aren't official members of the Armed Forces. Meaning they won't be considered prisoners of war if caught. The protections afforded by the convention won't necessarily apply."

"Seems like something that should have been thought about earlier," says Dominic. "I'm proud of her, you know, for doing her bit. Finding a way to contribute that felt meaningful to her without betraying her principles."

Theo is dumbstruck by this statement, years of bitterness—the bitterness of the less favored child—rising like the dark. You two, he thinks. Your *club*. He is gripping his teacup too tightly. Tessa could tell when he was struggling with his temper. She'd reach out and place a hand on his; sometimes she could calm him with just a look.

"What exactly do you think she was doing in France?" Theo says. "Trying to get the Germans to see the error of their ways through the persuasive power of conversation?"

His father clicks his tongue but says nothing.

"The weapons might have been different, but make no mistake, we were both of us fighting out there," Theo continues. "We both saw violence—

witnessed it, engaged with it, and almost certainly visited it upon others. I'm glad you're proud, you should be, but there was nothing passive about Tessa's role, I can assure you of that."

They sit quietly for a moment, letting his words settle. Theo stands up, hiding the effort as best he can, and carries on with the washing-up his father left soaking in the sink. "I keep coming back to a memory from when we were little. Swimming in the Cam, with you on the bank, reading a book. We were seeing how long we could hold our breath under water."

He can picture it now. Tessa enjoying floating on her back, not really keen to play. For a while they'd floated together, hand in hand, but that wasn't enough for restless Theo, who knew full well Tessa never could resist a dare. They plunged down into the water, fingers pinched on noses, cheeks puffed out. Tessa won the first round, of course. He can see her now, her wide, delighted eyes glorying in her triumph.

"Best of three," he'd said. But because he'd felt cross and because he knew Tessa hated to open her eyes under water, this time when they plunged beneath the surface he glided over to the bank. In one fluid movement he pushed his body against the wet earth and hauled himself free of the clear, grey water.

His father looked up from his book, annoyed, because didn't they realize this was his time too? Theo put a finger to his lips, crouching down beneath the low trunk of a weeping willow. He heard her resurface. Heard the disappointed "Oh!" which made the moment all the sweeter.

"Theo?" she said, and again but with more urgency, "Theo?"

From his hiding place, he spied her body disappear again beneath the water. When she reappeared, her eyes were wide with panic. "Theo? Theo!" she shouted. "Papa, he's not here!"

He watched his father look up from his book. There was no cross look for Tessa. "I'm sure he's here somewhere," he said.

But Tessa became frantic. Diving into the river, resurfacing in a spluttering, uncontrolled way. "He's gone!" she called. "Papa, he's gone!"

Then she'd started to cry. Still Theo didn't move. It was astonishing, this reaction. It quickly proved too much for their father. "That's enough, Theo," he said, shooting him an irritated look.

Tessa followed his gaze toward the tree and Theo stood up, waving sheepishly.

"It was only a joke," he said, but she'd already made it to the bank, heaving her body from the water. Then she was striding across the mud and grass toward him, and shoving her hands against his shoulders.

"You beast!" she screamed, sending birds from the trees. "I thought you were dead!"

This seemed, even for Tessa, an overreaction of enormous proportions. He laughed, even though she'd started to scare him.

"How could you do that to me?" she said.

"Calm down, will you? It was a joke."

She stalked off toward their father, who was standing by his chair, impatiently holding out towels for them. "I would never do that to you," she spat over her shoulder. "*Never.*"

In the present, Theo hands his father a dishcloth, and they stand together at the kitchen window. The garden is a patchwork of browns and muted greens. He wants his sister to appear, now, poking her head around the kitchen door, eyes bright. "Tricked you," she'd say. "Got you back, finally."

It is quiet in the kitchen. A dripping tap, a bird in the garden.

"I don't remember that at all," his father says.

He sleeps for most of the afternoon. It's dark when he wakes, and the house is quiet. Yellow light seeps under the gap beneath the sitting-room door. Theo pours himself a glass of water from the kitchen tap and drinks it down in a series of slow, steady gulps. He doesn't want to go back to bed, so he opens the door to the sitting room, where his mother lies sprawled on the sofa, asleep. There is an overturned glass on the floor, red wine leaching into the rug, burgundy spooling into the woven scarlet and ochre. An empty bottle sits on the coffee table, an open one, almost full, beside it. Theo watches her for a moment. Perhaps it would be best to close the door and leave her to sleep it off. But that would mean closing his eyes, his brain, to the truth that has led to this mess.

He kneels down beside her and sweeps the hair from her eyes. "Maman?" he whispers. "Mum, it's time to go to bed."

Slowly she opens her eyes. "I thought you were a dream," she mumbles.

"Come on, let's get you upstairs. Time for bed." He drapes her arms around his neck and peels her from the sofa. "You've got to hold on or I'll drop you."

Burning embers spark in his leg, but he keeps going. His mother nuzzles into the collar of his shirt. She is speaking; low, incomprehensible strings of words. He nudges open the door to his parents' bedroom, laying her on the bed as gently as he can. "Where's Papa?" he says.

"I don't know," she murmurs, so softly he has to lean in to hear. "Working, walking . . . he is always walking." She takes Theo's hand. "Do you know, sometimes I felt that as long as you and your sister had each other, you had no need of me. You can't know what that's like for a mother, or what it felt like when she came to me. *Me.*"

"Came to you about what?" he says, quickly. But it's too late, her eyes are closed, her breath deepening again.

Theo pulls the eiderdown up to her chin and, thinking back on his own experiences, places a wastepaper bin on the floor next to her. Then he goes downstairs, sits on the sofa and drinks the remaining wine straight from the bottle.

Paris, 1945

Twenty-six

More and more of the missing begin to turn up, not from French hideouts but from Germany, fleeing prison camps as the regime collapses around them. There are others, the missing tell Theo and his colleagues, giving them names and aliases which he crosses off Miss Jones' list. The Americans cross the Rhine into Germany. The Soviets come upon a camp near to a nothing town in Poland. Thousands of emaciated prisoners, abandoned; thousands more believed to be marching—or rather, being marched, by their Nazi jailers—toward the front. Then there are more camps, and more atrocities, the photographs lodging in Theo's brain with the brutal memories of his own recent past. Weimar—or Buchenwald as it is called in the press—Belsen, Ravensbrück and Dachau. Ravensbrück, Theo notes, is a camp for women.

The situation descends into chaos. One day in spring, Theo arrives at the hotel to find the lobby full of people, some looking stricken, some furious. As he forces his way through the crowd, people start pulling at his sleeve, begging him to listen, to get them home. He spies Mabel by the lift, white-faced, her hand across her mouth. Michael climbs onto the front desk, the elderly concierge swatting at his ankles and imploring him to get down.

"We ask that you register your name with my colleagues here at the desk," Michael says, "and we will interview and debrief each of you in turn." When the noise fails to subside, he says, louder this time, "We want to help you, but you must help us. Please remain calm and form an orderly queue at the desk."

Theo manages to reach Mabel. "They've all come via the Red Cross," she says. "From the camps. There's even more in the courtyard."

He scans the crowd. Mabel squeezes his arm. "I'll come and get you if she turns up, I promise."

Theo nods, not trusting himself to speak his thanks aloud. This is why Miss Jones and Michael thought him unsuitable for this work. "Unsuitable" is a euphemism. "Inappropriate" fits better; "a grotesque dereliction of duty on the part of his superiors" better still. Theo should not be the one to find Tessa. It is right for the families to be spared the details in this situation. General Patton had photographs taken of Buchenwald because he felt no one should be spared this truth. But perhaps it should be filtered out, the worst of it, the details that cling. The crowded bunks. The piles of bodies, legs like sticks. No one should see their loved ones in this condition. It will finish his parents, he thinks.

"Do we have an up-to-date list of the missing from London?" he says.

Mabel nods. "Miss Jones wired it through first thing."

Marianne and Isabelle, those were Tessa's aliases. The Baker Street staff knew her as Genevieve. What were they like, these characters she'd played, and how closely did they align with his sister's true self? Sometimes he wonders if he'd recognize her now, if she were to appear among these thin-haired, hollow-cheeked apparitions. Theo keeps one eye on his office door at all times. It is unbearable, the waiting, the not-knowing, when so much, suddenly, is becoming known.

As soon as Theo makes it upstairs, he collects a copy of Miss Jones' updated list.

"There are no women on here," he says to Michael, who is frantically searching through his own notes, trying to cross-reference names and details to make the pieces fit. "What is the point of a new list if it still excludes a portion of the missing? How does that help anyone?"

"Request from up high. We're sharing the list with the Red Cross. It's bound to be leaked if we include the women's names." Michael doesn't even bother to look up. "British women lost behind enemy lines. Theo, dear chap, imagine the questions we'd get. It'd be a scandal, as you well know. After all, it's exactly what you used to blackmail me into getting you this job, isn't it?"

"Things have moved on since then."

"Have they?"

Theo is incensed. It takes him a moment to gather his thoughts. "So, we don't give women the necessary commissions to grant them Geneva protections if they're taken prisoner, which they have been, and then we make it as difficult as possible for them to be found when they go missing. Do I have that right?"

"We have the women's photographs. The powers that be don't want us circulating their names to anyone on the outside, that's all."

"Because they think it looks incriminating for them?"

"Well, it does, rather."

Theo cannot believe it. "And that's the priority, is it? That's how we've decided to treat these women, the missing, who've shown the most astonishing bravery in the service of their country? We should be doing everything in our power to find them but no, hang on, instead let's pretend they don't exist in order to save the reputations of the suits in Whitehall.

Tell me, does that sit right with you? Because it seems bloody shameful to me."

Michael is terse. "We don't make the orders, we just follow them."

Theo is given the interview of a Free French agent, brought before the security directorate because, the agent claims, he was deported to Buchenwald in the company of several British agents. There is skepticism about this among Theo's colleagues, a rejection of rational thought; it is a kind of exceptionalism on their part, the refusal to believe that the appalling fates captured in Patton's black and white images might be shared by British subjects. It is beyond the pale. Several of the men named by the agent are on Miss Jones' list of the missing, and Theo notes the Free French agent is identifying them by their real names and not their aliases. Did they crack and reveal their true identities or were they blown, he wonders.

"I was transported to the camp in August 1944," says the agent, whose name is Landry.

"By what means?" Theo is scribbling in his notebook.

"A bus, a train, and then by lorry."

"And where were you before that?"

"In prison, in Paris. Fresnes."

"And the men were in prison with you?"

"Most of them, I believe."

"And you were with them on the train?"

"*Oui*, and about twenty women."

Theo looks up and Landry nods. Theo writes this down and underlines it. His hand is shaking.

"The train line had been bombed, so we could not go on. We stopped for a while . . ."

"How long?"

"About a day. Then they took us back to a small station and we were placed in two lorries. One for the men, and one for the women. We took the road to Châlons-sur-Marne, where we changed lorries before going on to Verdun. We stayed the night—"

"You slept at Verdun?"

The man shakes his head, incredulous. "Monsieur, I doubt anyone slept. We left for Metz and remained there for about four hours. I saw the women there again."

Theo opens a folder and takes out a stack of black and white photographs and hands them to Landry. He is able to identify the men well enough, but only one of the women sparks his memory. When he holds Tessa's photograph in his hand Theo forces himself to look away, lest the Frenchman read anything into his expression. When Landry shakes his head, placing Tessa's photograph face down on the pile, Theo fears he might be sick, even though it was a long shot. The transport was almost a year after Tessa left her cell in Paris.

How can people just disappear?

"I did not see the women again after this," the man says. "We were driven to Saarbrücken station and taken by train to Weimar. We were at this point chained together, in groups of five."

Theo gathers himself to continue his questioning. "And do you recall the date you arrived at Buchenwald?"

"The sixteenth or seventeenth of August, I believe. We were told we were to be gassed but we were not. They took everything we had, shaved our heads and sent us off to a prison block."

"Which block?"

"Block 17."

"And these other men, are they still in the camp as far as you are aware?"

Landry prods a scrawny finger at one of the names, a British agent named Argyle.

"I think he is still alive."

Another lurch in Theo's stomach. "And the others?"

The man shakes his head. "There was a list. Fourteen names. The men were taken to the prison in the center of the camp."

"Sorry, when was this?"

"Early September 1944. They were beaten first and then hanged—"

Theo interrupts him. "How do you know?"

"It was the talk of the camp. They were strung up by ropes attached to hooks on the ceiling. It didn't snap their necks, oh no, that would have been too merciful. It took them five, ten minutes to die. Then their bodies were burned in the crematorium. In October, another list appeared and the named men were shot that afternoon. They were brave, defiant even, until the moment of death."

Theo writes this down. He likes to maintain a calm, even cool exterior during this process, but inside his heart is pounding. "These lists . . . Do you mean to suggest it was an order from the camp authorities?"

Landry points at the ceiling. "Or above," he says. He leans forward in his seat. "There's one more thing you should know."

"What's that?" says Theo.

"All of them, every man I met, believed you had a rat in your ranks. You should probably do something about that, shouldn't you? Your rat, your traitor, is as guilty of murder as any Nazi."

It is late when Mabel appears in the doorway of Theo's office. Late enough for the room to glow with a triangle of light from his desk lamp.

"Everyone's gone," he says, without looking up. He gestures at the pile of paperwork, reports and interrogations on his desk. "I'll be here for a while. You may as well go."

"It's not that," she says, and the nerves in her voice make him put down his pen. "Major Crawley is here to see you. He's next door."

The directorate's commanding officer. "Crawley's here . . ." Theo pushes his chair away from his desk, alarmed. "Why wasn't I informed he was in Paris?"

"We didn't know."

Theo dismisses her more curtly than he intends. He steals a minute to inspect his appearance in the bathroom mirror, smoothing down his hair and willing away the tell-tale grey beneath his eyes. Crawley will think he's been having a good time.

The older man, a barrister too before the war, nods as Theo enters the room. "Armstrong, good man."

"Sir. I didn't know you were in Paris."

"A flying visit. Good to keep people on their toes. Best to make the most of it—talk is of this all being wound down any day."

They've been saying this for months. It's becoming apparent the authorities want the problem of the missing agents to go away. Women lost behind the lines, women possibly executed, is a scandal the government can ill afford. Crawley—all those men, in fact—want it swept under the rug and never spoken of again. Theo thinks, is that what you want for her? A file stamped "Missing, presumed dead" and no answers, because that is the way the tide is moving.

Crawley directs Theo to the chair facing the desk. So this is an interview, he thinks. He wishes they'd had a moment to tidy. There are half-drunk cups of tea on desks, papers left out, pens lined up ready for the morning.

"When were you called to the Bar?" says Crawley.

It is an unexpected question. "In 1938," he says, after a pause.

"Goodness, what appalling timing."

"Why do you ask, sir?"

"Armstrong, you've done good work here, and in unimaginably difficult circumstances."

Theo's heart sinks. This is a professional "goodbye," if ever he's heard one. "Thank you, sir."

"I see on your file you speak German."

"Some, yes. I took lessons at school."

"Now look, this is in confidence, but it seems the Foreign Secretary's had his head turned at the San Francisco conference."

"Meaning what, sir?"

"Meaning he's capitulated to pressure from the Americans and there is likely to be a trial. War crimes. Crimes against humanity."

Suddenly this feels like quite the opposite of matters being swept under the rug. "As you know, sir, I think it the right course," Theo says.

"Yes, I thought you'd be pleased. Look, you've shown yourself to be an excellent investigator, Armstrong, and you have a decent working knowledge of international law. If I have to lose you to anything, at least it's this."

Gossip about a possible trial has raged for months; longer, even. Hitler, Goebbels and Himmler are dead, but other senior Nazis are falling into Allied hands.

"Do you *have* to lose me, sir?" he says.

Crawley smiles, but he doesn't answer the question. "It's the trial of our lifetime. It'll be the making of you. Now look, as to other matters, how have you taken this news about your sister? Awfully well, by the looks of you. Good man. Impressive."

All energy drains from Theo's body and he feels his mouth drop open slightly. In the brief, shocked silence that follows, Crawley reddens, looking back and forth to the door, but there is no one around to save him. "Has no one told you?"

Theo shakes his head. He doesn't trust his voice. She must be dead. Tessa is dead. Crying is not the done thing in these situations. Stoicism is a virtue, there is dignity in strength, but he wants to tear up the room. He wants to scream.

Recovering his composure, Crawley clears his throat. "Last week a woman was handed over to the Swedish Red Cross from the women's camp, Ravensbrück, a few days before the Russians liberated it. She identified herself as a British agent and spoke of several other British women known to have been held in the camp. I'm sorry to tell you that one of them was Tessa."

The awkwardness of the moment sits heavy between them. Crawley fears Theo's emotions, Theo can tell, so he puts a good deal of effort into keeping his features calm and still. Later he realizes this probably came across as cold, not stoic as he had hoped. Alone in the office, he allows his fingers to rest upon a stack of folders. Transcripts of interrogations, margins scribbled with notes. Tessa might be in there, it might be all that's left, an observation across a hut, a passing word.

Or she might be alive.

Theo goes to a little bar in the Latin Quarter, a throwaway mention in one of her letters almost a decade ago. Tessa would laugh. She'd say, "You, there?" and she'd be right. This is not his place. The bar is dark, and undoubtedly geared toward students, or at least it had been before the Germans ripped the heart out of the city, swamping the language with their own, plastering signs and shopfronts with their words. Luc lives nearby. Sometimes Theo thinks he'll knock on his door but he doesn't, because it's begun to feel like a violation, unearthing these secrets that Tessa kept to herself.

"Quite a trek for a place like this," says Michael, sitting down on the bar stool next to him and making him jump.

Theo sips his whisky. "Are you following me?"

"I am, yes. I'm dreadfully worried about you. You know, you could invite the others here. They'd like that, Mabel especially." Michael signals to the barman, pointing at Theo's drink and holding up two fingers. "Besides, aren't you celebrating? The war crimes tribunal, my good fellow—you'll dine out on this for the rest of your life."

"If I take the job."

"Why wouldn't you?"

"Crawley told me about Tessa," he says, although part of him doesn't want Michael to know. He doesn't want anyone to know. He wants to sit alone with this knowledge, burning red in his brain.

Michael grimaces. "Which part?"

"Which part . . . ?"

The bartender puts down their drinks, and Theo flexes his knuckles before saying, because it seems such a reasonable request, that he might as well just bring the bottle. "He told me she'd been seen in Ravensbrück. Why, what else do you know?"

"A woman, one of ours, says Tessa was held for a quite a while at avenue Foch. Secondary confirmation of what Tessa told us herself when she carved it into the wall. It's probably nothing, but what we're learning is that it's unusual. König tended to work fast and send the agents elsewhere."

Theo doesn't say anything to this.

"We hardly know anything about Ravensbrück, of course. The Russians aren't proving too forthcoming." Michael chuckles, sourly. "Not sure our alliance with the East is going to last long in peacetime."

"We know about Buchenwald, and Belsen and Dachau. The state of the prisoners in those camps. Barely alive. Skin and bones, and riddled with pestilence."

Michael breathes in sharply. "I don't know why you're doing this to yourself."

"I wouldn't expect you to understand, being as you're an only child." He watches as Michael absorbs the blow.

"Crawley's finally agreed to circulate the names of the missing women to the Red Cross," Michael says, after a while.

"Good. That means her name will be out there. I don't want this kicked into the long grass. I want her found and I want to know what happened. I mean it, Michael."

"You think I'd—"

"I think you do what you're told. Besides, I've seen Miss Jones' little notes to the families, the euphemisms. I don't want to be spared the worst, I've decided. And if she's found, whatever state she's in, I want to be the one to bring her home."

Nuremberg, 1945

Twenty-seven

The war was a pin in everything else, Stephen had said that day by the river, their flesh stippled with mud and twigs. Theo is thinking about this as the bus inches along a patched-up road, weaving around rips and craters. He set out to find his sister but ended up an onlooker anyway, tantalizingly close to the action but always waiting for someone else to tell him what was going on. The inescapable truth of the matter is, he's not on the road to Nuremberg for Tessa, and this feels so selfish, that he gets to move on and she is stuck wherever she is.

His mind is a busy place. There are thousands of corpses beneath enormous heaps of debris in Nuremberg, or so says someone on the army bus. Paris was all tight smiles and narrowed eyes. In Nuremberg nothing is hidden, there is no pretense, the sheer scale of the damage makes that an impossibility. Don't drink the water, someone says and they laugh, but it's a grim sound.

He could get to Ravensbrück in four hours. He knows, he's checked.

The next stop in his moving-on tour is the Palace of Justice. The people on the street wear their anger at the destruction wrought by the Allies in glares and hisses, and he wants to say to them, no, don't you see, loss goes both ways and I am angry at *you*. He accepts it now as a loss; even if she returns, she will never be the same, not after what she's seen in the camps. He knows because he's seen it too, at a step removed, in photographs and news reels.

Sherman tanks stand ready outside the Palace of Justice, where the trial is to be held. There are building materials piled high in the corridors, hammers and drills echoing from the principal courtroom. Theo is wandering around, trying to get his bearings. There is nobody to ask and he doesn't want to disturb the workmen, recommissioned soldiers who can barely spare him a glance. From a corridor lined with windows, Theo has a view of a barren garden, in which prisoners are taking exercise. There goes Hermann Göring, there goes Rudolf Hess, a group of American guards keeping a watchful eye on them. Theo stops in his tracks, unable to look away.

"A rum business, isn't it?" says a voice behind him. "One thinks of them as monsters but then you realize, isn't it more terrifying them being mere men?" Theo turns around and the man sticks out his hand. "Major Page. I'm on the staff with the International Military Tribunal. Are you by any chance Group Captain Armstrong?"

Theo concurs, shaking the man's hand.

"Good, excellent, I've been trying to track you down. Call me Jeremy, won't you? We'll have our heads buried in enough formalities as it is. And sorry about the noise, it's the Americans crashing about. Have to make the courtroom bigger, you see, to squeeze in the crowds."

Theo knows he is supposed to move, but he still cannot tear his eyes from the window panes.

"Best to get it out of your system before you find yourself in a room with them," Jeremy says.

Theo turns back to him reluctantly. "Have you?"

"I have, yes. Fascinatingly banal creatures given what they've done."

He puts his hand on Theo's elbow, gently moving him away. "Shall I show you to our chambers? It's all a bit of a hodgepodge around here, I'm afraid. Procedure decided on the fly, that sort of thing. Not that I'm saying we're making it up as we go along, you understand, just that none of us have done anything like this before."

"How are they, the prisoners out there?" Jeremy's long stride means he has pulled ahead, and Theo is hurrying to keep up.

"Very defensive, unsurprisingly. Disbelieving of the notion they'll get a fair trial, and of course, Stalin's already decreed their guilt, so you can see their point. But still, let's try and prove them wrong, shall we? Ah, here we are."

When Theo has been introduced to the others in chambers and shown to his desk, Jeremy says, cryptically, "Afraid you've drawn the short straw."

"Oh dear," Theo says, peeling off his jacket and wondering what this means.

"Yes, rather. One of the defendants wants to make an application to the tribunal judges. Happens most days and we do need to take it seriously. Can you go now? We've a meeting with the judges later where you can present whatever it is he wants this time."

Theo is regathering his things, putting his jacket back on, all fingers and thumbs, his pen sliding from his pile of folders, his arm getting stuck in his sleeve. "Who is it?" he says.

"Ribbentrop."

The prison at the Palace of Justice is guarded by the United States Army, big burly fellows who—to Theo's mind—look upon him with scorn.

"You're new," says the governor of the prison, when Theo arrives. "And young."

Thick iron doors sit at the end of a covered walkway. The governor rings a bell and the door is opened immediately by guards who snap to attention and salute. I'm going to meet Ribbentrop, Theo thinks. I'm going to write this down. Then he wonders what Tessa would do, because his sister is always just outside the light of his thoughts, and decides that she would relish this opportunity. He looks up at the prison, three floors and a spiral staircase, doors with metal grilles, guards patrolling because suicide attempts are common. Theo is led to one of these doors, the master-sergeant with his jangling keys rapping on the metal and shouting "Stand back, stand back." Theo can hear the shuffle of feet inside the cell, and when he sets eyes on Ribbentrop, a wave of disgust washes over him. The Foreign Minister of the Third Reich is disheveled, his hair askew, his eyes tired. His cell is as messy as Theo's room in his billet, with a small desk covered in sheets of paper.

Ribbentrop looks Theo up and down with black, beady eyes. "And you are?" he says, in accented English. Theo introduces himself, and Ribbentrop starts shaking his head. "No, I mean your title. You are English, yes?"

Theo is perplexed. "I'm Group Captain Armstrong," he repeats.

"No, no!" Ribbentrop is furious now. "Your *title*."

It dawns on Theo what Ribbentrop, once so popular with the St. James set, means by this. "I'm afraid you won't find me in *Debrett's*," he says.

The American governor looks from one to the other, seemingly mystified by the strange language of the English upper classes tripping off their tongues. Ribbentrop slumps sullenly, his shoulders slipping forward. He reminds Theo of a rat caught in a torch beam. Although he knows he should be enjoying it—Tessa would certainly enjoy it—he finds no joy in the spectacle. She once called Ribbentrop "a peacock draped in a swastika," but to Theo he just seems pathetic.

Ribbentrop sits on his small metal chair. "Every time it is someone new, and every time the rank descends." He puffs out his chest and levels his gaze at Theo. "I have connections to the British aristocracy, you know."

Ah yes, thinks Theo, a peacock. "I'm told you have an application to make. Perhaps you might get on with it."

Ribbentrop crosses his arms. "I wish to see my doctor."

Theo glances back at the governor. "Are you unwell?"

Ribbentrop shoots Theo a look of utter loathing. "That is between me and my physician, is it not?"

"You've seen the doctor. He says there's nothing wrong with you." The governor pulls a face as he says this. To Theo he says, "He's wasting your time, I'm sorry."

Theo starts to say, no, don't worry—even if he is, it's still a story for the ages—when Ribbentrop jumps up.

"Wait," he snaps. He scrabbles around on his desk until he finds the piece of paper he's looking for and thrusts it toward Theo. "These are witnesses for my defense. I demand they be summoned." Then he turns his back and refuses to engage further.

And so that evening, before the judges given the task of adjudicating the biggest tribunal in history, Theo finds himself putting forth Ribbentrop's application. "Herr Ribbentrop requests His Majesty King George VI attend the trial and give evidence on the defendant's 'desire for peace,'" he says, trying to keep his voice steady. He can see Jeremy at the back of the room, his shoulders shaking as he tries not to laugh.

Lord Justice Lawrence, the British judge, furrows his thick eyebrows and settles a hard stare on Theo. Theo can see the corners of his mouth twitching. "I think not, Captain Armstrong," he says, and that is that.

Despite the occasional absurdities of his role, it feels good to be awakening his muscle memory of the law. He revives another part of his brain too, surprising himself greatly by accepting when he's invited out with colleagues at the end of a working day. They head to the Grand Hotel, one of the only buildings in the city with electricity. The Americans have torn down walls, knocking through to the building next door for more space, although looking around, one senses they didn't have to work too hard. In Nuremberg, demolition came top-down from the sky. I would have been part of this, thinks Theo.

In the hotel's Marble Room, Theo taps his fingers on the bar and orders a whisky. The others—Jeremy, the staff and a group of WRENs—are at a table covered with glasses and cigarette papers. Everyone is chatting as if they're in a bar in Soho—about the weather, what's on at the flickers. Life is paper-thin and dressed up as a step back toward the norm, but it's not really, what with the monsters from the newspapers exercising in the yard.

"Were you in Normandy?" Jeremy asks, and Theo is nodding and reenacting his fall from the sky, hearing himself describe the evacuation hospital where they fixed up his leg as "damned impressive." Then Jeremy is telling them his own stories of the push into Germany, and Theo can hear that it's too neat, no light and shade; just like his own tale, it's a surface-wash. A woman, Laura, asks him to dance and he cries off, pointing at his leg when she protests. Most of the table pair off and take to the dancefloor, and Theo finds himself sitting next to Jeremy. In a mirror on the wall he can see the red in his cheeks—signs of life, after all. He's enjoying himself, he thinks, surprised. He's enjoying talking to Jeremy.

"Thing is," says Jeremy, not looking at him, "I don't think the Marble Room is quite your thing." Beneath the table, he presses his leg against Theo's.

Because he's been here before, Theo knows these conversations can go one of two ways. It's either a trap or an invitation, and with Jeremy he assumes the latter. He wants to say, no, don't you know how torn up I am, because he's hidden it too well. Jeremy, it seems, hasn't noticed.

Jeremy's arm is right next to his. "It's not my thing either," Jeremy says.

It hangs there between them. And how strange it feels to say it with words as opposed to a look or a nod of the head, even if it's not quite the right words, a roundabout way to inch toward a point. A waiter chooses this moment to stop at their table and ask if he is, perchance, Theo Armstrong, telling him there's a telephone call for him in the lobby. Theo thinks he must have done something wrong in chambers. Or perhaps it's his mother, because Lord knows that woman is persistent, and she's not going to let a little thing like the obliteration of a city stop her from speaking to her son.

"For God's sake, do you know how long it's taken me to track you down?" says the voice on the other end of the line.

Michael. Theo's heart starts racing. "What is it? Have you found her?" he says, because he's been kidding himself. There's no moving on, his feet have been glued to the spot all this time.

"What? No, no, sorry." He can hear Michael's raggedy breathing, as if he's stopped for a conversation mid-sprint. "I've been trying to get hold of you for days. Half the time the line just goes dead."

"We bomb the place to smithereens and the next day expect it to be orderly and efficient. They've only just got a line in here. What do you want?"

There's a staticky pause. "It's about your father."

Surely there is a limit to how much Theo can reasonably be expected to take. "What is it?" he says. "What's happened?"

"Nothing's happened as such, at least not yet. We have it on good authority that he's planning on speaking to the press. Have a word, will you? We need him stopped."

Theo puts his head down on the wooden lobby desk and groans. "Which newspaper?" he says.

"That rag, the *Manchester Guardian*. Not that anyone reads it."

"Clearly enough people do for you to get in a stew about it."

"Theo, it's a bad time, matters are sensitive." There's a beat. "He wants to talk about Tessa."

Of course he wants to talk about Tessa. "He does what he wants," Theo says.

"Yes, as do you, as did Tessa—"

"As *does* Tessa." The correction is automatic. There's another pause on the line, a sigh.

"Your father needs to think very carefully about his position."

This is a change in both tone and temperature. Theo raises his head. "What does that mean?" he says, quickly.

"In fact, given what we know about your sister, I'd suggest it's in both of your interests to cooperate entirely from here on in," says Michael. "I think we both know you have secrets you'd rather keep hidden."

Theo feels the air leave his body. He swallows. "What do you know about my sister?" he says.

"I mean it, Theo. Stop him, and do it now."

Michael hangs up.

Theo swears, louder than he intends. Too loud, too quiet, he's forgotten how to relax around other people, he's forgotten what it means to be himself. Tessa, he thinks, squeezing his eyes closed as if he might truly possess some form of summoning power. Tessa, Tess, Tee. Her absence is a screaming silence. It is the loss of a limb.

He has to get a grip on himself but he can't marshal his thoughts. Your father needs to consider his position, he says to himself; it's a very sensitive time. *Given what we know about your sister* is new, because what does that mean, what do they know that hasn't been said before? What has Tessa done? He looks back toward the Marble Room but it's too late, there's no pretending to be normal now. He's been kidding himself, all these notions of moving on. He's never going anywhere again.

Twenty-eight

When the trial begins in November, it takes two full days for the junior members of the prosecution to read aloud the indictment against the accused, their voices now four, English then Russian, German and French, translated into the headphones of those looking on, nodding their heads at the appropriate moments. Theo keeps looking over at the twenty-one men in the dock, trying to gauge their reactions, but aside from Göring's smile they all sit there impassive, unmoved. Hess has even brought a novel to read. Theo strains his neck, trying to see what it is, but he's too far away.

Outside the court a crowd is battling for access to the public gallery, which although enlarged isn't quite big enough for all the eyes wishing to gawp at the spectacle below. When Theo tries to get back into court after lunch he has to dodge elbows and shoves because his youth is misleading, and people don't realize he's not one of them. This is when his eyes catch her, midtussle.

"Miss Jones! Emmeline?" he calls, waving.

He knows she hears him because of the way her body stills and her eyes dart toward him but not at him. There's no way she could ever be accused of *seeing* him because she doesn't let it get that far, but there's nothing natural in the squaring of those shoulders. He watches her press through the crowd away from him. In court when he locates her and looks up to where she's sitting, she turns her head away.

Hitler's 1941 order to destroy Leningrad is read aloud to the court. The words "we are not interested in preserving even a part of the population of this large city" are so simple, so clinical, and yet what a glimpse it is, Theo thinks, into darkness. The third part of the indictment, war crimes, is read by a Frenchman who is not long out of a concentration camp. How steady he keeps his voice, given the close proximity of the men who put him there. The judges instruct the men in the dock to stand and they do, and Theo thinks it is quite a thing, to lace such a simple movement of the body with arrogance, with indifference. The men are asked how they plead.

"Not guilty," says Göring.

"Not guilty," says Speer.

"Not guilty," says Ribbentrop, the peacock.

"Nein," says Hess.

On and on it goes, twenty-one denials. Theo is there to fetch papers and witnesses, pass messages, a small cog in the machine. Outwardly he is a picture of restraint, but inside he wants to see these men hang. It's what she'd want.

In the second week of the trial, the Americans present footage filmed in a series of concentration camps. It's the busiest he's seen the court, people crammed onto the benches, men in white helmets lined up around the walls. The lights go down and the film begins. A map showing the camps dotted across the continent, a white rash of evil. Theo has seen photographs, of course, everyone has by now, but naturally the film is worse. Splayed bodies on concrete at Ohrdruf and Nordhausen. The prisoners, the court is told, are "human skeletons, too weak to move." At Mauthausen, the camera tracks the disbelief on a liberated prisoner's face, his naked form more bone than flesh, angles where there should be none. It tracks German civilians on a "forced" tour at Buchenwald, smiling for the camera as they enter the camp and then later, amid piles of bodies, their smiles wiped clean by the truth they'd ignored at the end of the road. There are so many bodies, piled top to toe, grotesque distortions of the human form, the charred ribcage of an inmate still visible in an oven. Dachau is a city with a gas chamber at its heart—never used, Theo's told, but there are clothes left hanging on pegs outside of it.

It is too much. It sucks the air from the room. People are sobbing into handkerchiefs; many have lost all color in their faces. This cannot be. He cannot comprehend that this was Tessa's fate, will not accept it as such. No, he thinks, I refuse. His stomach lurches. He covers his mouth with his hand, a warning bell sounding in his head telling him to move, and quickly. Theo stands up, and his colleagues look at him in confusion and then are distracted by a kerfuffle in the public gallery where a woman has fainted. For some, the stuttering images on screen are their recent technicolor reality. They are Tessa's reality. He feels his way along the bench, inching his way past his colleagues. Opening the door sends a shaft of white light into the courtroom, and people look around and then back to the screen. He pushes his way through a queue of people still hoping for a space inside. In a cubicle in the men's lavatory, Theo drops to his knees and vomits into the toilet bowl. He can hear the man at the urinal behind zipping up his trousers, muttering in disgust, and leaving. Theo vomits once more. He hears the door open again but he doesn't look round. A hand, warm from the heat of the courtroom, rubs his lower back.

"Are you all right?"

Theo wipes his mouth with the back of his hand.

"Of course you're not," says Jeremy. "What a stupid question."

Theo shakes his head. He cannot say more than "My sister." The rest is in the look they exchange.

Jeremy leans back on his haunches against the cubicle wall. "Jesus. Where?"

"Ravensbrück."

Jeremy puts his hand to his mouth. Theo knows, he feels it too. Any connection to those images on the screen, however tenuous, is unbearable.

"She hasn't come back," says Theo. "She'd be back by now, wouldn't she?"

Jeremy's expression is part pity, part discomfort. "I don't know. As you're aware, the Russians haven't told us much about the camps they liberated. Besides, those conditions will have done all sorts of things to people's memories. They've forgotten who they are, and who can blame them. We could speak to the Russians here, if you'd like? I don't know if I can get you into the camp, but we might be able to get some information."

Theo nods gratefully. "Please don't tell me I shouldn't be here." He leans back next to Jeremy, resting his head against his colleague's shoulder, surprised at how natural it feels.

"On the contrary, you're exactly who those men should face in court." Jeremy looks out of the cubicle, just in case, then squeezes Theo's hand.

Theo is summoned from the court during Göring's performance on the stand.

"Someone to see you—says it's urgent," whispers Max, one of the clerks, and Theo reluctantly rises from his seat. He can see how thrilled Max is to take his place.

Emmeline Jones is in the lobby, in her neat WAAF uniform. She's going to rag on me for not speaking to my father, he thinks, because he hasn't and he doesn't intend to.

"Speaking to me now, are you?" he says.

She doesn't respond to this, only says, "Might we go somewhere private?" and Theo knows then that this is it. He takes her to his office, moving piles of folders so she might sit down, but remains standing himself.

"A few days ago," she begins, "at the prison in the British zone, I interrogated an SS man named Johann Kraus. He identified your sister from a photograph and stated that not only had she been an inmate in Ravensbrück Concentration Camp, but that in January 1945 her name had featured on a list of persons to be executed drawn up by the Gestapo in Berlin."

His insides crumble and he sits down heavily on the closest chair. January 1945, he'd been at home in Cambridge. Almost from the off, he'd been too late.

"I should tell my parents," he says.

Miss Jones shakes her head. "It's taken care of. I've asked Michael."

"Michael," he repeats dully.

"It seemed appropriate."

"You didn't speak to your father, as requested," she says.

"It would have been instantaneous, wouldn't it? If they killed her, I mean. She wouldn't have felt a thing."

She hesitates. "No, I expect not."

"Although she'd have known it was coming. Did this man . . ."

"Kraus."

"Yes, did he say any more—how she'd been in the camp, for example; the conditions?" Theo looks straight at her. He's been staving off the grief for so long, where has it gone now? There is nothing. Perhaps he has nothing left. How strange it is, that something so inevitable can still come as such a shock.

"I know very little. She'd been in a subcamp, working . . ."

He knows what this means. "Forced labor."

Miss Jones nods.

"She probably tried to unionize."

"Theo, I'm afraid there's something else," she says.

Theo wipes his eyes with the back of his hand, unembarrassed at his sudden emotion. "I know you asked me to speak to him, but my father and I are our own men. We don't interfere." Or speak, he thinks. Or show any interest. "Whatever the implied cost to me."

"Your father's not going to speak to the press, after all."

Theo is pulled up short. "Really, is he not? How did you achieve that?"

"That's just it, it's what I need to speak to you about. There's been an accusation."

He leaves the office and takes the stairs, not turning toward the courtroom—although he's no doubt expected back—but leaving the Palace of Justice by the front door. It is a bright day of white winter sun. He looks about for more details, adding light and shade to this, the day he found out. In the street, rubble is being shifted by massive earth movers. Everything is darker, greyer, in this world reclaimed, despite the sun. Can he still call himself a twin? There is no word to describe a person who loses half of themselves. Tessa is his blood, but he doesn't know her, not any more. How can he? The woman Emmeline Jones described is a stranger. He can't go back inside, not yet. He has a difficult road ahead, navigating the very worst of human nature, the gulf between what was and what is, and who he was and is: a person, once complete, now halved.

London, 1949

Twenty-nine

A finger peels back his eyelid. A voice says, "You're alive, at least."

Opening his eyes, Theo can see Graham staring at him, hands on hips, all pinched cheeks and concerned eyes. The dank stench of old water permeates the flat and Theo too, when he puts his nose to his armpit. He half sits up, clamping a hand to his mouth. Graham sits down on the bed, breathing out a deep sigh, which will never do. Theo doesn't want any sympathy, least of all Graham's.

Graham takes Theo's hand, places a small white pill into his palm and curls his fingers into a fist around it. "This is to get you through the day," he says, nodding at a glass of water on the bedside table. Theo tips back his head and downs the pill. He doesn't ask what it is. He doesn't care.

"Don't tell me you're working today," Graham says.

"Why?" he snaps. He starts hunting through the mess on the floor for his clothes, unearthing his suit, crumpled in a ball. Where did they go last night, how did he get here? He wonders, not for the first time, if Graham is his real name, or if it's just what he tells his customers.

"Just thinking that maybe you shouldn't, that's all. You were all over the place last night, tossing and turning in your sleep. Frightening, it was."

Theo can feel himself coming back to life and starting to make sense of what came before. His head is full of memories he doesn't want and has no idea what to do with. The hearse pulling up outside his parents' house. The weight of the coffin on his shoulder. The faces of the others as they walked into the church. He couldn't look at his mother.

"I don't need you to give me advice," he says now. "We're not friends." He is pulling on his trousers as quickly as he can, getting into a muddle with his shirt buttons. "You're a drug pusher. Every time I wake up here, it means something has gone wrong. Do you understand that?"

Graham is smiling his toothy smile. It makes Theo's stomach turn. "It goes wrong quite a lot, doesn't it?" he says, his laugh like nails on a blackboard.

Theo's leaving, he's stalking toward the door, his eyes are on the stairs, on escape. Turning back, he takes a few notes from his wallet and slaps them onto the bedside table. "Don't expect to see me again," he says, which makes Graham laugh even harder.

There is a distinct whiff of urine in the tenement hallway. An old lady walks past and shakes her head, looking him up and down, muttering beneath her breath. Concerned that it might be worse than he'd feared, Theo finds the nearest window, scraping his fingers through his hair, pinching his cheeks, deciding that any sign of life will do. It's early but the streets of Kennington are busy; Theo has to wind his way around people coming and going, his eyes searching out the right bus. But when he sees it, he lets it go past. He's rooted to the spot, trying to make sense of the feeling in his belly. He flags down a taxi, the words out of his mouth before he can grasp what they mean. Tossing and turning all night, he thinks. He'd put money on him having spoken in his sleep and it's always the same, always Tessa.

Theo hasn't been to Petersham Place since the war. He remembers the first time he came here, his leg more metal than bone after Normandy. He remembers hovering across from Michael's front door, trying to make himself cross the street and ring the bell. This time there's no hesitation. His fingers are on the button, three sharp bursts. Michael answers, dressed for a day's work, whatever it is he does now. Presumably more of the same.

"My God," says Michael, in surprise. He's irritated but there's a pinch of concern too. Looking down at his creased suit, aware of how his face must look, Theo can see why. Normally he has time to go home and bathe and change his clothes, but there's no disguising it today.

"Aren't you going to let me in?" says Theo. "I know how much you dislike people hovering on your doorstep. Neighbors gossiping and whatnot."

"I couldn't care less about what the neighbors think," Michael says, curtly. But he stands back to let Theo inside.

In the flat, Michael pours Theo a cup of strong coffee and a glass of water. Theo sits down on the sofa, breathing deeply and holding his sides. Without a word, Michael picks up the wastepaper basket and places it at Theo's feet.

"You might not want to hear this, but your mother is dreadfully worried about you," Michael says. Theo can see the effort it's taking for him to keep his annoyance from his tone, but it's all there in the tight lines around his mouth. "You disappeared from the wake without a word." Michael sits down in the armchair opposite. Theo keeps his eyes low, knowing he's in for a ticking-off. "You're still wearing your suit from the funeral. Where the hell have you been, or do I not want to know?"

"I went to see a friend." He knows Michael won't believe this. Theo doesn't have any friends, not any more. He hasn't spoken to Stephen in years, he's scared everyone off. Except for leeches like Graham, who give him what he needs—which is oblivion—when he needs it.

Michael leans forward. "Look, I'm sorry about your father. He was a good man, a fine man. I admired him. More to the point it's damned unfair, coming so soon after Tess. But look, old pal, you need to pull yourself together . . ."

Theo scowls, spoiling for a fight. "I can almost hear a dash of guilt in your voice, *old pal*. Don't tell me you're finally going to take some responsibility for what happened? For what's happened since? For my father, I mean, because the grief killed him—you know that, don't you? Poor sod didn't stand a chance. I'm only surprised my mother's still with us, and Christ knows how, given she spends most of the day passed out drunk on the sofa."

"Stop this, Theo."

"Thing is, I can't. I want to talk to you about Tessa."

Michael closes his eyes.

"I've been writing to Emmeline Jones."

"I know you have."

"Only she never replies. Rather rude, wouldn't you say?"

"She's moved on."

"But I haven't. I want to know what happened to my sister. I want the details. I want to challenge what's been said."

"You know the details."

"I want to speak to this chap, the one who accused her."

"That won't be possible."

"Why, is he dead?"

Michael puts a hand to his mouth, pinching his lips between his fingers.

Theo downs his glass of water, thinking it might settle his stomach, which is suddenly full of knots. "She didn't betray anyone, Michael."

"People did."

Theo shakes his head. "Not Tessa."

"But you don't know that, not for sure. The evidence is . . . compelling, to say the least. Miraculous escapes, ignoring direct orders from her seniors, the enemy having inside information on drops and ops she was involved in. Not to mention the SD holding her in Paris for longer than anyone else. It all speaks to someone cooperating, I'm sorry to say."

"No," insists Theo, calmly. "Tessa wouldn't do that."

Michael stands up abruptly, making Theo jump. "What is it going to take to make you understand? Honestly, do you have any idea what you're risking here?" Michael clasps his hands together but it's all for show, it always is. "Look, I'm begging you, let this go, for everyone's sake. Tessa would hate to see you like this."

"Don't tell me what she'd think."

Michael hesitates. "Word on the street is that despite your current appearance—you look dreadful, by the way—you're doing rather well. Isn't that what you've always wanted? A successful career, the respect of your peers? I know Adela is incredibly proud of you."

"And stop talking about my mother."

"Fine. Let me be clear then, yes? Because it seems that nothing else is working. Carrying on down this road will not end well for you, I guarantee it."

Theo stiffens. "That sounds rather like a threat."

Michael looks down at him. "I'd be minded to take it seriously, if I were you."

Theo slumps back on the sofa. A noise, a low moan, slips out of his mouth. It's been four years of this going around and around in his head. "I still look for her, in the street I mean. Everywhere. I still expect her to walk in the door as if nothing is amiss." He starts to cry. Michael rocks back on his heels, as if unsure whether to comfort him or not, then an odd look crosses his face, one Theo can't comprehend. Michael sits down next to him, tentatively laying his hand on Theo's arm, then his leg. Theo stands up, unable to tolerate the closeness, but Michael follows him.

"It's not that I don't want to help," Michael says.

"Then help, for God's sake," Theo says, squaring up to him. "I always thought you loved her."

Michael steps toward him. "I . . ."

"Say it, go on, I dare you." Theo pushes Michael's shoulder. "Say you loved her."

"Theo, please."

Theo pushes him again. "Say the words. Go on, do it. Or are you a coward? Say you loved her."

Michael is angry now. Theo can see it in his eyes. "I've always loved you both, you know that. I love you."

Theo gives in to his own fury. He can't help it. He wants Michael to feel even a tenth of what he is feeling. "Are you mad? You must be if you think this is love. Torturing me for years, sending Tessa to her death."

Michael seems struck dumb.

"That isn't fucking love, Michael," Theo rages. "It's nowhere near. No, on the contrary, you must hate me to do what you've done. You must—"

"Don't say that," hisses Michael.

Theo pushes him again. "If you loved us . . ."

"I mean it . . ."

"If you actually *loved* either of us, then you'd do everything in your power to put me out of my misery. Love! Fuck off. Do you hear me? Just fuck off with your talk of love."

Michael kisses him, his lips hard against Theo's. Theo pushes his hands against Michael's shoulders as roughly as he can, until the connection breaks.

Theo is rubbing his lips, and Michael delicately places a finger to his own, as if he can't quite believe what those lips have just experienced.

"That's not . . . I don't want that, not from you. Do you hear? I don't want that." Theo sits down and cradles his head in his hands. "It's Tessa you loved. Tessa. And look what you did, what you've done."

Michael shakes his head and arranges himself gingerly in a chair across from Theo. They sit in silence for a while. Then Michael says, his voice almost a whisper, "I know someone in the Cabinet Office. What if I get them to speak to you? Just to run you through what we know, again?"

Theo looks up, wiping his eyes on his sleeve. "Really?" he asks, wary.

"But after that, you have to promise to let it go. I mean it. Let it go."

It starts with a brief letter. "Dear Mr. Armstrong," it begins, thanking him for his continued interest in the work of Tessa's organization. It explains the basics of Tessa's case, dropped into France on this date, believed to have been working in this area of France (why don't they *know?*), arrested around this date, imprisoned between these dates, last sighted in Ravensbrück and believed to be dead. The author, a Sir Peter Jenkins, goes on to say that unfortunately, due to a fire, it is impossible for him to supply further details. The records have been destroyed. End of story, Theo thinks. *Fin.*

No. He's been in this game long enough to know when he's being fobbed off. He writes back, requesting a meeting, and when he doesn't receive a reply he writes again. When no answer is forthcoming, he begins to telephone Sir Peter's office. At work, Theo displays all the hallmarks of prodigious success. A busy roster of clients at a prestigious chambers—he's a sought-after barrister despite his youth. Everything is going right, is going well. One thing, at least, is just as it's supposed to be. Except that in the pocket of his Savile Row suit is a small flask of whisky. He keeps mints stocked up in his desk drawer. Theo doesn't get drunk at work, he's not as far gone as that, he just drinks enough to keep him on an even keel. He lives alone, in a small flat just off Kensington High Street, so there's no one to witness the nightmares or hear him shouting out in his sleep. When it gets too much, he sees Graham for medicinal relief that can't be purchased from a pharmacy counter. Theo can lose whole chunks of time in Graham's flat.

Only when Theo escalates to telephoning the Cabinet Office several times a day does the mysterious Sir Peter yield to a meeting. Theo makes sure he arrives there in good time and is shown to a small office, not the grand affair he was expecting for a Knight Commander of the British Empire. His fingers brush against a piece of folded paper in his pocket. A letter from Jeremy, which arrived that morning. Jeremy, who is in London, and is so sorry to read of Theo's father's death. Jeremy, who would love to catch up.

They haven't seen each other since Theo left Nuremberg to take up his new position, despite them swearing they'd stay in touch. The letter has a return address—Jeremy doesn't live far from Theo's flat. He's noted his telephone number at the bottom of the letter. Theo could telephone, couldn't he? It doesn't take much effort to say hello. Maybe they'd have a drink, reestablish themselves as friends. Maybe they'd become more, explore that frisson of possibility that's always been there.

But no, this is a distraction. Jeremy would be *distracting*. Theo crumples the letter into a ball but finds he cannot throw it away. He smooths the paper out against his thigh, folding it neatly before he places it back in his pocket.

He's been waiting for twenty minutes when a young civil servant slips into the room.

"So sorry to keep you waiting," he says, sticking out his hand for Theo to shake. "Andrew Clarke, secretary to Sir Peter. I'm sorry to say he's been called away on some rather urgent business."

Theo frowns. "Has he? What a shame. Perhaps I ought to come back when it's more convenient."

The man smiles, his lips pulled tight over his teeth. "Not at all, Mr. Armstrong. I'm sure I can be of help in Sir Peter's absence. Now, let's see what we have here . . ." He flips open a folder and begins to read out the scant details of Tessa's recruitment and time in France.

"I already know all this," says Theo. "I want to see the evidence against her."

"Ah, yes. Unfortunate business. I believe Sir Peter explained in his letter to you that the records pertaining to that time have been destroyed in a fire. We're lucky no one was killed."

"But surely you know what was in them? We're hardly speaking about ancient history."

"I'm afraid—"

"Fine. I want to speak to the man who accused my sister."

"That won't be possible either. We have no way of contacting Monsieur Aubert."

Theo looks up. "Aubert?"

The man reddens. "He's not been heard of since the war."

"And if I go public?"

The man smiles his tight smile again. "Well, I'd of course advise against it."

"I'm sure you would, only you're not giving me much of a choice, are you?"

"Mr. Armstrong, I'd advise—"

Theo doesn't wait to hear whatever trite excuse he's going to reach for next. He won't be able to sleep until he knows what happened, he can feel it in his bones. The not-knowing killed his father, shattered his mother, and is the source of his nightmares, of never being able to get things straight in his head. What's more, the pretense of being fine day after day is exhausting.

Theo thinks, enough.

Two weeks later, and there's no slinking off home to his flat to lose himself in any way he can, not on this evening. In his hand he carries an invitation, the paper hand-painted in vibrant pinks and yellows, the name of the event in bold white, "*Tee.*" Theo has to pause at the door, summoning courage, wishing he'd thought to bring along the bottle of whisky he keeps in his desk drawer for support. He takes a deep breath, counts to three, and pushes open the door to the gallery.

Luc Langlois is in the middle of the room, holding court. A crowd of journalists and others whose very demeanor shrieks wealth are milling around him, trying to catch the artist's eye and find a way into his conversation.

Theo ducks his head, pulling his lips into a grateful smile when a waiter proffers a glass of champagne in his direction. Almost at once, an American woman is upon him, large ornate earrings and red lips, offering a catalog and sales advice. Theo politely shakes his head, eyes down, waiting for a group to move on from a large canvas, an array of colors in broad, purposeful strokes. The works are strange, abstract—which seems to be the new thing. None of them look like anything, but then perhaps that is the point. It is not what one sees but what one feels that matters. Tessa would love it. She'd explain it in a way he understood, she'd make it make sense.

"*Est-ce que celui-ci vous plaît?* How interesting that you have paused here."

Theo turns around and there he is: Luc, looking much the same as he did in 1944; a little thicker around the middle, perhaps, but brighter in the eyes, his skin less grey. Theo sticks out his hand and Luc pulls him into a hug, wrapping his arms around him. Stiffening, Theo wonders if Luc can sense how difficult he finds physical contact with another these days.

"How are you, dear Theo?" says Luc, his grin wide. "You are well, yes? You look well." He stumbles momentarily on this obvious lie, then recovers and says, "I heard you were living in Germany."

"Yes, for about a year. I've been home since '47."

"You did a good thing in bringing those men to justice. You held them accountable."

Theo demurs. "Yes, well. I'm not sure I really—"

"No, no. I won't accept modesty. Not when it comes to Nuremberg." Luc looks about the gallery. "I wasn't sure you'd come."

"I wasn't sure I would. But it's good of you to invite me. You seem to be making quite a name for yourself."

Luc gestures dismissively toward the other guests, who Theo realizes are glaring enviously. "It's just noise, Theo. Noise. All that matters is the work. Come, let me show you around."

Theo follows Luc, trying to keep up with his rapid-fire running commentary. "Normally I don't like to explain my paintings. What do *you* think, you know? That's what is important. That is the *point*. But look, I explained in my letter what this is all about. It is for her. All of it. It is the beginning of our relationship, it is the confusion I felt when she left, the pain of our meeting in Paris—yes, with you, Theo. You are here too. This is how I comprehend that time."

Theo can't look at him, but he's also finding it hard to look at the works, which are vibrant in places, dark and discomfiting in others. Just like Tessa, he thinks. He finds if he focuses on the bottom corner of each canvas, he can nod along and smile, and even contribute appropriate verbal expressions at intervals. Eventually, Luc takes him by the arm and positions him in front of the final piece.

"And this is how I say goodbye. The courage it takes to do so. To move on." Luc bites his lip. "For the longest time such a thing felt impossible."

Theo casts his eyes over the painting, the entirety of it this time. It is a colossal work, more than six feet high and twice as wide, painted in different shades of warm yellow. It is a summer's day, he thinks. The sun on your skin.

"Goodbye," he echoes, softly, but the thought is jarring. Immediately his mind resists any notion of letting go. Theo realizes then that they're not alone. A woman has joined them, her hair swept back from her face with a thin fabric headband. She has an open, questioning smile. Her hands cradle her pregnant belly.

"This is my wife, Louisa. Louisa, this is Tessa's brother Theo."

"Theo, I've heard so much about you. I'm truly glad you could make it," she says, taking his hand and squeezing it.

"Wife?" says Theo.

He receives the word like a blow to the stomach; instinctively, he wraps his arms around himself. Luc hasn't noticed, too taken by Louisa and the festivities. He is telling Theo about his new life in New York. About Louisa and the apartment they share. Theo isn't listening. The gall of the man, doesn't he know? There's no moving on from Tessa. There are questions, yes; endless, endless questions, and riddles and mysteries that Theo has to solve, with the answers moving further and further out of reach. And there is time, of course, which keeps slipping between his fingers, and everyone is getting older, and the past is a line in the distance and that distance keeps growing. There is no time, he wants to say, to shout. He wants to tear the paintings from the walls. *Don't you know what they're saying about her?* he wants to scream. *Don't you know what's happened?*

And then Luc is asking if he's all right, and Theo is outside, gasping for air, shrugging off his sister's one-time lover because he can't look at him, he won't, ever again. He leaves him to his paintings, grotesquely thin tributes to Tessa which exist only to assuage Luc's guilt at forgetting.

Theo is trying to get his bearings. Knowing he needs to wash this experience from his face, he slips into a public lavatory next door to the Tube station. The only other person inside, a young man standing at a urinal, looks up at Theo and smiles briefly. Theo nods and looks away, because sometimes these things have meaning and sometimes it's not what he wants. Then he feels a hand on his shoulder, a hard smack to the back of his head. Theo drops to his knees, crying out, while the young man shouts, "What's this, what's this?" in a high, panicked voice. Hauled to his feet, Theo finds himself face to face with a policeman, who grips Theo's arm with one hand and raises a truncheon in the other.

"People like you are a menace," the policeman spits, taking a pair of handcuffs from his pocket. "Get out of here!" he shouts at the young man, who runs out, zipping up his flies as he goes.

"Christ," says Theo. "Shit." His head is throbbing. It is happening so fast. "This isn't . . . we weren't . . ." he's saying, but the policeman is snapping the handcuffs shut around his wrists.

The street is busy outside, he knows. He has colleagues who live in this area, people he knows from other chambers; his boss's house is just a minute away from where he stands, hands now bound in metal. He thinks of Barnes, and Jeremy, and all the love he holds inside himself, remembering Jeremy's letter, still folded neatly inside his jacket pocket.

He thinks, shit.

Cambridge, 1956

Thirty

It's bright in the garden. Theo is sitting beneath the oak tree, his cat Jasper in the shade beneath his chair. No sound but the birdsong and the gentle lap of the river at the bottom of the garden.

In his mind he is decades in the past, racing across the lawn, swerving between his parents' guests, shouting, "Go, go!" at Tessa who is sprawled on the grass, ignoring her friends. Tessa's on her feet now, sprinting toward the tree—of course she gets there first. Arms above her head, pulling herself up branch by branch, she makes it to the top in what he's sure is record time. He can see her looking down at him, smile wide. Yes, he thinks, I've missed you too.

"I've brought you a lemonade, though you'll have to forgive me, there's no ice."

In the here and now Theo snaps to attention, squinting at Jeremy over his sunglasses.

"You're away with the fairies." Jeremy's smiling, but he has a pinched look of concern.

"I was, rather." Theo feels caught out. Sometimes his memories are so vivid, as if they are playing out in real time around him.

"It's a charming picture, you sitting here in the sun. You're even handsomer in this light."

Theo lets his gaze linger on Jeremy. The present dispels the past, which temporarily fades into the background. Happiness is a warm sensation in his chest, one he must force himself to embrace because for so long he was afraid of feeling anything at all. Numbness was a blessing. Numbness was the goal.

Their relationship happened gradually, then suddenly. A friendship that grew over years, until one day, it became more. Upon him before he'd realized what had happened. Perhaps Theo couldn't have welcomed love any other way.

"You'll never make a dent in your marking if you spend the entire afternoon staring up at that tree."

"You know," Theo tells him, "you can see so much from the top of that tree. Right into Cambridge. You can see the spires of my father's college. Tessa and I used to wave a red flag from the top branches to summon him home for supper. Of course he couldn't really see it, but he always pretended he had."

Jeremy nods. Theo has told him this before.

"We used to race each other to the top."

"I thought we might dine out tonight," says Jeremy, abruptly. "There's a new Italian place in town. I've heard good things."

Theo taps the pile of marking on his lap with his pen, and Jeremy sighs.

"Darling, we have so little time together. We have to make the most of these weekends."

"You're the one traveling all the time." Theo regrets it as soon as he says it. He owes Jeremy so much. He owes him more than snippy asides, at any rate.

"Yes, well. Someone has to pay for all this."

It is a shock to hear Jeremy say it aloud. Normally they dance around Theo's reduced circumstances.

"I'm sorry," says Theo. "I don't want to fight."

Jeremy grimaces, but it takes him a moment to answer. "I shouldn't have said anything."

"Of course you should. I want us to be open with each other."

"You want us to . . ." Jeremy shakes his head. "I worry about you."

"There's no need."

"It feels like you're only half here. I'm not sure being in this house is good for you. Perhaps you ought to sell it. Your mother wouldn't care. In fact, I rather think she'd be happy to see it gone."

"What do you mean? It's not as if we're here often." It's a weekend place, more a holiday home than anything else these days. What's more, it's a place where they can be together—he can't believe Jeremy would want to give that up.

"But is it doing you any good? Being here, surrounded by . . ."

Theo waves this away: this is dangerous territory. No man's land. "Let's not talk about it."

"I realize this is an uncomfortable subject for you. But Tessa is everywhere here. You haven't touched her room. Her raincoat's still hanging on a peg in the downstairs cloakroom, for pity's sake."

Theo shifts against his cushion. "I'm hardly here. We're both so busy. I really ought to spend more time in London. That's where the work is, and like you say, you can't pay for everything—"

"I didn't say that, actually."

"And you're back to the Hague, when—tomorrow or the day after?" Jeremy spends his weeks putting despots on trial. Theo doesn't know how he can stand it, listening to horror week in and week out. We did our bit, he thinks. We saw the bastards hang. Nazi after Nazi, necks snapping. It's a sound he hears in his dreams, the sickening crunch of a neck breaking. Theo has developed a steady rotation of nightmares. Sometimes he is in his Spitfire, observing Barnes' fiery death over and over. Sometimes he sees his sister in a dark room, or he is back at Nuremberg, listening to the testimonies of those who suffered the worst of humanity, his brain painting pictures to match the words.

"I'm in Brussels first for a couple of meetings," Jeremy replies. "You should come with me. Have a city break—we always talk about it. The neighbors are happy to look in on the cats."

Theo shakes away the memory of the hangman's noose. "It's tricky with the university. It's a busy time."

"We could stop off in Paris. Visit your mother."

Theo flinches. "That's not really my idea of a holiday, you know. Look, I *want* to be here—don't you? I certainly don't want to waste what little time we have together sorting . . ." He swallows. Sometimes it hurts to even say her name. ". . . Tessa's things into suitcases."

Theo knows he's being manipulative, turning Jeremy's point around and using it himself.

Jeremy takes a deep breath. "I don't think you'll be at peace until you find out what happened to your sister."

Theo pushes the pile of essays from his lap, and Jasper flees from beneath his chair. No man's land. "I told you, I don't want to talk about this."

"And I don't know how we'll make it when you spend most of your time daydreaming about the past. I am here, Theo. Now. This is our life, and it could be so good if only you'd let it. After everything we witnessed, everything you went through with the arrest, don't you want to make the most of it?"

"Please—"

"It's been a decade. Your sister is dead."

Theo's insides turn ice cold. "Probably dead, but—"

"No, Theo. She is dead."

"But if I accept that, then . . ." Don't cry, he thinks.

"Then what?"

Theo can't answer. He shakes his head, blinking. That he still has tears for his sister, all these years on, takes his breath away.

Jeremy's tone is gentle now. He kneels down next to Theo's chair. "Is it that if you accept her death, you'll have to accept the rest, too? Because I don't think anyone can judge Tessa, not really, for what she may or may not have done in the most desperate of times. She wasn't a Nazi. She wasn't evil to the core. She was trying to survive. That's the strongest human instinct we have."

No, no. Theo will not have this conversation.

"Darling, you must think me the most frightful bore," he says, forcing lightness into his tone and looking around to make sure the neighbors aren't peering over the garden fence before he takes Jeremy's hand.

Jeremy is undeterred. "I want you to see the psychiatrist again. I think it will help you."

For God's sake, thinks Theo. The psychiatrist and his endless bloody theories. But he says, "Of course I will. I promise I'll do better."

He hasn't had a drink in three months. Doesn't that count? Doesn't Jeremy know how much effort that takes? Perhaps he doesn't believe it will last, and he'd be right, because it's never lasted before. "Do you know what, I've changed my mind. Let's eat out tonight."

Jeremy's mouth twitches. He doesn't look convinced. "I'll leave you to your marking, then. So we don't have to rush."

Theo glances at the essays, spread haphazardly across the grass. "I'll do it on the train on Monday morning. It won't take long. These students, they all write the same bloody thing."

The love for teaching will come, he's sure. He just needs to be patient.

"I'll telephone for a table."

Theo nods, fixing his smile at Jeremy's departing back until he hears the back door slam. He looks back at the tree, squinting into the sun, his hand shielding his eyes. Tessa looks back at him.

I know you didn't turn, he thinks. And I don't want to be at peace, if it means letting you go. I just need to get better at hiding it.

Tessa nods. She always understood him better than anyone else.

Part Three

EDIE

London, 2003

Thirty-one

Edie gets off the train at Kew Bridge. It means a longer walk but she likes peering into the big houses that flank the roads in this part of the city, imagining the lives lived within. It's warm out. Edie takes off her headphones and in the moment it takes for her ears to adjust there is just her breath, calm and steady. Then comes the traffic, children playing in a garden somewhere. A plane roars overhead, then another and another. Beautiful Kew, trapped beneath a motorway in the sky.

When she arrives, once she's shown her card to the security guard and left most of her belongings in the cloakroom, she submits her request to the archivist at the main desk. It's still a thrill, all these times on, when the stack of cardboard binders appear in her allotted glass-fronted locker. Today she's come for the personnel files, each folder neatly tied with ribbon or string, a single name typed on the cover. The topic of her PhD is ever-morphing, but she knows it will involve the women of the Special Operations Executive. It takes her back to childhood, when Saturdays meant a day with her gran watching black and white films (as a child, Edie believed the entire world had existed entirely in black and white before her time, until one day, like the scene change in *The Wizard of Oz*, it had simply exploded into technicolor). Her grandmother's favorite film had been *Carve Her Name with Pride*, in which Virginia McKenna as Violette Szabo goes tearing through France on a secret mission, meeting her end in a very neat-looking Ravensbrück. Family lore said Edie's grandfather had been in the French Resistance, though he was just sixteen when war broke out. "This is what it was like," her grandmother would say, nodding at the television, "this was his life"—though she'd also say this when watching *'Allo 'Allo*. Here is Edie, fifteen years on, just as enthralled by these stories, and especially these women swept into extraordinary situations by the war. Edie often wonders if she could put her life on the line for the good of others, deciding that she's glad she doesn't have to make that choice, which even she can admit is a bit of a cop-out.

Edie takes the first file from the stack. Somehow the women agents feel like old friends, although it's hard to get a sense of them from these files, which cover just the basics, maybe a note on recruitment and training, an operational report if she's really lucky. Most of the good stuff, assuming there ever was any, is supposed lost in a mysterious fire at the end of the war. Of course there are books, countless numbers of them now, which read like *Boys' Own* adventure yarns. But Edie wants it all, not just the heroics.

She slides a blue ribbon from the folder. Tessa Armstrong. There are no films about Tessa and she never gets more than a mention in books. It strikes Edie how odd this is, to champion the other thirty-eight women who went behind the lines in France, and leave one out. The first document in the file is a brief summation of Tessa's recruitment interview. She'd been recommended to the service by an unnamed MI6 operative. Simon Joyce, although impressed by her linguistic skills, found her attitude "somewhat chippy," writing, "Miss Armstrong is prone to long fulminations when challenged." Chippy, sure, Edie thinks. Or perhaps she had a healthy disregard for authority like any woman worth her salt in SOE.

Next is a summary of Tessa's training at a list of country houses, and although Tessa appears to have acquitted herself well, many of the instructors resented being asked to train women, thinking it both beneath them and rather pointless. Tessa "performed adequately" in the physical training. She was an excellent shot, security-minded, "rather shrewd," but an "atrocious jumper." Edie can only sympathize, having never felt the urge to throw herself out of a plane either.

The file contains a surprising level of detail. *Strange*, she writes in her notepad, underlining the question, *why?* Tessa had been recommended for the George Cross in 1945 but this was later withdrawn. Why, Edie writes in her notepad, would anyone not want to honor her? Perhaps the family didn't want the attention. Perhaps they wanted to be alone in their grief. There's a handwritten report of a weekend in Manchester, a dummy mission, in Tessa's neat cursive.

I set about acquiring a room. The first boarding house, on Albion Street, I quickly discounted due to the inquisitive nature of the landlady. The next house had what I considered to be inadequate means of escape should my cover be blown. Finally, I accepted a room in a terraced house on Medlock Street. The room is at the rear of the property and on the ground floor, with a window leading onto a small yard, with easy access to other yards on both sides and an alleyway at the rear leading to a main road. The landlady said, without prompt, that she "didn't mind comings and goings as long as I get a quiet life," which I judged to be truthful.

Edie sits back in her chair, smiling, because it's so unusual to have a glimpse into these women's thoughts. They are names on a page, memories recalled by those who knew them, usually men. She feels a connection to Tessa through this—her own words in her own handwriting—much more than she'd experienced when looking at her photograph in the Imperial War Museum. Edie flicks back to the first pages in the file, the basics. Tessa Camille Armstrong, born and raised in Cambridge, educated in Paris. Father was an academic with "questionable" politics, shared by

Tessa. Her mother was French. She had a twin brother, Cambridge educated, a barrister who'd served as a pilot during the war. Nice, thinks Edie. Posh. Tessa had worried about deceiving her brother, according to a scrawled note next to his name. Had she succumbed to her worries and told him, Edie wonders, because plenty of agents must have let the truth slip.

Edie takes out a bundle of A4 sheets from the file, on which someone has noted at the top of the first page TROUBLING VIEWS? And then, underlined to emphasize alarm, IS THIS PERSON A MARXIST????? Edie reads on. The document appears to be an essay from Tessa Armstrong's school days—Edie does the sums on her fingers, calculating that Tessa must have been about sixteen at the time of writing. In it, Armstrong writes:

In the English education system, as evidenced in this very school, children are conditioned to revere authority and take pride in following rules, indoctrinating them with a sense of "false class consciousness" in which respect is due to their "betters" because of the status afforded to them in a capitalist society, as opposed to any deserving attributes they might actually possess.

Edie snorts in surprise. A couple of other researchers look around, one man shaking his head as if personally offended by Edie's lack of decorum. Edie clamps her lips together and reads on:

Like Marx, Gramsci believed that education could in fact be a useful tool of change . . .

A thoroughly middle-class grammar-school girl (at least, so it seems from Tessa's personnel file) quoting Gramsci—Edie likes Tessa already. At the bottom of the essay Tessa's teacher has written in large letters See me at once, Armstrong. I wonder how much trouble she got into, Edie thinks, stifling another laugh—clearly enough for the school to keep the essay on file and offer it up to the authorities as evidence of Tessa's troublesome left-wing views.

At the back of the file Edie finds four typed pages of messages sent to

Baker Street from Tessa, via a wireless operator code-named PHOTO. Genevieve, Tessa's own Baker Street code name, is printed at the top, and beneath is the same message sent several times over the course of a day. "LUNA MALA EST." Someone has drawn a large question mark in red ink at the top of the page. Luna Mala Est, she thinks, The Moon Is Bad. She stares at the message, as if it will help decipher it. It must refer to a drop—perhaps they had to cancel it because of bad weather? Edie makes a note of the date, hoping she'll be able to line it up with an aborted operation. But she keeps looking back at the page. It's an awful lot of transmissions. The wireless operator had put himself in enormous danger with such frequent repetitions—whatever it was, it must have been urgent. Edie taps her pencil against her notepad. A good researcher, her tutor Charlotte says, always detects a scent. As she puts the messages back into the file, a slip of paper falls out onto the table. It is rough around the edges, as if it had been torn from a notebook. On it, Tessa has signed the name Marianne Bonaly over and over in blue ink, clearly trying to get it right, trying to make it stick. In the bottom right-hand corner is a fingerprint, lightly smudged.

Edie holds the paper up to the electric light. There you are, she thinks. Hello, Tessa.

The problem, she discovers, is that although many agents and operatives are still alive, none of them wants to speak to her. *I'm not allowed to talk about that* is the popular refrain, and despite Edie's urgings—the SOE files have been opened! It's been in all the newspapers! Not to mention the countless books already in existence!—no one is convinced. Telephones are slammed down. Letters and emails go unanswered. *Please don't contact me again*, whisper former operatives—to which Edie wants to say, but you did something incredible, you served your country, take some credit! But no one wants to hear it. What do they think will happen if they speak?

What's been drilled into them over the years to make them so worried? Or is it just about having a secret and not wanting to share it?

In her tutor's office one day, she bemoans her lack of progress. If no one will speak to her she'll have to change her subject; after all, a thesis like this—written relatively close in time to the events in question—cannot be written on secondary sources alone. Edie needs personal testimony. She wants to ask her questions, her way.

"Do you think it's because, you know . . ." says Edie.

Charlotte looks at her quizzically. "Because what?"

"I worry that I'm not from the right background," she says. "I think they can hear it in my voice."

Her tutor frowns. "A class thing?"

"Yeah."

"You have a place on a prestigious PhD program, Edie. You need to own it. There's a good reason why you're the one asking these questions."

And how do I do that, Edie thinks, how do I *own* it? Are there written instructions? Given the crispness of Charlotte's accent, Edie's sure it's not something she's ever had to grapple with.

"But I understand. It's a closed world—you need an in," Charlotte says.

"I do, but the problem is I don't know anyone."

Charlotte has a brainwave—a colleague in the history department has a friend who is married to a civil servant whose mother did *something* for the SOE, she's sure of it. Perhaps she might be willing to speak? Edie blinks, trying to absorb the link from one person to another.

"How exciting," she says. "To have a relative involved in this."

The older woman smiles. "If they're a certain type of person of a certain age, and attended a certain type of school, you can be sure their parents either did *something* important during the war, or knew *someone*. The double-barreled surnames. They mingle with one another."

You've just proved my point, thinks Edie.

Charlotte taps out an email on her computer and promises to keep in touch.

Edie goes to the library, feeling invigorated yet stalled, because how long will it take? A group of women she vaguely knows from her program are at a table, books out in front of them, notes strewn everywhere. They all did their master's degrees at the university together. She is the interloper.

"Hey," says one, vaguely.

"Do you mind me sitting here?" Edie feels self-conscious. If they wanted her here, they would have invited her in the first place. "I mean, I don't have to. If you guys are really getting into it, I wouldn't want to interrupt your flow, or anything."

"Sure," says another, "I think we're leaving soon anyway."

They clear her a space and Edie takes out her own notes, but it's hard to concentrate. The others have reached saturation point with their research that day and are whispering, gossiping about the undergraduates in the seminars they lead, two lecturers they're sure are having an affair, a film they're going to see that evening.

"Oh, that looks great," says Edie. "I want to see that."

They nod and smile. "We'll let you know what it's like," says one.

With a sigh, Edie starts making preparatory notes for the next day, a meeting she's managed to arrange with an ex-SOE staffer—a Mrs. Andrews—the only one, in fact, who's agreed to meet her. She lists questions, abstract thoughts—trying to work out where she wants the interview to take her, what exactly it is she wants to know.

The Special Forces Club looks like every other Knightsbridge mansion block, but what else would you expect for a club for spies, for people used to slipping unnoticed in between the folds of life? Inside, a man in a suit directs her to leave her jacket in a cloakroom marked "Cloaks and Daggers."

"That's clever," she says. The man's expression suggests every person who walks into that foyer says the same thing.

"Mrs. Andrews is in the lounge," he says, pointing to a room off the lobby, where smart velvet armchairs are arranged around a grand fireplace. Mrs. Andrews is in a chair facing the open doorway, so she's had a view of Edie since she stepped into the building. She is a formidable-looking woman, with grey hair swept up into an immovable style that makes Edie think of Margaret Thatcher.

Edie holds her hand out and Mrs. Andrews stares at it before submitting, briefly, to the most minimal of contact, a graze of fingers, the lightest touch.

"Thank you so much for agreeing to meet with me," Edie says, taking her notepad and pen from her bag. "As you know, I'm looking into—"

"I'm hungry, aren't you?" the old woman says. "I thought we'd have lunch."

"Yes, OK, lovely," Edie says, thinking of the egg sandwich and cheese and onion crisps she'd devoured less than twenty minutes earlier. "Is there a dining room . . . ?"

"Of course there's a dining room, it's a club. But before we go up, I want to ask you something. Have you read the novel *Agent Femme*?"

This wrong-foots Edie. Obviously she's read it, everyone has. It's a bestseller.

Mrs. Andrews nods. "Thought so. It seems to have brought so many of you out of the woodwork. Tell me, then, what did you think of it?"

Edie hesitates, because she can't read Mrs. Andrews' expression. She might have consulted on the novel. There might be a character based on her. "Well, OK," Edie says, holding up her hands in submission. "On the surface, it's a faithful retelling of the SOE story—the French section, at any rate. But look, I hope this isn't too controversial, but I thought it was pretty terrible. I appreciate it was trying to explore the sexist treatment of women by Whitehall—"

"Oh, that occurred at every level in this game, I think you'll find."

"Right, and yet it still ended up being completely misogynistic in its portrayal of the central characters."

There's a pause. A frown. "Go on," Mrs. Andrews says.

"I mean, the women agents spend half the book in tears, needing to be rescued by their male colleagues, and the other half getting everyone killed through sheer idiocy."

Edie's not sure if she passes the test or if Mrs. Andrews decides the topic isn't worth pursuing. Perhaps she shouldn't have mentioned misogyny; perhaps Mrs. Andrews didn't see it that way. Sometimes Edie thinks her greatest skill lies in doubting herself. Mrs. Andrews gestures for her to lead the way upstairs to the dining room, which is at the top of a winding staircase. On the walls are faces Edie felt she knew well, until encountering them in the presence of someone who actually did.

"Here's Violette," Mrs. Andrews is saying. "Diana, Noor, France Antelme . . ."

They are not characters in a novel, they are people who did extraordinary things, brave things. Some lived, and some didn't. At the top of the wall, hung so high it is hard to see, is the familiar sepia photograph of Tessa Armstrong.

The dining room is empty save for a trio of Americans, the man at the center of the group in a blue blazer and beret, regaling them with stories from the war. Edie can see this is a place where members feel safe in their history. Perhaps they think you can only understand if you were there, she thinks. Perhaps this is why no one wants to speak to me; I'm an outsider.

"We'll have the fish," Mrs. Andrews says to the waiter, adding in a stage whisper to Edie, "It's the only thing worth having. She's a student," she continues more loudly, "so I suppose I'm expected to pay."

Edie is asking the waiter for a glass of water and shaking her head at Mrs. Andrews, all at the same time. "No, no," she says, quickly. "I wouldn't dream of making you pay." In her head, she mentally trawls through the contents of her purse, the number of figures behind the minus sign on her bank statement.

"You should probably ask your questions," says Mrs. Andrews, apparently happy to move on, having settled that pressing matter. "Get them out of the way before the food turns up. I don't care to talk when I'm eating."

Edie smiles gratefully at the waiter as he sets down her glass of water. "I'd love to hear about your work in the Baker Street signals room. It must have been fascinating to receive word from the agents abroad."

Edie phrases the question lightly, but the change in Mrs. Andrews' demeanor is instantaneous. "I'm not allowed to talk about that," she says, glancing around the room.

"No, it's all right. It's all public now," Edie says, nodding encouragingly.

Mrs. Andrews doesn't look convinced, but she says, "Besides, I wasn't the first to receive the messages, they went to the Home Station to be decoded first."

"Is that MI6?"

"Who told you that?"

Edie fixes her face with what she hopes is a patient smile. "It's in several books. Don't worry, it's not a secret. But look, I'm happy to move on. Are there any particular messages you remember receiving?"

"Well, not exactly. You see I wasn't supposed to read them, just make sure they got in front of the right people." The older woman appears to relent a little, and says, "I suppose it was a bit of a thrill, when the little machine whirred into life as a message came through. Every operative out in the field had a set time they were supposed to make contact and sometimes if they were very late, and it could be days, you'd feel an enormous sense of relief when their call-sign—their code name—appeared on the board." The waiter appears and places two plates in front of them. Rainbow trout, new potatoes and steamed vegetables.

"Did you get to know the agents before they left for Europe?" asks Edie.

"No, never. They didn't come to Baker Street. It was all kept very separate for security reasons. I'll have to stop now," she says, glancing down at her food.

"So you never met Tessa Armstrong?"

Mrs. Andrews draws a sharp breath. "No, I never met her."

"But you took down messages from her?"

"Via others, I suppose. Yes. She was a courier, so she wouldn't send messages herself."

Edie pulls a sheet of paper from her notebook, a photocopy of the messages she'd found in Tessa's file, "The Moon Is Bad." "I'm so interested in Tessa. I mean, there's hardly anything written about her and yet her file contained some really interesting information, like this, and—"

"I don't know why you're asking me about her." Mrs. Andrews looks crossly at her meal, clearly keen to eat. "I've told you, I never met her and I don't know anything about it."

"About what?"

The woman emits a tiny snort of frustration. "I'm not saying anything. I've told you, I'm not allowed to talk about it."

"Did something happen to Tessa?" persists Edie, aware she is testing her interviewee's patience.

"I should imagine plenty of things happened to her, but I've no idea what they were."

Edie sits with this for a moment. "OK, fair enough. But look, going back to this message, Luna Mala Est. It means 'The Moon Is Bad.'"

"I know what it means."

Edie is nodding, and trying to smile. "I'm interested in the reception a message like this would have got in the signals room. Would it, along with the frequency of the transmissions—I mean, the wireless operator was taking a hell of a risk—but what I'm asking is, would this have triggered alarm in the signals room, and if so, what would have happened? Do you remember these transmissions arriving?"

Mrs. Andrews shakes her head. "I wouldn't have been a part of it. I just passed things on."

Edie tries a different approach. "Right, OK, OK. But would it be typical for operatives in the field to send messages like this as a warning?"

Mrs. Andrews pops a tidy forkful of fish into her mouth and chews deliberately. Edie can't let it go. "It's just the frequency makes it seem like a warning, don't you think?"

Mrs. Andrews, seeming to come to a decision, puts her cutlery back down. "Armstrong was clever, I'll give her that. You can see it in her photograph—look at her eyes. There was a row, I believe, when they hung it here, only Miss Jones insisted. She's got a lot of sway, Miss Jones, even now."

Edie is trying to keep up, scrawling notes on her pad as her own lunch cools on the table. "Is that Emmeline Jones?"

Mrs. Andrews nods.

"Why would people object to Tessa's portrait going up on the wall?"

"I don't know much about it. Only what I've heard."

"Only, it feels like you're hinting at something."

Mrs. Andrews reddens. "Does it? Perhaps you're reading too much into it."

"Am I?"

"Or perhaps it's just not my story to tell. You should ask that brother of hers."

"Tessa's brother?" Edie flicks through her notepad. "That's . . . Theo Armstrong?"

"That's the one. A bad sort, if you ask me. At least, that's what people said. He was up to his neck in it."

"In what?"

Mrs. Andrews smiles as she takes up her knife and fork again. Edie's half convinced she's enjoying this. "I told you, I've no idea."

Thirty-two

Edie rushes home in time to meet her friend Hellie, down from Leeds to do her own research in the Imperial War Museum. Hellie's subject involves the French Resistance, and they often find themselves texting each other helpful tidbits of information. They meet at Elephant and Castle Tube station, Edie hugging Hellie harder than she means to because, God, she's missed her mates.

Within ten minutes of Edie slotting her key into her front door, they are shimmying around the kitchen to The White Stripes, chicken browning in a pan on the hob. In the six months Edie has lived in this terraced house, she's probably spoken to her housemates about ten times, save for "hello" and "good night" which don't count because those are things you have to say. A postgraduate degree is a lonely business, her tutor had warned her, and she's right, but this is London and Edie had assumed she'd meet people, because that's how it is in London, isn't it? Outsiders forging their own paths, together.

"I think the brother's in the bloody phone book," says Edie, pausing her shimmying to run her fingers down the telephone directory listings until she comes to Armstrong, TD—which could be him. She's cleared a small space on the kitchen table in between dirty cups and Saturday supplements, even though it's a Wednesday.

Hellie spins around, holding a wooden spoon in the air. "Obviously you have to call him."

"Obviously," says Edie. "Should I, though? I mean, it feels a bit intrusive to just ring an old man out of the blue."

"I bet you a tenner he'll be happy to chat. These old chaps love banging on about what they did in the war."

"What his sister did," Edie corrects.

"That too." Hellie stops and looks around, suddenly concerned. "It's so quiet here, Edie. Where are your housemates?"

"At work probably." Edie doesn't want to admit that they barely know one another. "This is nice though, isn't it? Like old times."

She stands up to turn the chicken in the pan and adds the bacon. Hellie gives her arm a squeeze. "Good old kitchen disco."

Edie takes a bottle of wine from the fridge and pours two glasses. "Too right."

"So, this old fella, this Theo . . ." says Hellie. "You *are* going to call him, right? I mean, you couldn't stop talking about his sister. Seems like there's something there?"

"Tessa. There's something a bit feisty about her, on paper at least. She has a real spark. She's barely mentioned in any of my SOE books though. And the woman I spoke to at the Special Forces Club seemed to be implying there was something iffy about her."

"So call him. Maybe you'll find out what happened."

The next morning, Edie picks up the phone and dials.

"Hello?" says a voice. It sounds raspy and old. It makes her think of red wine and cigarettes.

"Hello," she says back. A tangible link, she thinks, that's what it is.

Theo Armstrong has a front door painted a cerulean blue that, on this particular day, matches the sky. Edie's never been to Finsbury Park before, with its wide artery road running through the center, the greengrocers and Afro-Caribbean haircare shops.

Theo Armstrong lives in the downstairs flat of a neat Edwardian house. Pots of earth sit by the doorstep, giving the house an air of mild neglect. Steeling herself to knock, Edie runs through the things she's learned about him in the past week, which are few. Before he retired, he'd been a lecturer at a north London university, no longer a barrister as was suggested in Tessa's wartime file. He appears to have published little during his academic career, and it is a shock when Edie finds his name listed as a staff member at the Nuremberg trials.

Edie takes a deep breath and knocks on the door. He's probably expecting a serious, cerebral academic, which Edie is sure she is not. The door opens and there he is, a shock of grey hair, deep lines around his eyes. He's looking at her in surprise, as if he hadn't heard her knock and wasn't expecting to find her there.

"Hello," she says. "I hope I'm not early."

There's no trace of warmth or welcome on his face at all. He looks downcast, in fact. "You're the first," he says. "The first researcher to get in touch, I mean, since they opened the files."

These words are a gift to any PhD student. She's smiling but it's starting to feel pinched and not a little bit awkward, because he's still looking at her in that strange, sad way. He's debating whether or not to let me in, she thinks; he's going to slam the door in my face. Eventually one side of his brain claims victory, and he stands back and gestures for her to come inside. The house is stark, with white floors, walls and ceilings, but in between are bursts of color. Tight-weave rugs on the floors; paintings, both abstract and surreal, on the walls.

"I like your paintings," she says.

"They're just cheap prints and posters." There is a long pause. "I should offer you a cup of tea. You'll have one, I expect?"

She says yes, and tries to make herself comfortable on a sofa, although she's feeling anything but. A few art books are arranged on the coffee table—Lee Miller, Robert Mapplethorpe, Sonia Delaunay—but the dresser is the place for family photographs and yes, there she is. Tessa and Theo as children, sitting in the branches of a large tree. Tessa dressed up for a party with the feathered wings of an angel strapped to her back and a crown on her head.

Theo returns with a tray of tea and follows her line of sight to the photographs, tensing slightly. Edie notices his slight limp as he walks.

"You have a lovely flat," she says, wincing at her unoriginality.

Theo looks about, as if unimpressed. "It'll do, I suppose. I've been here a long time."

Theo is stirring milk into the tea and offering her sugar, to which she shakes her head. To her surprise, he takes a Dictaphone from his pocket, flicks "record," and puts it on the coffee table in front of her. "I feel it best," he says.

Edie trails a pen down her list of questions. Faced with a Dictaphone and Theo's stern expression, they suddenly seem entirely inadequate.

"Do you intend to focus the entirety of your thesis on my sister? I don't recall the specifics."

"No, it's more to do with how women like your sister subverted prescribed gender roles. I don't know if you're familiar with the idea of gender performativity . . ."

Theo shrugs. "Not my field."

"No, well. OK."

"And what brought you to this subject? You're a little young, aren't you, to be bothered by the war?"

"Well, I don't see it as being that long ago—I mean, relatively speaking it isn't. But my grandad was in the French Resistance, and—"

"Was he really, or did he just say he was?" He sniffs. "Because every Frenchman and his dog took part in the Resistance, it seems, and I can assure you that wasn't the case."

This wrong-foots Edie. Why is she letting him interview her? "Well, I'm not sure. It's what was said. We found some papers in the attic after he died and . . . well, he found it difficult to talk about, actually."

"Did he, indeed?"

"Yes. He was a socialist. A trade unionist. He always stood up for people, always wanted to help."

She can spy him softening, a hint of a smile—or is it guilt?—crossing his features. "Yes, well . . ." He coughs into his fist. "Good man."

"But to get back to the matter in hand. I wrote my MA thesis on women in the Resistance, which led me on to female agents of the Special Operations Executive. Although, I've always had a fascination. *Carve Her Name with Pride . . .*"

He sniffs, again. "A Hollywood movie."

"Yes. Well, no, it was a British film. I mean to be honest, I'm not even sure I'll be able to feature Tess . . . your sister . . ."

"Her name was Tessa."

"Right, yes, sorry. Tessa." Christ alive, get a hold of yourself, she thinks. "There's so little written about her."

"So, you thought you'd get there first and fill in the gaps?"

"I'd like to. People should know what she did."

"I beg your pardon?"

Edie wants to shrink back into the cushions. He looks momentarily furious. "I think what these women did was extraordinary, and they should be commemorated accordingly. And that goes for your sister, too."

He sits back in his chair, crossing his legs. He's wearing leather slippers, which look worn but expensive. "But who are you to decide that? What gives you the right to say what is revealed and what stays hidden?"

Edie frowns. "Why should anything be hidden?" Perhaps he doesn't want to be overshadowed.

He purses his lips. He reminds her of her father just before he properly loses his rag.

"It's not my intention to upset you," she says.

Then Theo sighs with his whole body. Edie watches as it ripples through him. Because she doesn't know where to put her gaze, she pretends again to admire the art on the walls, especially the pieces by people with names she recognizes from Tate Modern. But then she wonders where the value is in that, in recognition without appraisal. Theo makes her jump by leaning forward and topping up her tea, even though she's probably only had a mouthful.

"I'm actually in favor of transparency, of accountability—it's something of a matter of principle to me," he says, his voice softening. "But it's hard, when it's so close to home. We were twins, did you know that?"

Edie takes a sip of tea and nods. "Did you know she'd gone to France?"

"Not till after, no, I was away in the RAF. My parents knew something, possibly more than they let on." He's speaking slowly, as if considering the ramifications of each individual word. "She'd never have admitted it to me."

Edie starts scribbling down notes in her pad but stops when she sees how uneasy it makes him. "What makes you say that?"

"Well, I'd told her not to do anything stupid, for a start."

"Do you think that's why she went to France? To be contrary?"

Theo sits back in his chair, clearly pained by the question. "No, I think she was bored. Tessa was frightfully clever, and she deserved to be more than someone's secretary. She knew it too, knew that she could be of more use. I wish I'd seen that—or, I think I did, actually. So I suppose what I'm saying is, I wish I'd taken it seriously." He clears his throat. "I don't mean to be obtuse, but I'm trying to work out what you know."

"I don't know anything."

"But you've been asking around, haven't you? I think you've set your sights on Tessa for a reason."

He looks so worried. Edie wants to put her things back in her bag and leave him alone to enjoy his cheap art and expensive slippers. "No one's said anything," she says.

He raises an eyebrow. "No one?"

Edie hesitates. "There was one woman," she says, and he sighs. "But she didn't really tell me anything. I don't think she knew anything, save for gossip and hearsay, and she was too scared of getting into trouble to take a punt on that. She was snippy from the off, but when I mentioned your sister's name, she became evasive. Cross, too."

He appears to ponder this for a moment, then says, "You must think I'm the most frightful hypocrite. All that talk about principles."

Edie opens her mouth and closes it again. She's not sure they're having the same conversation. "I suppose I'm curious as to why Tessa's been overlooked."

Theo nods at this. He looks so tired, as if he hasn't had a good night's sleep in years. Then he takes a deep breath and says, "The reason for the vagueness surrounding Tessa's mission in particular, and for the lack of recognition, is because anything else would have been terribly embarrassing for the government. It was an enormous thing, sending women behind the lines like that. The press were highly critical when it came out."

She is making notes now whether he likes it or not. "What exactly would have been an embarrassment to the government?"

"Even though it was never heard in court, even though no one was ever granted the opportunity to challenge the evidence, as far as the British government is concerned, my sister was a traitor."

Edie can almost hear her heart beating in the silence following his statement.

Slowly she looks up. "But . . . how could something like that have remained a secret?"

He shoots her a thin-lipped smile. "Quite easily, it turns out. But then it was in a lot of very important people's interests to keep it quiet, and believe me, they went to enormous lengths to ensure it did. Her innocence—or guilt—didn't seem to matter; the notion of a British woman turning against her country was so beyond the pale, so scandalous—and it was already a scandal, dropping women behind enemy lines—that they didn't even pause to consider the possibility of my sister's innocence. So yes, it was buried to protect the people who employed her with no regard for Tessa and her sacrifice in the service of her country. My sister died for them, and this is how they repaid her."

Thirty-three

Edie finds herself growing protective of Tessa. It goes one of two ways in her research interviews: a few of her subjects can't denounce Tessa fast enough, finally unleashed from the shackles of the past by Edie's knowledge of the accusation, but the rest won't say anything at all, a steely silence lingering over any remaining proceedings. In time, Edie learns to wait until the end of each interview to mention Tessa. She knows something is amiss. None of those who accuse Tessa have any details; it's all surface, it's "the look in Tessa's eyes," as if this alone is a characteristic worthy of suspicion.

Two weeks after her meeting with Theo in his flat, Edie takes the train to Cambridge and a cab out to "the sticks," as Theo calls it on the telephone, the sort of neighborhood that makes her wish she'd dressed better. He opens the door and beckons her into the house, which looks smart from the outside but has a worn, stale feel inside. In the sitting room, he doesn't offer her a seat, nor does he take one for himself. They stand at opposing ends of the room. It is uncomfortable, the allegations against his sister in the air between them.

"Is this where you grew up? It's lovely," she says, trying to relax the mood. "Like an academic's house in a film."

He laughs, which breaks the tension. "A cliché, you mean. But yes, I did grow up here, happily so. My mother left it to me when she died. I probably should have sold it. Christ knows I needed the money."

She decides to take charge, sitting down in an armchair which looks to have seen fifty years of sunlight and cats' claws.

Theo is looking thoughtful. "It's a family home, really, a place for children to grow up and move on from. But when it came to it, I couldn't part with it. I've found myself spending more time here recently rather than in London, and actually, I'm glad to have it. I'm making myself sound like a miserable old sod but I'm not at all, I assure you." He changes position, moving his weight from one foot to another. "I am, however, being terribly rude. Let me get you a drink." Theo has visibly relaxed, and Edie is glad it hasn't taken long for him to drop his guard this time.

He leads her into the garden, although Edie is desperate to explore the house, which seems, at first sight, to be a warren of corridors and small rooms. There are shelves dotted with ornaments and trinkets, and almost everything is lightly covered in dust and cobwebs—less a film set and more something out of Dickens. It's the sort of house she always wished she resided in as a child, although now she's older she can see that the 1960s semi her family lived in had a character of its own. Straight lines and modernity, and not enough storage. A new type of life for the working class.

They sit on a bench beneath an enormous oak tree and drink glasses of lemonade. The garden slopes down toward the river, where a small wooden boat bobs alongside a jetty. A woman in a blue rubber cap swims past in a rhythmic breaststroke, her eyes focused firmly ahead, seemingly oblivious to her two-person audience.

"It's so peaceful here," says Edie. "What an amazing place to grow up."

"There'll be fifty punts full of students along in a minute, don't you worry."

"Do you live alone?" she says, between sips of bitter lemonade. It is like an itch she cannot help but scratch, the desire to know more, to intrude.

"I do now, yes. I lived with a very nice man called Jeremy for a long time, but he died last year." Theo hesitates, looking out over the water. "He lived here with the cats and I lived in London, and of course it had to be that way for a while, but it worked for us."

"Had to be that way because it was illegal?" It might be legal now, she thinks, but Edie is a child of Section 28. No promotion or teaching of homosexuality in schools, by government decree. As such, she'd grown up thinking no one at her school was gay, surely a statistical impossibility.

Theo nods. "As far as the outside world was concerned, Jeremy was my tenant, nothing more."

"I'm sorry," she says, but he dismisses her sympathy.

"What about you? Was that your boyfriend who answered the phone?"

Edie feels oddly embarrassed. "No, one of my housemates. I don't really know them, it's not that sort of house."

"No? That's a shame."

"I did my undergrad and my MA up north. Most of my friends are still there. I hardly know anyone in London. Sometimes I think I should have stayed where I was. Better the devil and all that."

"A woman who is tired of London . . ." he begins and then stops himself. "God, I'm old," he says, but he is laughing, which makes Edie think it's OK to do the same. "You just haven't found your place there yet. Sometimes we can't see the woods for the trees."

"Perhaps that's it."

Eventually he takes her back inside. Stalling, taking time to point out paintings, his father's study, his mother's writing table. He doesn't want to begin whatever this is. He offers innocuous queries about her upbringing, asks more about her housemates, which she knows she's invited through her own nosiness.

When he runs out of steam, he takes her up to a large attic bedroom.

There are leather trunks and piles of crates and cardboard boxes. "Well, this is Tessa," he says.

Tessa, packed away and caked in dust and spider skins. He opens the nearest trunk, full of neatly folded clothes wrapped in tissue paper. "I imagine people would wear these now. Fashion is a funny thing."

His hands are shaking. It brings on a lump in her throat. It is the neatness of the packing, despite the cobwebs. It is the very fact that it remains, after all this time.

Another box is filled with notebooks and postcards, yet another with Labour Party leaflets. Theo draws out a plastic folder. "Here, you'll be interested in this. These are some of her letters to me. Of course, the ones written after May 1943 are invented, by which I mean she wrote them before she left for France. I always wondered why they seemed so odd. Why she never commented on anything outside of her own—pretend, it turns out—experiences and never on anything I'd written, especially after I was injured. I just reasoned my letters weren't getting through. In hindsight it's absurd how easily I explained away things that didn't make sense."

He shows her a pile of books, well read, spines broken, the pages permanently fanned out.

"She had good taste," says Edie.

"Tessa was a ferocious reader. She'd read a book a day during the summer vac."

Edie is flicking through a battered first edition of *Persephone* by Ephra Laurent. The margins are annotated with notes and drawings. "Wow. Did you know this is signed?"

"Is it?" He takes it from her, turning it over in his hands. "Tessa moved in quite interesting circles in Paris."

"It must be worth a fortune." Edie looks up. "Not that I'm suggesting you sell it."

"She was involved with a friend of his, Luc Langlois."

"The painter? There was an exhibition of his work at the Whitechapel Gallery last year."

"Yes, I remember. I couldn't bring myself to go. Stupid, really. I met him a few times, at the end of the war. He had a show in London then, too, inspired by Tess. I did go to that one." He stares down at the book, lost in thought.

"Have you kept everything?" she says.

"My mother did. My father died in the late '40s. I think it was too much for her to contemplate, first Tessa and then Dad. Eventually she moved to Paris and left it all behind, which was probably easier for her, to be honest."

"What about you?"

"I wasn't in a brilliant state of mind after the war." Theo takes a deep breath. "When we took over the house . . . I didn't come up here for a long time, I couldn't. Jeremy didn't think it was healthy being here but . . . I couldn't let go." As he speaks, he presses his hand against the neat pile of clothes, wrapped in white paper.

Edie kneels down next to him. "If this is too hard . . ." she says. Her thesis isn't even about Tessa; all she's doing is torturing an old man in his grief.

"Are you still speaking to people about her?" he says.

"A few. Most won't entertain the subject."

"And those who do?"

Edie huffs out a breath, which makes him laugh.

"I see. Yes. One would think the anger would dissipate after all this time but it doesn't, it hardens. In some ways that's why I keep all this. This is my Tessa, *mine*. Ah, she'd hate that—*my Tessa*. One thing I've learned is that the human brain has an enormous capacity for self-protection. It cloaks itself, only allowing what it can tolerate to seep in. Sorry, you must think I'm spouting the most incredible nonsense."

"When you say, 'my Tessa,' do you mean as opposed to the courier Tessa, to Marianne?"

He shakes his head thoughtfully. "I'd say I didn't know Marianne, but what I mean is I don't feel as if I really knew Tessa toward the end. I'd call it a change but it was deeper than that—it had to be with a relationship as close as ours. It was hard for me when she took off to Paris for university, but we moved on, we got over it, we visited one another. We wrote an unfathomable number of letters. Then in her final year, I don't know—it's difficult to explain, but everything changed. She distanced herself from me, deliberately. She closed herself off. It felt as if she wanted to hide a part of herself from me. Even the way she spoke changed."

"How do you mean?"

"The flat, controlled reactions. The guardedness. It was only when I began to recognize the same behavior in myself—and believe me, it took decades for that to happen—only then did I realize."

"Realize what?"

"She was traumatized. Something terrible happened to my sister. It took our understanding of how trauma affects the brain many years to catch up with my symptoms. It came far too late for Tessa."

Edie puts the Ephra Laurent book back in its cardboard box. "What happened to traumatize her?"

"I have absolutely no idea. She never told me."

She hesitates, then takes the plunge. "Theo, do you think Tessa was a traitor?"

He closes his eyes, briefly. "No, I never have."

"Never?"

"No."

"Then why do other people believe it?"

"I'd imagine because there's evidence to support that view."

"What evidence?"

"Well, I was rather hoping you might be able to find that out for me."

He makes her lunch, a Greek feta salad bathed in a dressing he whips together in a small ceramic bowl. They eat on the terrace, as punts of students float past on the river below. In the garden there are borders of wallflowers and box hedging sculpted into ornate shapes. They tread carefully with their words. He asks about her family; she asks about his teaching career.

"My family are just really normal," she says.

He scoffs. "There's no such thing."

"No?"

"There's a spectrum, certainly, but all families are complex."

"Do you mean a bit nutty? Because I'd agree with that. They probably are boring, though."

"See, what people don't realize is that boring is good." She raises her eyebrows, and he says, "Trust me, you don't want to live in interesting times. That's famously a euphemism for bloody awful."

"In Tessa's file it said you were a barrister. What made you give up practicing law?" she asks, sipping her lemonade. She's surprised to see his expression change as he looks over at the river, wringing his hands.

"Well," he says, eventually. "I had a brush with the law, and it made the whole thing quite tricky."

Edie waits for him to go on, but he doesn't. Instead, they speak about the Nuremberg trials: it says quite a lot about the strangeness of their meeting that this is considered the easier topic of conversation. They make no further mention of the cardboard boxes upstairs, the signed books and the life cut short, until they've finished their food.

"I have to ask you something," he says. "If you only came upon these suspicions about Tessa as your research went on, why were you so interested in her in the first place?"

Edie is aware that she is choosing her words carefully. It must be catching.

"This is going to sound strange, but it was two things: the essay she wrote at school, and her inky fingerprint on the paper where she practiced her new signature. It felt like she was right there, and I didn't get that from the other files. And, of course, the wireless messages. Of all the personnel files, hers was the only one containing the actual voice of the person it represented."

Theo puts down his glass, squinting against the sun. "What wireless messages?"

He looks so confused that Edie goes to fetch her folder from the hallway. She hands him the photocopied messages.

"Luna Mala Est," he says, under his breath.

"It means 'The Moon Is Bad.' Have you never seen this before?"

Theo's eyes stay on the paper. "No, I haven't." He laughs, although the sound doesn't match the expression on his face. "Latin, that's so very Tessa."

"I thought you'd seen her file when it was being cleared for release?"

A pause. "I did."

Edie shrugs. "I suppose it's only one sheet. Easy to overlook. Perhaps it was stuck to another piece of paper, or tucked inside . . ."

Theo seems affronted. "I can assure you I was meticulous in my study of the contents of her file. I didn't miss a thing."

There is another brief silence. "Are you saying someone put this in her file after it was cleared?"

"Evidently," he replies, "as it wasn't there and now it is."

"But who, and why?"

"I've no idea," he says. She can almost see thoughts forming behind his eyes. Forming before being discarded, re-forming, being reconsidered. "But I know someone who might."

The house is Arts and Crafts in style, surrounded by neat lawns and box hedging. Edie cannot help but exclaim, "Wow!" as Theo parks the car on the gravel drive.

"Michael's done very well for himself," he says.

"I can't believe you know him. I mean, I never would have guessed. *Agent Femme* is such a . . ."

His eyebrows rise. "Yes?"

Edie bites her lip, unsure if she's about to commit a terrible faux pas. "Everyone I've interviewed absolutely loathes that novel," she says, quickly.

"Really?" Theo is smiling, and for the first time looks as if he means it. "What do you think of it?"

"I agree with them. I mean, the female characters are barely capable of making it through a day without getting someone killed, and most of them are only involved in the war in the first place to find a husband, which seems obscenely insulting to the real female agents." Edie can't resist asking the question. "Why, what do you think?"

He puts his hands over his mouth, as if he's about to say something he shouldn't. "I think it's the most god-awful trash. But look, it bought him this house, it delivered him a very nice life, I should think."

Edie makes a show of looking out of the car window. "No kidding. Maybe I should write novels. How do you know him?"

"From way back: school, university, then the Intelligence Service for a short while." She notices that Theo closes his eyes, just briefly. "It almost felt like he was following me, but then I imagine he'd say the same about me."

A gardener is attempting to tame a trailing rose against the front of the house.

"Why do you think he'll know about Tessa's file?" she says.

"Michael always took an interest in my sister. He recruited her in the first place. I sometimes wonder if the book is his way of atoning for what happened." Clearly sensing Edie's skepticism, he says, "All those women in need of rescue, and then actually *being rescued*. Whenever they get into trouble or make a mistake . . ."

"Which they frequently do."

"Indeed, but there's always a man—and that man is undoubtedly Michael, ready to save the day—to save *them*. It's Michael saving Tessa, again and again. I think he feels very badly about what happened, and so he should. But look, why don't we ask him? It'll be an interesting experience at the very least."

"Why do you say that?"

"Because I haven't spoken to him in decades."

A woman comes to the door. Her hair is cut into a neat bob and kept in place with a padded velvet headband. "Yes?" she says, looking them both up and down.

"Is Michael—" Theo begins, but the woman has already set off down a hallway carpeted in a plush cream, calling, "Mike, Mike, the door!"

Theo moves from one foot to the other.

"We can always get back in the car," says Edie.

He shakes his head. "It's in motion."

A man with grey hair and small round glasses perched on his nose appears at the end of the hallway. "Good God," he says, in a plummy, not quite real voice, pressing his fingers to his lips.

"Hello, Michael," says Theo. Edie sees the effort it takes for him to step over the threshold.

Michael leads them into a sitting room, decorated in the same off-white as the hallway. It reminds Edie of her mum's *Country Living* magazines. She'd mentally borrow from the photographs—that rug, that Knole sofa, that lamp—concocting a child's vision of the perfect grown-up abode, and now she is sitting in it.

"You have a lovely home," she says, in case either of them can read her thoughts.

"And who is this?" says Michael to Theo, which incenses her because has she not just that minute demonstrated she has a voice of her own? He has an annoying habit, she notices, of tilting his head forward when he looks at people, allowing his spectacles to slide down his nose before he pushes them back into place.

"I'm Edie," she says, tersely.

Theo shoots her a steadying look and she thinks how nice it is, that they can already communicate in glances and nods. "She's a student, looking into Tessa," he says.

Before Michael can respond, the woman with the headband returns with a tray of tea and biscuits. "This is my wife, Mary," he says to Theo.

Theo shakes her hand. "Yes, I heard you'd got married," he says, and Edie is surprised to see Michael blush.

"I'll leave you to it," says Mary. Edie smiles but the woman doesn't look in her direction.

"How's retirement—bored yet?" says Michael to Theo. "I hear you're at the house a lot."

"I'm fine, Michael."

Michael hesitates. "I heard about Jeremy too," he says. "I'm sorry."

"Are you?" says Theo, and the sharpness of his tone surprises Edie. She watches Michael shift in his seat. "Yes, well. Thank you."

"Interesting that you've come today. I've just heard that *Agent Femme* is to be adapted for the BBC." Michael pushes his glasses up his nose again, and Edie feels an irritated shiver rush across her shoulders. "I've been asked to write the script, of course."

"How *fabulous*," she says, and there's Theo shooting her that look again.

Theo takes the photocopied wireless messages from his pocket, unfolds the paper and hands it to Michael, who glances at it without appearing to read it.

"These are wireless messages sent on Tess's behalf," Theo says. "But you knew that already, didn't you?"

Michael smiles, an expression so smug it brings to Edie's mind thoughts of violence. "Latin, that's so her," he says, and Edie can feel Theo tensing up next to her.

"Did you put it in her personnel file after it was cleared for release?" he says.

"Now why on earth should I do that?"

"So that someone like me would find it," says Edie.

Michael shrugs, but he's still smiling. "It's a theory, I suppose, but not one I can help you with, I'm sorry to say."

Edie ignores this. "What does she mean by 'The Moon Is Bad'?" she says, and finally Michael turns his gaze and his displaced spectacles toward her.

"You're the student." He passes her the piece of paper. "What do you think it means?"

Edie resists the urge to curl her fingers into a fist. She glances at Theo and is amused to see his hands clasped tightly together, as if he is fighting a similar battle. "Obviously it's a warning," she says.

"That's interesting. Why *obviously*?"

"The repetition. It gives the message a sense of urgency."

"How do you know repetition wasn't commonplace?"

"I don't. I haven't come across any other messages yet. But it seems unlikely given how dangerous it was to transmit them in the first place. Surely the operators would want to stop transmitting as quickly as they could and do so as few times as possible."

"She's done her homework," Michael says to Theo.

"She has, but you're the expert. That's why we're here," says Theo. Edie can see this comment pleases Michael.

Michael takes back the piece of paper and studies it. Or pretends to—everything he does has an air of theatricality. "It could be about the weather. The moon was crucial to drops—people, weapons, supplies. Or . . ." He raises his eyebrows.

"Yes?" says Theo.

"Well, and I mean this is just a hypothesis, but could it be referring to a person?"

"What makes you say that?" says Edie, thinking, he *knows*, he bloody well knows what it means.

"I wonder if it's code," he says, pacing out each word as if it's only just occurring to him. "I wonder if 'Luna Mala Est' refers to a person."

"Who?" says Theo.

"How the devil should I know? And even if I did, to be perfectly frank, the Tessa situation remains something of a sticky wicket in certain circles, and I'd rather my name wasn't attached to it. No, I think your best bet is to head back to the personnel files. Agent code names, nicknames, that sort of thing."

Edie thinks of the stack of folders on her desk in the National Archives. Suddenly it doesn't feel quite so thrilling.

"Or . . ." says Michael.

Theo drums his fists against his legs. "Or?" Theo and Edie say, at the same time.

"Well, I can think of someone who might know."

"Who?" says Edie.

Theo shakes his head. "He means Emmeline Jones."

"Exactly. A woman with perfect recall. She'll have answers for you."

"She hasn't replied to any of my letters," says Edie.

Michael smiles, again. "I don't think for a second she'll talk to you, but I guarantee she'll talk to *him*." He nods at Theo and adds, softly, "Guilt can be the most astonishing motivator."

Thirty-four

It is arranged in a short conversation on the phone. Theo, in his office, hunched over his desk, one hand against his temple. Edie needs to go home, the frequency of the trains tails off the later it gets, but she doesn't want to leave him. The visit to Michael has exhausted him, it's obvious. He could barely raise a word on the journey back.

Theo places the phone down and she hears him take a series of deep breaths.

"Theo, is everything—"

He looks up sharply. "It's all arranged. Next Saturday with Emmeline." He hesitates. "I should have checked with you before I said yes."

"No, no, it's fine. Of course I can make it. Thank you so much for arranging it."

Edie wonders what other plans she should have. Drinks, dinner with friends, a visit home perhaps? She can't remember the last time she did that.

"Shall I make some supper?" he says. "Do you eat fish?"

She glances at the wall clock. "I do eat fish, it's just . . ."

"You need to go. Of course, of course. I'll drive you to the station."

She's bone tired. She could lie down right now and sleep. "It's not that I don't want to stay, it's just the trains . . ."

"Of course, of course. You're very welcome to stay, though."

Edie frowns. It's almost seven. "Do you mean, stay the night?"

"I didn't mean to suggest anything improper."

"Oh! I would never have thought that." Mortified, she puts her hand to her chest, until she realizes he is smiling, teasing.

"Do you want to, then? We could make a plan for Emmeline and talk some more about Tessa. I'd like to do that. I can drop you at the station in the morning."

Edie does want to talk more about Tessa. She puts her hands on her hips. It is her thinking position. "Are you all right, Theo? I'm not forcing you to do this, am I? Dig into the past, I mean."

He smiles, but too brightly for it to be of any comfort. "It's time for digging, I realize that."

Edie prepares steamed vegetables while Theo bakes cod with lemon and dill. It smells delicious, like a posh restaurant and Mediterranean holidays rolled into one.

"It must have been strange for you today, with Michael," she says, when they are seated in the dining room—another room of books, this time piled in heaps on the floor.

"I suppose it was. He hasn't changed. Well, no, that's not quite true. He's a little grander, perhaps. Tessa couldn't stand him."

Edie laughs, although she's not sure why. "How come?"

"He was keen on her and he didn't hide it—that was always guaranteed to set my sister against a chap. In actual fact, I think he was rather in love with us both, or perhaps just the idea of us. Michael was an only child, you see. He envied our bond. Sometimes I think he wanted to be the third in our relationship but, you see, that's the thing with twins. There's only room for two. Tessa didn't trust him. Tessa put great weight on instinct, and instinctively she didn't trust him. And look, she was right. We all know what happened when she let her guard down."

"Do you blame Michael?" She really wants a glass of wine but Theo is sticking religiously to water. Earlier in the kitchen, she'd opened a cupboard looking for a dish and it was stacked high with bottles, all mineral water.

Theo doesn't say anything for a while. "I did for a long time. I blamed everyone and anyone because I couldn't face my own guilt. Being so close to the actual perpetrators in Nuremberg was . . ." He grimaces. "I want to say cathartic, but it wasn't; it made me feel worse because they just seemed so pathetic. All that loss, that destruction, the cruelty that humanity is capable of—everything we went through—and what was it for? What were they doing, these little feeble men, unleashing the worst of humanity, and I say that because that's how they seemed to me—small. I became what you'd call an angry young man."

"What happened to your sister was hardly your fault," Edie tells him. "Tessa had her own mind and her own agency."

"Yes, but I should have known what she was up to. She should have confided in me and perhaps if I'd been more open with her, she would have."

"Open about what?"

He swallows a mouthful of food. "About myself." He laughs, but it's a hollow sound. "Wisdom comes with age. Age, and giving up some bad habits, working less."

"Do you mean when you switched to teaching?"

Theo puts down his fork.

"Sorry," she says. "I didn't mean to pry."

"No, no it's fine." Theo is shaking his head. He lifts his glass to take a big swig of water. "It's just, that was . . . something different." He coughs, and Edie watches a blush creep up his neck. "You see, a few years after the war I was arrested. In a public lavatory, with another man. He wasn't arrested, by the way, the policeman let him scarper. Not that we'd done anything," he says, quickly, "and we weren't going to either. But a policeman had followed me in and he thought he read something in a look between us."

"A look?"

"Yes, that was often all it took, you see. I wasn't convicted. I was bound over—incarcerated for a few days to scare me senseless, and then released. Jeremy helped me—it's actually what put us back in contact. We had worked together at Nuremberg." He goes to the mantelpiece and picks up a photograph in a frame, handing it to her. It is Theo with another man, salt and pepper hair, arm in arm in the garden. They are looking at each other and smiling.

"Our relationship was an entirely delightful and unexpected consequence of my arrest. I mean, I suppose in many ways I was lucky . . ." Here, he sighs. "But it made my profession difficult. People talk, as they say. So, in the absence of other options I became a lecturer—a great profession, as it happens. My father's profession too."

"Theo, that's appalling. I mean, to go through that on top of everything else. Jesus."

He shrugs. "I certainly never saw teaching as a step down, although undoubtedly many did. But look, a busy career can mask an awful lot of unpleasantness beneath the surface, believe me. I was a mess. Problem is, it gets out. It leaches from you, trauma like that."

"How did it . . ." Edie cringes. "I'm being so nosy. I'm sorry."

"It's all right. Bad behavior, mainly. I wasn't a nice person for a while."

"What changed?"

"A lot of very thorough and very expensive therapy—a useful by-product of making a life with an extremely successful barrister. And Jeremy became quite taken with yoga and chanting, getting up early, that sort of thing."

Edie puts her hand to her mouth to stifle the laugh. "You're a yogi?"

"I'm partial to a slow sun salutation of a morning, yes. There's probably a few books on meditation in here, if you want to take a look." He gestures at the books on the floor. "These are all Jeremy's. He wanted me to give them to charity but as you can see, I'm not very good at getting rid of belongings. Or anything, really."

"It's sort of incredible, what you've been through," says Edie. "It seems like too much for one person. I mean, it's amazing you've survived it as well as you have."

Theo is kneeling on the floor now. He flicks open a book, reads an inscription and smiles. "We don't get to choose," he says.

"No, I know. But I'm worried about bringing this up again."

"You've said that before. But look, it was never settled. Not a day has gone by where I haven't thought about what happened to my sister. I just became very adept at pretending I'd moved on." He smiles. "I have very effective coping strategies because darling Jeremy paid an awful lot of money for them."

They are quiet for a moment.

"We should probably talk about Emmeline," she says, softly.

"Now that was odd."

"What was?" Edie sits on the floor next to him and he starts passing her books with names like *Light on Yoga*, and *Psycho-Yoga*.

"Speaking to Emmeline for the first time since, let me think . . . yes, probably about 1946."

Edie puts down the book she's holding. "Wait, what? I did not get that vibe from your conversation."

"Well, Emmeline and I are nothing if not professional."

"But Michael said she'd agree to see me if you asked. I assumed that meant you were friends."

"I believe he was referring to the way in which we parted, which was not on particularly good terms. My sister had just been accused of treason, after all."

"God, Theo, this is too much. I'll go and see her on my own."

He shakes his head. "Certainly not. Besides, there's plenty I want to ask her."

Edie is torn between packing it all in and running to fetch her notebook from her rucksack. "So Emmeline is the one who accused Tessa of betrayal?"

"I should think it went much higher than Emmeline. She was just the mouthpiece."

"But she believed it?"

"Who knows? People like Emmeline got to where they did by knowing when to voice opinions and when to keep mum. But look, I can't be too cross at her."

"Why?"

"Because I expect when she closes her eyes at night, the thought of what happened to those women must tear her apart. It destroys you, a responsibility like that. Whether you choose to admit it or not, it destroys you."

It is a week later, and Theo is in his battered Morris outside the house. Edie gathers up her notepad and her Dictaphone. Tomás, one of her housemates, is washing up in the kitchen. He'd had a friend over last night and Edie had thought of joining them, if they'd stayed in the kitchen. Just introducing herself and barreling her way into their evening. But they ate in his room. She could hear the movie they watched through her bedroom wall.

"I'm off out," she says now, and he looks at her, almost bemused, before waving his hand which is clad in a pink Marigold. Edie closes the front door behind her and presses her back and hands into the cold wood. She just wants someone to ask her about her day. A conversation that doesn't happen at a supermarket checkout. Theo is watching from the car, but she doesn't care.

"Good morning!" he says, when she gets in. "Should be in Sussex in a couple of hours. Fingers crossed the car makes it."

Edie's only just shut the car door. She looks at it in alarm. "Is that in any doubt?"

"Of course, Christ, just look at it. Anyway, let's hope Emmeline hasn't gone and died in the meantime."

"What?"

"Well, she is in her nineties. It'd be typical of Emmeline to die just to spite us."

It takes an age for the car to wind through London. Theo pulls onto the M25, and begins weaving back and forth between the middle lane and the slow lane. Her hands grip her seat, either side of her legs. "Not to be a nag, but could you slow down a little bit?"

"What are you talking about, I'm an excellent driver."

"I didn't say you weren't."

"Besides, the car always shakes like this."

They drive in silence then, Edie giving a little cheer as the rolling downland comes into view. She's always loved the countryside, but it's different where she's from. It's scraggy peaks and waterfalls. Sussex has an openness to it, but it's greener, somehow fresher, despite the trunk roads tarmacked through ancient field systems, and the cars and people spilling onto the roads and pavements. Tractors roam fields dragging heavy machinery first one way and then the other. Combine harvesters spray wheat into metal containers. The turning of the earth, the turning of the seasons.

Two hours after the journey began and Theo is still sitting in the driver's seat, his fingers tapping out some unknown tune against the steering wheel. They are parked in a village car park, a square of independent shops and cafés between them and Emmeline Jones' small cottage, which they can see from the car. Edie imagines Emmeline glaring back at them from the window. She sounds like someone who doesn't like to be kept waiting.

"I wonder what she looks like," says Theo, eyes on the cottage. "She's not going to look how she appears in my head, is she? I suppose she might say the same about me."

Edie looks from Theo to the cottage and back again. "Only one way to find out," she says.

"I think this a lot about Tessa. I mean, I think about her all the time. Her face is always in my mind. But if she suddenly appeared, Tessa, as I last knew her, I wonder how different she'd look. I wonder what time has altered in my image of her without me even realizing. Do I still have her eyes, her nose, her mouth, or is everything a little off?"

"I don't know, Theo."

"No, no of course you don't. She's just a photograph to you."

"That's not true." The atmosphere in the car is oppressive. She wants to wind the window down and gulp in the fresh air, but she's worried the car door would fall off. "Theo, I think we should go over."

He walks slowly across the road, even though she knows he has more get up and go than she does. He seems reluctant to ring the bell, so she does it for him. It takes Emmeline a while to open the door, but they can see her shape approaching through the speckled glass, her form growing into a distorted outline of a person. They can hear her snapping locks back, one, two, three.

"Christ, what's she got in there, the Crown Jewels?" says Theo.

Emmeline opens the door and gives him a hard stare. "No, but one likes to feel safe, all the same."

Theo is uncharacteristically mute.

"You've come, then," says Emmeline. "It's taken you much longer than I thought it would."

"I did try before," says Theo. "I wrote to you, do you remember?"

Emmeline's lips squeeze into a frown. She steps away from the door and they follow her inside. The cottage is low-beamed, and almost half the sitting room is swallowed by a deep inglenook fireplace. The walls are sparse, an oil painting and several framed sepia photographs the only real decoration. The room has a smell, not unpleasant, which makes Edie think of making pomanders with her grandmother at Christmas, thick orange peel pierced with cloves.

Emmeline disappears into a narrow kitchen, calling behind her, "I'll make tea—that's all I've got, so it's that or water."

Theo quirks an eyebrow at Edie. "Tea would be marvelous, thank you," he says.

Five minutes later Emmeline is back, carrying an overloaded tray. Theo moves to take it from her hands, and she makes a sound like a cat hissing.

"There are biscuits, but I don't eat that rot, so I really can't say if they're any good. I normally have a girl come in but naturally you've come on her day off. Why are you standing up? Sit down, for God's sake. You're behaving very strangely."

Emmeline places the tray on a low table and sits down in an armchair, as if showing them how it's done. She pours three cups of tea, hands them round and then settles her eyes on Edie. "I've been getting phone calls about you."

Edie thinks, oh dear.

"Awkward so-and-so, I hear."

"Emmeline," says Theo.

"No, it's true." Edie helps herself to a biscuit. "I have been a bit awkward."

"You might as well hop to it. I haven't got long," says Emmeline.

"Do you have another appointment?" says Theo.

"No, but I'm ninety-four and I don't want to spend whatever time I have left doing this." Emmeline takes a cigarette from a long leather case. "I can't think what I can tell you anyway. That business with your sister was sixty years ago."

"I'm confident you remember it as if it were yesterday," says Theo.

"I've been listening to your interviews in the Imperial War Museum's Sound Archive," adds Edie. "They're fascinating. Your contribution—"

"No, no, not that way. I won't be buttered up," says Emmeline, but she looks pleased none the less.

Theo looks at Edie, who pulls the piece of paper from her notebook.

"We want to ask you about these messages," she says.

Emmeline goes very still. Edie has the impression she is a woman not easily rattled.

"Where did you get this?" she says.

"Tessa's personnel file."

"No, you didn't."

"Yes, she did, Emmeline," says Theo, gently.

"What does it mean?" says Edie.

Emmeline exhales a slow trail of smoke into the air. "I've no idea. It was more than half a century ago, and we received thousands of wireless messages."

"Of course you did. But we wondered if you might be able to help understand the code. Specifically, does 'Luna Mala Est'—'The Moon Is Bad'—refer to a person?" says Edie.

Emmeline looks taken aback. "What makes you say that?"

Edie shrugs. "It's just a question," she says, thinking, yes, a person.

Emmeline doesn't say anything for a while. She stares at the fire blazing red in the grate, despite the warmth of the day outside.

"Do you believe Tessa was a traitor?" she says to Theo.

"No," he says.

"Did you ever?"

Theo hesitates. "No."

Emmeline considers this for a moment. "There was plenty of evidence, you realize. Your sister went underground for a while. Ordered home but ran off to the south instead. It never struck me as the actions of an innocent—

and that's before we received the specific accusations, of course. The networks she'd interacted with were rounded up as soon as she was arrested. The Germans had to get that information from somewhere."

Theo looks like he's searching for the right response. "If she was a spy, then why send her to the camp?"

"Perhaps she'd outlived her usefulness. The Nazis were hardly known for their loyalty." She drags on her cigarette. "You took the news so calmly that day in Nuremberg."

Theo looks down at his hands, stretched over his thighs. "I couldn't put my parents through it. The exposure."

"Couldn't put them through it, or you?"

"My parents," he says, but it takes a moment.

"Did it make a difference, do you think? That it never came out."

Edie wonders if Emmeline has forgotten she's there.

Theo shakes his head. "No, it killed them anyway."

Theo's face is changing; it's etched with pain; she's watching it happen. It's the pull of the past, she thinks. It's never being able to move on, not really.

Emmeline stubs out the cigarette in an enameled dish already thick with ash, and immediately takes another from her case. "His name was Paul Aubert," she says.

Edie looks at Theo, who doesn't take his eyes from Emmeline. He's breathing quickly, and Edie can see his hand is shaking.

"Sorry, this is the person referred to in Tessa's messages?" says Edie, and Emmeline nods.

"She knew him as Jean. They met in the field, although if memory serves, they trained in England together for a short time. He was nicknamed 'The Moon' because of his appearance. A shock of white hair and a big round face, like a full moon." She looks as if she's about to go on, but instead she sits back in her chair.

They sit in silence for a moment. Edie hears a hiss of brakes at the bus stop outside. She hears people getting off, chattering, it's nice to see you, oh yes, the weather's on the turn.

"Who was he?" she says.

"He was our man on the ground, organizing drops, welcoming committees, that sort of thing, in the Loire and then later, when our manpower became stretched further south too."

"Why would Tessa send so many messages about him?" says Edie.

"I really can't say."

"'Bad Moon,' the moon is bad. It was a warning," says Edie.

"Perhaps," says Emmeline.

"Paul Aubert is the man who accused my sister of betrayal," Theo says, his fingers gripping the fabric of his trousers.

"What?" says Edie. She turns to Emmeline. She feels like a spectator at a tennis match. "Is that true?"

Emmeline has closed her eyes, but she nods.

"Fuck," says Edie, which causes Emmeline's eyes to snap open. "Sorry," says Edie.

Theo stands up and begins pacing the room. "What happened when these messages arrived? What happened in Baker Street?"

"Nothing happened. The drop that evening, which Tessa and her wireless operator thought should be canceled, was not. It went ahead."

Theo sits back down and winds his arms around his head. "Nothing happened," he repeats.

"What happened at the drop?" says Edie.

Emmeline sighs. "There was an ambush. Everyone involved was rounded up." Theo unwinds his arms from his head, and she says, quickly, "There had already been an investigation, by your friend Crawley, as it happens. Aubert was cleared."

"There had already been . . ." Theo begins, then trails off.

"You mean there were other accusations against Aubert, before these wireless transmissions arrived?" says Edie.

"There were . . . concerns. Aubert was believed killed in a drop. He reappeared in London a while later and yes, it raised eyebrows. A thorough investigation was conducted and—"

"This investigation unearthed no evidence?" says Theo.

"It was not thought to be convincing."

"By whom?"

She hesitates, then says, "The head of our section, Ronald Stenwick."

"And was there any connection between the two men?" says Theo.

"What do you mean? Aubert was an agent assigned to Stenwick's section, he—"

"Who recruited him?"

Edie knows the answer to this. "Stenwick did," she says, flicking through her notebook. "Aubert is mentioned in Stenwick's autobiography—I knew I'd heard the name somewhere. They were friends before the war."

Emmeline purses her lips. "I believe they worked together in France."

"Jesus Christ," says Theo.

"It simply means Stenwick could speak to the man's character."

"Yes, despite all the evidence to the contrary. Shame no one thought to do that for my sister. What a shame I didn't—" Theo breaks off and looks down.

"Aubert lived, didn't he?" says Edie. Emmeline nods.

"So he could say whatever he wanted." Theo is blazing, furious. "Did you believe him?"

"It was not my judgment to make," says Emmeline firmly.

Theo starts pacing again; he looks distraught. Edie wants to reach out and squeeze his hand.

"You said there was concrete evidence against my sister. You said it was damning," he says. "Was there ever any evidence, any at all, outside of Aubert's claims?"

"I told you; she went underground for a time. Disobeyed a direct order to return home. Other than that, well, quite frankly Aubert's word was enough." She takes a long drag on her cigarette. "I believe it's what politicians these days call 'optics.' The press were gunning for us. All those women missing. Violette Szabo's appalling father running his mouth all over Fleet Street, and your father didn't exactly help the situation. We couldn't risk a protracted inquiry into a female agent going rogue behind the lines."

"So you buried it," says Theo.

Emmeline nods. She looks defiant, thinks Edie, but not powerful. She looks small.

"We buried it," she says.

Thirty-five

London is in the grip of an Indian summer. Edie can feel the heat of the pavement through her sandals. Passing buses are steamed up and she can imagine how uncomfortable it is, the heat from the engine, the warmth of all those bodies squished together. It's airless and still. A woman outside a newsagent holds a wrapped ice lolly against her forehead, bliss in her shut-eyed expression. Edie's head is swimming with desired sensations: a plunge into the Ladies' Pond, or a circuit of the Serpentine, mouth bolted shut against whatever else might be in the water. Instead, she treads on past the market stalls and haircare shops, past the pubs spilling clientele onto the pavements, where they crouch on the curb with plastic pint glasses.

"I'm so jealous," says Hellie, down the phone from Leeds. "I mean, it's nice here but it's not, like, Spain hot."

"I'd happily swap. Spain hot is too hot. Hellie, I'm not sure about this."

"What do you mean?"

"Wouldn't it be better to just leave him alone? Haven't I messed with his head enough by dragging this up?"

"I think if you're going to miss my birthday weekend by swanning off to Berlin, the least you can do is talk it out with Theo."

Edie grimaces. "Oh, I see. You're encouraging me to see him *as a punishment*. Got it."

It's been a month since Edie last spoke to Theo. "I'll call you," had been his last words, shouted from the wound-down car window, but he hadn't and it hadn't felt right to push him, though she'd countless times picked up the phone. She'd decided to write a letter, but hadn't done that either, being the master of coming up with ideas and not following them through.

"Hellie, I'm actually really nervous about this."

"You're fine. You'll be fine. He's a nice man, isn't he?"

"He's lovely."

"Well, there you go, then."

Edie rings off and presses the doorbell. She sees his shape in the glass, the pause when he recognizes her. He smiles when he opens the door, but she can tell it's forced. Theo gestures for her to go into the garden.

"How did you know I was in London?" he says, a moment later, emerging from the kitchen with two glasses of orange juice, ice cubes clinking against the side. She resists the urge to scoop one out and hold it against her temple.

"Thought I'd chance it," she says.

He won't look at her. "I'm actually about to get in the car and go back to—"

"Seeing as I haven't heard from you in a while . . ."

Theo sits back in his chair. It's a nice garden, a small courtyard designed for someone who doesn't have the time to deal with more than a handful of pots. But it's light and he has a large garden umbrella for shade, which makes her think she might stay for the afternoon whether he likes it or not.

"I've been working really hard, as it happens," she says. "I even got a smile out of my tutor the other day, which is certainly a turn-up for the books."

Theo closes his eyes and says nothing.

"I know it's difficult." The words are tumbling out in a nervous rush. "I do get it. But I need to tell you this: I've changed my PhD. It's going to focus solely on Tessa. I wanted to tell you face to face."

Theo nods. "Yes, that makes sense, given what you've heard so far."

"The second thing is, I've been speaking to lots of people. Ex-agents, former members of the French Resistance. Listen—whenever I mentioned Paul Aubert, the atmosphere changed. Loads of people had suspicions about him, which they swore they'd passed on to London at the time—only they were fobbed off, told their fears were unfounded. One man had been imprisoned in Paris and said Nazi officials even named Aubert, and the British still didn't take it seriously. Theo, they knew he was a traitor, but Stenwick refused to believe it. Despite being warned about Aubert over and over again, they did nothing. Not a thing. And then they let him throw your sister under the bus."

Theo looks utterly defeated as she waits for him to process her words. Perhaps that's what anguish does to a person. It sucks the life out of you, like a parasite.

"I would say it seems evident, yes, that the British authorities chose one narrative over the other," he says finally.

This isn't enough. Edie wants him to acknowledge her anger and match it, because he has more of a right to it than she does. "An institutional cover-up," she says.

"That's a big accusation, Edie."

"Aubert framed Tessa and I think there was enough reasonable doubt around her actions for the mud to stick. I mean, we've heard it over and over, haven't we, and it's always the same. 'Tessa seemed to get lucky quite a bit'; 'Tessa and her miraculous escape.' I mean, maybe she *did* get lucky? Maybe she *did* outwit the enemy? People do, sometimes. Perhaps she went underground because she realized the organization had been corrupted. I mean, Theo, what this did to your sister's reputation!"

Theo takes a drink and places the glass back on a coaster, his fingers lingering. "Within a very small circle. She's never been publicly denounced. There were too many careers on the line for that."

Edie can't understand how he's being so reasonable. "By seeking to hide his own betrayal, Aubert denied Tessa the posthumous honors she deserved. If I had a sister I'm not sure I'd be so relaxed about her being robbed of her rightful place in history, but OK."

He bristles at this. "Well, I'm not sure I—"

"And why did they go along with it—the powers that be?" she persists. "Because they were already facing criticism for sending women behind the lines and didn't want to fuel the fire. Because they'd been told, repeatedly, about the traitor in their midst and they did nothing, not one thing, and how many people died because of their inaction? Plus, they messed up in another way, didn't they? Aubert was recruited by the top dog, who didn't want anyone knowing that it was his agent who went rogue. People *died*! It's a scandal."

She is on her feet, gesticulating indignantly, and now Theo laughs. "I like this side of you. This confidence. Where've you been hiding it?"

"Perhaps you've brought it out of me. You and Tessa."

"Give yourself some credit. I should warn you, you'll put some noses out of joint if you go around writing things like that."

"It's not my crowd. I don't have anything to lose."

He settles his eyes on her and waits. She wonders if this is one of his expensive coping techniques, waiting for the wave to peak, deep breath, deep breath. "It's not as if I'm not angry," he says, eventually. "Because of course I am. I have been for a very long time. This is . . . this is really very difficult for me, Edie."

When Theo begins to speak, it rushes from him with such speed that she wonders how long he's been waiting to say it, waiting for someone to listen. "Except the truth is, that despite knowing my sister better than anyone, when the accusations were first put to me, I doubted her innocence. I doubted *her*. My fiercely loyal and passionately anti-fascist sister."

Edie opens her mouth to protest and he raises his hand.

"I know, Edie. Believe me, I know. The thing is, people behave in the most inexplicable ways during war. They'll do the most unfathomable things if they think it'll save their life, or the lives of the people they love. But I *knew* her, better than anyone else. And I should have fought for her, for the truth, for the Tessa *I* knew—whatever she may or may not have done. And if I had, perhaps there wouldn't be this ridiculous question mark hanging over her head. She'd be celebrated for her bravery and honored for her contribution to the war, for the astonishing things she did."

"But even if you had asked questions, even if you'd advocated for Tessa, there's no certainty you'd have got to the truth, especially given who you were up against," Edie says.

"But I did ask questions," he says, quietly, pulling a handkerchief from his pocket.

Edie realizes he is crying and reaches out to touch his arm. "Theo, no . . ." But after all, she cannot stop herself from asking, "What do you mean?"

"After the war. It was a bad time, my father had just died, and . . . and I was struggling. I thought if I could just solve this, if I could just clear her name then maybe . . ." He covers his face with his hands. "Maybe it wouldn't be such a mess. Maybe my mother would be all right and I'd be—I don't know, Edie—a better person. Happy, even."

"Theo, who did you speak to?"

"Most of the people I knew had gone back into civilian life. Michael put me in touch with someone in the Cabinet Office . . ."

"Michael."

"Yes. No one would tell me anything—well, nothing new anyway. But I couldn't let it go, rather like you, now. I kept asking questions and the more I did, the more certain I felt that something wasn't right. Sometimes you just know, don't you? I imagine it was around this time they started having me followed."

"What?"

"Call it paranoia, if you will. The delusions of a drunk—because that's what I was back then. I had a new job, a new chambers, and Christ knows how I was holding it all together—looking back, I barely was. And that's when it happened, the incident in the gentlemen's lavatory."

Edie gapes at him. "You mean, you think . . . are you saying it was a set-up?"

"I don't *think*, Edie, I know. When they brought me from the cells after days of leaving me there to think the worst, I wasn't questioned by the policeman who'd brought me in, but by a couple of fellows in smart suits. Spooks, I suppose, although I doubt I'll ever know for sure. They told me to stop making a nuisance of myself, that things would get much worse if I kept on asking questions of people who had much more important matters to deal with, thank you very much." He's still crying. Edie is watching the tears running down his face, wondering how many years' worth they are.

"It's hard to explain to someone of your age what it was like. How frightening it was to love in a way that wasn't just seen as wrong, but criminal. I mean, Christ, look at what they did to Alan Turing: he won the war, and they castrated him."

"What did you do?" she asks.

"I did what they asked. I backed off, instead of prison, instead of whatever hideous medical procedures they wanted to inflict on me and my so-called urges. I chose cowardice. And then I lost it all anyway, except Jeremy." He smiles. "It wasn't always easy, but we had each other. They couldn't take that away. It was a defiance of sorts, our relationship. The happiness we shared."

Edie tries to speak but the words won't come. Instead, she bursts into tears. Theo reaches out and squeezes her arm. When her breathing steadies, he goes on.

"I've spent years, *years*, Edie, feeling utterly furious with my sister. Because her decisions, decisions she didn't even bother to share with me, look at what they did to my parents, to me, to the people she left behind. I feel awfully guilty about that. About my anger, and . . ." He hesitates. ". . . and the fact I never quite managed to vanquish my doubts about Tessa's conduct. It was always there, the creeping suspicion that she did turn. That she was as guilty as they said."

They sit in silence for a moment.

"I've never admitted that before," he says.

"Those feelings seem completely understandable," she says, softly.

"But did she deserve my doubts, that anger? I'm not sure she did. And if I had kept going, if I'd pushed, then you wouldn't be here now. Perhaps this would all be known. Perhaps if I'd just been braver—"

"Braver from your prison cell? Come on! You didn't have a choice."

Edie takes a deep breath as Theo wipes his eyes.

"Theo, I spoke to Emmeline Jones again. If I'm going to write about Tessa, then I need to know what happened to her after she was captured."

He raises his eyebrows. "How did that go?"

"Terribly. She told me she'd said everything she intended to on the matter and that was that. So I went back to basics, back to my notes. Then I read the books again, collecting the names of anyone connected to SOE, however loosely, and tried to follow the trail."

"And?"

"And then it occurred to me that perhaps the clue to this might not be with the people who sent Tessa to France—who have, it seems, invented plenty of reasons for sticking to their version of the truth. No, perhaps the clue might lie with the people who discovered her there."

Theo looks up. "The people who . . . you mean . . ."

"The German officers who captured her in Paris."

"But most of them are—"

"Dead, yes, or disappeared. The men, at least. Which leaves the women who worked for them. The secretaries. The record-keepers. Theo, these were young women, some of them barely out of their teens. A lot of them are still alive."

"That may be, but I don't know how you'd track them down. I doubt they'd admit to such a past these days."

"Yes, well, luckily for me the transcripts of the Nuremberg trials have proved to be very thorough and really quite fruitful. One name in particular caught my attention, a woman named Gerta Müller."

Straight away, Theo is nodding. His eyes are bright. "Yes, yes of course. She worked for Hans König, the head of the SD in Paris. She was his secretary."

Edie smiles. It is oddly touching how fresh the memory seems to be for him. "The Nuremberg prosecutors probably had her name thanks to your investigations in Paris."

But he's too modest to accept this, muttering about the others on his team, the group effort. Theo rubs his eyes, sits back in his chair and looks up, and Edie does the same. Together they watch a plane carve a white line across the sky.

"I visited avenue Foch, König's headquarters, when I was in Paris at the end of the war," he says. "I saw Tessa's name carved into the wall of a cell. I stood in this woman's office. I probably placed my hands on her desk. But what makes you think she knows anything specifically about Tessa?"

"I tracked her down," she tells him. "I called her. Emmeline Jones interviewed her at the end of the war when she was investigating the missing women agents. It wasn't easy—my German isn't great and she only has a little English. But Theo—she remembers your sister."

He is quiet for a moment, then he says, "König spoke, you know, when he was finally arrested. He didn't have much to say about Tessa, just that he'd questioned her. I'm sorry, Edie, but I doubt this woman will tell you anything we don't already know."

"I think it's worth making the trip."

"To Germany?"

"Yes," she says. "Müller wants to talk face to face. You could be my translator—God knows I need one. I mean, why not? You said you've never been told much about Tessa's time in prison. I can't imagine how difficult it is to not know that—or what happened to her in Ravensbrück." Lightly, Edie places her hand on his. "I don't think your sister did anything wrong and I'm going to try and prove it. And look, I know what this means to you, I've *seen* how important this is. I don't think you'll find peace unless we can somehow find out for sure what happened all those years ago. Please, come with me."

Above them, the plane continues carving a streak of white through all that blue.

Thirty-six

Edie is in the toilets at Gatwick, pinching her cheeks, splashing herself with cold water, anything to bring color to her face. She's never been an early riser and it shows, but this was the cheapest flight and she can't let him pay. He was gracious enough to not object.

Her phone beeps. She flips it open and reads the message. It's a woman from university—a group of them are meeting for a drink later and would Edie like to join them? *I hear you're making great strides with your research—the entire department is agog*, the woman adds.

Edie writes back at once, heart racing: *I'm away but next time, yes please—count me in!*

A drink. A drink with colleagues. She texts Hellie: *Guess who's found their social life?*

A woman nudges her, jostling for mirror space. She has in hand a fat makeup bag, setting out each stage in the process on the cheap, utilitarian sinktop. Edie snatches up her small carry case and makes her way out into the busy departure lounge, where Theo sits square-shouldered on a metal seat. As she approaches, he takes a small blister strip from his pocket, small because it's been cut from a larger pack, pops two pills and downs them with the water she bought him as part of a meal deal in Boots. A chicken sandwich is no breakfast, he'd said, but it is the only complaint ventured so far in a morning deserving of more.

"Headache?" she says, knocking her case into the bank of metal chairs and making him wince. "The gate's open, we should probably get going. I hate queuing."

"You have no patience. I'll go when I'm good and ready, thank you," he snaps.

In the ensuing startled silence, a tinny voice calls out over the tannoy: a child is unattended in Pret a Manger, has anyone lost one?

Theo exhales. "Right then," he says, slapping his hands against his thighs. He stands up and starts marching toward the wrong gate. It's all Edie can do to place her hands on his shoulders and spin him in the right direction. Of course, there is a queue. Two queues, in fact. One for people who've paid marginally more for the privilege of competing in the first scrum for seats and one for the rest.

It is a miracle they find seats together, although staring into Theo's increasingly pin-pricked pupils she questions if this is something to be truly grateful for.

"Fell out of my plane on D-Day," Theo announces to their neighbor, a young woman with headphones clamped over her ears as a first line of defense. The surrounding rows go quiet. "That's why I can't stand flying."

"Theo," Edie says quickly. "You fell out of your plane?"

He nods, wide-eyed. "Went straight through a barn, thank Christ for the parachute. I survived but a beautiful man called Barnes did not. God, I loved him. Gorgeous, inside and out. I sometimes wonder what happened to it—the parachute, I mean. All those French brides wearing British silk. Tessa's parachute, too." He nods. "That's one for you. You and your questions. I should get you to track down the woman in Normandy."

"Who?" Edie is rather enjoying this new, stoned version of Theo.

"My savior. She'll be dead now. I wish I'd gone back and told her about Tessa. She'd have had some answers, she was very wise."

By the time they take off he is asleep.

He's groggy in Berlin. They take a taxi to the hotel, which he had chosen after catching her browsing a youth hostel website. Too many turns about the sun for that, he'd said. But his hotel is nothing grand, the price point chosen with her in mind, another polite but unspoken sop toward her circumstances. They ditch their bags and he books them a taxi to a sushi restaurant in Mitte, "an old favorite of Jeremy's." Before her eyes he emerges from his medicated fug, his expression lighter.

Edie hasn't eaten sushi before and though it galls her to do so, she allows him to order for them both.

"We weren't very adventurous with food growing up," she says. "It's stuck with me. It's a bit British, I suppose, to never feel the need to venture too far outside of your comfort zone."

"Is that a British thing?"

"Well, a class thing then. I can almost guarantee no member of my family back home has tried sushi. A Chinese, maybe, because there's a takeaway round the corner from my dad's house. It was the height of exoticism growing up."

"Your family must be very proud."

"Why?"

Theo looks up from his menu. "Well . . ."

"It's just a thing you say, isn't it? I'm not sure if my family are proud of me. Confused by me, sure. I'm the first person in my family to go to university. They're gregarious people, on the whole, whereas I'm quiet and bookish. To be honest, I think they think I'm a bit up myself, because of the choices I've made."

Theo lays his menu down on the table. "That's terrible."

"It is what it is."

"I find it hard to believe they don't see you for who you are."

"Oh God, I don't think I want to know."

"On the contrary, I can't think of anyone I'd rather be here doing this with. You should have some faith in yourself, Edie. You spend so long mired in doubt, I rather think you miss your own brilliance."

Edie feels the heat in her cheeks. "Jesus, Theo."

"Yes, well. There's no need to make a thing of it. I've said it now."

She nods. "Thank you, though," she whispers.

A waitress appears, eager to take their order and get to her next table. Theo reels off a list of items from the menu in rapid German.

"You're good," she says when the waitress has bustled away.

"I studied German at school, and of course I lived in Nuremberg for a time. I came to love this country, although I didn't for a long while. I hated it for a time."

"That seems fair, considering. Do you come here a lot?"

"Berlin? Not as often as I used to. Jeremy loved it here. I don't go back to Nuremberg. Have you been here before? No? Well, you should come again. You'd like the Bauhaus Museum, great stuff. The Stasi Museum is extraordinary. Maybe we'll squeeze it in. I think the youngsters hang out in Kreuzberg, think strange bars and colorful drinks. You'll excuse me, I hope, if I don't accompany you there."

The waitress returns, placing down a large wooden tray of neat rows of sushi rolls.

"Did you ever visit Ravensbrück?" she says.

He pops a salmon roll into his mouth without answering, holding up his chopsticks to show her what to do. She drops her first roll three times.

"You can't ask for a knife and fork," he says. "You just can't." Then he shakes his head. "To answer your question. I went once to Ravensbrück with my mother, which remains one of the single most awful experiences of my life. It's very quiet there—as in, there's never many people. But also, it's just quiet, like the trenches of the Western Front, green and still. The birds don't sing. Besides, she's not there; not the Tessa I knew. A woman who'd been briefly incarcerated with Tessa—make sure I give you her name—told the Red Cross my sister was very depressed in the camp, very subdued. It makes it worse, somehow."

The sushi is cold as it slides down her throat. It is both disgusting and completely delicious and it astonishes her how one can exist alongside the other.

"It makes it worse, how?"

"Because my sister always had such spirit, such fight. And as soon as I heard those words, I knew that they'd broken her."

Gerta Müller's house, in a suburb outside Berlin, is small and cramped. They are led from the front door through a room in which the curtains are drawn. China sits on shelves, lace coverings on the backs of chairs. It is pristine and untouched, a room for best.

It is not a room for them. They are taken to the kitchen, a long thin space with an inglenook at one end, a wooden table in the center, and a small kitchenette at the other end. The table is laid with a thick waxed cloth that sticks to Edie's elbows, and plates of cakes in an array of colors, enough to feed twenty. Müller whisks away an embroidery loop, in which she is two thirds of the way through a scene from Disney's *Pocahontas*. On the train, Edie has given Theo this woman's past, or the bullet points at least. König was a family friend. She began working for him when she was seventeen and traveled with him as he rose through the ranks in the Nazi party, all the way to Paris.

"Eat, eat," says Gerta Müller in German, waving her hand toward the spread.

Edie looks at Theo and he nods. The cakes are rich and filled with whipped cream. Gerta Müller returns with a ceramic jug of coffee and sits down on the opposing bench. Edie sets her Dictaphone on the table, so she can transcribe and translate the conversation later, if needed.

"And so the circle turns," says Gerta Müller, softly. "It is to be dragged into the light, after all."

"She says it will now become known," Theo translates. "Dragged into the light." He snorts. "Dragged!"

"You don't have to speak to us," says Edie, slowly, ignoring Theo's sharp look. "There's no pressure. Theo, tell her."

Theo speaks in hurried German, too fast for Edie to grasp the words. She hopes he's saying what she wants him to.

"Do you tell people what you did during the war?" asks Theo. He translates his question for Edie. Now it is her turn to shoot him a look.

Gerta Müller shrugs. "I was a secretary."

She pours coffee into three small cups and, without asking, thick cream from a small jug. Edie feels her stomach turn.

"Eat more cake," says Gerta Müller.

"I'm told you might know something about my sister, Tessa Armstrong." Edie can read his impatience in the small movements of his body, the fidgeting fingers and feet.

"*Ja*, *ja*," says the old woman.

"And this is something you couldn't tell the Allied authorities in the aftermath? We know you were interviewed." He says it once in German, then translates for Edie, who is just about grasping the conversation.

"Keep it slow," she says. "Then I get it."

Gerta Müller snorts. "I was barely questioned. They didn't care about me, I was just a secretary. I didn't know anything."

"Then why are we here?"

"Because I knew *them*. The captured. I heard them speaking among themselves. I read their interrogations. I typed up König's notes. I was there."

"Were you in the office on the fifth floor, next to the cells?"

Edie can hear the edge in Theo's voice. Gerta Müller looks surprised. "I was, *ja*. Have you been there?"

"Yes, not long after you shredded everything. Go on then, let's hear it."

Edie puts her hand on his arm, but he won't look at her.

"It's what we're here for, isn't it?" He addresses Gerta Müller again. "Do you tell people you were a Nazi?"

"Theo!" says Edie, mortified, because there's no mistaking that word.

"Your sister was angry too. A live wire, always throwing off sparks. Many of her accomplices assessed the situation and realized they had to bargain for their lives. But your sister was defiant."

"A lot of people think she was a double agent. A traitor," says Edie. "Theo, tell her."

The woman looks astonished. "Tessa Armstrong? *Nein, nein*. Absolutely not, she was too bloody-minded for that."

"Absolutely not," Theo echoes. It takes him a moment to collect himself. How does it feel, Edie wonders, to hear his sister's innocence described so plainly.

"König did his best to convince your sister to turn against her organization, to work for us, even, but she refused. She spoke a lot about her principles. König admired her for it, I think. But he liked to sow seeds of mistrust among his prisoners, it was a tactic. It made people talk, to make them doubt themselves and each other."

"He turned them against each other," says Theo. He looks disgusted.

"He made himself appear to be the most reasonable person in the room, and often he was."

Edie can't eat any more cake, not even for politeness's sake.

"And you think he did that to Tessa? Made people think she couldn't be trusted?" Theo asks.

"Perhaps, or he exploited something that was already there. He'd do that too. So perhaps she was useful to him even though she refused to talk." Gerta Müller mimes a zip across her lips, to make her point clear to Edie. "He certainly kept her around longer than most."

Theo takes another cake. Edie doesn't know how he can stand the sweetness. Perhaps he just needs something to do with his hands.

"Why did he do that, do you think?" she says, and Theo translates.

"At first because of her connection to Agnès Roue. She was causing a lot of problems. The SD were desperate to track her down. It made Tessa very vulnerable."

Edie gasps. "Did she just say Agnès Roue? Is she saying Tessa was involved with Agnès Roue?" She looks at Theo, incredulous.

"The French Resistance woman?" he says.

"Yes—she's a legend! Managed to smuggle countless Jewish children out of France, hid the ones she couldn't, and practically ran a Resistance network single-handedly."

Theo turns back to Gerta Müller. "Sorry, Tessa was connected to this remarkable woman how?"

"It was believed she sheltered your sister after she escaped capture, not long after she arrived in France," Müller answers, hesitantly. "It was a matter of great frustration that Tessa did that: under arrest and yet she manages to walk out of the police station—unfathomable! But I heard it from König myself."

Theo repeats this in English for Edie.

"And that's why people thought she'd turned, because it was unfathomable?" she says. The mud had stuck, just as she'd thought.

The old woman nods at Theo's translation. "There was no deal. No turning. I am certain of it."

"Tessa did that?" says Theo. Edie watches his lips briefly curve into a proud smile and feels her heart break.

Müller nods, again. "*Ja*, and then Agnès Roue hid her and sent her south to stay with some contacts of hers."

"So, Tessa didn't go underground," says Edie, writing rapidly in her notebook. "Agnès Roue was helping her. I can't believe this!"

Theo says, quietly, in a wavering voice, "All these years this woman was here, and I could have asked her what happened. I could have just *asked*. It's been there, all along, just a plane ride away." He puts his hand to his mouth.

"Theo, where did Agnès Roue send Tessa?" says Edie, quickly. "Where did she stay?"

Theo asks the question.

"A farm in the south, I think. I don't know more. They were picked up far from there, in the Loire."

Edie is scribbling down Theo's translations as fast as she can. It is astonishing, she thinks, that so much can remain unknown, and how easily the truth can be hidden.

"She was arrested at your grandmother's house, wasn't she?" she says.

Theo nods, but his eyes remain on Gerta Müller. "You said 'they.' Do you mean Tessa wasn't alone?" He is keeping his voice level, but Edie can see he is shaking.

"I believe she was with someone from her circuit. But he wasn't held at avenue Foch for long."

"You said her connection to Agnès Roue was the initial reason for König's interest in Tessa. Why else did he keep her at avenue Foch for so long?"

Gerta Müller pulls her lips tight across her teeth. "He was a good man," she says.

Glancing at Theo as he translates this, Edie watches a flash of incredulity cross his face.

"He had daughters," says Gerta Müller.

"*Und?*"

"And I think he saw a lot of his children in your sister. He wanted to help her."

"But he didn't, did he?" says Theo. "He sent her to her death." He leans forward, eyes blazing now. He's forgotten to speak German, the words spilling out in English. "And because no one's ever told me what happened to my sister, not definitively anyway, my imagination has spent these past sixty years conjuring her death thousands of times over, in innumerable different ways. Can you comprehend what that's like for a person? To have that playing out in your mind every time you close your eyes?"

Gerta Müller comes alive, arms waving. "König was a good man, a good and honest man. It is not simple, not black and white, it never is. He and I, we simply wanted to do what was right."

Theo takes Edie to a bar, where he orders an inexplicably neon green beer for her and a sparkling water for himself. His eyes follow glasses of wine and spirits floating past their table, carried by waiters in cropped tops and baggy trousers. She wants to say, just have one, you've earned it, but she can't because the truth is the opposite, is hard-won sobriety, and she just wants him to be OK when it is obvious that he is not. Instead she sticks to her current mission, head down over her mobile phone, as he gazes at booze and passersby. A waiter plops two bowls of fries and bratwurst onto their table, because Theo's given in to the tourist in her. She can see it's hard for him. The patient smiles, the hesitation before he takes a bite. She can't imagine what this experience must be like for him, this fragmenting of what he knew and what he was told, the divide between the two opening wider with every conversation dragged from the past. On their walk to the bar, he'd pointed out signs of the war, still there but masked by time. Bullet holes, shrapnel wounds carved into buildings. It is not just *the* past, it is his past. Her phone beeps and she flips it open.

It is unbelievably good news.

"My God, I've found her," she says.

Theo pauses midbite. "Who?"

"Agnès Roue. I've got her telephone number. She lives in Paris."

"But, how?"

"I sent a text to my friend Hellie. The French Resistance is her specialism so I figured it wouldn't hurt to ask. Turns out she knows someone who interviewed Roue in the past. Should we call her?"

"Should we?"

"Don't you want to?"

Theo takes the proffered phone and hands it straight back. "I can't deal with these things. Can you make it work?"

Edie types in the number and presses "call." After two rings, a man answers. Edie turns up the volume, sits as close as she can to Theo and holds the phone up in the space between their heads.

"Hello, may I speak to Agnès Roue?" she says, in tentative French.

There is a long pause. "Who is calling, please?" the man says, immediately switching into English.

"My name is Edie, I'm an academic researcher. I'm looking into the story of Tessa Armstrong, an agent with the—"

There is a muffled noise on the other end of the line, but the connection stays open. Edie decides to continue.

"We've just come across some information that leads us to think there was a connection between Tessa and Agnès, and we'd love to ask her some questions, if at all possible."

There is a pause. "Agnès is in a retirement home," says the voice. "We're just sorting out her apartment. I'm sorry, but we normally ask that interview requests go through her lawyer."

Edie looks at Theo in dismay.

"We are so sorry to have troubled you," says Theo. "We'll leave you to it, but before we do, perhaps you might have a telephone number for her lawyer?"

She can hear the man breathing on the other end of the line. "Sorry, I'm confused. Who am I speaking to now, please?" he says.

"My apologies, perhaps this is a bad time. We should let you—" says Theo, even though Edie is furiously shaking her head.

"Get the number," she hisses.

"But who is this?" says the man.

"I'm Tessa's brother. I'm helping Edie with her research."

There is another pause.

"We're trying to fill in the gaps in Tessa's story," says Edie. "For numerous, complicated reasons, it seems the whole story has never been told."

"You're Theo," says the man. He pronounces it the French way—*Théo.*

Theo goes very still. Edie nudges him, but he seems incapable of speech.

"You should come here, if you can, to Paris," the man says, quickly. "I'm going through Agnès' papers, there might be something . . . And I'm sure she'll want to meet you."

"Who are you?" says Theo, quietly.

"I'm Agnès' brother," says the man. "My name is Gabriel."

THEO

Berlin, 2003

Thirty-seven

Some things never change. One thing that has never changed: when Theo feels anxious, he disappears into the past. For a long time, this meant his childhood. The bond between the twins that only they could understand. Nightingales, and made-up languages, and always having someone by his side, always. Since Jeremy's death, Theo has started folding himself inside the past he shared with him.

He's settling into his seat on the plane, the first flight they could get to Paris. He's less anxious this time; the journey is more of a distraction, he supposes, imbued as it is with urgency and purpose. This Gabriel, waiting on the other side. Edie's next to him, already snoring lightly. He has no idea how she can sleep, given he can hear the tinny thud of music leaking from her headphones.

Thud thud thud.

Theo closes his eyes. He has a neat, orderly list of memories he likes to revisit, so tidily curated because Jeremy—always so fanatically organized—gave them to him.

Jeremy's illness crept up on them, as cancer does. For a long while he hadn't even appeared ill, despite what the doctors said. The grave prognosis, the gloom of the hospital waiting room and all those endless tests. Almost before they realized what was happening, visiting London became too much, as did the garden, then reading. Before Theo knew it, the hospital had delivered a bed, a great hulking thing, for the sitting room, because Jeremy could no longer manage the stairs.

Theo took up a vigil; the cats, too—curled up at the bottom of the hospital bed. The doctor was generous with the morphine, and Jeremy would sleep for hours at a time, waking for soup—the only thing he could manage—which Theo spooned into his mouth. They made their way through a steep pile of old favorites. *Mrs. Dalloway*, *Wuthering Heights*, *Maurice*, *Anna Karenina*. Theo reading, Jeremy butting in because somehow he had whole passages of these books memorized.

"I surprised you," he said, one afternoon. "The first time I kissed you."

Theo squeezed his hand. "I thought I'd missed my chance."

"You almost did. Got bored waiting for you to pounce."

On the plane, Theo smiles. They'd been in the garden in Cambridge, planting a tree at his mother's request. Theo was knee-deep in a muddy hole with a shovel.

"Not your natural state this, is it?" said Jeremy, stubbing his cigarette into the grass so he could offer Theo a hand out of the hole.

"I don't know why she even wants the bloody thing in the garden; she keeps saying she's off to Paris." Theo cast a look toward the house, but there was no sign of his mother.

Theo took one side of the giant root ball, Jeremy the other, Theo skidding in the mud at the first *heave* and landing flat on his back. The momentum sent Jeremy flying. They ended up lying shoulder to shoulder, laughing so much Theo began to wheeze. That was when it happened. Jeremy glanced around to make sure no one was looking and planted a gentle kiss on Theo's lips.

Theo never forgot it, the sensation of Jeremy's lips on his.

Then there was the time they stayed for six weeks in North Africa, spending the GDP of a small country in the souk. Rugs and pots and spices. The fortnight in Greece in '63, where Jeremy turned a glorious golden-brown in the sun. The endless hours they spent chatting in the garden in Cambridge.

Even when times were hard, they had each other.

"It's been a lovely life, really," said Jeremy, one day near the end. "Despite its ups and downs."

Not long after that, Jeremy stopped speaking altogether, the silence that descended on the house broken only by Edie a year later.

"You saved me, you know," said Theo to Jeremy, on the last day. Whenever the darkness threatened, it had been Jeremy who'd pulled him free. Dusted him off and given him a reason to carry on.

Fifty years. Fifty years is a lifetime. Fifty years of love is luck.

Paris

Thirty-eight

He can see she's getting irritated with him.

"We can't turn up empty-handed," he says. But he can't make a decision.

Edie points at a neat blue cardboard box of colorful macarons. "We'll take these, please," she says.

"I'm not sure . . ."

"We'll be late otherwise. Where does that fall on the spectrum of rudeness? Is it better or worse than showing up *sans* treats?"

Agnès Roue lives in a smart cream apartment building in the Marais, fronted by a large oak door. Theo stalls, pointing out bookshops he thinks Edie might like, but she's eager to go on.

"Third floor—there's a lift, don't brave the stairs," says a low voice on the intercom. The door buzzes and Edie ushers him through. He wants to tell her to slow down; to say this is my story, not yours; but he's giving it away, he's letting her lead because he knows himself by now. Nothing will get done otherwise.

"Hi, I'm Gabriel," says a man outside the lift. He must be of a similar age to Theo but he wears it better, with an expensive suit and haircut. Jeremy always used to beg him to dress better but it didn't matter, it doesn't matter. It doesn't matter, he says under his breath, and Edie shoots him an odd look. They introduce themselves and the man politely thanks them for the macarons in excellent English. The apartment is open plan and a mess, with papers spread across every surface.

A woman of about fifty peers around the bedroom door and waves.

"This is Eliana, my niece," says Gabriel.

"I'm starting on the wardrobe," she says. "Make yourselves at home, won't you?"

"Excuse the chaos," says Gabriel. "My sister is desperate for us to get her papers in order."

"How is she?" asks Edie.

"Frail, but still as sharp as anything. She wants to write a book, and knowing Agnès, that's exactly what she'll do."

He passes them each a small cup of black coffee and sits down facing them, one leg swung over the other. "I cannot tell you how strange it is to finally be sitting opposite you," he says, studying Theo's face intently.

Theo is thrown by this. Edie, clearly scenting a story, whips out her notebook and biro. "We'd love to hear more about you," she says.

"About me? OK, well, I'm not sure what to tell you. I'm retired, of course. But I taught literature and journalism at universities for many years." He nods at Theo. "A professor, like your father, I believe."

Theo puts down his cup with such force that coffee spills over the side and soaks into a folded copy of *Libération*. Gabriel shoos away his apologies. "It's fine, it's fine. It's nothing, just a newspaper."

Edie is watching them both. Theo feels momentarily jealous of her innocence, her surprise at every twist and turn. He thinks, I'm glad she's here. I must tell her that.

"Did you know Tessa?" she says.

Gabriel's head dips, just slightly. "I wondered how much they'd told you. I could tell on the phone you didn't know who I was."

"Who are 'they'?" says Edie, at the same time as Theo says, "Who are you?"

"As you know, my sister Agnès knew Isabelle—Tessa. I'm sorry, I always thought of her as Isabelle. But my sister took her in soon after she arrived in France. Tessa was in bad shape. She'd been roughed up by the police not long after she arrived, but escaped—"

"Yes—how exactly did she escape?" says Edie, pen poised.

"The local resisters had someone on the inside, although we weren't sure of it at the time. The police were hard to turn—many of them welcomed the Germans with open arms—but it wasn't impossible. We all had our own ideas of what it meant to be 'for France.'"

"And this person, this policeman, helped her get out?"

"They created an opportunity, but Tessa had a nose for it. I doubt they'd have caught her at all if your grandmother's neighbor hadn't given us up."

Theo is aghast. "You surely can't mean Madame Daunay?"

Gabriel nods.

"Good God, my family paid that woman to look after the house until the day she died. She always said she'd had no idea Tessa had been there." He shakes his head. "She said she was with the Resistance," he says, and Gabriel laughs, but it is a sharp, cruel sound.

"Wait, so you were with Tessa when she was caught?" says Edie.

"I think you need to go back to the beginning," says Theo. All those years, all those years and Madame Daunay never said a word.

Gabriel says, "Tessa found her way to Agnès. She'd been pretty much abandoned by the British at that point. They didn't buy the story of her escaping. It was a massacre, you know, what happened at her drop site when she first arrived in France. There's no other word for it. They butchered them all."

"So how come Tessa walked away?"

"She missed the drop. She hesitated, she hated parachuting. I feel like she'd be furious at me for telling you that."

Theo looks at Gabriel in astonishment. "You're saying she missed her spot and survived?"

"Exactly. Agnès had already helped me to escape to a farm in the south and sent Tessa there too. There was an SOE circuit nearby and Agnès convinced them to give Tessa a shot. If Agnès trusted someone it meant something, you see, no matter what your British HQ said. It was different on the ground. Chaos. I don't think they ever grasped that."

"Your sister sounds like an incredible person," Edie tells Gabriel.

He takes a short breath and pushes his hair back from his face. They both spot at the same time the chain of numbers tattooed onto his wrist.

"She is brilliant," he says. "We aren't deserving of her."

"This circuit was headed by a man with the alias Victor?" says Theo.

"Yes. I liked him, but he was ambitious. Sometimes it helped but often it meant he got ahead of himself."

"Where was this farm?" says Edie.

"Just outside Saint-Martin-d'Ardèche," says Gabriel. "It's still there, still in the same family, although I expect they make more money from holiday lets than the actual farm these days. They were friends of my grandparents." He hesitates. "I could take you there, perhaps. I'd like to, although the barn where we all would meet fell down years ago. I used to go back every year. I had to, really."

He stops, suddenly. "I have something to show you."

His loafers slap against the parquet flooring as he disappears into the bedroom. They can hear him speaking softly to Eliana.

"Are you OK?" says Edie.

"Why didn't I ask these questions?" Theo says. "Why did I just accept it?" He thinks, because I was a coward, that's why. He has to keep it together, doesn't want to cry in front of a stranger; he is biting his lip, steadying his breath. Edie places a hand on his arm, and he pats it, grateful.

Gabriel returns and drops a handful of black and white photographs onto the table.

"This was a stupid thing to do, really, given we were hiding. I suppose we felt we needed proof of our reality. I was amazed to find the film still there when I returned. All of my books, everything, the family kept them until I came back after the war. They'd buried the film in the herb garden."

Theo picks up a photograph. It is his sister, in a jumper and slacks, a machine gun slung casually over her shoulder. Her hair, cropped to chin length, is tucked beneath a black beret.

"My God," says Theo. "Her hair."

Darling Tess, I wish I'd known this version of you, he thinks.

Gabriel laughs. "Agnès cut it for her. I was surprised to see her photograph in your Imperial War Museum, that long wavy hair."

There are other photographs. Tessa in a large farmhouse kitchen, kneading dough with her fists. She has flour on her nose and is laughing. In another, Tessa and Gabriel, side by side, stretched out on a patch of grass. Theo feels a strange sensation in his chest. He wants to laugh because look at her, look at his sister, the bread-baking is more surprising than the gun, but instead he starts to cry.

"You were lovers," he says.

Gabriel coughs. Edie puts down her pen.

"Were you?" she says.

"I loved her," says Gabriel, simply.

"That's why you were together at my grandmother's house," says Theo.

"You should know, I tried to find you after the war. I tried your British War Office but no one ever called back. When I finally managed to speak to someone on the telephone they told me Tessa's case was closed, that she was presumed dead. They didn't want to know. I wasn't British, I was

French Resistance, and I think they'd had quite enough of us by then. I told them I wanted to speak to you, I had read you were in Germany and I said I'd go to Nuremberg myself if I had to. But they said no, that someone would contact you on my behalf."

Theo is still staring at the photographs of his sister. Tessa as he had never known her—the short hair, the gun. He'd never contemplated just how far she'd traveled from the image he had of her in his head. "They never did."

"Then they told me you didn't want to speak to me. That you and your family had taken it very badly and wanted to be left alone. So I did, I left you alone and I've always regretted it. So many times I wanted to pick up the phone to you but I didn't. I figured I was too late, that you knew everything. It took me a long time to get back into a position where I was capable of anything after the war."

"What happened to you?" asks Edie.

"Mauthausen, then Dachau," he says. He smiles, and Theo knows why. Sometimes it is the only way to brace against the past.

"Somehow König failed to connect me to Agnès. If he had, I imagine it would have been even worse. Nowadays we call it PTSD, but back then people just told you to have another drink."

Theo nods, because he knows this, too.

"What would she say, if she could see us here together?" says Gabriel.

"I bet she'd be thrilled," says Edie.

"She'd laugh," says Theo. "And tell us not to talk behind her back."

It is the seasons rolling across the hills. It is the turning of the wheel, the meaninglessness of time. Sixty years gone and she is still forming links and bonds.

Gabriel smacks his leg with his hand. "I can't believe I almost forgot to ask this, but I have to know. Did you ever find the child?"

Theo has picked up the topmost photograph of Tessa. He can see that beyond the sepia, her eyes are blazing. He remembers himself through this image: same eyes, same nose, same mouth. Practically the same person, except the roots that traveled far beneath the earth. He can picture her now, smiling at him, shielding her eyes from the sun as he strides across the garden.

Finally, the words sink in and he meets Gabriel's gaze. "What child?" he says.

It takes a moment for Gabriel to respond. His face pales.

"Child?" says Edie, nose scrunched in confusion.

"Oh," says Gabriel.

Theo can feel his heart beating in his chest—there it goes, thudding against his ribs. This isn't the time for a heart attack, he tells himself, willing his body to behave.

"What child?" he asks, again, trying to keep his tone light.

"I think I should make some more coffee," says Gabriel. "Or perhaps you'd prefer some tea?"

They nod, both stunned into silence.

Eliana appears behind them. She's a short woman, with a mass of greying curls tied in a ponytail. "*Je m'en occupe*," she says, smiling at Edie, nodding at Theo as she collects the cups.

"Jesus," says Gabriel.

"Just spit it out." Theo's getting impatient now.

"Theo," Edie says, quietly.

Gabriel is still white as a sheet. "Your sister never told you . . ."

"Evidently not."

Gabriel takes what Theo presumes is a steadying breath. "Tessa had a child, a girl named Béatrice."

In his mind, Theo sees the rough letters carved into the wall of Tessa's cell.

Two Ts and a B.

Theo, Tessa *and Béatrice*.

"What?" says Edie, eyes like saucers. "Are you serious?"

Theo sees Eliana pause in her tea-making, a spoon hovering above the steaming pot. "Edie, why don't I show you some of Agnès' papers?" says Eliana. "I hear you're a researcher. They might be of interest to you."

Edie shoots Theo an uncertain look, and he nods. Eliana places the teapot on the table, and the two women disappear into the bedroom.

"*Théo*," says Gabriel.

"Please go on." Theo doesn't mean to be terse, but he can't help it.

"Your mother arranged for the child to be adopted. Tessa only spent a few days with her, I believe, at your grandmother's house."

Tessa gave birth at their grandmother's house. It is almost too much for Theo to comprehend.

"When did this happen?" he asks. Gabriel looks so wretched. Theo wants to shrug and say, it's all right, I'm all right, no worries, but he can't. It isn't true.

"Her final year at the Sorbonne, I believe."

Of course, of course. Theo closes his eyes. There it is. The answer he's been searching for since 1938. This is what divided them all those years ago. The Tessa from before, the Tessa that came after, and in between the two—a child.

Béatrice.

The silence between his mother and Tessa. The strain Theo himself felt with his mother that he could never understand. Pieces slot into place. The light that stood between them. The puzzle is laid out before him, almost complete.

"God, Tee, I wish you'd told me," he says, speaking into the past. He could have helped. He would have helped. He'd have supported his sister in any way she needed. "The father was Luc Langlois, I presume?"

But Luc hadn't mentioned any of this. Luc had been as baffled as Theo by Tessa's behavior.

Gabriel shakes his head.

"No? Not Luc?"

"It was the author, Ephra Laurent." A dark look flashes across Gabriel's face.

Theo sees the book with its green cover, wrapped in white paper in Tessa's trunk.

It takes him a moment to respond. "I had no idea they were involved." Theo's head is spinning. What else had she kept from him?

"They weren't. The encounter was . . . not consensual."

"It was . . . you're saying . . ."

"That man violated your sister. Béatrice was a child of rape. Tessa didn't want to give her up—I don't think she ever forgave herself for going along with it. *Théo*, I am sorry."

A new door opens in Theo's mind. The change in Tessa takes on a new meaning.

A man violated my sister, he thinks, and she didn't tell me. Theo starts to cry, he can't help it, fumbling in his pocket for his handkerchief.

"Tessa loved you more than anything," says Gabriel. "She must have wanted to protect you from this."

"Is Laurent still alive?" Theo notices Gabriel glancing at his fists, which he realizes are clenched.

"He died in the eighties. He'd rather faded into obscurity by then, although his novels have gained something of a cult following of late."

Theo knows this. Radio 4 ran a program on him not long ago.

"Tessa probably didn't tell you because she felt ashamed. It was a different time back then. A different world."

"Tessa had *nothing* to be ashamed of." He says it forcefully, although he knows Gabriel agrees.

He thinks, of course you had to go to France, Tess. Your daughter was there.

His niece, Béatrice.

At least I know now, he thinks. But if it had been different, if he had been different back then, if Tessa had trusted him and turned to him instead of their mother. If all this had been known. *What if, what if, what if.*

More than sixty years of darkness. Finally, the past is bathed in light.

It is late when they return to their hotel. Edie moves stiffly along the corridor, trying to catch a yawn with her hand. But still, she hovers at her door, asks a quiet "Are you all right?," to which he can only nod an affirmation.

"This doesn't have to be the end, you know."

"What do you mean?"

"The child. Béatrice. She might still be out there somewhere. We can try to find her. There are ways and means."

"I wouldn't know where to start."

"No, but I've got a few ideas."

He hesitates. "You'll help?"

Edie nudges him with her elbow. "You don't even have to ask."

"Yes," he says. Not an ending, but a beginning.

"It's settled, then." She turns to go, but he stops her with a hand on her shoulder.

"I want to thank you. None of this would've happened without you." He coughs, embarrassed. "You've given me my sister back."

Alone in his room, he pulls the French doors open and steps out onto the balcony. Clasping his hands around the iron railing, he looks out over the street below. The evening is so clear, the air still warm. There is a new feeling in his bones. This is what it feels like to be released from the past, he thinks. His past, theirs. The not-knowing had felt like a trailing thread, but the truth is a connection after all.

Béatrice, he says aloud.

Part Four

TESSA

Ravensbrück, 1945

Thirty-nine

"Hope" is the thing with feathers

Roll call is at 4 a.m. at the Appellplatz. Hours and hours and hours pass but time is nothing here, it is grains of sand, a bottomless crow-black hole. Winter in Germany is so cold. A woman in her row whispers, "*Don't move*," but Tessa cannot stop, shivering, teeth chattering. Teeth-chattering percussion thousands of times over through neat lines of humans. Don't fall, wait your turn, don't fall, they think as one. The path between the huts is marked with poplar trees. A button falls off her thin jacket, the thread just giving way. It rolls across the earth and a guard, the woman with the thin lips and the little yapping dog, picks it up and pockets it. Sometimes the small, petty cruelties shock you the most.

"Is there," she asks aloud, "a second before death, between the thud and the black, where reality hits and you know what is upon you?" The others in her hut tell her to quieten down and not be so morbid. It got me in the end, the people on the floor might think in that quick second, as they take their last glimpse not of hell, not of a nightmare, but of the logical conclusion of everything that's gone before. "Think about it," she says. She thinks about it every night. The logical conclusion of words and bile, and division, and anger, and how it used to make her shudder, and how it used to make her angry too. "Look at what it means," she says to her bunkmate, "when morality is swept aside."

In the hut she sleeps on a bed of straw. Warmth might be scarce in winter, but two bodies squashed together in one cot is enough to draw out the lice. Itch is a word with meaning here. Skin, hair, eyes, red streaks against the skin, itch scratch itch scratch.

Her bed-mate Nanette squeezes her hand but the movement splits open a sore, oozing blood and pus into the straw. The lice will eat well tonight, she says, and Nanette laughs, not because it's funny but because it's a relief to think of something other than death for just one moment—even when that something is lice.

Most often she disappears inside her head. Theo on his back in the river, arms outstretched. Gabriel, that evening in the barn. The feeling when the armaments factory exploded in flames. Sometimes she thinks of linen sheets and dancing sunlight. The room in her grandmother's house that she hadn't been able to stop herself from entering all those months ago with Gabriel. The bedroom had looked the same but not, the light different, shadows where on that day in 1938 there had been none.

Sometimes she disappears into the worst parts of the past. Sometimes she cannot keep those cruel black eyes from her thoughts. Then she sees him, feels him, feels it, because Ephra Laurent is an *it*. He'd known she was alone that weekend in Paris. Luc had told her as much himself. "Just telephone him if you need anything," he'd said, one foot out of the door, his mother waiting in Chartres. On occasion the water might fail or a window get stuck. But don't worry, no fear, Ephra was on hand if she needed help. Ephra, Luc said, might in fact stop by to make sure she was all right.

"Just a little drink," he'd said, when he inevitably did. "Seeing as it's just the two of us."

She'd agreed because she thought it would make him leave faster. Even though he made her skin crawl. Even though she remembered so clearly the sensation of his fingernails digging into her waist that first time they'd met. Even though, even though, even though . . . She let him in and that was all that mattered, *after*.

He held her by the wrists as he did what he did, a cushion over her face, his legs pinning her own open against Luc's sofa. She turned her head to the side before the cushion came down, so at least she could breathe, at least she had that. Her view was of Luc's tiny kitchenette, the open bottle of wine on the counter, dirty dishes piled up. She took in every detail of that scene, as he did what he did.

The others in the billet think liberation is just around the corner. King George won't stand for it, they say. British women treated like this? The Russians are just across the River Oder. (*"Hope" is the thing with feathers*, said Emily Dickinson.) Nanette squeezes Tessa's hand every night before she falls into a fitful, restless sleep. One dream becomes another. It is lighter, behind Tessa's eyes, it is ten fingers and ten toes. You say names in your sleep, says Nanette. Who is Theo? Who is Gabriel? Who is Béatrice? Béatrice is what I called her, she says, smiling, because if she'd done this during training, spoken in her sleep, she wouldn't be there. They'd have given her another role, she'd be someone else.

Only once does she allow herself to wonder, if she'd talked in her Paris cell, if she'd sold her colleagues down the river and given König what he wanted, would this still have been her fate?

What if, what if, what if.

She silences the thought. Extinguishes it like a match caught between two fingers.

The camp's punishment block has two floors of identical cells. She is not allowed to stand up straight or sit down. If she stretches out her hands in the pitch darkness, they hit the walls. It triggers a memory two-fold, muscle and mind. The journey from Paris to the transport camp at Saarbrücken, a ring around her wrists, a ring around her ankles, a chain in between. The metal rings cut into her flesh and bloodied her legs. She couldn't stand up straight.

Every day for three days a man drags her from the punishment box and holds her head beneath icy water over and over again. They don't usually do this to the British women; perhaps they think she's French. Perhaps they just think she deserves it. There is a ringing in her ears, a sharp pain, and panic. The fight for life is instinctual, no matter what the mind might want.

Outside the camp are pine forests and a lake. Sometimes the smell of pine needles breaches the stench.

At Saarbrücken, waiting for the cattle-train to the camp, the women were expected to fight for scraps. Tessa decided she'd rather starve, but soon hunger became yearning, then pain, and then she was in the middle of it all, hair-pulling, scratching, and all for a piece of moldy bread.

She will not make munitions, that is the problem, that is what lands her in the punishment block in the first place. Other women refuse, too. They say, "We won't kill our brothers," but where they say *our* Tessa means *my*. Theo in a box in the sky. Tessa in a box with no windows. That she knows her rights is another problem. "I am a prisoner of war," she says, and they laugh or turn away.

The black box kills the thing with feathers and there is no coming back from that.

"Fine," says a man, eventually. "You'll build us a road instead."

Gabriel was on the prison transport from Paris. He'd mouthed words but her brain couldn't fathom his meaning in that moment, because all she'd wanted to do was fling her arms around him. Purple around his eyes, his mouth, a kink in his nose. Remember the barn, lips wet not split, not purple but just the right color. "Keep going," she'd mouthed back at him. "Where are we going?" said someone else.

She'd said it aloud at her grandmother's house, her great confession, Gabriel listening in silence. He'd looked briefly appalled; she'd noticed that. It had taken him a minute to mask it.

It was the first time the words had passed her lips: "A few years ago I had a baby, and I gave her away." How simple it was to say it aloud.

It had happened early morning, she said, picturing sunlight on her grandmother's yellow sheets, and outside, a puckered white-blue sky. The pile of bloody muslins on the floor. If she closes her eyes she can still see the midwife, her disapproving frown as Tessa reached for the child. Her mother standing with her back to her, unable to look Tessa in the eye. The heat of the baby against her breast, suckling for the first milk. I've changed my mind, she'd said, but it could not be undone, her mother wouldn't hear of it. There is no father, her mother said, as if that put an end to it, but there was, there is. She can picture his face so clearly.

The frozen sods of earth won't sit flat against the snow but keep going, keep going, they say. The road the women are failing to build is a long way from the camp. In fact it is a different camp, a work camp, and here the billet has a stove. There is one loaf of bread for fourteen women. This, she now knows, is a lot. One loaf, fourteen women, a few spoonfuls of peel soup, potato, beetroot, don't ask, don't care. A woman, French, a capital "P" for "Political Prisoner" inside a red triangle on her arm, one day stops trying to get the sods of earth to lie flat and takes off running across the fields. The guards shoot her in the back, as she must have known they would, and throw her in the ditch but take her clothes. There are always new arrivals to dress.

As Tessa works, she thinks about her guilt. What matters to her, but hadn't mattered to anyone else, including Ephra Laurent, is that she'd said no. She'd kept on saying no, but it hadn't mattered because he had decided and that was that. And despite her saying no, it somehow still ended up being entirely her fault. "You shouldn't have been nice to him if you didn't want him to take advantage" is what her mother said.

Gabriel was the first one to put words to what Ephra did. A crime, he said, that's what it was.

Men summon them away one morning at roll call. The English women are to return to the main camp, they say, where the others wait with hollow eyes and the hissed "don't fall down"s, and the guard with the yapping dog. Tessa knows what this means, but the others speak quickly about liberation this, and finally that. *The Russians.*

At the main camp, thick white smoke pours from the crematorium chimney.

The woman with the dog isn't there. It's the top brass instead. I'll see you hang, she thinks, as the Commandant reads out the final pronouncement—then she realizes she won't. There are four women in a row, and two start crying. No one begs and Tessa feels glad of it. On your knees, says a different man. The air is thick with smoke. Tessa holds Nanette's hand and gives it a squeeze, and no one stops them. A man forces her head down but she shakes him off. She looks up to the light, just a momentary glimpse, one last look.

Tessa thinks of her brother, and of herself as a young woman, not quite formed. The twins, two Ts, on their backs in the river with their arms outstretched.

Acknowledgments

The phrase "It takes a village" has never felt more apt than in the birth of this novel. I feel incredibly lucky to have delivered a book into the world surrounded by the best of people.

Thank you to my wonderful agent Susan Armstrong, for your support and kindness. I simply could not have hoped for a better guide through this process. Huge gratitude to Catriona Paget and all at C&W. Thanks too to Gráinne Fox at United Talent Agency for working such magic in the USA.

I am endlessly indebted to Suzie Dooré, and to Beth Coates, Jabin Ali and all at The Borough Press for championing this book. To Pamela Dorman, Lara Hinchberger, Marie Michels, Natalie Grant and everyone at Pamela Dorman Books and Penguin Random House, thank you for having such faith in me. The editorial team of dreams. Together you transformed my novel several times over, molding my words with such intelligence and care into something beyond my wildest dreams. Thanks too to Amber

Burlinson for your incisive copy-editing, and to everyone involved in the production of the novel.

Thank you to all the international editors and translators working on this book.

My profound gratitude to Anna South for spotting something in an early draft and encouraging me to keep going. Thanks also to Gillian Stern for your enthusiasm and generosity, and for introducing me to the best agent out there.

Love and thanks to my family (especially my dad with his encyclopedic knowledge of military history) and to my wonderful friends. Special thanks to Holly Dawson, my first reader, and to Richard, Christine, Penny, Gudrun and Julian for your unwavering support.

My Farleys Family. Kerry, Antony, Ami, Kate, Lance, Sophie, Tom, Elaine and Tracy, and all at the Lee Miller Archives and Farleys House & Gallery, thank you for cheering me on from the off and calming my *many* freak-outs. It meant the world to me.

To my GCSE English teacher Dave Claricoates. I doubt you realized it at the time, but your early encouragement set me on this path. Thank you.

And finally, Antony, Arthur and Polly—for *everything*. "The love that I have of the life that I have, is yours and yours and yours" (from Leo Marks' code poem for SOE agent Violette Szabo).

Author's Note

Thirty-nine British women traveled behind the lines in enemy-occupied France in the Second World War. Sixteen paid with their lives. Like many authors writing fiction about this period, I have liberally plundered real events. The Nazis did indeed play a "radio game" with the wireless sets of captured agents—and the SOE French section did really break their own security rules by pointing it out, and reminding one agent to use his "true check," condemning him and the rest of his party. The British authorities' refusal to accept what had happened led to the widespread infiltration of SOE networks in France, with weapons, money and people sent straight into enemy hands. Captured agents did scratch their names into the walls of the cells in avenue Foch. The British did refuse to release the missing women's names to the Red Cross, initially at least, to avoid drawing attention to the fact that women had been sent behind enemy lines. The French saboteur Robert de La Rochefoucauld is rumored to have bombed a munitions plant with plastic explosives smuggled inside loaves of French bread. As a student, I read an account of a female French resister who managed to escape from a police station by presenting an injury from a beating as a simple nosebleed. Though I read this testimony with my eyebrows raised—like Edie, marking my notes with a question mark—it is not the most fanciful account of an escape I encountered.

The personnel files of the women who went to war behind the lines in France are available to read at the National Archives in Kew. In Noor Inayat Khan's file is a piece of paper upon which she had practiced the signature of her alias. Although the characters presented here are fictitious, several are loosely inspired by real-life counterparts and their testimony is—for the most part—recorded in the Imperial War Museum's brilliant sound archive.

I'm grateful to the former SOE staffers who spoke with me when I conducted academic work on this subject. Particularly Mrs. Blair and her son, Ian, who treated me to a delightful lunch at the Special Forces Club in London, which I remember as being the antithesis of Edie's experience with Mrs. Andrews. I'm indebted, too, to the wealth of research on this subject. I'd like to draw particular attention to Rod Kedward's invaluable works on the French Resistance in rural France and Sarah Helm's extraordinary books *A Life in Secrets* and *If This Is a Woman*. Also, *Violette Szabo* by Susan Ottoway, *Sisters in the Resistance* by Margaret Collins Weitz, and Jean Overton Fuller's three books *Madeleine*, *Déricourt: The Chequered Spy* and *The German Penetration of SOE: France 1941–44*. Theo's experience in Nuremberg is inspired in part by Airey Neave's *Nuremberg* (and Neave really did have to ask the tribunal judges if Ribbentrop could call witnesses from the British royal family and aristocracy). Paul Roland's *The Nuremberg Trials: The Nazis and Their Crimes Against Humanity* and Hilary Gaskin's *Eyewitnesses at Nuremberg* also proved invaluable. Thank you to the staff of Mahn- und Gedenkstätte Ravensbrück for so patiently answering my questions. The camp is now a memorial, and like all camps must be seen to be truly comprehended. The huts are gone, marked instead by indentations, like shallow graves in the earth. The crumbling remnants of the Siemens plant, where the inmates were forced to make armaments for the company, go on and on through the pine woods.

And finally, I must mention the war correspondent Lee Miller, whose visceral records of liberated Europe will remain with me for the rest of my life.